Dream into Nightmare

When young Linda Martin came to the stately old Château Valmy as English governess to the nine-year-old Comte Philippe de Valmy, it seemed like a dream come true. *At first.*

Everyone seemed so wonderful, so charming, so very elegant. *At first.*

Then bit by bit she became aware of a strange tension in the air. Odd things began to happen. Little things, unaccountable things. But they were so imperceptible that Linda decided it was just her imagination playing tricks—

Until the accident that nearly killed the boy.

> Everyone insisted it was an accident. Everyone but Linda. She knew now that something was wrong at Valmy. Very wrong. Valmy was no longer a dream come true—it was a nightmare.

Nine Coaches Waiting

by Mary Stewart

FAWCETT CREST • NEW YORK

For Elizabeth Manners

NINE COACHES WAITING

THIS BOOK CONTAINS THE COMPLETE TEXT OF
THE ORIGINAL HARDCOVER EDITION.

Published by Fawcett Crest Books, CBS Educational and
Professional Publishing, a division of CBS Inc., by arrangement with William Morrow & Co., Inc.

ISBN: 0-449-23988-8

Printed in the United States of America

46   45   44   43   42   41   40   39   38   37

First and Second Coaches

Chapter I

O, think upon the pleasure of the palace!
Securèd ease and state! The stirring meats
Ready to move out of the dishes, that e'en now
Quicken when they are eaten. . . .
Banquets abroad by torchlight! music! sports!
Nine coaches waiting—hurry, hurry, hurry—
Ay, to the devil. . . .

Tourneur: *The Revenger's Tragedy.*

I WAS thankful that nobody was there to meet me at the airport.

We reached Paris just as the light was fading. It had been a soft, gray March day, with the smell of spring in the air. The wet tarmac glistened underfoot; over the airfield the sky looked very high, rinsed by the afternoon's rain to a pale clear blue. Little trails of soft cloud drifted in the wet wind, and a late sunbeam touched them with a fleeting underglow. Away beyond the airport buildings the telegraph wires swooped gleaming above the road where passing vehicles showed lights already.

Some of the baggage was out on the tarmac. I could see my own shabby case wedged between a brand-new Revrobe and something huge and extravagant in cream-colored hide. Mine had been a good case once, good solid leather stamped deeply with Daddy's initials, now half hidden under the new label smeared by London's rain. Miss L. Martin, Paris. Symbolic, I thought, with an amusement that twisted a bit awry somewhere inside me. Miss L. Martin, Paris, trudging along between a stout man in impeccable city clothes and a beautiful American girl with a blond mink coat slung carelessly over a suit that announced discreetly that she had been to Paris before, and recently. I myself must have just that drab, seen-better-days shabbiness that Daddy's old case had, perched up there among the sleek cabin-class luggage.

But I was here, home after ten years. Ten years. More than a third of my lifetime. So long a time that now, pausing in the crush beside the Customs barrier, I felt as strange as I suppose anybody must feel on their first visit abroad. I found I even had to make a conscious effort to adjust my ears to the flood of French chatter going on around me. I even found myself, as all about me people uttered little cries of recognition, excitement and pleasure, and were claimed by waiting friends and relations, scanning the crowd of alien faces for one that I knew. Which was absurd. Who would there be to meet me? Madame de Valmy herself? I smiled at the thought. It was very good of Madame de Valmy to have provided me with the money for a taxi into Paris. She was hardly likely to do much for the hired help. And that was what I was. I had better start remembering it, as from now.

The *douanier*, chalk in hand, was pausing over my shabby case. As I stepped forward to claim it an airport official, hurrying past, bumped against me, sending my handbag flying to the floor.

"Mille pardons, mademoiselle. Excusez-moi."

"Ce n'est rien, monsieur."

"Je vous ai fait mal?"

"Pas du tout. Ce n'est rien."

"Permettez-moi, mademoiselle. Votre sac."

"Merci, monsieur. Non, je vous assure, il n'y a pas de mal . . ." And to my repeated assurances that nothing was lost and that I was not irretrievably damaged, he at length took himself off.

I stared after him for a moment, thoughtfully. The trivial little incident had shown me that, after all, that ten-years' gap had not been so very long. Ear and brain had readjusted themselves now with a click that could be felt.

And I must not let it happen. It was another thing I must remember. I was English. English. Madame de Valmy had made it very clear that she wanted an English girl, and I hadn't seen any harm in letting her assume that my knowledge of France and things French was on a par with that of the average English girl who'd done French at school. She had made rather a lot of it, really . . . though probably, I thought, I'd been so anxious to get the job that I'd exaggerated the importance of the thing out of all measure. After all, it could hardly matter to Madame de Valmy whether I was English, French or even Hottentot, as long as I did the job properly and didn't lapse into French when I was supposed to be talking English to young Philippe. And I could hardly be said to have deceived her, because in fact I *was* English; Daddy had been English and Maman at least a

6

quarter so . . . and even to me those early years were faded and remote. The years when Maman and I lived out at Passy with Grand'mère, and the Boche was in Paris, and Daddy was away somewhere unspecified but highly dangerous and we never allowed ourselves to speak or even think in English . . . even for me those years had sunk well back into the past, so far back that now they seemed hardly to belong to me at all. Infinitely more real were the last ten years in England—seven of them spent at the Constance Butcher Home, an orphanage in North London, and the last three in a qualified independence—a travesty of freedom—as general help and dogsbody at a small prep school for boys in Kent. Those endless green-linoleum corridors, the sausage on Mondays and Thursdays, the piles of dirty sheets to count, and the smell of chalk and carbolic soap in the classroom . . . these were a very much more present memory than the lovely old house at Passy or even the top flat in the Rue du Printemps, where we had gone after the war was over and Daddy came home. . . .

The douanier said wearily, "Vous n'avez rien à déclarer?"

I started and turned. I said firmly, in English, "Nothing to declare. No, none of those things. Nothing at all. . . ."

There were taxis waiting outside. To the driver I said, "Hôtel Crillon, please," and derived my third twinge of amusement from the slight air of surprise with which he received the august address. Then he heaved the old brown case in beside me; the car door slammed, the gears raced, and we were off.

If there had been any strangeness left in me, it would have vanished now. The taxi swung around into the main road with a screech of brakes, skidded as a matter of course on the wet tarmac, and roared toward Paris. I sat back in the familiar reek of Gauloises, distintegrating leather, and stale exhaust, and the old world closed around me in a cloud of forgotten impressions which seemed in a moment to blot out the last ten years as if they had never been. The taxi was Pandora's box, and I had not only lifted the lid, I was inside it. These sweet, these stinging memories . . . things I had never before noticed, never missed, until now I saw them unchanged, part and parcel of that life that stopped ten years ago. . . .

The driver had been reading a newspaper; it was thrust into a compartment beside the dashboard. I could see the familiar black blurred print, and the corner of an out-of-focus

7

picture. A bus approached, its direction board already lighted: SENLIS. I saw the crowd of girls and workmen standing on the rear platform, crushed together and lurching with the movement against rails and rope. And now the ugly suburbs were closing in; tall houses with wrought-iron balconies and slatted shutters; hoardings with their peeling posters, Bonbel, Sunil, Ancre Pils; shabby little *tabacs* with their lights reflected orange and gold in the damp pavements; in a café-bar, bright light on rows of glittering bottles and a huddle of metal tables behind steamy glass; Dubo, Dubon, Dubonnet . . . and there ahead of us, down the long straight stretch of the Route de Flandre, Paris was lighting up.

My eyelids stung suddenly, and I shut my eyes and leaned back against the shabby upholstery. But still through the open window Paris met me, assailed, bombarded me. The smell of coffee, cats, drains, wine and wet air . . . the hoarse voices shouting *France-Soir*, *Paris-Presse* . . . someone selling lottery tickets . . . the police whistles . . . the scream of brakes. Something was missing, I thought vaguely, something had changed . . . but it was only when the taxi swerved violently and I opened my eyes to see it miss a pack of cyclists by inches that I realized what it was. He wasn't using his horn; the incessant blare of Paris was gone. I found myself looking about me all at once as if I were a stranger and this were a new town and a new experience.

Something inside me welcomed the change. Quite deliberately I turned my thoughts away from the easy path they were treading, and made myself think about the future. I was back in France; that much of the dream of the past ten years had come true. However prosaic or even dreary my new job might be, at least I had come back to the country I had persisted in regarding as my home. If I had deceived Madame de Valmy, I had done so under a pressure that was to me a necessity. Well, here I was. This was France. The lighted suburbs that were swimming past me were those of my home. Not very long now and we would be in the heart of Paris, thrusting our way down the confusion of the Rue Royale to shoot out into the great glittering spaces of Concorde, where the windows of the Crillon look out through the still-bare chestnut branches toward the Seine. Then tomorrow we would set off again, deeper into France, across her pastures and vineyards and hills and high Alps till we reached the Château Valmy, perched above its forests by the little village of Soubirous in High Savoy. . . . I could see it in my mind's eye now, as I had pictured it a hundred times since the journey

8

started—the fairy-tale castle of a dream, something remote and romantic and impossible—a sort of Walt Disney advertisement for Gibbs Dentrifice. Of course it wouldn't be like that, but all the same. . . . The taxi checked, then ground to a reluctant halt behind a stationary bus. I clutched my handbag tightly on my knee and leaned forward, staring out of the window. Now that I was here, even this tiny delay became suddenly intolerable. The bus moved a yard or so and pulled to the right. The taxi shot past with three centimeters to spare, did a quick in-and-out between two terrified pedestrians, and tore on its way. *Hurry. . . .*

Suddenly, unbidden, verses were spinning in my brain. *Nine coaches waiting—hurry, hurry, hurry—* But here, surely, the quotation was desperately inappropriate? What was it, anyhow? I racked my brain, remembering. . . . Something about *the pleasures of the palace, secured ease and state . . . banquets abroad by torchlight! music! sports! nine coaches waiting—hurry, hurry, hurry . . .* some tempter's list of pleasures, it had been, designed to lure a lonely young female to a luxurious doom; yes, that was it, Vendice enticing the pure and idiotic Castiza to the Duke's bed. . . . *(Ay, to the devil).* . . . I grinned to myself as I placed it. Inappropriate, certainly. This particular young female was heading, I hoped, neither to luxury nor the devil, but merely to a new setting for the same old job she'd abandoned in England. Miss Linda Martin, nursery-governess to Philippe, Comte de Valmy, aged nine.

In a few minues now I would be there. Madame de Valmy, silver and elegant and so upright in her chair that you thought a draft would sway her—Madame de Valmy would receive me. I abandoned fairy tales, dragged a mirror from my bag, and began to tidy my hair, making myself recall, as if it were a lesson, what I could remember of my new employers.

Madame de Valmy, when I had talked to her in London, had not told me a great deal about the family I was to serve, but I had gathered the essentials of what seemed to have been a fairly complicated story. The old Comte de Valmy, Philippe's grandfather, had been enormously wealthy, and on his death the property had been divided between his three sons, the new Comte Étienne, Léon, and Hippolyte. To Étienne went the bulk of the fortune, the Château Valmy, and the Paris house; to Léon, among other things, a lovely little estate in Provence called Bellevigne, and to Hippolyte a large property on the edge of Lac Léman, a few kilometers below the Valmy estate. At the time of the old

Comte's death the eldest son, Étienne, had not been married, and had been thankful when his brother Léon offered to stay on at Valmy and run the estate for him. Étienne preferred Paris, so to Paris he went, while Léon stayed on at Valmy and managed it, running his own Midi property from a distance. The younger brother, Hippolyte, who was, I gathered, an archaeologist of some standing, lived quietly at his house in Thonon-les-Bains, in between bouts of traveling and "digging" abroad.

So things had gone on for some years. Then, long after anyone had ceased to expect him to do so, Étienne had married, and within a couple of years Philippe had been born. The family had stayed on in Paris until last year, when Philippe was almost nine years old, tragedy had struck at him even as it had struck at me. His parents had been killed together in an air crash on their way back from a holiday in Spain, and Philippe had left Paris to live with his uncle Hippolyte in Thonon. Hippolyte was still unmarried, "but," said Madame de Valmy to me, poised in that silver elegance of hers beside a Regency mirror in her sitting room at Claridge's, "but the child had seen a lot of him, and is very fond of him. Hippolyte—my brother-in-law—wouldn't hear of his coming to us at Valmy, even though, officially, Valmy is Philippe's home. . . ." She smiled then, that remote sweet smile of hers that was about as cosy as an April moon, so that I thought I saw Hippolyte's point. I couldn't exactly picture the exquisite Héloïse in a romp with a nine-year-old boy. Philippe was certainly better off at the Villa Mireille with Uncle Hippolyte. Even an archaeologist, I thought, must be more approachable than Madame de Valmy. At least he would share the normal small boy's passion for grubbing in the mud.

But an archaeologist must occasionally grub to order. Philippe had been only a few months at the Villa Mireille when Monsieur Hippolyte had to fulfill an engagement which took him to Greece and Asia Minor for some months. The Villa Mireille was perforce shut up, and Philippe went up to Valmy to stay with his other aunt and uncle for the duration of Hippolyte's tour. And his Paris-bred nanny, restless enough in the little town of Thonon, had struck at the prospect of perhaps half a year's sojourn in the remote Savoyard valley, and removed herself, with tears and reproaches, back to Paris. . . .

So here was I. And it was curious that, in spite of the familiarity with which Paris invaded me, I didn't yet feel at home. I was a stranger, a foreigner, going to a strange house and a strange job. Perhaps loneliness was nothing to do with place or circumstance; perhaps it was in you, yourself. Perhaps, wherever you were, you took your little circle of loneliness with you. . . .

The taxi swerved across the Rue Riquet and swung right-handed into streets I knew. Away on the right I could see the dome of Sacré Coeur sharp against the daffodil sky of evening. Somewhere below it, in the spangling blue dusk of Montmartre, was the Rue du Printemps.

On an impulse I leaned forward, my hands tight on the clasp of my shabby handbag.

"Do you know the Rue du Printemps? It's off the Avenue Verchoix, Eighteenth Arrondissement. Take me there, please. I—I've changed my mind."

I stood on the damp pavement outside the open door and looked up at Number 14, Rue du Printemps. The paint was peeling off the walls; the wrought-iron of the balconies, that I remembered as a bright turquoise, showed in this light as a patched and dirty gray. A shutter hung on one hinge beside the first-floor window. Monsieur Bécard's canaries had long since gone; there wasn't even a patch of darker color on the wall where the cage had hung. The top balcony, our balcony, looked very small and high. There were pots of straggling geraniums arranged around its edge, and a striped towel hung over the railing to air.

How stupid to have come! How unutterably stupid to have come! It was like finding the glass empty when you lifted it to drink. I turned away.

Someone was coming down the stairs. I could hear the click of high-heeled shoes. I waited, perhaps still in some faint hope that it might be somebody I knew. It wasn't. It was a young woman, cheap and smart, with that tight-black-sweater-and-skirt smartness made to look very Place Vendôme with ropes of improbable pearls. She was blonde, and chewed gum. She eyed me with slight hostility as she crossed the lobby to the concierge's desk by the door and reached to the rack for a bundle of papers.

"You looking for someone?"

"No," I said.

Her eyes went beyond me to my suitcase on the pavement. "If you're wanting a room—"

"I wasn't," I said, feeling suddenly foolish. "I was just—I used to live hereabouts, and I thought I'd just like to

11

look at the place. Is—is Madame Leclerc still here? She used to be the concierge."

"She was my aunt. She's dead."

"Oh. I'm sorry."

She was leafing through the papers, still eying me. "You look English."

"I am English."

"Oh? You don't sound it. But then I suppose if you lived here . . . . In this house, you mean? What name?"

"My father was Charles Martin. The poet Charles Martin."

The blonde said, "Before my time," licked a pencil, and made a careful mark on one of the papers she held.

I said. "Well, thanks very much. Good evening," and went back to where my case stood on the pavement. I looked up the now darkening street for a taxi. There was one coming, and I lifted a hand, but as it came nearer I saw that it was engaged. A street lamp shone into the back as it passed me. A middle-aged couple sat there—a wispy woman and a stoutish man in city clothes; two girls in their early teens sat on the drop seats. All four were laden with parcels, and they were laughing.

The taxi had gone. The street was empty. Behind me I heard the blonde's footsteps receding up the stairs of Number 14. I glanced back over my shoulder once at the house, then turned back to the street to watch for another taxi. Neither house nor street looked even remotely familiar any more.

Quite suddenly I ceased to be sorry I had come. It was as if the past, till then so longed after, so lived over, had slipped off my shoulders like a burden. The future was still hidden, somewhere in the lights that made a yellow blur in the sky beyond the end of the dark street. Here between the two I waited, and for the first time saw both clearly. Because of Daddy and Maman and the Rue du Printemps I had made myself a stranger in England, not only bereaved, but miserably dépaysée, drifting with no clear aim, resenting the life I had been thrust into with such tragic brutality; I had refused to adapt myself to it and make myself a place there, behaving like the spoiled child who, because he cannot have the best cake, refuses to eat at all. I had waited for life to offer itself back to me on the old terms. Well, it wasn't going to. Because of my childhood I had rejected what England had for me, and now the Paris of my childhood had rejected me. Here, too, I had been dispossessed. And if I was ever to have a place, in whatever country—well, nobody ever wanted you anyway unless you damned well made them. And that was what I would have to do. I had my chance in front of me now, at the Château Valmy. As yet I knew nothing of the family but their names; soon those names would be people I knew, the people I lived with; the people to whom I would matter. . . . I said their names over slowly to myself, thinking about them; Héloïse de Valmy, elegant and remote with that chilly grace that would—surely—melt in time; Philippe de Valmy, my pupil, of whom I knew nothing except that he was nine years old and not very strong; his uncle, the acting master of the château, Léon de Valmy. . . .

And then a queer thing happened. Whether it was because now for the first time I said the name over to myself, coupled with the fact that I was standing in the street where a million unconscious memories must be stirring, I don't know; but now, as I said the name, some trick of the subconscious drew some of those memories together as a magnet draws pins into a pattern so that, clear, and till now unrecollected, I heard them speak. "Léon de Valmy," Maman was saying, and I think she was reading from a newspaper, "Léon de Valmy. It says he's crippled. He's cracked his back at polo and they say if he recovers he'll be in a wheel chair for the rest of his life." Then Daddy's voice, indifferently: "Oh? Well, I'm sorry to hear it, I suppose, though I can't help feeling it's a pity he didn't break his neck. He'd be no loss." And when Maman said, "*Charles!*" he added impatiently, "Why should I be a hypocrite about the man? You know I detest him." And Maman said, "I can't think why," and Daddy laughed and said, "No. You wouldn't. . . ."

The memory spun away into silence, leaving me tingling with something that might have been apprehension, wondering if I had really remembered it at all, or if it were some new trick of that romantic imagination of mine. A taxi had appeared and I must have signaled it because here it was swerving in toward the curb with a screech of brakes. Once again I said, "Hôtel Crillon, please," and climbed in. The taxi moved off with a jerk, swung left out of the Rue du Printemps and accelerated down a dark shuttered street. The sound of the engine swelled and echoed back from the blind houses. *Nine coaches waiting, hurry, hurry, hurry. . . . Ay, to the devil . . . to the devil. . . .*

It wasn't apprehension, it was excitement. I laughed to myself. To the devil or not, I was on my way. . . .

I rapped on the glass. "Hurry," I said.

Third Coach

Chapter II

. . . his form had not yet lost
All her original brightness, nor appeared
Less than Archangel ruin'd . . .

MILTON: *Paradise Lost.*

My first thought was, he lied in every word,
That hoary cripple, with malicious eye
Askance to watch the working of his lie
On mine. . . .

BROWNING: *Childe Roland.*

THE little town of Thonon-les-Bains lies some twenty miles northeast of Geneva, on the southern shore of Lac Léman. Our plane had been met at Geneva by the big black Daimler from Valmy, which wafted us smoothly through the expensive streets of the city toward the French frontier and Thonon.

Madame de Valmy had talked very little to me on the journey from Paris, for which I was grateful, not only because my eyes and mind were busy with new impressions, but because—although she had been kind and pleasant in the extreme—I could not yet feel quite at ease with her. There was that curious remoteness about her which made her difficult to approach, or even to assess. Conversation with her had an almost long-distance touch about it, far from feeling that she had come halfway to meet you, you found her suddenly abstracted, all contact withdrawn. I wondered at first whether she was deliberately keeping me at a distance, but when she had twice asked me a question, only to lose interest before I had answered, I decided that she had graver matters on her mind than Philippe's governess, and myself retired contentedly enough into silence.

The car was purring along through prosperous, densely-cultivated country. To our left, through thickets of poplar and willow, the gleam of water showed and hid and showed again. On the right the country rolled green and gradual to wooded foothills, then swooped dramatically up to the

14

great ranges of the Alps and the dazzle of the colossal snows. One of them, I supposed, was Mont Blanc itself, but this, I thought, stealing a glance at Héloïse de Valmy beside me, was not the time to ask.

She was sitting with shut eyes. I thought as I looked at her that I had been right. She looked both tired and preoccupied, though nothing, it seemed, could impair her rather chilly elegance. She was, I supposed, about fifty-five, and was still a beautiful woman, with the sort of beauty that age seems hardly to touch. Bone-deep, that was the phrase; it was in the shape of her head and temples and the thin-bridged, faintly aquiline nose with its fine nostrils; it was only at another glance that you saw the fine wrinkles etching eyes and mouth. Her skin was pale and clear, and expertly tinted; her brows delicately drawn and arched with a faint arrogance above the closed lids. Her hair was sculptured silver. Only her mouth under the curve of its expensive rouge, and the hands which lay gray-gloved and still in her lap, were too thin for beauty. She looked expensive, a little fragile, and about as approachable as the moon.

I sat back in my corner. In front of me were the square shoulders of Madame's chauffeur. Beside him, equally square and correct, sat Madame's maid Albertine. If I—as the classic tales of governessing led me to expect—was to be insecurely poised between the salon and the servant's hall, at least I was now at what might be called the right end of the car. For which I was grateful, as I didn't much like what I had seen of Albertine.

She was a dark sallow-faced woman of perhaps forty-five, with a sullen, secretive expression and ugly hands. Although she had been most of the time about Madame de Valmy's rooms last night when I had been there, she had not once spoken to me and I had seen her watching me with a sort of stony resentment which had surprised me, but which I now realized was probably habitual and without meaning. She sat rigidly beside the chauffeur, gripping Madame's jewel case tightly on her lap. Neither she nor the man spoke. Neither, as far as I could tell, was remotely aware of the other's presence. They seemed so admirably suited that I found myself wondering, quite without irony, if they were a married couple (I found later that they were, in fact, brother and sister). Bernard, the chauffeur, had impeccable manners, but he, too, looked as if he never smiled, and he had the same dark-visaged, almost resentful air as the woman. I hoped it wasn't a common Savoyard characteristic. . . . I

15

stole another look at Madame's still face. It didn't look as though, for gaiety, there was going to be much to choose between the drawing room and the servants' hall. . . .

We had crossed the frontier, and were climbing now toward Thonon, where our road would turn south toward the mountains. As we climbed, the ground fell sharply away to the left, spilling a huddle of bright roofs and budding fruit boughs down toward the belt of trees that bordered the water. Through the mist of still-bare branches, showed, here and there, the chimneys of some biggish houses. One of these—Madame de Valmy surprised me by rousing herself to point it out—was the Villa Mireille, where the third Valmy brother, Hippolyte, lived. I could just see its chimneys, smokeless among the enveloping trees. Beyond, mile upon glimmering mile, stretched Lac Léman, lazily rippling its silk under the afternoon sun, with here and there a slim sickle of white or scarlet sail cutting the bright field of water.

It was a warm afternoon, and the little town through which we drove was gay in the sun. Pollarded trees lined the streets, linking trained branches where buds were already bursting into green. Shops had spilled their goods onto the pavements; racks of brightly printed dresses swung in the warm breeze; red and green peppers shone glossy among last season's withered apples; there was a pile of gaily-painted plant pots and a small forest of garden tools in brilliant green. And at the edge of the pavement there were the flowers; tubs of tulips and freesias and the scarlet globes of ranunculus; box after box of polyanthus, vivid-eyed; daffodils, sharply yellow; the deep drowned-purple of pansies; irises with crown and fall of white and ivory and blue and deeper blue . . . oh, beautiful! And all packed and jammed together, French-fashion, billowing and blazing with scent as thick smoke in the sunlight.

I must have made some exclamation of pleasure as we slid past them and into the square, because I remember Madame de Valmy smiling a little and saying, "Wait till you see Valmy in April." Then we had swung to the right and the road was climbing again through a sparse tree-crowded suburb toward the hills.

Very soon, it seemed, we were in a narrow gorge where road, river, and railway, crossing and recrossing one another in a fine confusion, plaited their way up between high cliffs hung with trees. After a few miles of this the railway vanished, tunneling away on the right, not to reappear, but the

16

river stayed with us to the left of the road, a rush of green-white water that wrestled down its boulder-strewn gully. The cliffs closed in. Above, the gray March-bare trees hung in clouds. The road began to climb. Away below us the water arrowed loud and white between its boulders.

A grim little valley, I thought, and a dangerous road . . . and then we rounded the bend called Belle Surprise, and away in front of us, like a sunlit rent in a dark curtain, lay the meadows of Valmy.

"That's Soubirous," said Madame de Valmy, "there in the distance. You'll lose sight of it again in a moment when the road runs down into the trees."

I craned forward to look. The village of Soubirous was set in a wide, green saucer of meadow and orchard serene among the cradling hills. I could see the needle-thin gleam of water, and the lines of willows where two streams threaded the grassland. Where they met stood the village, bright as a toy and sharply focused in the clear air, with its three bridges and its little watch-making factory and its church of Sainte-Marie-des-Ponts with the sunlight glinting on the weathercock that tips the famous spire.

"And Valmy?" I said, as the car sailed downhill again and trees crowded thickly in on either side of the road. "We must be near it now?"

"Those are the Valmy woods on your left. They stretch most of the way back to Thonon. The Merlon—that's the name of the river—marks the boundary between Valmy and Dieudonné, the estate to the right of the road. We cross the river soon and then—" she smiled faintly—"you'll see Valmy."

She spoke as usual in that cool, flute-clear voice, with nothing ruffling the silvery surface. But I thought, suddenly, she's excited—no, perhaps nothing so strong as that, but there's anticipation there and something more. . . . I had been wrong in my judgment of her a while back; in spite of the rather fragile urban charm, she loved this lonely valley, and came back with pleasure to it. I felt a little rush of warmth toward her, and said impulsively, "It's lovely, Madame de Valmy! It's a beautiful place!"

She smiled. "Yes, isn't it? And you're lucky, Miss Martin, that spring has come early this year. It can be bleak and grim enough in winter, but it's always beautiful. At least, I think so. It has been my—our home for many years."

I said impetuously, "I shall love it here! I know I shall!"

The gloved hands moved in her lap. "I hope you will, Miss

Martin." The words were kind, but formally spoken, and the smile had gone. She was withdrawn again, cool and remote. She looked away from me. I might be at the right end of the car, but it seemed I must keep to my own side.

I threw her a doubtful little look that she didn't see, and turned again to my own window. And at that moment I saw the château.

We had been running for a little time along the bottom of the valley, with the Dieudonné plantations—tall firs with the sun and wind in their crests—on our right, and beyond the river the steep woods of Valmy, a wild forest where holly gleamed among oak and birch, and great beeches rose elephant-gray from a tangle of hawthorn and wild clematis. Above these banked and raveled boughs hung a high plateau; and there, backed by more forest and the steep rise of another hill, stood the Château Valmy, its windows catching the sunlight. I had only a glimpse of it, just enough to show me that here was no romantic castle of turrets and pinnacles; here was the four-square classic grace of the eighteenth century, looking, however, wonderfully remote, and floating insubstantially enough up there in the light above the dark sea of trees. It also looked inaccessible, but I had barely time to wonder how it was approached when the car slowed, turned gently off the main road onto a beautiful little stone bridge that spanned the Merlon, swung again into a steep tunnel of trees, and took the hill with a rush.

The Valmy road was a zigzag, a steep, rather terrifying approach which the big car took in a series of smooth upward rushes, rather like the movement of a lift, swooping up through woodland, then open hillside, and running at last under the high boundary wall that marked the end of the château's formal garden. At the top was a gravel sweep as big as a small field. We swung effortlessly off the zigzag onto this, and came around in a magnificent curve to stop in front of the great north door.

The chauffeur came around to open Madame de Valmy's door and help her to alight. Albertine, without a glance or a word for me, busied herself with wraps and hand luggage. I got out of the car and stood waiting, while my employer paused for a moment talking to Bernard in a low rapid French that I couldn't catch.

I did wonder for a moment if her instructions could have anything to do with me, because the man's little dark eyes kept flickering toward me almost as if he weren't attending to what his employer said. But it must only have been a natural

18

interest in a newcomer, because presently he bent his head impassively enough and turned without a further glance at me to attend to the luggage.

Madame de Valmy turned to me then. "Here we are," she said unnecessarily, but with such grace that the cliché took on almost the quality of a welcome. She gave me her sweet, fleeting smile, and turned toward the house.

As I followed her I got only the most confused impression of the size and graciousness of the place—the great square façade with the sweep of steps up to the door, the archway on our left leading to courtyard and outbuildings, the sunny slope beyond these where orderly kitchen gardens climbed toward another tree-bounded horizon. . . . I saw these things only vaguely, without noticing. What met me with the rush almost of a wind was the sunlight and space and the music of the trees. Everywhere was the golden light of late afternoon. The air was cool and sweet and very pure, heady with the smell of pines and with the faint tang of the snows.

A far cry, certainly, from North London.

I followed my employer up the wide flight of steps and past a bowing manservant into the hall of the château.

At first I did not see the woman who waited for us a few paces inside the great door.

The hall seemed immense, but this was mainly because it was very high and full of shadows. The floor was a chilly chessboard of black and white marble, from which, opposite the door, a staircase rose to a wide landing lit by a window whose five tall lancets poured the sun downward in dazzling shafts. At the landing the staircase divided, lifting in twin graceful curves toward a gallery. So much I saw, but the light, falling steeply through the speartips of the high windows, threw all but the center of the hall into deep shadow.

I was still blinking against the glare when I heard a voice greeting Madame de Valmy, and then a woman came toward us in welcome. I supposed she was the housekeeper. She was a stout body of sixty-odd, with a fat comfortable face and gray hair worn neatly in an old-fashioned bun. She was dressed in severe black, her only ornament—if it could be called that—being a pair of gold-rimmed pince-nez which stuck out of a pocket high on her bosom, and was secured by a chain to a plain gold pin. Her pleasant face, her plodding walk, her whole appearance were solid respectability personified. This was no secret dark Savoyard, at any rate.

She looked at me curiously as she greeted Madame de

Valmy. She had a cheerful voice that sounded perpetually a little out of breath, and surprisingly, her French, though fluent, was atrociously bad.

Madame answered her greeting absently. In that merciless cascade of light the lines in her face showed up clearly. She said abruptly, her eyes sliding past the woman in black toward the dimmer background of the hall, "The Master—he's well?"

"Oh yes, madame. He's been—oh, quite his old self the last few days, madame, if you'll forgive my saying so . . . interested in what's going on, the way he hasn't been for long enough, and full of plans. Oh, quite like old times, madame."

She spoke with the ease of an old servant, and her face showed her very real pleasure in the good news she could give her employer. More pleasure, indeed, than Madame de Valmy's own face reflected. I thought I saw a shadow pass over it as she said, "Plans?"

"Yes, madame. I don't rightly know what they are, myself, but he and Armand Lestocq were talking it over for long enough, and I do know there's extra hands busy in the garden, and a man came today to look round the place and give his estimate for the jobs the Master was talking about last winter. He's here now, as it happens, madame. He went up to take a look at the stonework on the west balcony, and I think the Master went with him. The Master's lift wasn't at the ground floor when Seddon made up the library fire."

Madame de Valmy was pulling off her gloves with quick nervous movements. She said abruptly, "Do you know if he has heard from Monsieur Hippolyte?"

"I think so, madame. There was a letter a week ago, on Tuesday . . . no, it was Wednesday; it was your letter came from London on Tuesday about the young lady." She paused, puffing a little, and then nodded. "That's right. The one from Athens came on the Wednesday, because I remember Armand Lestocq was up here that very day, and—"

"Very well, Mrs. Seddon, thank you." Madame de Valmy might hardly have been listening. "You said the Master was upstairs? Please send someone to tell him I'm here with Miss Martin."

"I've already done that, madame. He most particularly asked to be told the minute you arrived."

"Ah, thank you." Madame de Valmy turned then toward me, still with those abrupt, slightly nervous movements, and spoke in English. "Now, Mrs. Seddon, this is Miss Martin. I wrote to you about her when I informed the Master. Miss Martin, Mrs. Seddon is the housekeeper here. She is English, so you need not feel too much alone. Her husband is our butler, and he and Mrs. Seddon will do what they can to help you."

"That we will," said Mrs. Seddon warmly. She beamed at me and nodded, so that the gold chain on her bosom bobbed and glittered. "You're very welcome, I'm sure."

"Miss Martin's rooms are ready?"

"Oh, yes, madame, of course. I'll take her up now, shall I, and then show her round myself, seeing that perhaps she's a little strange?"

"Thank you, yes, if you will, but not straight away. She will come upstairs presently. Perhaps you will wait for her?"

"Oh course, madame." Mrs. Seddon nodded and beamed again, then retreated, puffing her way steadily up the stairs like a squat determined tug.

Madame de Valmy turned as if to speak to me, but I saw her eyes go past my shoulder, and her hands, which had been jerking her gloves between them, stilled themselves.

"Léon."

I heard nothing. I turned quickly. Even then it was a second or so before I saw the shadow detach itself from the other shadows and slide forward.

Though I had known what to expect, instinctively my eye went too high, and then fell—again by instinct, shrinkingly —to the squat shape that shot forward, uncannily without sound, to a smooth halt six feet away.

Pity, repulsion, curiosity, the determination to show none of these . . . whatever feelings struggled in me as I turned were swept aside like leaves before a blast of wind. The slightly dramatic quality of his entrance may have contributed to the effect; one moment a shadow, and the next moment silently there. . . . But, once there, Léon de Valmy was an object for no one's pity; one saw simply a big, handsome, powerful man who from his wheel chair managed without speaking a word to obliterate everyone else in the hall—this literally, for almost before the wheel chair stopped, the servants had melted unobtrusively away. Only Mrs. Seddon was still audible, steaming steadily up the right-hand branch of the staircase toward the gallery.

It was a tribute to Léon de Valmy's rather overwhelming personality that my own first impression had nothing to do with his crippled state; it was merely that this was the hand-somest man I had ever seen. My experience, admittedly, had not been large, but in any company he would have been conspicuous. The years had only added to his extraordinary good looks, giving him the slightly haggard distinction of lined cheeks and white hair that contrasted strikingly with dark eyes and black, strongly-marked brows. The beautifully-shaped mouth had that thin, almost cruel set to it that is sometimes placed there by pain. His hands looked soft, as if they were not used enough, and he was too pale. But for all that, this was no invalid; this was the master of the house, and the half of his body that was still alive was just twice as much so as anybody else's. . . .

He was smiling now as he greeted his wife and turned to me, and the smile lit his face attractively. There was no earthly reason why I should feel suddenly nervous, or why I should imagine that Héloïse de Valmy's voice as she introduced us was too taut and high, like an overtight string.

I thought, watching her, she's afraid of him. . . . Then I told myself sharply not to be a fool. This was the result of Daddy's intriguing build-up and my own damned romantic imagination. Just because the man looked like Milton's ruined archangel and chose to appear in the hall like the Demon King through a trap door, it didn't necessarily mean that I had to smell sulphur.

It was disconcerting to reach downward to shake hands, but I hoped I hadn't shown it. My self-command, as it happened, was a mistake. He said gently, "You were warned about me?" The dark eyes, with a question in them, slid to his wife standing beside me.

I felt rather than saw her small movement of dissent. A glance passed between them and his brows lifted. He was too quick by half. With a guilty memory of my own secret I said uncertainly, "Warned?"

"About Lucifer's fall from heaven, Miss Martin."

I felt my eyes widen in a stare. Was the man a thought-reader? And was he determined I should smell sulphur? Or . . . did he really see himself as the thunder-scarred angel he quoted? Oddly, the last thought made him more human, more vulnerable.

Before I could speak he smiled again, charmingly. "I'm sorry. I shouldn't have tried to be so cryptic. I was referring to the accident that, as you see—"

I said hastily, and a bit too ingenuously, "I know. I was only surprised because that's what I was thinking myself."

"Was it indeed?" His laugh held a tiny note of self-mockery, but I thought he looked pleased. Then the laugh died and his eyes were on me, intent, appraising. I remembered perhaps rather late that I was a servant and this was my employer. I

22

felt myself color, and said quickly, almost at random, "Someone told me about your accident—someone I met on the plane from London."

"Oh? An acquaintance of ours, perhaps?"

"I think so. We talked. When I told her I was coming here she remembered having met you."

"She?" said Héloïse de Valmy.

I said, "I never knew her name. She was elderly, and I think she came from Lyons or somewhere like that. I don't remember."

Léon de Valmy abandoned the catechism abruptly. "Whoever it was, it's just as well she told you." He hesitated a moment, looking down at his hands, then went on slowly, "You must think this very odd of us, Miss Martin, but I believe my wife does not care to speak of my . . . deformity. Consequently it is apt to meet people with a shock. And I myself—even after twelve years—am absurdly sensitive of meeting new people and seeing it in their eyes. Perhaps both my wife and I are foolish about this. . . . Perhaps already you are condemning me as a neurotic. . . . But it is a very human folly, Miss Martin. We all of us spend some of our time pretending that something that *is*, is not—and we are not grateful to those who break the dream."

He looked up and his eyes met mine. "One day, perhaps, it will cease to matter." He shrugged, and smiled a little wryly. "But until then. . . ."

He had spoken quite without bitterness, only that small wryness touched his voice. But the speech was so little what I would have expected from him that I found myself, embarrassed and disarmed, shaken into some stupid and impulsive reply.

I said quickly, "No, please—you mustn't mind. Deformity's the wrong word, and it's the last thing anybody'd notice about you anyway . . . honestly it is."

I stopped, appalled. From Linda Martin to Monsieur de Valmy the words would have been bad enough. From the new governess to her employer they were impossible. I didn't pause then to reflect that it was the employer who had—deliberately, it seemed—called them up. I stood biting my lip and wishing myself a thousand miles away. Through my sharp discomfort I heard myself stammering, "I—I'm sorry. I shouldn't have said that. . . . I only meant—"

"Thank you, my dear." His voice was still grave, but I saw the unmistakable flash of amusement in his eyes. Then he was saying easily, "It seems, Héloïse, that your excessively silly friend Lady Benchley has justified her existence at last in recommending Miss Martin to us. We were indeed lucky to find you, Miss Martin, and we're delighted to welcome you to Valmy. I hope we'll manage to make you feel at home." He paused. That gleam again. "Not perhaps quite a felicitous expression. Shall I say rather that I hope Valmy will become a home for you?"

I said rather stiffly, "Thank you. You're very kind. I was happy to have the chance to come, and I'll try my best to—"

"Endeavor to give satisfaction? That's the usual bromide, isn't it? What are you staring at?"

"I'm sorry. It was impertinent of me. It was just—your English is so frightfully good," I said lamely. Damn the man; was I never to regain my lost poise? I finished the sentence coldly—"Sir."

He laughed outright then, a quite delightful laugh that at once conceded a point and abandoned the game, whatever it was. He began then to inquire quite naturally and very kindly about the journey and my impressions of the valley; Madame de Valmy joined in, smiling, and soon, under their renewed phrases of welcome, I found my embarrassment relaxing into naturalness once again. More, into liking. The man's charm was palpable, and he had taken the trouble to turn it on full blast . . . and I was all the more vulnerable for being tired, lonely, and a bit bewildered. By the time the three of us had talked for a few minutes longer I was back on top of the world again with my shattered poise restored and all the tensions and uneasinesses of the past half-hour dismissed as figments. Monsieur and Madame de Valmy were a handsome and delightful couple and I was going to like them and love living at Valmy and belonging even in this humble sort to a family again.

Sulphur? Poppycock.

But all the same, I reflected, it hadn't taken me long to see what had been implied in that remembered snatch of conversation. "*You wouldn't,*" Daddy had said, and I saw what he meant. The man was damnably attractive, no doubt of that . . . and I used the adverb deliberately; it was the *mot juste.* And, charm or no, the faintest of resentments still pricked me. Léon de Valmy had played a game with me, and I hadn't liked it. I had been shaken into offering pity and comfort where none was needed . . . and he had been amused.

Nor did I attempt to explain, even to myself, why I had launched so unerringly on that sea of lies about the elderly lady from Lyons, or how I knew I would never, never have the courage to tell Léon de Valmy that I spoke French even better than he spoke English, and had understood perfectly well what he said to Héloïse when, at length dismissed, I had gone upstairs to meet Mrs. Seddon on the gallery landing.

He had said softly, and I knew he was staring after me, "All the same, Héloïse, it is possible that you've made a very great mistake. . . ."

Chapter III

The castle hath a pleasant seat; the air
Nimbly and sweetly recommends itself
Unto our gentle senses. . . .

SHAKESPEARE: *Macbeth*

The raven himself is hoarse
That croaks the fatal entrance of Duncan
Under my battlements. . . .

IBID.

MY rooms were lovelier than anything I had imagined, certainly than any I had ever been in. They had tall windows facing west, which gave onto a balcony and the view across the valley.

This drew me straight away. I stood leaning on the stone balustrading and looked out over that incredible view. So high-perched we were that I seemed to be looking level at the crest of the Dieudonné forest beyond the Merlon; below, along the zigzag, the bare tree tops moved like clouds. The balcony was afloat in a golden airy space. Soubirous, to the south, glinted like a jewel.

I turned. Mrs. Seddon had followed me to the window, and waited, smiling, plump hands clasped under plump bosom.

"It's . . . wonderful," I said.

"It's a pretty place," she said comfortably. "Though some don't like the country, of course. Myself, I've always lived in the country. Now I'll show you the bedroom, if you'll come this way."

I followed her across the pretty sitting room to a door in the corner opposite the fireplace.

"These rooms are built in a suite," she said. "All the main

rooms open onto this corridor, or the south one. You saw how the balcony runs the whole length of the house. These rooms at the end have been made into the nursery suite, and they open out of one another as well. This is your bedroom."

It was, if possible, prettier than the sitting room. I told her so, and she looked pleased. She moved to a door I had not noticed, half-concealed as it was in the ivory and gold paneling. "That door's to the bathroom and Master Philip's bedroom opens off it the other side. You share the bathroom with him. I hope you don't mind?"

At the Constance Butcher Home we had queued for baths. "No," I said, "I don't mind. It's beautifully up to date, isn't it? Baths behind the paneling. Did all the ghosts leave when the plumbing was put in, Mrs. Seddon?"

"I never heard tell of any," said Mrs. Seddon, sedately. "This was a powder closet in the old days; it runs the whole way between the two rooms. They made half of it into a bathroom and the other half's a little pantry with an electric stove for making nursery tea and Master Philip's chocolate at night. Here's the pantry." The door she opened showed a small immaculate room which seemed to share the functions of pantry and broom closet. Beside the door was an orderly stock of housemaid's tools—vacuum cleaner, stepladder, brushes, mops—and beyond these was a small electric stove in what looked like a very efficiently planned nest of fitted cupboards and gleaming shelves. I must have looked surprised, because she added, "This was always the schoolroom wing; the Master and his brothers were brought up here, you see, and then these alterations, with the electricity and all that, were done when Mr. Rowl was born."

"Mr. . . . Raoul?" I queried.

"The Master's son. He lives at Bellyveen. That's the Master's place in the Midi."

"Yes, I knew about that. I didn't know there was a son, though. Madame de Valmy didn't—well, she didn't talk to me much. I know very little about the family."

She gave me a shrewd look, and I thought she was going to make some comment, but all she said was: "No? Ah well, you'll find everything out soon enough, I dare say. Mr. Rowl isn't Madame's son, you understand. The Master was married before. Mr. Rowl's mother died twenty-two years ago this spring, when he was eight. It's sixteen years ago now that the Master married again and you can't blame him at that. It's a big place to be alone in, as you may well imagine. Not that," said Mrs. Seddon cheerfully, chugging across the room to twitch a curtain into place, "the Master was ever one in those days for sitting alone in the house, if you take my meaning. Fair set Europe alight between them, him and his oldest brother, if all tales be true; but there, wild oats is wild oats, and the poor Master'll sow no more of them even if he wanted to, which I doubt he doesn't, and poor Mr. Étienne's dead, God rest him, and long past thinking of the world, the flesh and the devil, or so we'll hope. . . ." She turned to me again, a little out of breath with these remarkable confidences; it appeared that Mrs. Seddon, at any rate, didn't share Madame de Valmy's habit of reticence: "And now would you like to see over the rest of the place, or will you wait till later? You'll be tired, I dare say."

"I'll leave it till later, if I may."

"It's as you wish." Again the shrewd twinkling glance. "Shall I send Berthe to unpack for you?"

"No, thank you." That look meant that she knew quite well that I wouldn't want a maid exploring my meager suitcase. Far from resenting the thought, I was grateful for it. "Where's the nursery?" I asked. "Beyond Master Philip's bedroom?"

"No. His bedroom's the end one, then yours, then your sitting room, then the nursery. Beyond that come Madame's rooms, and the Master's are round the corner above the library."

"Oh, yes. He has a lift there, hasn't he?"

"That's so, miss. It was put in soon after the accident. That'd be, let's see, twelve years ago come June."

"I was told about that. Were you here then, Mrs. Seddon?"

"Oh, yes, indeed I was." She nodded at me with a certain complacency. "I came here thirty-two years ago, miss, when the Master was first married."

I sat down on the edge of the bed and looked at her with interest. "Thirty-two years? That's a long time, Mrs. Seddon. Did you come with the first Madame de Valmy, then?"

"That I did. She was from Northumberland, the same as me."

"Then she was English?" I said, surprised.

"Indeed, yes. She was a lovely girl, Miss Deborah. I'd been in service at her home ever since she was a little girl. She met the Master in Paris one spring, and they was engaged in a fortnight, just like that. Oh, very romantic it all was, very romantic. She said to me, she said: 'Mary—' that's my name, miss—'Mary,' she said, 'you'll come with me, won't you? I won't feel so far from home then,' she said." Mrs. Seddon nodded at me, with an easy sentimental moistening of the eye.

27

"So, seeing as I was courting Arthur—that's Mr. Seddon—meself at the time, I married him and made him go along, too. I couldn't let Miss Debbie adventure all by herself to foreign parts, like."

"Of course not," I said sympathetically, and Mrs. Seddon beamed, settling her arms together under the plump bosom, obviously ready to gossip for as long as I would listen. She gave the appearance of one indulging in a favorite pastime whose rules were almost forgotten. If I had been delighted to see her pleasant English face after the secret countenances of Albertine and Bernard, it was obvious that Mrs. Seddon had been equally pleased to see me. And the governess, of course, was not on the proscribed list: this could not be called Gossiping with the Servants. I supposed that, for me, Mrs. Seddon was hardly on the proscribed list either. At any rate I was going to gossip all I could.

I prompted her. "And then when your Miss Debbie . . . died, you didn't go back to England? What made you stay on, Mrs. Seddon?"

As to that, it seemed that she was not quite sure herself. Miss Debbie's father had died meanwhile and the house in England had been sold, while here at Valmy Mrs. Seddon and her husband had excellent jobs which "the Master" seemed quite disposed to let them keep. . . . I also gathered that Miss Debbie's interest had lifted them into positions which in another house they might never have filled; Seddon himself had been on my one sight of him impeccably polished, neutral and correct; Mrs. Seddon, too, had all the trappings of the competent and superior housekeeper; but her voice and some of her mannerisms had, gloriously defying gentility, remained the homely and genuine voice and ways of Mary Seddon, erstwhile second-gardener's daughter.

I listened to a long description of Miss Debbie, and others of Miss Debbie's home, father, pony, clothes, jewelry, wedding, wedding presents and wedding guests. When we appeared to be about to launch (via how much Miss Debbie's mother would have liked to be at the wedding if only she had been alive) on a description of Miss Debbie's mother's clothes, jewelry, wedding, and so on, as observed by Mrs. Seddon's mother—then I thought it was time to prod her gently back to foreign parts.

"And there was Miss Debbie's son, wasn't there? Of course you wanted to stay and look after him?"

"Mr. Rowl?" She primmed her lips a little. "French nurses they had for him. Such a quiet little boy as he was, too—a bit

28

like Master Philip here, very quiet and never a mite of bother. You'd never have thought—" But here she stopped, sighing a little wheezily, and shook her head. "Eh, well, miss, he's half foreign, say what you will."

There was all rural England in the condemnation. I waited, gravely expectant, but she merely added, maddeningly, "But there, I never was one to gossip. And now, if you'll excuse me, I'll have to be getting about my work and leaving you to unpack. Now, miss, if there's anything you want you've only to ask me or Seddon and we'll do our best to help you."

"Thank you very much. I'm awfully glad you're here, Mrs. Seddon," I added naïvely.

She looked pleased. "Well, now, that's very nice of you, miss, I'm sure. But you'll soon feel at home and pick things up. I couldn't speak a word of French when I came here first, and now I can talk it as fast as they can."

"I heard you. It sounded wonderful." I stood up and clicked back the locks of my suitcase. "As you say, thirty years is a long time, especially when one's away from home. You didn't feel tempted to go back to England, say, when Monsieur de Valmy married again?"

"Oh, we talked of it, Seddon and I," she said comfortably, "but Seddon's that easygoing, and we liked the new madame, and she was satisfied, so we stayed. Besides, I've had the asthma terrible bad since a girl, and, say what you like, none of these new-fangled things they give you, anti-hysterics and suchlike, seem to do me any good. I used to get it terrible bad at home, but up here it cleared up something wonderful. It still comes now and again, but it soon goes off. It's the air. Wonderful healthy it is up here, and very dry."

"It's certainly lovely."

"And then," said Mrs. Seddon, "after the Master had his accident, she wouldn't hear of us going. He couldn't stand changes, you see."

"I did gather that from what he said to me in the hall. Does he—does he have much pain, Mrs. Seddon?"

"Pain? No. But he has his days," said Mrs. Seddon cryptically. "And you can't blame him, the way things are."

"No, of course not. He's bound to get depressed at times."

"Depressed?" She looked at me blankly. "The Master?"

I was still trying to equate the self-confessed "neurotic" with the impression of easy and competent power that Léon de Valmy gave. "Yes. Does he get sort of sorry for himself at times?"

She gave a sound suspiciously like a snort. "Sorry for him-

self? Not him! Mind you, this last few years he's not been just
as sweet-tempered as he might be, but he's all there, miss,
you may be sure. He'd never be the one to give up because
of a little thing like being crippled for life!"

"I think I can see that. In fact you never think of that when
you talk to him." (I didn't add "unless he reminds you," but
the thought persisted.)

"That's so." She nodded at me again. "And he forgets it
himself, most times. What with that electric chair of his, and
the lift, and the telephone to every corner of the place, and
that there Bernard to be the legs of him, there's nothing he
can't do. But now and then, just like that, something'll bring
it home to him, and then. . . ."

I said, still thinking of the scene in the hall, "What sort of
thing?"

"Dear only knows. It might be a bad night, or a report
coming in that something's gone wrong or been neglected in
some place he can't get to himself to see to it, or something
that needs doing and no money to do it with, or Mr. Rowl—"
As before, she stopped abruptly.

I waited. She pulled unnecessarily at a chair cover to
straighten it. She said vaguely, "Mr. Rowl runs the other estate
for him, Bellyveen, in the Midi, and there's always trouble
over money, and it upsets the Master, and besides . . . ah, well,
he's not often here, which is as it should be, seeing he's the
one that reminds the Master most often that he's a helpless
cripple for all the powerful ways he has with him."

I stirred. "Reminds him? That's rather beastly."

She looked shocked. "Oh, not on purpose, you understand.
I didn't mean that! It's only that he—well, Mr. Rowl might
be the Master like he was twenty years ago, you see."

"Oh, I see what you mean. He does all the things his father
used to like doing. Polo, for instance?"

She shot me a surprised look. "Did they tell you about
that?"

"No. I heard it from someone who knew them—someone
I met on the plane."

"Oh, I see. Yes, that sort of thing. He could put his hand
to anything, the Master." She smiled reminiscently and a
little sadly. "Miss Debbie always did say he'd break his neck
one day. He was such a one for sport—all sorts, motorcars,
horses, speedboats . . . fighting with swords, even. He's got a
shelf of silver cups for that alone."

"Fencing?"

"That's it. But cars and horses were the chief thing. I've

30

often thought he'd break his own neck and everyone else's, the way he'd come up that zigzag from the Valmy bridge. Sometimes," added Mrs. Seddon surprisingly, "you'd think a devil was driving him . . . like as if he had to be able to do everything—and do it better than anybody else."

Yes, I thought, I can believe that. And even crippled he has to be a crippled archangel. . . .

I said, "And now he has to sit and watch his son riding and driving and fencing. . . ?"

"As to that," said Mrs. Seddon, "Mr. Rowl hasn't got the money . . . which is just as well, or maybe he'd go the same way as his father. And like I said, he's not here very often anyway. He lives at Bellyveen. I've never been to Bellyveen myself, but I've heard tell it's very pretty."

I said "Oh?" with an expression of polite interest as she began to tell me about Bellevigne, but I wasn't really listening. I was reflecting that if Raoul de Valmy was really a younger copy of his father it was probably just as well he visited Valmy only rarely. I couldn't imagine two of Léon de Valmy settling at all comfortably under the same roof. . . . I stirred again. There was that same damned romantic imagination at work still. . . . And what had I to go on, after all? A vague snatch of memory twelve years old, and the impression of an overwhelming personality in some odd way playing with me for its own amusement, for some reason concerned to give me a picture of itself that was was not the truth. . . .

It struck me then, for the first time, that there had been a notable omission from my welcome to the Château Valmy.

And that was the owner of all this magnificence, the most important of the Valmys, Monsieur le Comte, Philippe.

And now Mrs. Seddon was preparing to go about her own affairs.

She plodded firmly away to the door, only to hesitate there and turn. I bent over my case and began to lift things out onto the coverlet. I could feel her eying me.

She said, "You . . . the Master . . . he seemed all right with you, did he? I thought I heard him laugh when I was waiting upstairs for you."

I straightened up, my hands full of folded handkerchiefs. "Perfectly all right, Mrs. Seddon. He was very pleasant."

"Oh. That's good. I'd like to have been able to have a word with you first and warn you what he sometimes was like with strangers."

I could well understand her slightly anxious probing. It was obvious that the emotional temperature, so to speak, of the Château Valmy, must depend very largely on Léon de Valmy and "his days."

I said cheerfully, "Thanks very much, but don't worry, Mrs. Seddon. He was awfully nice to me and made me feel very welcome."

"Did he now?" Her eyes were anxious and a little puzzled. "Oh, well, that's all right, then. I know he was very pleased when Madame's letter came about you, but as a rule he hates changes in the house. That's why we were so surprised when Master Philip's Nanny was dismissed after being with the family all those years, and they said a new girl was coming from England."

"Oh, yes, Madame de Valmy told me about her." I put the handkerchiefs down and lifted some underwear out of the suitcase. "But she wasn't dismissed, surely? I understood from Madame that she didn't want to live in the wilds at Valmy and, as Madame was in London at the time, Monsieur de Valmy wrote urgently and asked her to find an English governess while she was there."

"Oh, no." Mrs. Seddon was downright. "You must have misunderstood what Madame said. Nanny was devoted to Master Philip, and I'm sure she broke her heart when she had to go."

"Oh? I was sure that Madame said she'd left because the place was so lonely. I must have been mistaken." I found myself shrugging my shoulders, and hastily abandoned that very Gallic gesture. "Maybe she was just warning me what it would be like. But she did seem very anxious to engage someone to teach him English."

"Master Philip's English is excellent," said Mrs. Seddon, rather primly.

I laughed and said, "I'm glad to hear it. Well, whatever the case, I suppose if Philippe's nine he's old enough to graduate from a Nanny to a governess of sorts. I gathered from Monsieur de Valmy that that was the idea. And for a start I'm going to try and remember to call the nursery the 'schoolroom.' I'm sure one's too old for a nursery when one's nine."

"Master Philip's very young for his age," she said, "though there's times when he's too solemn for my liking. But there, you can't expect much after what's happened, poor mite. He'll get over it in the end, but it takes time."

"I know," I said.

She eyed me for a moment and then said, tentatively, "If I might ask—do you remember your own folks, now?"

"Oh, yes." I looked across the room and met the kindly inquisitive gaze. Fair was fair, after all. She must be every bit as curious about me as I was about the Valmys. I said, "I was fourteen when they were killed. In an air accident, like Philippe's. I suppose Madame told you I'd been at an orphanage in England?"

"Indeed, yes. She wrote that she'd heard of you through a friend of hers, a Lady Benchley, who comes up every year to Evian, and Lady Benchley thought very highly of you, very highly."

"That was very nice of her. Lady Benchley was one of the governors at the orphanage for the last three years I was there. Then when I left to be assistant at a boy's school it turned out she had a son there. She came up to me on Visitors' Day and talked to me, and when I told her I hated the place she asked me if I'd ever considered a private job abroad, because this friend of hers—Madame de Valmy—was looking for a governess for her nephew and had asked her if she knew of anyone from the Home. When I heard the job was in France I jumped at it. I—I'd always fancied living in France, somehow. I went straight up to London next day and saw her. Lady Benchley had promised to telephone about me, and—well, I got the job." I didn't add that Madame must have taken Lady Benchley's recommendation to be worth a good deal more than it actually was. Lady Benchley was a kindly scatterbrain who spent a good deal of her time acting as a sort of private labor-exchange between her friends and the Constance Butcher Home, and I doubt if she had ever known very much about me. And I had certainly got the impression that Madame de Valmy had been so anxious to find a suitable young woman for the post during her short stay in London that she hadn't perhaps probed as far back into my history as she might have done. Not, of course, that it mattered.

I smiled at Mrs. Seddon, who was still eying me with that faintly puzzled look. Then all at once she smiled back, and nodded, so that the gold chain on her bosom glittered and swung.

"Well," she said, "well," and though she didn't actually add "You'll do," the implication was there. She opened the door. "And now I really will have to be going. Berthe'll be up soon with some tea for you; she's the girl that looks after these rooms and you'll find she's a good girl, though a bit what you might call flighty. I expect you'll make yourself understood to her all right, and Master Philip'll help."

"I expect I shall," I said. "Where is Master Philip?"

"He's probably in the nursery," said Mrs. Seddon, her hand on the door. "But Madame particularly said you weren't to bother with him tonight. You were to have a cup of tea— which I may say is *tea*, though it took near thirty years to teach them how to make it—and settle yourself in before dinner and you'll be seeing Master Philip tomorrow. But not to bother yourself tonight."

"Very well," I said. "Thank you, Mrs. Seddon. I shall look forward to that tea."

The door shut behind her. I could hear the soft plod of her steps along the corridor.

I stood where I was, looking at the door, and absently smoothing the folds of a petticoat between my hands.

I was thinking two things. First that I was not supposed to have heard Mrs. Seddon mentioning the lift in her conversation with Madame de Valmy, and that if I was going to make mistakes as easily as that I had better confess quickly before any real damage was done.

The second thing was Mrs. Seddon's parting admonition: "not to bother with him tonight." Had that really been Héloïse de Valmy's phrase? *"Not to bother with him."* And he was "probably" in the nursery . . . I laid the petticoat gently in a drawer, then turned and walked out of my pretty bedroom, across the roses and ivory sitting room, toward the schoolroom door. There I hesitated a moment, listening. I could hear nothing.

I tapped gently on the door and then turned the gilded handle. It opened smoothly.

I pushed it wide and walked in.

My first thought was that he was not an attractive little boy.

He was small for his age, with a thin little neck supporting a round dark head. His hair was black, and cut very short, and his skin was sallow, almost waxen. His eyes were black, and very large, his wrists and knees bony and somehow pathetic. He was dressed in navy shorts and a striped jersey, and was lying on his stomach, reading a large book. He looked small and a little drab on the big luxurious rug.

He looked around in inquiry and then got slowly to his feet.

I said, in English, "I'm Mademoiselle Martin. You must be Philippe."

He nodded, looking shy. Then his breeding asserted itself, and he took a short step forward, holding out his hand. "You are very welcome, Mademoiselle Martin." His voice was small and thin like himself, and without much expression. "I hope

34

you will be happy at Valmy."

It came to me again, sharply, as I shook the hand, that this was the owner of Valmy. The thought made him, oddly enough, seem even smaller, less significant.

"I was told that you might be busy," I said, "but I thought I'd better come straight along and see you."

He considered this for a moment, taking me in with the frankly interested stare of a child. "Are you really going to teach me English?"

"Yes."

He said, "You do not look like a governess."

"Then I must try and look more like one, I suppose."

"No, I like it as you are. Do not change."

The de Valmys, it seemed, started young. I laughed. "Merci du compliment, Monsieur le Comte."

He gave me a swift look upward. There was glimmer in the black eyes. But all he said was, "Do we have a lesson to-morrow?"

"I expect so. I don't know. I shall probably see your aunt tonight, and no doubt she'll tell me just what the program is."

"Have you seen . . . my uncle?" Was there, or was there not, the faintest of changes in that monotonous little voice?

"Yes."

He was standing quite still, small hands dangling from their bony wrists in front of him. It came to me that he was in his own way as un-get-at-able as Héloïse de Valmy. My task here might not be a very easy one. His manners were beautiful; he was not, it was patent, going to be a "difficult" child in the sense of the word as usually used by governesses; but would I ever get to know him, ever get past that touch-me-not electric fence of reserve? That, and his unchildlike habit of stillness, I had already met in Madame de Valmy, but there the re-semblance ended. Her stillness and remoteness was beautiful and poised; this child's was ungraceful and somehow dis-turbing.

I said, "I must go and unpack now, or I'll be late for dinner. Would you like to help?"

He looked up quickly. "Me?"

"Well, not help, exactly, but come and keep me company, and see what I've brought you from London."

"You mean a present?"

"Of course."

He flushed a slow and unbecoming scarlet. Without speaking, he walked sedately past me through my sitting room

35

toward my bedroom door, opened it for me, then followed me into the room. He stood at the foot of the bed, still in silence, staring at my case.

I stooped over it, lifted a few more things out onto the bed, then rummaged to find what I had brought.

"They're nothing very much," I said, "because I haven't much spare cash. But—well, here they are."

I had brought him, from Woolworth's, a cardboard model of Windsor Castle—the kind that you cut out and assemble, together with a box, as big as I could afford, containing a collection of men in the uniform of the Grenadier Guards.

I looked a little uncertainly at the silent owner of the Château Valmy, and handed him the boxes.

"An English castle?" he said. "And English soldiers?"

"Yes. The kind they have at Buckingham Palace."

"With the fur hats, to guard the Queen. I know." He was still looking raptly at a picture of a full regiment of Guards, drilling in an improbable fashion.

"They're—they're not much," I said. "You see—"

But I saw he was not listening. He had opened the lid, and was fingering the cheap toys inside. "A present from London," he said, touching one crudely-painted toy soldier. It came to me, suddenly, that it would not have mattered if they had been homemade paper dolls.

I said, "I brought you a game, too, called Peggitty. You play it with these pegs. Later, I'll show you how. It's a good game."

From the schoolroom a girl's voice called, "Philippe? Où es-tu, Philippe?"

He started. "It's Berthe. I have to go." He shut the boxes and stood up, holding them tightly to him. He said, very formally, "Thank you. Thank you, mademoiselle." Then he turned and ran to the door. "Me voici, Berthe. Je viens." On the threshold he stopped and swung around. His face was still flushed, and he clutched the presents hard.

"Mademoiselle."

"Yes, Philippe?"

"What is the name of the game with the pegs?"

"Peggitty."

"Peg-it-ee. You will show me how to play it?"

"Yes."

"You will play this Peg-it-ee when I have had my supper before I go to bed?"

"Yes."

"Tonight?"

"Yes."

He hesitated as if he were going to say something else. Then instead he went quickly out, and shut the door gently behind him.

Chapter IV

O my prophetic soul!
Mine uncle?

SHAKESPEARE: *Hamlet.*

HOWEVER strange and luxurious my new surroundings, life at Valmy soon settled itself into a simple and orderly routine. Every morning Monsieur Bétemps, Philippe's tutor, arrived, and the two were closeted together till lunchtime. Once my various morning jobs about the schoolroom suite were finished I could count myself free, and for the first few days I occupied myself happily in exploring the gardens and the nearer woods, or in reading—hours and hours of reading, a luxury so long denied me at the Home that I still felt guilty whenever I indulged in it.

The library at the château almost certainly contained English books, but since it was Léon de Valmy's private study-cum-office, I could not—or would not—ask permission to use it. But I had brought as many of my own books as I could carry, and in the schoolroom there were shelves to the ceiling full of an excellent miscellany—children's books thrust cheek by jowl with English and French classics and a good deal of lighter reading. I wondered a little at the odd collection until I saw in some of the volumes the name *Deborah Bohun,* or the message "To Debbie," and once I took down a battered old copy of *Treasure Island* to find it inscribed in a flamboyant young hand *Raoul Philippe St. Aubin de Valmy* . . . of course, Léon's son was half-English and had used these very rooms. I found Buchan, too, and Conan Doyle, and a host of forgotten or never-known books that, gratefully, I devoured—forcing myself to ignore the irrational feeling drilled into me in the seven years at the Home that Reading was a Waste of Time.

On one occasion my guilty feeling was justified. When I read French, I read it in secrecy, and once I was nearly caught out over *Tristan et Iseut.* I was devouring it, rapt and oblivious

37

in my bedroom, when Berthe knocked and, receiving no reply, came in to dust the room. She noticed nothing, but I cursed myself and vowed yet again to be careful and wished for the hundredth time that I had never embarked on the silly deception that had seemed at the time to matter so much, and became daily more difficult to confess.

I no longer imagined seriously that anyone would mind; Philippe and I got on well together, and Madame de Valmy, in her aloof way, seemed to like me; I was certainly very completely trusted with Philippe's well-being. But I didn't particularly want her to know that I had deceived her—systematically, as it were, schemed to deceive her. And, as with all deceptions, the thing grew bigger daily. I had to make myself understood to Berthe, the schoolroom maid, and did this in elementary schoolgirl French which amused her and even made Philippe smile. Luckily, I never had to do this with my employers; invariably in my presence they spoke in their flawless and seemingly effortless English. And so the days went by and I said nothing. I dared not risk their displeasure; I loved the place, I could easily cope with the job, and I liked Philippe.

He was a very quiet, self-controlled child, who never chattered. Every afternoon, unless it rained too hard, we went for a walk, and our "English conversation" mainly consisted of my comments on the country or the gardens where we took our walks. That electric fence of his was still up: it was not a consciously erected barrier—the gift of the toys had won his alliance if not his heart—but it was there, the obstruction of a deep natural reserve. I imagined that his naturally undemonstrative nature had been made even more so by the sudden loss of his parents, to whom he had never referred. This was not a child one could readily "get to know." I soon stopped trying, and kept both his and my own attention on things outside ourselves. If I was ever to win his confidence, it would only be done by very gradual and natural degrees: by custom, as it were. And there was, indeed, no reason why I should push my way into his fenced and private world; I had suffered so much from lack of privacy in the Home that I deeply respected anybody's right to it, and would have looked on any attempt at intimacy with Philippe as a kind of mental violation.

His reserve showed itself not only toward me. Each evening, at half-past five, I took him down for half an hour to the small salon where his aunt sat. She would politely put aside her book or writing paper, pick up her exquisite and interminable petit point, and hold conversation with Philippe for the half-hour. I say "hold conversation" advisedly, because that phrase does perfectly imply the difficult and stilted communication that took place. Philippe was his usual quiet and withdrawn self, answering questions readily and with impeccable politeness, but asking none and volunteering nothing. Madame de Valmy was the one, it seemed to me, who had to violate her personality here; she, also naturally withdrawn, had to unbend, almost to chatter.

I suppose, though, that it was I who loathed those half-hours most, and who suffered the most. Madame de Valmy and Philippe talked, naturally, in French, and this exchange I was supposed not to understand. But occasionally she would revert to English, either for my benefit or to test my pupil's knowledge of that tongue, and then I was drawn into the conversation, and had the awkward task of betraying no knowledge of the exchange in French to which I had just been listening. I don't remember if I made any mistakes; she certainly appeared to notice none, but then, she never gave the appearance of more than the most superficial attention to the whole routine; it was, for her, the discharge of a duty to a charge she hardly knew. Madame de Valmy, certainly, could not be accused of trying to violate anybody's confidence.

Her husband was never there. His only meetings with Philippe seemed to be the purely chance ones of encounters in corridors, on the terrace, or in the gardens. At first I found myself blaming Philippe's uncle for his lack of interest in a lonely and recently bereaved little boy, but soon I realized that it wasn't entirely Léon de Valmy's fault. Philippe systematically avoided him. He would only go down the library corridor with me when we had seen the wheel chair safely out beyond the ornamental ponds or at the far side of the rosery; he seemed to have the faculty for hearing the whisper of its wheels two corridors away, when he would invariably drag at my hand, persuading me with him to vanish out of his uncle's sight.

There seemed to be no good reason for this steady aversion; on the two or three occasions during my first week when we did, unavoidably, meet Monsieur de Valmy, he was very nice to Philippe. But Philippe was, if possible, more withdrawn than ever; in front of his uncle the child's reserve appeared to be little more than the sulks. This was natural enough in a way; in Léon de Valmy's overwhelming presence anyone as awkward and unattractive as Philippe was bound to be made to feel doubly so, and, consciously or not, to resent it.

Moreover his uncle's tone toward him was kind with the semi-indifferent indulgence he might have accorded to a not-very-favorite puppy. I could never make out whether Philippe noticed or resented this; I know that on one or two occasions I found myself resenting it on his behalf. But I still liked Léon de Valmy; Philippe, on the other hand—and this I came only gradually to realize—disliked his uncle very much indeed.

That this was irrational I tried on one occasion to tell him. "Philippe, why do you avoid your uncle Léon?"

The stonewall expression shut down on his face. "Ne comprends pas."

"English, please. And you do understand quite well. He's very good to you. You have everything you want, don't you?"

"Yes. Everything I want I have."

"Well, then—"

He gave me one of his quick, unreadable looks. "But he does not give it to me."

"Who then? Your aunt Héloïse?"

He shook his head. "It is not theirs to give to me. It was my father's and it is mine."

I looked at him. This, then, was it. Valmy. I remembered the little gleam in the black eyes when I had laughingly addressed him as Count de Valmy. This was another thing at which it seemed the de Valmys started young. "Your land?" I said. "Of course it's yours. He's keeping it for you. He's your trustee, isn't he?"

He looked puzzled. "Trustee? I do not know trustee."

"He takes care of Valmy till you are older. Then you have it."

"Yes, until I am fifteen. Is that trustee? Then my Uncle Hippolyte is also trustee."

"Is he? I didn't know that."

He nodded, with that solemn look that sat almost sullenly on his pale little face. "Yes. Tous les deux—both. My uncle Léon for the property and my uncle Hippolyte for me."

"What do you mean?" I asked involuntarily.

The gleam in the look he shot me might have been malice or only mischief. "I heard Papa say that. He said—"

"Philippe," I began, but he wasn't listening. He was wrestling with a translation of what papa had said, only to abandon it and quote in French in a rush that spoke of a literal and all-too-vivid memory.

"He said, 'Léon'll keep the place going, trust him for that. God help Valmy if it was left to Hippolyte.' And Maman said, 'But Hippolyte must have the child if anything happens

40

to us. Hippolyte must look after the child. He is not to be left to Léon.' That's what Maman—" He stopped, shutting his lips tightly over the word.

I said nothing.

He slanted that look at me again and said in English, "That is what they said. It means—"

"No, Philippe, don't try and translate," I said gently, "I don't suppose you were meant to hear it."

"N—no. But I wish I had not had to leave my uncle Hippolyte."

"You're fond of him?"

"Of course. He has gone to la Grèce. I wanted to go with him but he could not take me."

"He'll come back soon."

"Yes, but it is a long time."

"It'll pass," I said, "and meanwhile I'll look after you for him, and your uncle Léon'll look after Valmy."

I paused and looked at the uncommunicative little face. I didn't want to sound pompous or to alienate Philippe, but I was after all in charge of his manners. I said, tentatively, "He does it very well, Philippe. Valmy is beautiful, and he cares for it, ça se voit. You musn't be ungrateful."

It was true that Philippe had no cause to complain of his uncle's stewardship. Léon seemed to me to spend his whole time, indeed, his whole self, on the place. It was as if the immense virility that was physically denied its outlet was redirected onto Valmy. Day after day the wheel chair patroled the terraces and the gravel of the formal gardens, the conservatories, the kitchen gardens, the garages . . . everywhere the chair could possibly go it went. And in the chateau itself the hand of a careful master was everywhere apparent. No plan was too large, no detail too small, for Léon de Valmy's absorbed attention.

It was also true that, as Comte de Valmy, Philippe might legitimately claim that he was a cypher in his own house, but he was only nine, and moreover a Paris-bred stranger. His uncle and aunt did ignore him to a large extent, but his daily routine with its small disciplines and lack of what one might call cosy family life was very much the usual one for a boy in his position.

I added, rather lamely, "You couldn't have a better trustee."

Philippe shot me one of his looks. The shutters were up in his face again. He said politely and distantly, "No, mademoiselle," and looked away.

41

I said no more, feeling myself unable to deal with what still seemed an unreasonable dislike.

But one day toward the end of my second week at Valmy the situation was, so to speak, thrust on me.

Philippe and I had, as usual, been down for our five-thirty visit to Madame de Valmy in the small salon. Punctually at six she dismissed us, but as we went she called me back for some reason that I now forget. Philippe didn't wait, but escaped without ceremony into the corridor.

A minute or so later I left the salon, to walk straight into as nasty a little scene as I had yet come across.

Philippe was standing, the picture of guilt and misery, beside a table which stood against the wall outside the salon door. It was a lovely little table, flanked on either side by a Louis Quinze chair seated with straw-colored brocade. On one of the hair seats I now saw, horribly, a thick streak of ink, as if a pen had rolled from the table and then across the silk of the chair, smearing ink as it went.

I remembered, then, that Philippe had been writing to his uncle, Hippolyte, when I called him to come downstairs. He must have come hurriedly away, the pen still open in his hand, and have put it down there before going into the drawing room. He was clutching it now in an ink-stained fist, and staring white-faced at his uncle.

For this time of all times he hadn't managed to avoid Monsieur de Valmy. The wheel chair was slap in the middle of the corridor, barring escape. Philippe, in front of it, looked very small and guilty and defenseless.

Neither of them appeared to notice me. Léon de Valmy was speaking. That he was angry was obvious, and it looked as if he had every right to be, but the cold lash of his voice as he flayed the child for his small-boy carelessness was frightening; he was using—not a wheel, but an atomic blast, to break a butterfly.

Philippe, as white as ashes now, stammered something that might have been an apology, but merely sounded like a terrified mutter, and his uncle cut across it in that voice that bit like a loaded whip.

"It is, perhaps, just as well that your visits to this part of the house are restricted to this single one a day, as apparently you don't yet know how to behave like a civilized human being. Perhaps in your Paris home you were allowed to run wild in this hooligan manner, but here we are accustomed to—"

42

"This is my home," said Philippe.

He said it still in that small shaken voice that held the suggestion of a sullen mutter. It stopped Léon de Valmy in full tirade. For a moment I thought the sentence in that still little voice unbearably pathetic, and in the same moment wondered at Philippe, who was not prone to either drama or pathos. But then he added, still low, but very clearly, "And that is my chair."

There was a moment of appalling silence. Something came and went in Léon de Valmy's face—the merest flick of an expression like a flash of a camera's shutter—but Philippe took a step backward, and I found myself catapulting out of the doorway like a wildcat defending a kitten.

Léon de Valmy looked up and saw me, but he spoke to Philippe quietly, as though his anger had never been.

"When you have recovered your temper and your manners, Philippe, you will apologize for that remark." The dark eyes lifted to me, and he said coolly but very courteously, in English, "Ah, Miss Martin. I'm afraid there has been a slight contretemps. Perhaps you will take Philippe back to his own rooms and persuade him that courtesy toward his elders is one of the qualities that is expected of a gentleman."

As his uncle spoke to me, Philippe had turned quickly, as if in relief. His face was paler than ever, and looked pinched and sullen. But the eyes were vulnerable: child's eyes.

I looked at him, then past him at his uncle.

"There's no need," I said. "He'll apologize now." I took the boy gently by the shoulders and turned him back to face his uncle. I held him for a moment. The shoulders felt very thin and tense. He was shaking.

I let him go. "Philippe?" I said.

He said, his voice thin with a gulp in it, "I beg your pardon if I was rude."

Léon de Valmy looked from him to me and back again.

"Very well. That is forgotten. And now Miss Martin had better take you upstairs."

The child turned quickly to go, but I hesitated. I said, "I gather there's been an accident to that chair, and that Philippe's been careless; but then, so have I. It was my job to see that nothing of the sort happened. It was my fault, and I must apologize too, Monsieur de Valmy."

He said in a voice quite different from the one with which he had dismissed Philippe, "Very well, Miss Martin. Thank you. And now we will forget the episode, shall we?"

As we went I was very conscious of that still, misshapen figure sitting there watching us.

I shut the schoolroom door behind me, and leaned against it. Philippe and I looked at one another. His face was shuttered still with that white resentment. His mouth looked sulky, but I saw the lower lip tremble a little.

He waited, saying nothing.

This was where I had to uphold authority. Curtain lecture by Miss Martin. Léon de Valmy had been perfectly right: Philippe had been stupid, careless, and rude. . . .

I said, "My lamb, I'm with you all the way, but you are a little owl, aren't you?"

"You can't," said Philippe very stiffly, "be a lamb and an owl both at the same time."

Then he ran straight at me and burst into tears.

After that I did help to keep him out of his uncle's way.

Chapter V

Ay, now the plot thickens very much upon us.

BUCKINGHAM: *The Rehearsal.*

THE spring weather continued marvelous. There was still snow on the nearer hills, and the far high peaks that unrolled below the clouds were great dazzling beds of white as yet untouched by the spring. But the valley was green, and yet greener; the violets were out along the ditches, and all the urns and stone tubs that lined the chateau terraces held their constellations of narcissus and jonquil that danced with the wind.

Philippe and I went out every afternoon, coated and scarved against the breeze that blew off the snow. The mountain air seemed to be doing him good; color came into the shallow cheeks: he even, occasionally, laughed and ran a little, though for the most part he walked stolidly at my side, and answered in his slow but excellent English my dutiful attempts at conversation.

One of our walks was a steep but easy track down through the meadows toward the village. At the foot of the slope a narrow wooden bridge crossed the Merlon, deep here and placid in its wandering from one wide and gleaming pool to the next. From the bridge the track led straight through water meadows and budding orchards to the village.

On the occasions when it was known that our walk would take us to Soubirous, we were given small commissions to execute there, usually for Mrs. Seddon or Berthe, and sometimes for Albertine, but occasionally for Madame de Valmy herself.

One morning—it was the first of April—Philippe and I set out for the village soon after breakfast. It was Monday, and as a rule on Monday morning Monsieur St. Aubray, the curé of Soubirous, came up to the château to instruct the young Comte in Latin, Greek and the Roman Catholic religion. But M. le Curé had twisted an ankle, and, since it did not seem desirable for Philippe to miss his instruction, I took him down to the presbytery beside the church and left him there.

It was the first time I had been on my own in the village, with time to spare. I stood in the little square outside the church and looked about me.

The day was warm, the sunlight as it beat up from flags and cobbles was bright and almost hot. There was a white cat sunning itself on top of a low wall below which someone had planted primulas. The single *bistro* had put out its red-and-black striped awning, and in spite of faded paint and peeling walls the houses looked gay with their open doors and the colored shutters fastened back from the windows. A canary in a small cage hanging outside a shop sang lustily. Some small children, black-haired and brown-limbed, were intent on something in a gutter. Outside a food shop cabbage and cheeses and tired-looking oranges made a splash of color. A boy on a bicycle shot past me, with a yard or so of bread under one arm.

It was a pleasant, peaceful, lighthearted little scene, and my own heart was light as I surveyed it. It was a lovely morning; I was free to do as I wished with it for two hours; I had some money in my pocket; the shadow of the Constance Butcher Home for Girls dwindled and shrank to nothing in the warm Savoyard light. It was also—as a stray warm breeze stirred fragrance from the primulas and brought a shower of early cherry blossom floating out over the presbytery wall— it was also spring.

I walked slowly aross the square, made sure that it was only marbles, and not a frog or a kitten, that was occupying the children in the gutter, then turned into the pharmacy

45

beside the *bistro* to carry out what commissions I had for the day.

"Mademoiselle Martin?" The apothecary came out of his dark cave at the back. He knew me well by this time. Mrs. Seddon, in the intervals of antihistamine, seemed to live exclusively on aspirin and something she called Oh Dick Alone, while I (after half a lifetime of White Windsor) had developed a passion, which had to be satisfied frequently, for the more exotic soaps.

I said gaily, in my most English French, "Oh, good morning, Monsieur Garcin. It is a fine day, is it not? It was a fine day yesterday. It will be a fine day tomorrow. Not? I am looking at the soaps, as usual."

I said *par usuel*, and the chemist's thin lips pursed. It was his weekly pleasure to correct my French, always with that pained, crab-apple face, and I didn't see why I should deny him anything.

"*Comme d'habitude*," he said sourly.

"*Plaît-il?*" I said, very fluently. He had taught me that one last week.

"*Comme d'habitude*," said Monsieur Garcin, raising his voice as to the slightly deaf.

"*Comme quoi?* I do not understand," I said carefully. I was behaving badly and I knew it, but it was a heavenly day and it was spring, and Monsieur Garcin was prim and dry and a bit musty, like herbs that had been kept too long, and besides, he always tried to put me in what he thought was my place. I raised my voice, too, and repeated loudly, "I said I was looking at the soaps, *par usuel*."

The chemist's thin nose twitched, but he restrained himself with an effort. He looked at me dourly across a pile of laxatives. "So I see. And which do you want?" He heaved up a box of Roger and Gallet from behind the counter. "There is a new box this week. Rose, violet, cologne, sandalwood, clove pink—"

"Oh, yes, please. The clove pink. I love that."

A slight gleam of surprise showed in the oyster-like eyes. "You know what flower that is? *Oeillet mignardise?*"

I said composedly, "The name is on the soap. With a picture. *Voilà*." I reached across to pick the tablet out, sniffed it, smiled at him, and said kindly, "*C'est le plus bon, ça.*"

He rose to that one. "*Le meilleur.*"

"*Le meilleur*," I said meekly. "Thank you, monsieur."

"You are doing quite well," said Monsieur Garcin, magnanimously. "And have you any little commissions for your employers today?"

"Yes, if you please. Madame de Valmy asked me to get her medicine and the tablets—her pills for sleeping."

"Very well. Have you the paper?"

"Paper?"

"You must give me the paper, you understand."

I puckered my brows, trying to remember if Albertine had given me a prescription along with the shopping list. The chemist made a movement of ill-concealed impatience, and his mouth drew up and thinned till it disappeared. He repeated very slowly, as to an imbecile, "You—must—have—a paper—from—the—doctor."

"Oh," I said evilly, "a prescription? Why didn't you say so? Well, she didn't give me one, monsieur. May I bring it along next year?"

"Next year?"

"I mean next week."

"No," he said curtly. "I cannot give you the drugs without the prescription."

I was already regretting having teased him. I said distressfully, "Oh, but Madame asked specially for the medicine. I'll bring the paper as soon as I can, or send it or something, honestly I will! Please, Monsieur Garcin, can't you trust me for a day or two?"

"Impossible. No." His bony fingers were rearranging the tablets of soap. "And what else do you want?"

I glanced down at the list in my hand. There were various things on it, listed—luckily for Monsieur Garcin's patience and my own ingenuity—in French. I read them out to him carefully: someone wanted tooth powder and Dop shampoo: someone else (I hoped it was the sour-faced Albertine) demanded corn plasters and iodine, and so on to the end, where came the inevitable aspirin, Eau de cologne, and what Mrs. Seddon simply listed as "my bottle."

"And Mrs. Seddon's pills," I said finally.

The chemist picked up the packet of aspirin.

"No," I said, "the others." (I wouldn't know the word for asthma, would I? And I genuinely didn't know the word for antihistamine.) "The pills for her chest."

"You got them last week," said Monsieur Garcin.

"I don't think so."

"I know you did."

His voice was curt to rudeness, but I ignored it. "Perhaps,"

47

I said politely, "she has need of more?"

"She cannot have, if she got them last week."

"Are you sure she did, monsieur? She put them herself on the list today."

"Did she give you the paper—the prescription?"

"No," I said.

He said impatiently, "I told you she got them last week. You took them yourself. You were in a hurry and you handed me a list with a prescription for Madame Sed-don. I sent the tablets. Perhaps you forgot to give them to her. I have an excellent memory, me; and I remember handing them to you. Moreover, I have a record."

"I am sorry, monsieur. I just don't remember. No doubt you're right. I thought—oh, just a minute, here's a paper in my bag! Here it is, monsieur, the prescription! Voyez-vous. Is this it?"

I handed him the paper, carefully keeping anything of I-told-you-so out of my voice. Which was just as well, because he said tartly, "This is not for Madame Sed-don. It is the paper for Madame de Valmy's heart medicine."

"Oh? I hadn't realized I had it. It must have been with the list. I came out in a hurry and didn't notice. I'm so sorry." I smiled winningly at him. "Then you can give me the medicine after all, monsieur. I'll get the tablets in Thonon on Friday."

He shot me a queer look out of those oyster eyes, and then, by way of teaching me, I suppose, that servants shouldn't argue with their betters, he proceeded to put on his spectacles and read the prescription through with exaggerated care. I watched the sunlight beyond the doorway and waited, suppressing my irritation. He read it again. You'd have thought I was Madeleine Smith asking casually for half a pound of arsenic. Suddenly I saw the joke and laughed at him.

"It's all right, monsieur. It's quite safe to let me have it. I'll see I deliver it promptly where it belongs! I don't often eat digitalis, or whatever it is, myself!"

He said sourly, "I don't suppose you do." He folded the paper carefully and pushed my purchases toward me. "There you are then. I'll give you the drops, and perhaps you will also see that Madame Seddon gets the tablets I sent up on Wednesday?" As I gathered the things up without replying I saw him throw me that queer, quick look yet again. "And I must congratulate you on the way your French has improved, mademoiselle," he added, very dryly.

48

"Why, thank you, monsieur," I said coolly. "I try very hard and study every day. In another three weeks you won't even guess that I'm English."

"*Anglaise?*" The word was echoed, in a man's voice, just behind me. I looked around, startled. I had heard nobody come in, but now realized that a newcomer's large body was blocking the door of the pharmacy, while his enormous shadow, thrown before him by the morning sun, seemed to fill the shop. He came forward. "Excuse me, but I heard you say '*Je suis anglaise.*' Are you really English?"

"Yes."

"Oh, I—that *is* a relief!" He looked down at me half shyly. Seen properly now, and not just as a colossal silhouette framed in the shop door, he still appeared a very large young man. He was dressed in khaki shorts and a wind-breaker. His head was bare, and covered with an untidy thatch of fair hair, very fine and thick. His eyes were blue in a tanned face. His hands and legs were tanned, too, and on them in the sunlight the fair hair glinted, pale as barley in September.

He groped in an inner pocket and produced a tattered old envelope. "I wonder—could you possibly help me, d'you think? I've got a whole list of stuff to get, and I was wondering how on earth to ask for it. My French is nonexistent, and yours seems terribly good—"

I said firmly, "My French may sound wonderful to you, but it sounds like nothing on earth to Monsieur Garcin."

I sent a bright smile to the chemist, who still watched me, sourly, from behind the stack of laxatives. No response. I gave it up and turned back to the Englishman, who was saying, unconvinced, "It seems to get results anyway." He gestured toward my purchases.

I grinned. "You'd be surprised what a fight it is sometimes. But of course I'll help—if I can. May I see your list?"

He surrendered it relievedly. "This is awfully good of you to let me bother you." He gave his disarmingly shy grin. "Usually I just have to beat my breast like Tarzan and point."

"You must be very brave to come holidaying here without a word of French."

"Holidaying? I'm here on a job."

"Paid assassin?" I asked, "or only M.I.5?"

"I—I beg your pardon?"

I indicated the list. "This. It sounds a bit pointed." I read it aloud. "Bandages; three, one-and-a-half, and one-inch. Sticking plaster. Elastoplast. Burn-dressing. Boracic powder . . . You've forgotten the probe."

"Probe?"

"To get the bullets out."

He laughed. "I'm only a forester. I'm camping off and on in a hut at four thousand feet, so I thought I'd set up a first-aid kit."

"Do you intend to live quite so dangerously?"

"You never know. Anyway I'm a confirmed hypochondriac. I'm never happy till I'm surrounded by pills and boluses and thermometers marked in degrees centigrade."

I looked at his six-feet odd of solid bone and muscle. "Yes. One can see that you should take every care. Do you really want me to struggle with sticking-plaster and burn-dressings for you?"

"Yes, please, if you'd be so good, though the only item I'm really sure I shall need is the last one, and I could ask for that myself at a pinch."

"Cognac? Yes, I see what you mean." Then I turned to Monsieur Garcin and embarked on the slightly exhausting procedure of describing by simple word and gesture articles whose names I knew as well as he did himself. Monsieur Garcin served me reservedly, and as with Philippe, his reserve sometimes bore a strong resemblance to the sulks. I had twice tried the *amende honorable* of a smile, and I was dashed if I would try again, so we persevered in chilly politeness to the last-but-one item on the Englishman's list.

At last we had finished. The Englishman, weighed down with enough pills and boluses to satisfy the most highly-strung *malade imaginaire*, stood back from the doorway and waited for me to precede him into the sunlight.

As I picked up my own parcels and turned to go the chemist's voice said, as dry as the rustle of dead leaves, "You are forgetting the drops for Madame de Valmy." He was holding out the package across the counter.

When I reached the sunny street the young man said curiously, "What's biting him? Was he being rude? You're—forgive my saying so—but you're as pink as anything."

"Am I? Well, it's my own fault. No, he wasn't rude. It was just me being silly and getting what I deserved."

"I'm sure you weren't. And thank you most awfully for being such a help. I'd never have managed on my own." He gave me his shy grin. "I still have to get the cognac. I wonder if you'd help me to buy that too?"

"I thought you said you could ask for that yourself."

"I—well, I rather hoped you'd come with me and let me buy you a drink to thank you for taking all that trouble."

"That's very nice of you. But really, there's no need—"

He looked down at me rather imploringly over his armful of packages. "Please," he said. "Apart from everything else, it really is wonderful to talk English to someone."

I had a sudden vision of him up in his lonely hut at four thousand feet, surrounded by pills and boluses and thermometers in degrees centigrade.

"I'd like to very much," I said.

He beamed. "That's fine. In here? It's Hobson's choice anyway—I think this is the only place apart from the Coq Hardi half a mile away."

The *bistro* with its gay awning was next door to the pharmacy. Inside it looked dim and not very inviting, but on the cobbles outside there were two or three little metal tables, and some old cane chairs painted bright red. Two small clipped trees stood sentinel in blue tubs.

We sat down in the sun. "What will you have?" He was carefully disposing his life-saving parcels on an empty chair.

"Do you suppose they serve coffee?"

"Surely." And it seemed, indeed, that they did. It arrived in large yellow cups, with three wrapped oblongs of sugar in each saucer.

Now that we were facing one another more or less formally across a café, my companion seemed to have retreated once more behind a rather English shyness. He said, stirring his coffee hard, "My name's Blake. William Blake." On this last he looked up with a trace of defiance.

I said, "That's a good name to have, isn't it? Mine's only Belinda Martin. Linda for short—or for pretty, my mother used to say."

He smiled. "Thank you."

"For what? Making you free of my name?"

"Oh—yes, of course. But I meant for not making a crack about the *Songs of Innocence*."

" 'Little lamb, who made thee?' "

"That one exactly. You'd be surprised how many people can't resist it."

I laughed. "How awfully trying! But me, I prefer tigers. No thank you, Mr. Blake—" this to a proffered cigarette— "I don't smoke."

"Mind if I do?"

"Of course not."

Across the spluttering flare of a French match he was looking a question. "If one may ask—what are you doing in Soubirous? Not a holiday, I take it?"

"No. I'm here on a job, too. I'm governess."

"Of course. You must be the English girl from the Chateau Valmy."

"Yes. You know about me?"

"Everybody knows everybody else hereabouts. Anyway I'm a near neighbor, as things go round here. I'm working on the next estate, in the plantations west of the Merlon."

"Oh," I said, interested. "Dieudonné?"

"That's it. The chateau—it's only a country house really, a quarter the size of Valmy—lies in the valley a bit beyond the village. The owner's hardly ever there. His name's St. Vire. He seems to spend most of his time in Paris or down near Bordeaux. Like your boss, he gets a lot of his money from his timber and his vineyards."

"Vineyards? Valmy?"

"Oh, yes. They own chunks of Provence, I believe."

"Of course," I said. "Bellevigne. But that's Monsieur de Valmy's own property, and Valmy isn't. Even he wouldn't spend its income on Valmy."

"Even he?"

To my surprise my voice sounded defensive. "I believe he's an awfully good landlord."

"Oh, that. Yes, second to none, I imagine. He's pretty highly thought of hereabouts, I can tell you. And the gossip goes that most of the Bellevigne income did get diverted up here until a few years back; there used to be plenty money, anyway."

"There still is," I said, "or so it seems."

"Yes. Things are waking up again, I gather. Two good vintages, and you get the roof repaired. . . ." He laughed. "Funny how everyone in the places minds everyone else's business, isn't it?" He looked at me. "Governessing. Now that's a heck of a life, isn't it?"

"In story books, yes; and I suppose it could be in real life. But I like it. I like Philippe—my pupil—and I love the place."

"You're not lonely—so far from home, I mean, and England?"

I laughed. "If you only knew! My 'home in England' was seven years in an orphanage. Governessing or not, Valmy's a wild adventure to me!"

"I suppose so. Is that what you want, adventure?"

"Of course! Who doesn't?"

"Me, for one," said Mr. Blake firmly.

"Oh? But I thought all men saw themselves hacking their

way with machetes through the mangrove swamps and shooting rapids and things. You know, all hairy knees and camp fires and the wide wide world."

He grinned. "I got over that pretty young. And just exactly what is a machete?"

"Goodness knows. They always have them. But seriously—"

"Seriously," he said, "I don't know. I'd like to get around, yes, and I like travel and change and seeing new things, but —well, roots are a good thing to have." He stopped himself there and flushed a little. "I'm sorry. That was tactless."

"It's all right. And I do see what you mean. Everybody needs a—a center. Somewhere to go out from and come back to. And I suppose as you get older, you enjoy the coming back more than the going out."

He gave me his shy, rather charming smile. "Yes, I think so. But don't listen to me, Miss Martin. I have a stick-in-the-mud disposition. You go ahead and chase your tigers. After all, you've done pretty well up to now. You've found one already, haven't you?"

"Monsieur de Valmy?"

His eyebrows lifted. "You were quick onto that. He *is* a tiger, then?"

"You did mean him? Why?"

"Only that he seems a little fierce and incalculable by reputation. How do you get on with him? What's he like?"

"I—he's very polite and kind—I'd even say charming. Yes, certainly he's charming. He and Madame seem terribly anxious that I should really feel at home here. I don't see an awful lot of them, of course, but when I do they're awfully nice. . . ."

I looked away from him across the square. Two women came out of the boulangerie, and paused to glance at us curiously before they moved off, their sabots noisy on the stones. Someone called, shrilly, and the group of children broke up, chattering and screaming like jays. Two of them raced past us, bare feet slapping the warm cobbles. The clock in the church tower clanged the half-hour.

I said, "And what made you come here? Tell me about your job."

"There's nothing much to tell." He was drawing little patterns on the table top with the handle of his spoon. And indeed, the way he told it, his life had taken a very ordered course. A pleasant, reasonably well-to-do suburban home; a small public school; two years in the Army, doing nothing more eventful than maneuvers on Salisbury Plain; then the

University—four years' hard work, with holidays (more or less of the busman variety) in Scandinavia and Germany; finally, a good degree and the decision to go on to a further two years' research on some conifer diseases, which he proceeded to explain to me very carefully and with much enthusiasm. . . . Far from lacking adventure, it appeared that (what with butt rot, drought crack, larch canker, spruce bark beetle, and things with names like *Phomopsis* and *Megatismus* and even *Ips*) life in a conifer forest could positively teem with excitement. I gathered that Mr. Blake himself was seriously involved with the Pine Weevil . . . there was a magnificent infestation of these creatures (*Hylobius*, mark you, not *Pissodes*), in a plantation west of the Merlon. . . .

But here he recollected himself and flushed slightly, grinning at me. "Well, anyway," he finished, "that's why I'm here. I'm busy getting the best of both worlds—thanks to Monsieur de St. Vire, who's a remarkably decent chap for a Frenchman." He added, seeming to think this phenomenon worth explaining, "My father knew him in the War. He's given me a job here of a sort—at any rate I'm paid a bit for doing what's really my own research program anyway. I'm getting some valuable material as well as experience, and I like working in this country. It's small-scale stuff hereabouts, but those people—at any rate the Valmys and St. Vires—really do care about their land. But there's a lot to learn." He looked wistful. "Including the language. It seems to escape me, somehow. Perhaps I've no ear. But it would be a help."

"If you're living alone, with thermometers," I said, "I can't see why."

"Oh, I'm not up at the hut all the time. I work up there mostly, because it's near the plantation I'm 'on' at present, and it's quiet; I keep all my stuff up there, and I sleep there when I'm short of cash." He grinned. "That's quite often, of course. But I do come down to the Coq Hardi pretty frequently. It's noisy, but the boss speaks English and the food's good . . . ah, is that your little boy?"

From where we were sitting we could see the high wall of the presbytery garden, and now the gate in it opened, and Philippe appeared in the archway, with the broad figure of the curé's housekeeper behind him.

"Yes, that's Philippe," I said. "I'll have to go."

I got to my feet, and the child saw me, said something over his shoulder to the woman, and then ran across the square in our direction.

"I'm glad you waited. I told Madame Rocher you would go—would have gone for a walk. But here you are."

"Here I am. You're early, aren't you, Philippe? Did Monsieur le Curé get tired of you?"

"I do not know tired of."

"Ennuyé."

He was solemn. "No. But he is not very well. He is tired, but not at—of—me. Madame Rocher says I must come away."

"I'm sorry to hear that," I said. "Philippe, this is Monsieur Blake, who works for Monsieur de St. Vire. Mr. Blake, the Comte de Valmy."

They shook hands, Philippe with the large gravity that sat on him rather attractively.

"What do you work at, monsieur?"

"I'm a forester."

"Forest—oh, yes. There are foresters at Valmy also."

"I know. I've met one or two of them. Pierre Detruche, Jean-Louis Michaud, and Armand Lestocq—he lives next door to the Coq Hardi."

"As to that," said Philippe, "I do not know them myself yet. I have not been here very long, vous comprenez."

"Of course not. I—er, I suppose your uncle manages these things."

"Yes," said Philippe politely. "He is my trustee."

The look he shot me was merely one of minor triumph that he should have remembered the word, but it tinged the reply with a sort of smug stateliness that brought the beginnings of amusement to Mr. Blake's face. I said hastily, "We'd better go, I think, Mr. Blake, thank you so much for the coffee. I'm awfully glad we met." I held out my hand.

As he took it, he said quickly, "I say, please—don't just vanish. When can we meet again?"

"I'm not a very free agent. Sometimes I've a morning, but I don't often get as far as this."

"Are you free in the evenings?"

"No, not really. Only Fridays, and a Sunday here and there."

"Then that's no good," he said, sounding disappointed. "I've arranged to meet some pals of mine this week end. Perhaps later on?"

Philippe had given a little tug to my hand. "I really must go," I said. "Let's leave it, shall we? We're sure to meet—the valley isn't all that big. And thank you again. . . ."

As we crossed the bridge I glanced back, to see him laboriously gathering up the bandages and the sticking-plaster and all the homely remedies which were to reassure life at four thousand feet.

I hoped he would remember to get the cognac.

Chapter VI

*Something will come of this. I hope it
mayn't be human gore.*

DICKENS: *Barnaby Rudge.*

THAT evening the quiet run of our existence was broken. Nursery tea was over; the early April dusk had drawn in against the uncurtained windows where lamp and firelight were cheerfully reflected. Philippe was on the hearthrug playing in a desultory fashion with some soldiers and I was sitting, as I often did at that time, reading aloud to him, when I heard a car climbing the zigzag. It was a mild evening, and one of the long balcony windows was open. The mounting engine roared, changed, roared again nearer. As I paused in my reading and glanced toward the window, Philippe looked up.

"Une auto! Quelqu'un vient!"

"English," I said automatically. "Philippe, what are you doing?"

But he took no notice. He jumped up from the rug, while his toys scattered unheeded. Then he flew out of the window like a rocket and vanished to the right along the balcony.

I dropped the book and hurried after him. He had run to the end of the balcony where it overlooked the gravel forecourt, and was leaning over eagerly and somewhat precariously. I stifled an impulse to grab him by the seat of his pants and said instead, as mildly as I could, "You'll fall if you hang over like that. . . . Look, the dashed thing's loose anyway—this coping moved, I'm sure it did. This must be one of the bits they were talking about repairing. Philippe—"

But he didn't seem to be listening. He still craned forward over the stone coping. I said firmly, "Now come back, Philippe, and be sensible. What's the excitement for, anyway?"

56

The car roared up the last incline, and swung with a scrunch of tires across the gravel. She had her lights on. They scythed around, through the thin dark thorns of the rose garden, the flickering spear points of the iron railings below us, the carefully-planted pots on the loggia, came to rest on the stableyard archway, and were switched off.

A door slammed. I heard a man's voice, low-pitched and pleasant. Another voice—I supposed the driver's—answered him. Then the car moved off slowly toward the stableyard, and the newcomer crossed the gravel and mounted the steps to the great door.

I waited with mild curiosity for the door to open and the light from the hall to give body, as it were, to the voice. But before this happened Philippe ducked back behind me and retreated along the balcony toward the schoolroom windows. I turned, to see in the set of the thin back and shoulders the suggestion of some disappointment so sharp that I followed him in without a word, sat down again in my chair by the fire, and picked up my book. But Philippe didn't settle again to his toys. He stood still on the hearthrug, staring at the fire. I think he had forgotten I was there.

I leafed through a few pages of the book and then said very casually, "Who was it, did you know?"

The thin shoulders lifted. "Monsieur Florimond, I think."

"Monsieur Florimond? Do you mean the dress designer?"

"Yes. He used to visit us a lot in Paris and he is a friend of my aunt Héloïse. Do you know of him in England?"

"Of course." Even in the Constance Butcher Home we had heard of the great Florimond, whose "Aladdin" silhouette had been the rage of Paris and New York years before and had, it was rumored, caused Dior to mutter something under his breath and tear up a set of designs. I said, impressed, "Is he coming to stay?"

"I do not know." His voice sufficiently also expressed that he did not care. But the general impression of poignant disappointment prevailed so strongly that I said, "Did you expect someone else, Philippe?"

He glanced up momentarily, then the long lashes dropped. He said nothing.

I hesitated. But Philippe was my job: moreover, he was a very lonely little boy. Who was it who could expect that headlong welcome from him?

I said, "Your cousin Raoul, perhaps?"

No answer.

"Is anyone else supposed to be coming?"

57

He shook his head.

I tried again. "Don't you like Monsieur Florimond?"

"But yes. I like him very much."

"Then why——?" I began, but something in his face warned me to stop. I said gently, "It's time we went down to the salon, petit. I haven't been told not to, so I suppose, guest or not, that we'll have to go. Run and wash your hands while I tidy my hair."

He obeyed me without a word or look.

I went slowly across to shut the balcony window.

In a small salon a log fire had been lit, and in front of it sat Madame de Valmy and Monsieur Florimond on a rose brocaded sofa, talking.

I looked with interest at the newcomer. I don't know what I expected one of fashion's Big Five to look like; only know that the great Florimond didn't look like it. He was vast, baldish, and untidy. His face in repose had a suggestion of tranquil melancholy about it that was vaguely reminiscent of the White Knight, but no one could ever doubt Monsieur Florimond's large sanity. Those blue eyes were shrewd and very kind: they also looked as if they missed very little. He wore his conventional, superbly cut clothes with all the delicate care one might accord to an old beach towel. His pockets bulged comfortably in every direction, and there was cigar ash on his lapel. He was clutching what looked like a folio-society reprint in one large hand, and gestured with it lavishly to underscore some story he was telling Madame de Valmy.

She was laughing, looking happier and more animated than I had seen her since I came to Valmy. I realized sharply how lovely she had been before time and tragedy had drained the life from her face.

On the thought, she turned and saw myself and Philippe by the door, and the gaiety vanished. The boredom and annoyance that shut down over it were humiliatingly plain to see. I could have slapped her for it, but then realized that Philippe had probably not noticed. He was advancing solemnly and politely on Florimond, who surged to his feet with noises indicating quite sufficient delighted pleasure to counter Héloïse's obvious irritation.

"Philippe! This is delightful! How are you?"

"I am very well, thank you, m'sieur."

"H'm, yes." He tapped the boy's cheek. "A little more color there, perhaps, and then you'll do. Country air, that's

58

the thing, and the Valmy air suits you, by the look of it!"
He didn't actually say "better than Paris," but the words
were there, implicit, and Philippe didn't reply. It wasn't
easy to avoid mistakes just then with him. Florimond reg-
istered this one, I could see, but he merely added amiably,
"Mind you, I don't wonder that Valmy's good for you!
When one is lucky enough to have a beautiful young lady
as one's constant companion, one must expect to flourish!"

The perfect politeness of Philippe's smile indicated how
completely this gallant sally went over his head. It had perforce, since they were speaking French, to go over mine too.
I looked as noncommittal as I could and avoided Florimond's
eye.

Héloïse de Valmy said from the sofa, "Don't waste your
gallantries, Carlo. Miss Martin's French improves hourly, so
I'm told, but I don't think she's reached the compliment stage
yet." Then, in English: "Miss Martin, let me introduce Monsieur Florimond. You will have heard of him, I don't doubt."

I said composedly as I shook hands, "Even in my English
orphanage we had heard of Monsieur Florimond. You reached
us perhaps some six years late, monsieur, but you did reach
us." I smiled, remembering my own cheap ready-made. "Believe it or not."

He didn't pretend to misunderstand me. He made a largely
gallant gesture with the book which was, I saw, *The Tale of
Genji*, and said, "You, mademoiselle, would adorn anything
you wore."

I laughed. "Even this?"

"Even that," he said, unperturbed, a twinkle in the blue
eyes.

"The size of that compliment," I said, "strikes me dumb,
monsieur."

Madame de Valmy said, sounding amused now, and more
naturally friendly than I had yet heard her, "It's Monsieur
Florimond's constant sorrow that only the old and faded can
afford to be dressed by him, while the young and lovely buy
dresses *prêtes à porter* . . . there's a phrase—my English is
slipping in the excitement of talking to you, Carlo—what's the
phrase you have for 'ready-made'?"

" 'Off the peg?' " I suggested.

"Yes, that's it. You buy your dresses off the peg, and still
show us up."

"Your English *is* slipping, madame," I said. "You're getting
your pronouns all wrong."

As she lifted her eyebrows Florimond said delightedly,

"There, chère madame, a real compliment! A compliment of the right kind! So neat you did not see it coming, and so subtil that you still do not see it when it has come."

She laughed. "My dear Carlo, compliments even now aren't quite so rare that I don't recognize them, believe me. Thank you, Miss Martin, that was sweet of you." Her eyes as she smiled at me were friendly, almost warm, and for the first time since I had met her I saw charm in her—not the easy charm of the vivid personality, but the real and irresistible charm that reaches out halfway to meet you, assuring you that you are wanted and liked. And heaven knew I needed that assurance. . . . I was very ready to meet any gesture, however slight, with the response of affection. Perhaps at last . . .

But even as I smiled back at her it happened again. The warmth drained away as if wine had seeped from a crack and left the glass empty, a cool and misted shell, reflecting nothing.

She turned away to pick up her embroidery.

I stood with the smile stiffening on my lips, feeling, even more sharply than before, the sense of having been rebuffed for some reason that I couldn't understand. A moment ago I could have sworn the woman liked me, but now . . . in the last fleeting glance before the cool eyes dropped to her embroidery I thought I saw the same queerly apprehensive quality that I had noticed on my first day at Valmy.

I dismissed the idea straight away. I no longer imagined that Madame de Valmy feared her husband; on the contrary. Without any overt demonstration it was obvious that the two were very close; their personalities shared a boundary as light and shadow do; they marched. It was probable, I thought pityingly and only half comprehendingly, that Héloïse de Valmy's keep-your-distance chilliness was only a by-product of the sort of Samurai self-control that she must have learned to practice elsewhere. With the inability of youth to imagine any temperament other than my own, I felt that life must be a good deal easier for Léon de Valmy himself than for his wife. . . .

And her attitude to me—to Philippe as well—must only be part of the general shutdown. . . . It would take time for the reserve to melt, the door to open. That look of hers wasn't apprehension; it was a kind of waiting, an appraisal, no more. It would take time. Perhaps, she was still only wondering, as I was, why Léon de Valmy thought she'd made "a very great mistake. . . ."

She was setting a stitch with delicate care. There was a lamp at her elbow. The light shone softly on the thin white hand. The needle threaded the canvas with moving sparks. She didn't look up. "Come and sit by me, Philippe, on this footstool. You may stay ten minutes . . . no, Miss Martin, don't slip away. Sit down and entertain Monsieur Florimond for me."

The mask was on again. She sat, composed and elegant as ever over her needlework. She even managed to appear faintly interested as she put Philippe through the usual catechism about his day's activities, and listened to his polite, painstaking replies.

Beside me Florimond said, "Won't you sit here?"

I turned gratefully toward him, to find him watching me with those mild eyes that neverthless seemed to miss nothing. He may have noticed the ebb and flow of invitation and rebuff that had left me silent and stranded; at any rate he now appeared to lay himself out to amuse me. His repertoire of gently scandalous stories was extremely entertaining and probably at least half true, and—as I knew his Paris better than he realized—I was soon enjoying myself immensely. He flirted a very little, too—oh, so expertly!—and looked slightly disconcerted and then delighted when he found that his gallantries amused instead of confused me. He would have been even more disconcerted if he'd known that, in a queer sort of way, he was reminding me of Daddy: I hadn't heard this sort of clever, oversophisticated chatter since I'd last been allowed in to one of Daddy's drink-and-verses jamborees ten years before. I may be forgiven if I enjoyed every moment of the oddly nostalgic rubbish that we talked.

Or would have done, if every now and again I hadn't seen Héloïse de Valmy's cool eyes watching me with that indefinable expression which might have been appraisal, or wariness, or—if it weren't fantastic—fear.

And if I hadn't been wondering who had reported on the "hourly" improvement of my French.

The entry of Seddon with the cocktail tray interrupted us. I looked inquiringly at Madame de Valmy, and Philippe made as if to get to his feet.

But before she could dismiss us Florimond said comfortably, "Don't drive the child away, Héloïse. Now he's said his catechism perhaps you'll deliver him over to me."

She smiled, raising her delicate brows. "What do you want with him, Carlo?"

He had finally put down *The Tale of Genji* on the extreme edge of a fragile-looking coffee table, and was fishing in one untidy pocket with a large hand. He grinned at Philippe, who was watching him with that guarded look I hated to see, and I saw the child's face relax a little in reply. "Last time I saw you, my lad," said Florimond, "I was trying to initiate you into the only civilized pastime for men of sense. Ah, here we are. . . ." As he spoke he fished a small board out of one pocket. It was a traveler's chess set, complete with tiny men in red and white.

Madame de Valmy laughed. "The ruling passion," she said, her cool voice almost indulgent. "Very well, Carlo, but he must go upstairs at a quarter past, no later. Berthe will be waiting for him."

That this was not true she knew quite well, and so did I. Though the conversation was now in French, I saw her give me a quick glance, and kept my face noncommittal. It was interesting that I wasn't the only one who schemed to keep Philippe out of his uncle's way.

Philippe had dragged his stool eagerly enough across to Florimond's chair and the two of them were already poring over the board.

"Now," said Florimond cheerfully, "let's see if you can remember any of the rules, mon gars. I seem to recollect some erratic movements last time you and I were engaged, but there's a sort of wild freshness about your conception of the game which has its own surprising results. Your move."

"I moved," said Philippe demurely, "while you were talking."

"Did you, pardieu? Ah, the king's pawn. A classic gambit, monsieur . . . and I, this pawn. So."

Philippe bent over the board, his brows fiercely knitted, his whole small being concentrated on the game, while above him Florimond, leaning back vast in his chair, with cigar-ash spilling down his beautifully-cut jacket, watched him indulgently, never ceasing for a moment the gentle, aimless flow of words, of which it was very obvious that Philippe, if indeed he was listening at all, would understand only one in three.

I sat quietly and watched them, feeling a warm, almost affectionate glow toward this large and distinguished Parisian who, among all his other preoccupations, could bother to make a lonely small boy feel he was wanted. From the couturier's talk you would suppose that he had nothing to do for the past year but look forward to another game with Philippe.

I noticed then that Madame de Valmy wasn't sewing. Her hands lay idle in the tumble of embroidery in her lap. I thought that she was interested in the game until I saw that she wasn't watching the board. Her eyes were fixed on the back of Philippe's down-bent head. She must have been deep in some faraway thoughts, because when Philippe made a sudden exclamation she jumped visibly.

He gave a little whoop of glee and pounced on the board. "Your queen! Your queen! *Regardez* monsieur, I've got your queen!"

"So I see," said Florimond, unperturbed. "But will you kindly tell me, Capablanca, by what new law you were able to move your piece straight down the board to do so?"

"There was nothing in the way," explained Philippe kindly.

"No. But the piece you moved, *mon vieux*, was a bishop. I'm sorry to be petty about it, but there is a rule which restricts the bishop to a diagonal line. Nugatory, you will say; trifling . . . but there it is. Medes and Persians, Philippe."

"A bishop?" said Philippe, seizing on the one word that made sense.

"The ones with the pointed hats," said Florimond tranquilly, "are the bishops."

"Oh," said Philippe. He looked up at his opponent and grinned, not in the least abashed. "I forgot. You can have your queen back then."

"I am grateful. Thank you. Now, it's still your move and I should suggest that you observe again the relative positions of your bishop and my queen."

Philippe concentrated. "There is nothing between them," he said, uncertainly.

"Exactly."

"Well—oh!" The small hand hastily scooped the lawless bishop out of the queen's path. "There. I move him there."

Florimond chuckled. "Very wise," he said. "Very wise." From the way he leaned forward to scan the board through a thoughtful cloud of tobacco-smoke you would have thought he was matched with a master instead of a small boy who didn't even know the rules.

I glanced at the clock. Sixteen minutes past six. I looked in surprise at Madame de Valmy, whom I had suspected of a clock-watching nervousness almost equal to my own. She had dropped her hands in her lap again and was staring at the fire. She was a hundred miles away. I wondered where . . . no pleasant place, I thought.

I said, "Madame."

She started, and picked up her embroidery so quickly that she pricked her finger. I said, "I'm sorry, madame, I startled you. I think it's time I took Philippe upstairs, isn't it?"

I had my back to the door so I neither saw nor heard it

open. It was the quick turn of Philippe's head and the widening of the black eyes that told me. Léon de Valmy's beautiful voice said, "Ah, Philippe. No, don't move. Carlo, how delightful! Why don't we see you more often?"

The wheel chair glided silently forward as he spoke. For such a quiet entrance the effect was remarkable enough. Philippe jumped off his footstool and stood staring at his uncle like a mesmerized bird, Monsieur Florimond hoisted himself again to his feet, Héloïse de Valmy dropped her embroidery and turned quickly toward her husband, while I slid out of my place as his chair passed me and retired toward my usual distant window seat.

I didn't think Léon de Valmy had noticed me, but Philippe had. He, too, made a movement as if to escape, but was netted, so to speak, with a word.

"No, indeed, Philippe. It's all too rarely that I get a chance to see you. We must thank Monsieur Florimond for bringing me in early. Sit down."

The child obeyed. The wheel chair slid up beside the sofa and stopped. Léon de Valmy touched his wife's hand. "Your devotion to duty touches me, Héloïse. It does really."

Only an ear that was tuned to it could have detected the taunt in the smooth voice. I saw their eyes meet, and Héloïse de Valmy smiled, and for the second time that evening I felt the scald of a little spurt of anger. Did they find even half an hour out of the day intolerably much to give to Philippe? And did they have to make it plain? This time Philippe didn't miss it. I saw the swift upward slant of his lashes at his uncle, and the too-familiar sullenness settle on the pale little face, and thought: why don't you pick someone your own weight, damn you . . . ?

The next second the incident might have been illusion. Léon de Valmy, obviously in the best of spirits, was welcoming Monsieur Florimond almost gaily. "It's very nice of you to look us up, Carlo. What brought you to Geneva?"

Florimond lowered himself once more into his chair. "I came on the track of a material." He made another of his large gestures, this time toward *The Tale of Genji*, which promptly fell onto the floor. "Take a look at those pictures some time, Héloïse, and tell me if you ever saw anything to touch that elegance, that courteous silverpoint grace just on the hither side of decadence. . . . Ah, thank you, *mon lapin*." This to Philippe, who had quietly picked up the book and was handing it to him. "Give it to your aunt, *p'tit. C'est formidable, hein?*"

She glanced at it. "What's this, Carlo?"

"A threat to your peace of mind and my pocket," said Léon de Valmy, smiling. "The 'mandarin' line, or some such thing, I don't doubt, and just on the hither side of decadence at that. I confess I can't see you in it, my dear."

Florimond laughed. "Only the material, I do assure you, only the material! And that's as much as I shall tell you. Rose Gautier and I have concocted something between us that ought to flutter the dovecotes next November, and I came up to keep a father's eye on it in the making." He grinned amiably at his host. "At least, that's the excuse. I always try to desert Paris at this juncture if I possibly can."

"How's the collection going?" asked Madame.

Florimond dropped a gout of ash down his shirt front, and wiped it placidly aside across his lapel. "At the moment it's hardly even conceived. Not a twitch, not a pang. I shall not be in labor for many months to come, and then we shall have the usual lightning and half-aborted litter to be licked into shape in a frenzy of blood and tears." Here his eye fell on Philippe, silent on his stool, and he added, with no perceptible change of tone, "There was thick mist lying on the road between here and Thonon."

Léon de Valmy was busy at the cocktail tray. He handed his wife a glass. "Really? Bad?"

"In places. But I fancy it's only local. It was clear at Geneva, though of course it may cloud up later along the Lake. Ah, thank you."

Léon de Valmy poured his own drink, then as his chair turned again into the circle round the hearth he caught sight of the chessboard on the low table.

The black brows rose. "Chess? Do you never move without that thing, Carlo?"

"Never. May I hope you'll give me a game tonight?"

"With pleasure. But not with that collection of dressmakers' pins, I beg of you. I don't play my best when I've to use a telescope."

"It's always pure joy to play with that set of yours," said Florimond, "quite apart from the fact that you're a foeman worthy of my steel—which is one way of saying that you beat me four times out of five."

"Hm." Léon de Valmy was surveying the board. "It would certainly appear that Red was playing a pretty shortsighted game in every sense of the word. I knew you were not chessminded, Héloïse, my dear, but I didn't know you were quite that bad."

She merely smiled, not even bothering to deny it. There was no need anyway. He knew who'd been playing, and Philippe knew he knew.

"Ah, yes," said Florimond calmly. He peered at the miniature men. "Dear me, I have got myself into an odd tangle, haven't I? Perhaps I need spectacles. You're quite right, my dear Léon, it's a mistake to underrate one's opponent. Never do that." The big hand shifted a couple of men with quick movements. The mild clever face expressed nothing whatever except interest in the Lilliputian maneuvers on the board.

I saw Léon de Valmy glance up at him swiftly, and the look of amusement that came and went like the gleam on the underside of a blown cloud. "I don't." Then he smiled at Philippe, silent on his stool. "Come and finish the game, Philippe. I'm sure your aunt won't drive you upstairs just yet."

Philippe went, if possible, smaller and more rigid than before. "I—I'd rather not, thank you."

Léon de Valmy said pleasantly, "You mustn't allow the fact that you were losing to weigh with you, you know."

The child went scarlet. Florimond said, quite without inflection, "In any case we can't continue. I disarranged the pieces just now. The situation wasn't quite as peculiar as your uncle supposed, Philippe, but I can't remember just what it was. I'm sorry. I hope very much that you'll give me the pleasure of a game another time. You do very well."

He pushed the board aside and smiled down at the child, who responded with one quick upward look. Then he leaned back in his chair, and, smiling amiably at his host, launched without pausing straight into one of his improbable stories, thus effectively forcing the general attention back to himself. Philippe remained without moving, small on his stool, the picture of sulky isolation. I watched him, still feeling in my damn-them mood. He must have felt my glance, because eventually he looked up. I winked at him and grinned. There was no answering gleam. The black lashes merely dropped again.

Then the door opened, and Seddon, the butler, came in. He crossed the floor to Madame de Valmy's side.

"Madame, a telephone message has just come through from Monsieur Raoul."

I saw her flash a glance at her husband. "From Monsieur Raoul? Yes, Seddon?"

"He asked me to tell you he was on his way up, madame."

The base of Léon de Valmy's glass clinked down on the

arm of his chair. "On his way? Here? When? Where was he speaking from?"

"That I couldn't say, sir. But he wasn't at Bellevigne. He said he would be here some time tonight."

A pause. I noticed the soft uneven ticking of the lovely little clock on the mantel.

Then Florimond said comfortably, "How very pleasant! I don't know when I last set eyes on Raoul. I hope he'll be here for dinner?"

Seddon said, "No, monsieur. He said he might be late, and not to wait for him, but that he would get here tonight."

Léon de Valmy said, "And that was all the message?"

"Yes, sir."

Madame de Valmy stirred. "He didn't sound as if there was anything wrong . . . at Bellevigne?"

"No, madame. Not at all."

Florimond chuckled. "Don't look so worried, my dear. They've probably had a week of the mistral and he's decided to cut and run for it. The original ill wind."

"He doesn't usually run in this direction," said his father, very dryly. "Very well, Seddon, thank you."

Madame de Valmy said, "Perhaps you'll be good enough to see Mrs. Seddon straight away about a room?"

"Of course, madame." Seddon, expressionless as ever, bent his head. I saw Héloïse de Valmy glance again at her husband. I couldn't see his face from where I sat, but she was biting her bottom lip, and to my surprise she looked strained and pale.

A nice gay welcome for the son of the house was, it appeared, laid on. Him and Philippe both. . . . As a cozy family home the Château Valmy certainly took some beating. The Constance Butcher wasn't in it.

Then the central chandelier leaped into a lovely cascade of light. Seddon moved forward to draw curtains and replenish drinks. Glasses clinked, and someone laughed. Philippe moved cheerfully to help Florimond pack away the tiny chessmen . . . and in a moment, it seemed, under the bright light, the imagined tensions dissolved and vanished. Firelight, laughter, the smell of pine logs and Schiaparelli, the rattle of curtain rings and the swish as the heavy brocades swung together . . . it was absurd to people the lovely Château Valmy with the secret ghosts of Thornfield.

The Demon King turned his handsome gray head and said in English, "Come out, Jane Eyre."

I must have jumped about a foot. He looked surprised, then laughed and said, "Did I startle you? I'm sorry. Were you very far away?"

"Pretty far. At a place in Yorkshire called Thornfield Hall."

The black brows lifted. "So we're en rapport? No wonder you jumped." He smiled. "I shall have to be careful. . . . And now will you take your charge away before Monsieur Florimond corrupts him with vermouth? No, Philippe, I do assure you, you won't like it. Now make your adieux—in English, please, and go."

Philippe was on his feet in a flash, making those adieux correctly, if rather too eagerly. I think I was almost as thankful as he was when at length, his hand clutching mine, I said my own quiet good nights and withdrew.

Léon de Valmy's "Good night, Miss Eyre," with its wholly charming overtone of mockery, followed me to the door.

Philippe was a little subdued for the rest of the evening, but on the whole survived the ordeal by uncle pretty well. After he was in bed I dined alone in my room. It was Albertine, Madame de Valmy's sour-faced maid, who brought my supper in. She did it in tightlipped silence, making it very clear that she was demeaning herself unwillingly.

"Thanks, Albertine," I said cheerfully, as she set the last plate down just a shade too smartly. "Oh, and by the way—"

The woman turned in the doorway, her sallow face not even inquiring. She radiated all the charm and grace of a bad-tempered skunk. "Well?"

I said, "I wonder if you can remember whether I got Mrs. Seddon's tablets for her last week, or not?"

"Non," said Albertine, and turned to go.

"Do you mean I didn't or do you mean you don't remember?"

She spoke sourly over her shoulder without turning. "I mean I do not know. Why?"

"Only because Mrs. Seddon asked me to get the tablets today and Monsieur Garcin said he gave them to me last week. If that's the case you'd think I must have handed them to her with her other packages. I've no recollection of them at all. D'you know if there was a prescription with the list you gave me?"

The square shoulders lifted. "Perhaps. I do not know." The shallow black eyes surveyed me with dislike. "Why do you not ask her yourself?"

"Very well, I will," I said coldly. "That will do, Albertine."

But the door was already shut. I looked at it for a moment with compressed lips and then began my meal. When, some little time later, there came a tap on the door and Mrs. Seddon surged affably in, I said, almost without preamble—

"That Albertine woman. What's biting her? She's about as amiable as a snake."

Mrs. Seddon snorted. "Oh, her. She's going about like a wet month of Sundays because I told her to bring your supper up. Berthe's helping Mariette get a room ready for Mr. Rowl seeing as how Mariette won't work along with Albertine anyhow and she's as sour as a lemon if you ask her to do anything outside Madame's own rooms. Her and that Bernard, they're a pair. It's my belief he'd rob a bank for the Master if asked, but he'd see your nose cheese and the rats eating it before he'd raise a little finger for anybody else."

"I believe you. What I can't understand is why Madame puts up with her."

"You don't think she has that sour-milk face for Madame, do you? Oh, no, it's all niminy-piminy butter-won't-melt there, you mark my words." Conversation with Mrs. Seddon was nothing if not picturesque. "But she's like that with everyone else in the place bar Bernard, and it's my belief she's as jealous as sin if Madame so much as smiles at anybody besides herself. She knows Madame likes you, and that's the top and bottom of it, dear, believe you me."

I said, surprised, "Madame likes me? How d'you know?"

"Many's the nice thing she's said about you," said Mrs. Seddon comfortably, "so you don't have to fret yourself over a bit of lip from that Albertine."

I laughed. "I don't. How's the asthma? You sound better."

"I am that. It comes and goes. This time of year it's a nuisance, but never near so bad as it used to be. I remember as a girl Miss Debbie's mother saying to me—"

I stopped that one with the smoothness of much practice. "I'm afraid Monsieur Garcin wouldn't give me the antihistamine today. He said I got it last week. Did I give it to you, Mrs. Seddon? I'm terribly ashamed of myself, but I can't remember. D'you know if it was with the other things I got for you? There was some Nestlé's chocolate, wasn't there, and some buttons, and some cotton-wool—and was it last week you got your watch back from the repairers?"

"Was it now? Maybe it was. I can't mind just now about

the pills, but I know there were a lot of things and the pills may have been with them." She laughed a little wheezily. "I can't say I took much notice, not wanting them till now, but Mr. Garsang's probably right. He's as finicky as the five-times-table, and about as lively. I'll have a look in my cupboard tonight. I'm sorry to give you the bother, dear."

"Oh, that doesn't matter. I did get you the aspirins and the eau de cologne. They're here, with your change."

"Oh, thanks, dear—miss, I mean."

I said, "Is Monsieur Florimond staying, or is he only here for dinner?"

"He only came for dinner, but I dare say he'll stay on late to see Mr. Rowl. It might yet be they'll ask him to stay the night if the fog gets any thicker."

I got up and went over to the balcony windows.

"I don't see any fog. It seems a fine enough night."

"Eh? Oh, yes. I think it's only down by the water. We're high up here. But the road runs mostly along the river, and there's been accidents in the valley before now in the mist. It's a nasty road, that, in the dark."

"I can imagine it might be." I came back to my chair, adding, with a memory of the recent uncomfortable session in the drawing room, "Perhaps Monsieur Raoul won't get up here after all tonight."

She shook her head. "He'll come. If he said he was coming he'll come." She eyed me for a moment and said, "Did they—was there anything said downstairs, like?"

"Nothing. They wondered what brought him, that was all."

"They've not much call to wonder," she said darkly. "There's only one thing'll make him set foot in the place and that's money."

"Oh?" I said, rather uncomfortably. There were limits to gossip, after all. "I thought—I got the impression it might be some business to do with Bellevigne."

"Well," said Mrs. Seddon, "that's what I mean. It's always Bellyveen and money." She sighed. "I told you, Mr. Rowl manages it for him and now and again he comes up and talks to him about it and then—" she sighed again— "there's words. It's trouble every time, what with Mr. Rowl wanting money for Bellyveen and the Master wanting it for Valmy and before you know where you are it's cat and dog, or maybe I should say dog and dog because nobody could say Mr. Rowl's like a cat, the horrible sneaking beasts, but a dogfight it's always been, ever since Mr. Rowl was big enough to speak up for himself and—"

"He—he must be a careful landlord," I said hastily.

"Oh, I don't deny he makes a good job of Bellyveen—he's too like his father not to, if you see what I mean—but they do say he rackets about the place plenty between times. There's stories—"

"You can't believe everything you hear," I said.

"No, indeed, that's true," said Mrs. Seddon, a shade regretfully, "and especially when it's about Mr. Rowl, if you follow me, miss, because he's the sort that'd get himself talked about if he lived in a convent, as the saying is."

"I'm sure you're right," I said.

"And where does he get the money, I ask you that?" Mrs. Seddon was now fully and enjoyably launched. "Where did he get the car he was driving last time he was here? As long as the Queen Mary and a horn like the Last Trump, and so I ask you, where?"

"Well," I said mildly, "where?"

"Ah," said Mrs. Seddon darkly, "you may well ask. I heard the Master ask him that very question, sharplike, the last time he was here. And Mr. Rowl wouldn't tell him; just passed it off in that way he has with something about a lucky night and a lucky number."

I laughed. "It sounds to me as if he won it at roulette. Good luck to him."

She looked a little shocked. "Well, miss! I don't say as how I think a little flutter does any harm and I'm as partial to a nice game of whist as anyone, but—well, many's the time I wonder what Miss Debbie would have said. Many's the time she said to me, 'Mary,' she said—"

"Forgive me," I said quickly, "but it's time for Philippe's chocolate. I left him reading in bed and I must put his light out."

"Eh? Oh, yes, to be sure, how time goes on, doesn't it?" And it's long past time I ought to be seeing if Berthe and Mariette have put that room properly to rights. . . ." She heaved herself onto her feet and plodded to the door, which I opened for her. "Have they remembered the milk?"

"It was on the tray."

"Ah, yes. That Berthe, now, do you find she does her work all right, miss? If there's anything to complain of, you must be sure to let me know."

"I've no complaints," I said. "I like Berthe very much, and she keeps the rooms beautifully. You've only to look in the pantry here."

71

She followed me into the tiny pantry, where the light gleamed on the spotless enamel of the little stove, and saucepan, beaker and spoon stood ready. I poured milk into the pan, set it on the stove and switched on. Mrs. Seddon ran a practiced eye over the tiny room, and an equally practiced finger over the shelf where the tins of chocolate, coffee and tea stood, and nodded her head in a satisfied manner.

"Yes, Berthe's a good girl, I must say, if she'll keep her mind on her work instead of running after that there Bernard. . . . The sugar's here, miss."

"No, not that. I use the glucose for Philippe, you remember—that's his special tin, the blue one. Oh, thank you. D'you mean to tell me there's something between Berthe and Bernard? I hope it's not serious? It would be an awful pity. He's too old for her, and besides—"

I stopped, but she took me up.

"Well, miss, you never said a truer word. A pity it is. If that Albertine wasn't his sister born, I'd have said why not them, they wouldn't spoil two houses, and them as alike as two hogs in the same litter. A sour-faced, black-a-vised sort of chap he is and all, for a bonny young girl like Berthe to be losing her head over. But there, human nature's human nature, believe it or not, and there's nothing we can do about it. What are you looking for now?"

"The biscuits. They've been moved. Ah, here they are." I put three into Philippe's saucer, looking sidelong at Mrs. Seddon. "Extra rations tonight. It was a slightly sticky session in the drawing room."

"That's right. He could do with a bit of spoiling, if you ask me. And now I'll have to go, really. I've enjoyed our little chat, miss. And I may say that Seddon and me, we think that Philip's a whole lot better for having you here. He likes you that's plain to see, and it's my belief that what he needs is somebody to be fond of."

I said softly, half to myself, "Don't we all?"

"Well, there you are," said Mrs. Seddon comfortably. "Not but what his other Nanny wasn't a very nice woman, very nice indeed, but she did baby him a bit, say what you will, which was only natural, seeing as how she'd brought him up from a bairn in arms. Maybe the Master was right enough like you said in thinking he ought to have a change, especially after losing his Mam and Dad like that, poor bairn. And you're making a grand job of him, miss, if you'll excuse the liberty of me saying so."

I said with real gratitude, "It's very nice of you. Thank

72

you." I lifted Philippe's tray and grinned at her over it. "And I do hope all goes well downstairs. At least there's one person who'll be pleased when Mr. Raoul arrives."

She stopped in the doorway and turned, a little ponderously. "Who? Mr. Florimond? Well, I couldn't say—"

"I didn't mean him. I meant Philippe."

She stared at me, then shook her head. "Mr. Rowl hardly knows him, miss. Don't forget Philip only came from Paris just before you did, and Mr. Rowl's not been over since he was here."

"Then Monsieur Raoul must have seen something of him in Paris, or else when he was with Monsieur Hippolyte."

"He didn't. That I do know. And I'd go bail him and Mr. Rowl hardly saw each other in Paree. Paree!" said Mrs. Seddon, reverting to form, "Paree! He'd not be the one to bother with Philip there. He had other kettles of fish to fry in Paree, you mark my words."

"But when we heard the car coming up the zigzag tonight with Monsieur Florimond, Philippe flew out onto the balcony like a rocket—and he certainly wasn't hoping to see him. He looked desperately disappointed . . . more than that, really; 'blighted' would almost describe it. . . . Who else could he be looking for if it wasn't his cousin Raoul?"

Then I looked at her, startled, for her eyes, in the harsh light, were brimming with sudden, easy tears. She shook her head at me and wiped her cheeks with the back of a plump hand. "Poor bairn, poor bairn," was all she would say, but presently after a sniff or two and some action with a handkerchief, she explained. The explanation was simple, obvious, and dreadful.

"He never saw them dead, of course. Nor he wasn't allowed to go to the funeral. And it's my belief and Seddon's that he won't have it they're really gone. They were to have driven back from the airport, you see, and he was waiting for them, and they never came. He never saw no more of them. It's my belief he's still waiting."

"That's dreadful." I swallowed. "That's . . . dreadful, Mrs. Seddon."

"Yes. Every car that comes up, he'll fly out yonder. I've seen him do it. It's lucky there's not more coming and going than there is, or he'd do it once too often, and end up on the gravel on his head, or else stuck on those spikes like a beetle on a pin."

I shivered. "I'll watch him," I said.

"You do," said Mrs. Seddon.

73

Fourth Coach

Chapter VII

*A Being, erect upon two legs, and bearing all
the outward semblance of a man, and not of a
monster.*

DICKENS: *Pickwick Papers.*

PHILIPPE was already asleep, curled in an extraordinarily
small bundle under the bedclothes. The light was still on,
and his book had slid to the floor. Something was clutched
in his hand, and I drew the sheet aside to see what it was—
one of the Queen's soldiers with the fur hats.

I picked up the book, straightened the bedclothes, turned
off the light, and went softly out, taking the unwanted
chocolate back to the pantry.

Back in my room, I walked straight through it onto the
balcony, letting the curtains fall behind me to cut off the
light. The night was calm, and unexpectedly warm. There
was still no sign of fog, but I thought that I could see a
paler darkness away in the valley's depths. The damp of
spring hung in the air. An owl called below me, down in
the woods; called again. Its muted melancholy found too
ready an echo in me. I felt tired and depressed. Too much
had happened today; and the pleasant things—the morning's encounter with William Blake, my gay little flirtation
with Florimond in the salon—had somehow faded back out
of mind and left me with this queerly flattened feeling.

I know what it was, of course. I'd lived with loneliness a
long time. That was something which was always there . . .
one learns to keep it at bay, there are times when one even
enjoys it—but there are also times when a desperate self-
sufficiency doesn't quite suffice, and then the search for the
anodyne begins . . . the radio, the dog, the shampoo, the
stockings-to-wash, the tin soldier. . . .

I bit my lip and took myself sharply to task. Just because
I had had two pleasantly off-duty encounters—not to men-
tion a cozy and entertaining gossip with the housekeeper—
I didn't have to feel let down and left out when they were

over and I had to put in the evening by myself. I didn't have to stand here glooming at the spring dusk and picturing myself for the rest of my life relegated to the edge of the room, the frame of the conversation piece.

And what did I want, for heaven's sake? To retreat on the illusion that Florimond's courtesy had created, that he and I and Madame de Valmy could share a fireside on equal terms? To be where Madame de Valmy was? Where I might still have been if the thing that happened ten years ago hadn't happened? Well, *that* was out, and the sooner I accepted once and for all the fact the jamboree was over, the sooner I would stop riding this uneasy seesaw of moods and memories.

I turned deliberately and walked along to the southern end of the balcony until I stood above the salon.

The light from the long windows, muted by gold curtains, streamed softly across the loggia and onto the terrace. The bare rose bushes stood out, thorn and twig in a naked mesh netting the light. Their shadows raked away like besoms over the freshly-dug beds. One window had been opened to the mild night, and here the light streamed out boldly, and with it the sound of talk and laughter. I could imagine the spurting glow of the log fire, the gleam of rummers, the smell of coffee and brandy and cigars. . . .

Good night, Miss Eyre . . . amusement supervened and with it sanity. I grinned to myself as I walked softly back to my own window. If I did have to spend the rest of my life sitting in the corner of someone else's drawing room, knitting and wearing black bombazine—whatever that was—then by God it would be the best bombazine. The very best bombazine.

Ignoring the anodynes of book, radio and stockings-to-wash, I got my coat and went out.

I went down the zigzag very slowly, for in the faint moonlight the slope was deceptive, and the slight dampness made the surface slippery. There was a way down through the wood itself—a steep track of alternate step and slope that short-circuited the zigzag—but it would have been too dark under the trees, so I avoided it and kept to the road.

The air was very still. Below me, in the valley depths where the river ran, I could see, quite distinctly now, the pale drift of mist. The owl cried again once, very sadly, from the wood. There was a strong wet smell of earth and growing things; the smell of spring . . . not softness, not balm-and-blossoms, but something harsh and sharp that pierced the

75

senses as the thrust of new life broke the ground . . . *the cruelest month, breeding/Lilacs out of dead land* . . . yes, that was it. That was it. Not for the first time I was sharply grateful to Daddy for making poetry a habit with me. *The best words in the best order* . . . one always got the same shock of recognition and delight when someone's words swam up to meet a thought or name a picture. Daddy had been right. Poetry was awfully good material to think with.

Something rustled in last year's beech leaves and poetry fled as, absurdly, I remembered that there were still bears in France. And boars. And probably wolves. And werewolves and vampires too, no doubt . . . by mocking myself I got at length safely down to river-level and the bridge to the main road.

The bridge was an elegant affair of the eighteenth century, with carved balustrading that opened in graceful curves toward the river banks. The mist was thick here, but only in patches. Where I stood it was waist-high, but beyond the parapet to my right it slanted down like a snowbank to lie low over the water, pinned through here and there by spikes of bulrush and the black spars of dead boughs.

The water itself was invisible. The sound of it was dark and deep, a lovely liquid undertone to the night. The owl's breathy call fell less sadly now, less hollowly through the dim boughs.

I stood still in the center of the bridge, my hands deep in my pockets, and gazed up at the steeply wooded slope on the other side of the main road. Rank upon rank of pines, I knew, crowded up those rocky heights, with here and there a bare crag jutting through, where in daylight the hawks mewed and circled. Now, in the faint moonlight, the forest was no more than a looming darkness, a towering cloud faintly luminous where the crescent moon feather-edged the rims of the pines. The scent drifted down, spicy and sharp and somehow dark like the pines themselves.

A car was coming up the valley. I heard the sound of the engine grow and fade and grow again as the curving road and the mist cut off and distorted the sound. It came round Belle Surprise, high above the mist, before I saw its lights. I saw them turn then, tilt, and drive down into the darkness, to bend this way and that among the trees, brightening and then blurring as the fog clouds blunted them. I watched the stems of the trees outline themselves sharply against the light, to reel away like logs tumbling over a waterfall, then swoop

76

back and up into the towering shadow behind the glare where still the tree stems blanched, drifted, and darkened. . . .

Only a late truck driving up to Soubirous . . . The headlights went steadily past the end of the bridge, and the mist tossed and whirled in the red of the tail lamp.

I was turning to go back up the zigzag, when my eye was caught by a tiny light high up among the Dieudonné trees. A minute before it had not been there, but now it pricked through the cloud of pines like a small yellow star.

I stopped and looked up at it. The trees along the roadside were busy in their ghostly dance as another truck roared up the valley, but that tiny light hung there high above them, warm and steady. No, not a star: a planet, and lived on at that. It might very well not be William Blake's little hut at four thousand feet, but somehow I thought it was. I smiled to myself picturing him sitting up there with his bandages and boluses (what was a bolus?) and thermometers in degrees centigrade.

The second truck thundered past the end of the bridge.

And the cognac—had he remembered the cognac?

I hadn't noticed the car traveling quietly behind the enormous truck. I didn't see it until it turned sharp onto the narrow bridge and came at me like a torpedo.

It was an easy corner, and he took it fast. The main beam leaped out and pinned me full in the glare. I heard his brakes shriek as they bit metal. I jumped for the edge of the road. The lights lurched and tires screeched and ripped the tarmac. One yard: that was all the leeway he had. Something grabbed at me; tore. I slipped on the greasy road and fell flat in the gutter under the parapet as the car went by with a foot and a half to spare and screamed to a skidding halt beyond the bridge.

The engine cut. The door slammed. Léon de Valmy's voice said, "Where are you? Are you hurt? I didn't touch you, did I?" Quick footsteps sounded on the tarmac. "Where are you?"

I had risen to my knees in the wet gutter, and was holding rather hard to the parapet. At the sound of the footsteps and that familiar voice I thought I must have been hit and gone mad. I was blind, too. I couldn't see anything, anyone. I was blinking in a dazed sort of panic as I pulled myself shakily to my feet. . . .

I wasn't blinded after all; the mist sank and dwindled and swirled waist-high again as I turned, leaning back for support against the parapet.

77

Nor was I mad. The man who was striding toward me in the moonlight was not Léon de Valmy, though thirty years ago Léon de Valmy had probably looked exactly like him. As with his father, my first impression of Raoul de Valmy was that he was remarkably good looking; but where age and illness had given the older man's looks the fine-drawn, fallen-angel quality he had mocked to me on our first meeting, there was nothing in the least fine-drawn about Raoul. He merely looked tough, arrogant, and, at the moment, furious. It wasn't exactly the time to judge whether he possessed the charm which his father could apparently radiate at will, though his personality certainly made—this without irony—as strong an impact. But the difference was there again: where Léon de Valmy kept himself banked down, so to speak, and burning secretly, Raoul was at full blaze. And just now he was blazing with something more than personality. He was as shaken as I was, and it had made him angry.

I sat down suddenly on the parapet, and waited. He loomed over me, tall and formidable looking in the misty moonlight.

Tall, dark and handsome . . . the romantic cliché repeated itself in my head—so automatically and irresistibly that I braced myself to dislike him on sight.

He said sharply, "Are you hurt?"

"No."

"Did I hit you?"

"No."

"Not even touch you?"

I was smoothing my coat down with unsteady fingers. "N—no."

"You're sure you're all right?"

"Yes. I—yes. Thank you."

I heard his breath expelled in quick relief. He relaxed and his voice warmed then into anger. "Then will you kindly tell me what the bloody hell you were doing standing in the middle of the road in a fog? You came damned near being killed and if you had you'd have deserved it!"

Shock was reacting on me too, and I wasn't used to being sworn at. I stopped fussing with my clothes and lifted my head to glare straight back at him. "It's not a public road and I've a perfect right to stand in the middle of it or sit in the middle of it or lie in the middle of it if I want to! I wasn't expecting you—at least I'd quite forgotten you were coming and in any case you've no business to come at that speed, whether it's a private road or not!"

78

There was a fractional pause, during which I had the impression that he was distinctly taken aback. Then he said mildly, "I was only doing fifty, and I know the road like the back of my hand."

"*Fifty!*" I heard my voice rise to a squeak, and was furious. "Why, that's—oh, kilometers, of course."

"What else?"

"It's still too fast and there was mist."

"I could see the way quite well and that car sits down on the corners like a broody hen." He was beginning to sound amused, and that made me angrier.

I snapped, "Broody hen or no, it very nearly ran me down!"

"I'm quite aware of that. But I would hardly expect to find anyone standing on the bridge at this time of night—"

He stopped and then went on, the amusement now clear in his voice, "I'm damned if I see why I should have to stand here defending myself for not having run you over! Perhaps now you'll be good enough to tell me why you consider you've a perfect right to stand—or was it lie down?— in the middle of this particular private road? This is my— this is the Valmy estate, you know."

I was busy wiping my muddy hands on a handkerchief. "Yes," I said, "I live here."

He made a little movement of surprise, and I saw his eyes narrow on me in the moonlight. "Surely," he said, "you're not one of the, er—?"

"Servants? In a way," I said. "I'm Philippe's governess."

"But," said Raoul de Valmy, slowly, "they told me she was to be an English girl."

I felt as if he had dealt me a sharp blow in the stomach. For the first time I realized that the whole of the exchange had been in French. Literally thrown off my balance as I had been, I had answered him without thinking in the tongue that he had first used.

I said feebly, "I—I forgot."

"You are English?" he said, in a tone of great surprise.

I nodded. "Linda Martin, from London. I've been here three weeks."

His voice was a little dry. "Then allow me to congratulate you on your progress, Miss Martin."

But this second shock had shaken me quite out of all composure. The dry note in his voice was so like Léon de Valmy's that I found myself saying, in a taut little voice that was pitched a shade too high, "You must know perfectly

79

well that I haven't learned all my French in the last three weeks, Monsieur de Valmy, so don't add insult to injury by baiting me as well as knocking me down!"

This was palpable injustice and I half expected the annihilation I deserved. But he merely said, "I'm sorry. And now do you feel recovered enough to move? I shouldn't keep you here talking any more. You must have had a nasty shaking. We'll get into the car and I'll drive you up to the house."

Like his father, he knew how to disarm. . . . I found myself obediently sliding off the parapet to my feet, while he put a steadying hand under my elbow.

"I'm all right," I said.

But when I tried to move toward the car I found that my knees were very shaky still, and I was thankful for his support.

He said quickly, "You're limping. You are hurt."

I found myself reassuring him. "Not by you. I slipped and fell when I tried to jump out of the way. It's only a bumped knee or something. Honestly, that's all."

He said, sounding worried, "Well, I think the sooner I get you up to the château and find you a drink, the better. You'll have to get in by the driver's door, I'm afraid. The other one's rather difficult of access just at present."

This was, I saw, only too true. The big car, in swerving to avoid me, had skidded slightly on the damp tarmac, and run up onto the right-hand verge of the road beyond the bridge. The verge at this point was a muddy grass bank, mercifully not very steep, but quite steep enough to cant the car at a crazy-looking angle.

I looked at it guiltily, and then up at Raoul de Valmy's impassive face.

"I—it isn't damaged, is it?"

"I don't think so. Would you rather wait on the road while I straighten her out, or had you better get in and sit down?"

"I think if it's all the same to you I'll sit down."

"Of course." He opened the nearside door. I got in—with just a little difficulty, as my knee was undoubtedly stiff, and got myself somehow past the wheel and into the passenger's seat. He leaned into the car and groped in the darkness under the dash. There was a click, and the headlamps flashed on, so that just in front of the car the first bend and slope of the zigzag strode forward at us, a ragged white wall of tree and rock, not six feet from the front bumper.

He didn't even glance at it. "Just a minute," he said. He

slammed the door and went around to the back of the car.

I closed my eyes to shut out the sight of that looming rock-wall, and lay back in the deep seat, relaxing as well as I could. The car was very big and very comfortable, even tilted as it was at that odd angle. It smelled faintly of cigarettes and expensive leather. I opened my eyes again. In the light reflected back off the rock ahead the bonnet gleamed long and black—plenty horses under that, I thought, and remembered Mrs. Seddon's description, "As long as the Queen Mary and a horn like the Last Trump." I wondered what Raoul de Valmy's lucky number was. . . .

I settled my shoulders back in the luxurious seat. The shaky feeling had almost gone. Suddenly out of nowhere I remembered something I had once heard at the Constance Butcher—a piece of servant girls' lore which had amused me at the time and now came back with an added point. If you ever get run over, be sure and pick a Rolls-Royce. . . . Well, there was something in that, I reflected . . . and a Cadillac was perhaps not a bad second choice, especially when it had as good a driver as Raoul de Valmy at the wheel. Now that the first shock had subsided I realized perfectly well how near I had been to being badly hurt, through my own silliness. Moreover it was no thanks to me that Monsieur Raoul's expensive Cadillac hadn't smashed itself against the parapet.

I became aware that Raoul de Valmy was still behind the car. I peered back through the swirls of mist to see him bending over a rear wing, while a flashlight moved slowly over the metal. I bit my lip, but before I could speak he had straightened up, switched off the torch, and come swiftly around to the driver's door.

He slanted a quick look at me as he slid in beside me. "All right?" I nodded. "We'll soon get you home. Hold tight."

He touched the starter button and the engine snarled to life. He thrust the big car very gently forward and to the left; she moved, jerked, hesitated, and then the front wheels swooped down with a plunge to the level of the road. The back wheels seemed to mount for a moment, then slid down after them, and the car rolled onto the level road and stopped there, rocking gently on her superb springs.

"Et voilà," said Raoul de Valmy, and smiled at me.

As his hand moved on the handbrake I said, in a small voice, "Monsieur de Valmy."

The hand paused. "Yes?"

"Before you take me back I—I'd like to apologize. I'm most awfully sorry, really I am."

"Apologize? And for what? My dear ma'am—"

I said, "Don't be so *nice* about it, *please!* I know it was really my fault and you're making me feel a *worm!*" I heard him laugh, but I went on doggedly and not very clearly, "I had no business to be in the road and you saved my life by doing what you did and then I went and was rude to you and you were nothing but nice to me when ninety-nine drivers out of a hundred would have blasted me from here to Madagascar, and it's true, I do feel a worm. An utter crawling worm! And—" I took breath and finished idiotically—"if you've damaged your car you can stop it out of my wages!"

He was still laughing at me. "Thank you. But it's not damaged, as it happens."

"Is that the truth?" I asked suspiciously.

"Yes. Not a scratch. I thought I heard something as she skidded, but it was only a bit of a fallen branch hitting the wheel. Not a mark. So no apologies please, Miss Martin. If anybody should apologize, it's I. I believe I swore at you. I'm sorry."

"That's all right," I said a little awkwardly. "We were both a bit shaken up, I suppose. I didn't quite know where I was or what I was saying."

He said nothing. He seemed to be waiting. He made no move to start the car. I stole a sidelong look at him and saw that he was watching me steadily, with the amusement gone from his face. It was an oddly daunting look, and, though he had been much nicer to me than I deserved, I found that I was gripping my hands between my knees to give myself courage to go on.

I said, "I knew so little about what I was saying that I'm afraid I gave myself away to you."

"When you spoke to me in French." It was not a question. "Yes."

His hand moved to the ignition, and the engine died. He cut off the headlights, so that the car stood islanded in the little glow of side and tail-lamps. He half-turned toward me, his shoulder propped back against the door. I couldn't see his face now, and his voice told me nothing. He said, "This is interesting. So I was right?"

"That they didn't know I was partly French when I got the job? Yes."

He said, "I'm not your employer, you know. You don't

have to explain. But as a matter of curiosity, do I understand that you did deliberately deceive my father and Madame de Valmy over this?"

"I—I'm afraid so."

"Why?"

"Because I wanted the job."

"But I don't see why—"

I pressed my hands tightly together, and said carefully, "I needed the job. I—I'll try and tell you why, though I don't suppose you'll understand. . . ." He started to say something but I went on quickly and not very coherently, "I'm partly French and I was brought up in Paris. When I was fourteen Maman and Daddy were killed in a plane crash. Daddy was writing a script for a film to be made in Venice, and Maman went with him for the holiday. The—oh, the details don't matter, but I finished up in an orphanage in London. . . . I don't know if you've ever been inside an orphanage?"

"No."

"Well, the details don't matter there, either. They were very kind to me. But I wanted—oh, to *live*, to find some place in the world that was mine, and somehow I seemed to be getting nowhere. My schooling was all to blazes, what with the war and—and everything, so I can't do much, but I got a job at a small private school. I—I wasn't very happy there, either. Then when one of our governors heard that Madame de Valmy wanted an English governess it seemed like a gift from heaven. I told you I'm not qualified to do much, but I can look after children and I knew I could make a good job of Philippe's English and I thought it would be so wonderful to be in France and living in a real home again."

He said, very dryly, "So you came to Valmy."

"Yes. That's all."

There was a pause. He said, "I do understand, I think. But there was no need to explain all this to me, you know. I've no right to question you."

I said shyly, "I felt I sort of owed you something. And you did ask me why I wanted the job."

"No. You misunderstand me. I asked you why you had deceived my father and Héloïse about it."

I began, rather stupidly, "I told you—"

"I should have said, rather, why you *had* to deceive them. I'm not concerned in the least with the fact that you did do so." I caught the glimmer of a smile. "I merely find myself wondering why it was necessary. Are you trying to tell

83

me that you concealed the fact you were partly French because you wouldn't in that case have got the job?"

"I—yes, more or less."

A little silence. "Indeed."

"It wasn't put like that," I said hastily, "not said in so many words. But—but I honestly did get the impression that it might have mattered. I mean, once we had got past the point where I should have told Madame de Valmy I couldn't very well go back and confess or she'd have thought there was something queer about me and she'd never have looked at me. And she'd made rather a lot of the fact that I wouldn't be tempted to lapse into French when I was talking to Philippe—I'm supposed always to talk to him in English, you see. I didn't really see that it mattered, myself, because I could have taken care to speak English with him anyway, but—well, she was so emphatic about it that I—oh, I just let it slide. I know I was silly," I finished miserably, "and it's such a stupid little thing, but there it is."

"And I suppose I'm to understand," he said, still rather dryly, "that they still don't know."

"Yes."

"I see." To my relief he was beginning to sound amused again. "Haven't you found that such a deception—I'm sorry I started by using such a harsh term for it—has its socially embarrassing moments?"

"You mean overhearing things I'm not meant to? No, because Monsieur's and Madame's manners are too good." Here he laughed outright, and I said rather confusedly, "I mean—when I meet them without Philippe they always talk English, and when I take Philippe to see them they talk about his lessons, which I know about anyway; and in any case I don't listen."

He said, "Well, I should stop worrying about it. As far as I can see it can hardly matter one way or the other." He turned in his seat and started the engine. The lights sprang up. I could see him smiling. "And I certainly didn't mean to add insult to injury by turning this into an inquisition! Forgive me; it's not my affair."

"Monsieur," I said quickly, in a rather small voice.

"Yes?"

"I—I wonder if you'd not—I mean—" I floundered and stopped.

He gave me a quick glance. "You wondered if I'd not give you away?"

84

"Yes. Please," I added, feeling even smaller.

There was a fractional pause. "For what it's worth," said Raoul de Valmy, slowly, "I shan't. . . . And now I think we'd better make tracks. . . ."

The car moved forward and took the first slope at a decorous speed.

He drove in silence, and I had time to reflect with wry surprise that shock produces some very odd aftereffects. What on earth had impelled me to blurt out that naïve and stumbling betrayal of my pathetic needs to Raoul de Valmy's no doubt hard-bitten sophistication? *Daddy and Maman . . . they were very kind to me at the orphanage.* . . . What did it matter to him? A dreary little fool, that was what he'd think of me. And that's what I was, anyway, I thought, remembering my depression of earlier that evening. I bit my lip. What did it matter anyway? He probably hadn't even been listening. He had more important things than Philippe's governess on his mind. Bellevigne, for instance, or whatever had driven him up to see his father in the face of what appeared to be his normal welcome at the Château.

I found myself remembering Florimond's presence with a species of relief, and then felt amused. Raoul de Valmy would hardly need the same kind of protection as Philippe.

I said, "Monsieur Florimond's here this evening."

"Oh? Is he staying long?"

"I think he only came to dine, but if the mist gets thicker he'll probably stay."

"Ah," said Raoul, "that's something else to put down to the fog's account. It's an ill wind, they say."

I was still working that one out when the Cadillac swung off the last rise and came to a whispering halt at the foot of the steps.

Seddon was crossing the hall as we came in. He turned when he saw Raoul and came hurrying to meet him, then his eye fell on me, and a slight twitch of dismay crossed his impassive features.

"Mr. Raoul! Miss Martin! Has there been an accident?"

"I nearly ran Miss Martin over on the Valmy bridge. I suggest that you get her some brandy now, and send someone upstairs—"

"No, please," I said quickly, "I don't want any brandy. I'm all right now, Seddon. Mr. Raoul never touched me; I slipped and fell as I was getting out of the way. It was all my fault. I'll just go have a bath then make some tea in the pantry."

Seddon hesitated, glancing at Raoul, but I said firmly, "It's all right, really it is. I don't want a thing."

"Well, miss, if you're sure. . . ." He looked at Raoul. "I'll have your things taken straight up, sir. You're in your usual room."

"Thank you. How are you, Seddon? And Mrs. Seddon? The asthma keeping away?"

"Yes, thank you, sir, we're both well."

"That's fine. I'll come upstairs in a moment. Where's everyone? The small salon?"

"Yes, sir. Monsieur Florimond is here, sir, and he's staying the night. Shall I tell Madame you've arrived?"

"If you will. Say I'll join them in a few minutes."

"Very good, sir." And, with a final glance at me, he went.

As I turned to follow him, Raoul said, "You've torn your frock."

I looked down, unable to suppress a movement of dismay. My coat was open. At the hem of my frock a tear showed. "Oh, yes. I remember now. I felt it catch on something. But it's nothing much. It'll mend."

He was frowning. "The bumper must have caught you. I really am most—"

"Raoul?"

The voice came from behind me. I jumped and spun around. Raoul must have been inured to his father's methods of approach, for he merely turned, said, "How d'you do, sir?" and held out a hand. As Léon de Valmy took it his brilliant dark gaze turned to me.

"What's this? Did I hear something about a bumper catching you?"

I said, "It's nothing."

"Miss Martin and I," said Raoul, smiling, "met—rather abruptly—down on the Valmy bridge."

His father's eyes went to the torn hem of my frock; went lower to a laddered stocking and the stain of a muddy graze on my leg. "You mean you knocked her over?"

I said quickly, "Oh, no, nothing like that! I fell down and bumped my knee, that's all. Monsieur Raoul didn't touch me. It—"

"That tear wasn't done by falling down. That stuff's been ripped. Was that done by that damned great car of yours, Raoul?"

Temper flicked suddenly, patently, through the words, like a whip. For a moment I was reminded of the way I had heard him speak to Philippe, pilloried beside the yellow-brocaded chair, and, damn it, Raoul was—what? thirty? I felt myself going hot with embarassment, and glanced at him.

But this was not Philippe. He merely said, unruffled, "I imagine so. I had only just noticed it. I was abasing myself when you came in." He turned back to me. "Miss Martin, I really am most terribly sorry—"

"Oh, please!" I cried. "It was nothing. It was my own fault!"

Monsieur de Valmy said, "What were you doing down on the bridge at this time of night?"

"I went out for a walk," I said. "It was damp in the woods so I went down the road."

"What happened?"

Raoul began to speak but I said hastily, "I stopped in the middle of the bridge. I was going to turn back and I stood for a minute or two listening to the water. It was a silly thing to do, because there was a drift of mist there over the river, and Monsieur Raoul ran slap into it. But I'd forgotten he was coming."

"Forgotten?"

I looked at him in faint surprise. Then I remembered that the conversation in the salon had been in French. I said steadily, hoping my color hadn't risen, "Mrs. Seddon told me this evening that he was coming."

"Ah. Yes." The dark eyes were unreadable under the heavy black brows. He looked at Raoul. "And then?"

I said quickly, "So of course Monsieur Raoul didn't see me —he couldn't have seen me till he was just about running me down. It was entirely my own fault and I'm lucky to get away with a bruise and a torn frock. If it was the car that tore it that's all it touched, honestly. The bruise I got myself slipping and falling in the gutter."

Léon de Valmy was still frowning. "That's a bad corner . . . as we all know." The cutting edge was back on his voice. "Raoul, if you must come up that road on a night like this—"

Raoul said gently, "I have already told Miss Martin how sorry I am."

Something sparked inside me. My employer had a perfect right to catechise me, but not to make his son look a fool in front of me. And I'd seen a little too much of his tactics tonight already. I said hotly, "And I have explained to Monsieur Raoul that the fault was mine and mine only. So please may we drop the subject? It isn't fair that he should be blamed. If he'd been any less brilliant a driver I'd have been killed!"

I stopped. I had seen the faintest, least definable shade of amusement in Raoul's face, and in his father's something that was, less mistakably, anger. He said smoothly, but with the edge still on the carefully pedantic words, "A brilliant driver should not have to call upon his skill to that extent at such a dangerous corner."

Raoul smiled at him and said, very pleasantly, "The corner was relaid last autumn . . . by the Bellevigne estate, remember? And are you sure you're qualified to criticize my driving? You forget that both roads and cars have altered considerably since you were last able to drive."

In the sharp little silence that followed I saw the lines around Léon de Valmy's mouth deepen, and the white hands moved on the arms of the chair. He said nothing. Raoul smiled lazily down at him. No, this was not Philippe. No wonder he'd been amused when I wildcatted to his defense. I thought, with an absurd rush of pleasure: *that for Philippe, Monsieur the Demon King!*

Raoul turned to me and said easily, "Are you sure you won't have something sent up to you, Miss Martin?"

"Quite sure." I looked from one to the other a bit uncertainly. "Good night, Monsieur de Valmy. Good night, Monsieur Raoul."

I went quickly upstairs, leaving the two of them together.

Fifth Coach

Chapter VIII

Thou art more deep damn'd than Prince Lucifer.
There is not yet so ugly a fiend of hell
As thou shalt be, if thou didst kill this child.

SHAKESPEARE: *King John.*

NEXT day all traces of mist had gone, and the trees moved lightly in their Lenten green. Since the winds of March had whipped some of the buds into tiny leaf, our favorite walk had been the way through the woods that stretched northward down the valley, and this afternoon we went that way again.

We started down the path that short-circuited the zigzag. For all its steepness it was not bad walking, as the path itself was ribbed across with sunken logs to give a foothold, and the occasional flights of steps were in good repair, with wide flat treads scored and clear of moss. Here and there the path crossed a trickle of water; sometimes the bridge was only a step, a slab of stone over a mossy trough where water chuckled; but in places some streamlet had cut deeply through the rock into miniature cascades, spanned by sturdy little bridges no more than two planks' width, with a single handrail of untrimmed pine.

It was on these bridges that Philippe loved to linger, gazing down at the ferns and grasses swaying in the wind of the cascade, and counting what he fondly imagined to be the fish attempting to leap up the spray. This morning we hung happily together over the biggest of the pools where fingers of bright sunlight probed the ferns and made an iridescent bloom of fine spray.

"Three," said Philippe, triumphantly. "Voilà, did you see her? Beside the stone there, where the waves are!"

I peered down at the whirling pool some fifteen feet below us. "I can't see anything. And it's not *her*, Philippe."

"It was. Truly it was. I am seeing her—"

"I'm sure you are. But a fish isn't *her*, it's *it*."

"A trout is her in French," said Philippe firmly. It was a

89

great source of pride to him that my French was worse than his English.

"No doubt," I said, "but not in English. Oh, look, there's one, Philippe, definitely! I saw her—it jump!"

"Four." Philippe knew when to pursue his triumphs and when to hold his tongue. "Four and a half, because I do not know if that shadow is a *truite*—trout, or a shadow." He gripped the rail and leaned over, peering eagerly down.

"Let's go on," I said. "If it's still there when we come back, it's a shadow. Let's go down into the big wood again."

He turned obediently off the bridge onto the wide level path that led along the hillside deeper into the trees. "All right. To look for wolves?"

"Wolves?"

He was trotting ahead of me. He turned, laughing. "Mademoiselle, you sounded quite frightened! Did you think there were really wolves?"

"Well, I—"

He gave a crow of laughter and a comic little skip that shuffled up last year's dead leaves. "You did! You did!"

"Well," I said, "I've never lived in a place like this before. For all I know Valmy might be crawling with wolves."

"We have got bears," confided Philippe, in the tone of one inviting congratulations. He looked earnestly up at me. "We truly have. This is not a *blague*. Many bears of a bigness incredible." His scarlet-gloved hands sketched in the air something of the dimensions of an overgrown grizzly. "I have never seen one, *vous comprenez*, but Bernard has shot one. He told me so."

"Then I hope to goodness we don't meet one today."

"They are asleep," said Philippe comfortingly. "There is no danger unless one treads on them where they sleep." He jumped experimentally into a deep drift of dead leaves, sending them swirling up in bright flakes of gold. The drift was, fortunately, bearless. "They sleep very sound," said Philippe, who appeared to find it necessary to excuse this failure, "with nuts in the pocket, like an *écureuil*."

"Squirrel."

"Skervirrel. Perhaps you prefer that we do not look for bears?"

"I would really rather not, if you don't mind," I said apologetically.

"Then we will not," he said generously. "But there are many other things to see in the woods, I think. Papa used to tell me of them. There is chamois and marmottes and the foxes, oh, many! Do you think that when I have ten years—"

" 'When I am ten.' "

"When I am ten years I can have a gun and shoot, mademoiselle?"

"Possibly not when you're ten, Philippe, but certainly when you're a bit older."

"Ten is old."

"It may be old, but it's not very big. You wouldn't be of a bigness—I mean you wouldn't be big enough to use the right gun for a bear."

"Skervirrels, then."

"Squirrel."

"Skervirrel. I could have a small gun for skervirrel when I am ten?"

"Possibly, though I should doubt it. In any case, it's what they call an unworthy ambition."

"*Plait-il?*" He was still jigging along slightly in front of me, laughing back over his shoulder, his face for once flushed and bright under his scarlet woolen ski cap. He said cheekily, "English, please."

I laughed. "I meant that it's a shame to shoot squirrels. They're charming."

"Char-ming? No, they are not. They eat the young trees. They cause much work, lose much money. The foresters say it. One must shoot them."

"Very French," I said dryly.

"I am French," said Philippe, skipping gaily on ahead, "and they are my trees, and I shall have a gun when I am older and go out every day to shoot the skervirrels. Look! There's one! *Bang!*" He proceeded, with gestures, to shoot down several squirrels very loudly, singing meanwhile an extremely noisy and shapeless song whose burden was something like:

> Bang, bang, bang,
> Bang, bang, bang,
> Got you, got you,
> Bang, bang, bang.

"If you don't look where you're going," I said, "it'll be you who'll—look out, you silly chump!"

Then three things happened, almost simultaneously.

Philippe, laughing back at me as he jigged along, tripped over a tree root and fell headlong. Something struck the tree

91

beside him with the sound of a hand smacking the back, and, a fraction later, the sharp crack of a rifle split the silence of the woods.

I don't know how long it took me to grasp just what had happened. The unmistakable crack of the gun, and the child's body flat in the path . . . for one heart-stopping moment terror zigzagged like pain through my blood. Then even as Philippe moved the significance of that sharp smack on the tree's bole struck me, and I knew he was not hit.

I found myself shouting into the silent woods that sloped above us, "Don't shoot, you fool! There are people here!" Then I was beside Philippe, bending over him, making sure. . . .

The bullet had not touched him, of course; but when I looked up and saw the hole in the tree just above where he lay, I realized how nearly he had been missed. The silly little jiggling song that had tripped him up had saved his life.

He lifted a face from which all the bright gaiety and color had gone. There was mud on one thin little cheek and his eyes were scared.

"It was a gun. Something hit the tree. A bullet."

He spoke, of course, in French. This was no moment to insist either on his English or my own false position. In any case he had just heard me shouting in French at the owner of the gun. I put my arms around him and spoke in the same tongue. "Some silly fool out with a rifle after foxes." (Did one shoot foxes with a rifle?) "It's all right, Philippe, it's all right. A silly mistake, that's all. He'd hear me shout and he'll be far more scared than we were." I smiled at him and got up, pulling him to his feet. "I expect he thought you were a wolf."

Philippe was shaking, too, and I saw now that it was with anger as much as fright. "He has no business to shoot like that. Wolves don't sing, and in any case you don't shoot at sounds. You wait till you can see. He is a fool, an imbecile. He should not have a gun. I shall get him dismissed."

I let him rage on in a shaken shrill little voice, a queer and rather touching mixture of scared child and angry Comte de Valmy. I was scanning the slopes of open wood above us for the approach of an alarmed and apologetic keeper. It was quite a few seconds before I realized that the wood was, apparently, empty. The path where we walked ran between widely-spaced trees. Above us sloped some hundred yards of rough grass—an open space of sunlight and sparse young beeches, where brambles and honeysuckle tangled over the roots of felled trees. At the crest of the rise was a tumble of rock and the dark ridge of a planted forest. Nothing moved. Whoever was at large there with a rifle had no intention of admitting the recent piece of lunatic carelessness.

I said, my jerking heart shaking my voice a little, "You're right. He shouldn't be allowed out, whoever he is. You wait here. Since he won't come out I'm going to see—"

"*No!*" It was no more than a breath, but he caught hold of my hand and held it fast.

"But Philippe—now look, son, you'll be all right. He's miles away by now and getting further every second. Let me go, there's a good chap."

"*No!*"

I looked up through the empty wood, then down at the small pinched face under the scarlet cap.

"All right," I said, "we'll go home."

We were hurrying back the way we had come. I still held Philippe's hand. He clutched at me tightly. I said, still shaken and angry, "We'll soon find out, Philippe, don't worry, and your uncle'll dismiss him. Either he's a careless fool who's too scared to come out, or he's a lunatic who thinks that sort of thing's a joke, but your uncle can find out. He'll be dismissed, you'll see."

He said nothing. He half trotted, half shuffled along beside me, silent and sober. No skipping now, or singing. I said, trying to sound calm and reasonable above the blaze inside me, "Whatever the case, we're going straight to Monsieur de Valmy."

The hand tucked in mine twitched slightly. "No."

"But, my dear Philippe—!" I broke off, and glanced down at the averted scarlet cap. "All right, you needn't, but I must. I'll get Berthe to come and give you some five-o'clock and stay with you till I get back to the schoolroom. I'll ask Tante Héloïse if she'll visit you upstairs instead of making you go down to the salon, and then we'll play Peggitty till bedtime. How's that?"

The red cap merely nodded. We trudged on in silence for a bit. We came to the bridge where we had counted the trout, and Philippe walked straight over it without a glance at the pool below.

The blaze of anger licked up inside me again. I said, "We'll get the stupid criminal fool dismissed, Philippe. Now stop worrying about it."

He nodded again, and then stole a queer little look up at me.

"What is it?"

"You've been talking French," said Philippe. "I just noticed."

"So I have." I smiled at him. "Well, I could hardly expect you to remember your English when you were being shot at like a *skervirrel,* could I?"

He gave the ghost of a little smile.

"You say it wrong," he said. "It's *squirrel.*"

Then, quite suddenly, he began to cry.

Madame de Valmy was alone in the rose garden. Early violas were already budding beside the path where she walked. There were daffodils out along the edge of the terrace. She had some in her hands.

She was facing in our direction, and she saw us as soon as we emerged from the woods. She had been stooping for a flower, and she stopped in mid-movement, then slowly straightened up, the forgotten daffodil trailing from her fingers. Even at that distance—we were still some hundred yards away—she must have been able to see the mud on Philippe's coat and the general air of dejection that dragged at him.

She started toward us.

"Philippe! What in the world has happened? Your coat! Have you fallen down? Miss Martin—" her voice was sharp with real concern—"Miss Martin, not another accident, surely?"

I was breathless from the hasty ascent, and still angry. I said baldly, "Someone shot at Philippe in the wood down there."

She had been half bending toward the little boy. At my uncompromising words she stopped as if she had been struck.

"Shot . . . at Philippe?"

"Yes. They only missed him because he tripped and fell. The bullet hit a tree."

She straightened up slowly, her eyes on my face. She was very pale. "But—this is absurd! Who could . . . did you see who it was?"

"No. He must have known what had happened, because I shouted. But he didn't appear."

"And Philippe?" She turned shocked eyes to him. "Comment ça va, p'tit? On ne t'a fait mal?"

94

A shake of the red cap and a quiver of the hand in mine were the only answers. My own hand closed on his.

"He fell down," I said, "but he didn't really hurt himself. He's been very brave about the whole thing." I didn't feel it necessary to insist in front of the child that, but for the tumble, he would probably now be dead. But Madame de Valmy understood that. She was so white that I thought she would faint. The pale eyes, watching Philippe, held a look, unmistakably, of horror. So she did care after all, I thought, surprised and a little touched. She said, faintly, "This is . . . terrible. Such carelessness . . . criminal carelessness. You . . . saw nothing?"

I said crisply, "Nothing. But it shouldn't be too hard to find out who it was. I'd have gone after him then and there if I'd been able to leave Philippe. But I imagine Monsieur de Valmy can find out who was in the woods this afternoon. Where is Monsieur, madame?"

"In the library, I expect." She had one hand to her heart. From the other the daffodils fell in an unheeded scatter. She really did look dreadfully shocked. "This is—this is a dreadful thing. Philippe might have—might have—"

"I think," I said, "that I'd better not keep him out here. Will you excuse us from coming down tonight, madame? Philippe had better have a quiet evening and early bed."

"Of course. Of course. And you, too, Miss Martin. You have had a shock—"

"Yes, but I'm angry, too, and I find it helps. I'll go and see Monsieur de Valmy as soon as I've taken Philippe in."

She was nodding in a shocked, half comprehending way. "Yes. Yes, of course. Monsieur de Valmy will be terribly . . . annoyed. Terribly annoyed."

"I hope," I said grimly, "that that's an understatement. Come on, Philippe, let's go and find Berthe. Madame . . ."

As we left her I glanced back to see her hurrying away, toward the corner of the terrace. To tell Léon de Valmy herself, no doubt. Well, the sooner the better, I thought, and swept Philippe into the house and upstairs to the haven of the schoolroom.

Berthe was in the pantry, busy with some cleaning. After a swift explanation that shocked her as much as it had Héloïse, I would have left Philippe with her, but he clung to me, and looked so suspiciously like crying again that I stayed with him. Madame de Valmy had certainly taken the tale straight to her husband, who would, no doubt, put the necessary ma-

95

chinery in motion to discover the culprit. For me, Philippe was the first concern.

So I stayed with him and talked determinedly lighthearted nonsense to distract him till at length, fresh from a hot bath, he was safely ensconced with a book on the rug by the schoolroom fire. He made no objection when Berthe brought in her mending and prepared to keep him company while I went down to see his uncle.

Léon de Valmy was alone in the library. I had not been in the room before. It was a high room, lit with two long windows, but warmed and made darker by the oak bookshelves lining it from floor to ceiling. Above the fireplace a huge portrait glowed against the paneling; my first glance told me that it was a young portrait of Raoul de Valmy, looking very handsome in riding clothes, one hand holding a whip, the other the bridle of a gray Arab pony with large soft eyes and a dark muzzle. I wondered why his father kept it there. Below the portrait a log fire burned in the open hearth, which was flanked by a single armchair. The room contained, apart from its thousands of books and a big desk beside one window, very little furniture. I realized the reason for this as Léon de Valmy's wheel chair turned from a side table where he had been leafing through a pile of papers, and glided toward the fire, there to stop in the vacant place opposite the single armchair.

"Come and sit down, Miss Martin."

I obeyed him. The first rush of my anger had long since ebbed, but nervousness tightened my throat and made me wonder a little desperately how to start.

Not that there was anything even slightly intimidating about him today. His voice and face were grave and friendly as he turned toward me. It came to me then, with a sense of almost physical shock, that the portrait above the mantel was not of his son, but of Léon himself.

He must have caught my involuntary glance upward, for his own followed it. He sat in silence for a moment, regarding the picture somberly, then he turned to me and smiled. "It seems we are an ill-starred race, we Valmys."

There was the same wryness in voice and smile that I remembered from our first encounter. The slightly dramatic phrasing, no less than the repeated and deliberate reference to a state he ostensibly wanted ignored, jarred on me sharply. Did he see everything then, purely in relation to his own misfortune? I said nothing, but looked away from him.

He said, "I am told we have barely escaped another tragedy this afternoon."

I looked up. (Another tragedy.) I said stolidly, "Has Madame de Valmy seen you?"

"She came straight to me. She was very much shocked and upset. It has made her ill. Her heart, I am afraid, is not robust." He paused and the dark eyes scanned my face. There was nothing now in his own but gentleness and concern. "You, too, Miss Martin. I think you had better have a drink. Sherry? Now supposing you tell me what happened." He reached a hand to the tantalus at his elbow.

"Thank you." I took the glass gratefully. My nervousness had gone. I was left with an empty feeling of reaction and fatigue. In a voice drained of any emotion I told him briefly of the afternoon's events. "Do you know who was out with a gun today?" I asked in conclusion.

He lifted his sherry glass. "Off-hand, no. Armand Lestocq told me—no, that won't do. He went to Soubirous this afternoon to the sawmill. In any case Armand is never careless with a gun."

"But you'll be able to find out, won't you? He shouldn't be allowed—"

"I am doing my best." A glance. "My active work is mainly done by telephone. And when I do find out he'll be dismissed."

He was turning the glass around and around in his long fingers, watching the gleam and shift of the firelight in the amber liquid. Behind him the mellow brown and gold of the books glinted in the firelight. Outside the dusk fell rapidly; the windows were oblongs of murky gray. Soon Seddon would come to draw the curtains and turn on the lights. Now in the flickering glow of the logs the room looked rich and pleasant, even—in this booklined bay where the fire burned—cozy.

I said, "Someone's been out already to look around?"

He glanced up. "Of course. But the chances are that the culprit would make straight back when he saw what he had done—or nearly done. He wouldn't want to be caught out with the gun." He gave a little smile. "You do realize that whoever it is is going to take quite a bit of trouble to cover his tracks, don't you? Good jobs aren't as easy to get as all that around here."

"If he's been going to come forward he'd no doubt have come running when he heard me shout," I said. "But I quite see why he's scared to. It might even be a question of police proceedings."

The dark brows rose. "Police? If there had actually been an accident—yes. But as it is—"

"I don't think it was an accident."

He looked considerably startled. "What in the world are you suggesting, then?" Then, as I made no immediate reply, he said in a voice where anger flickered through derision and disbelief, "What else, Miss Martin, what else? Deliberate murder?"

Mockery—but through it I felt anger meeting me, palpable as the beat of a hot wind. The words bit through the air betweeen us. I merely gaped at him, surprised.

Then it drew off. He said, his voice smooth and cold, "You're being a little hysterical, aren't you? Who would want to kill a child? Philippe has no enemies."

No, I thought, and no friends either. Except me. I sat up and met Léon de Valmy's hard stare. I said coolly, "You take me up too quickly, Monsieur de Valmy. I wasn't suggesting anything quite as silly as that. And I am not hysterical."

His mouth relaxed a little. "I apologize. But you gave me a shock. Go on. Explain yourself."

I drank sherry, regarding him straightly. "It's only that I can't quite see how it could have been pure accident. The place was so open and he *must* have been able to hear us fairly easily. I think it was some silly prank—some youth, perhaps, showing off or trying to startle us. And he got nearer than he meant to, and then was so scared of what he'd done that he made off."

"I see." He was silent for a moment. "You had better fill in the details for me. Exactly where were you?"

"We went down the path that short-cuts the zigzag toward the Valmy bridge. We left it about halfway down, where you cross a deep ravine and turn right down the valley."

"I know it. There's a cascade and a trout pool."

Some fleeting surprise must have shown in my face, for he said quietly, "I have lived at Valmy all my life, Miss Martin."

It was an almost physical effort to keep from looking at the picture above our heads. I said quickly, "Of course. Well, you know how the path runs along the hillside down the valley? After about half a mile it's quite wide, and flat, and there are thick trees on the left going down toward the river, but on the right, above you, they thin out."

"I know. An open ride, with grass and beech rising to a ridge of rock. Above the rock is the planted forest."

I nodded. "The pines are about twenty feet high now, and very thick. We were going along the path; Philippe was singing and hopping about ahead of me, not looking where he was going."

"Fortunately, it seems," said Léon de Valmy dryly.

"Yes. Well, just as he tripped and fell flat, a bullet went slap into the tree that had tripped him, and I heard the report from above us, to the right."

"From the ridge?"

"I suppose so. It was the best cover, and where it happened there was nothing between us and the ridge except brambles and a few stumps covered with honeysuckle."

"You saw nothing?"

"Nothing. I shouted, and then, of course, I had to attend to Philippe. I suppose I assumed that whoever it was would have had a bad fright, and would come pelting down to see if we were hurt. But he didn't. I'd have gone up to investigate, only I thought I ought to get Philippe straight home."

He was watching me curiously. "You would have done something as dangerous as that?"

"Of course. Why not?"

He said slowly, "You are a courageous young woman, are you not?"

"Where's the courage? We both know it couldn't have been deliberate. Why should I be afraid of a fool?"

A pause, then all at once his face lighted with that extraordinarily charming smile. "A young woman might well be afraid to approach a fool armed with a rifle. Don't be angry with me, mademoiselle. It was meant as a compliment."

"I'm sorry." I swallowed, and said as an afterthought, "Thank you."

He smiled again. "Tell me, just how much do you know about guns?"

"Nothing whatever."

"I thought as much. You seem, when you talk of an 'accident,' to be picturing a singularly unlikely one. You think, in fact, that this fool with the gun fired more or less at random through the trees at a barely-seen target, or even at a sound?"

"Yes. And I can't quite see how he didn't know—"

"Exactly. The place was open and you said Philippe was shouting or singing."

"Yes. That's why I thought it must have been meant as a joke."

"Some unauthorized youth with a talent for excitement? Hardly. No, the explanation's far simpler than that. An 'accident' with a gun usually only means one thing—a carelessly-held gun, a stumble (as Philippe stumbled) over a

99

stone or a root . . . and the gun goes off. I think, myself, that he must have seen Philippe fall, and have thought he had hit him. So . . . he panicked, and ran away."

"Yes, of course. That does seem to be the answer."

"Well, you can be sure it'll be looked into. The culprit may even come forward when he hears that no damage was done —but personally, I don't think he will." The long fingers toyed with the glass. He said, kindly—it could surely not be amusement that so faintly warmed his voice?—"My poor child, you've had a strenuous couple of days, haven't you? We're very grateful to you, my wife and I, for your care of Philippe. I'm sorry it's been such a frightening burden today."

"It's not a burden. And I'm very happy here."

"Are you? I'm glad. And don't worry any more about this business. After all, whether we find the man or not, it's not likely to happen again. Has Philippe got over his fright?"

"I think so."

"There's no need to call a doctor, or take any measures of that kind?"

"Oh, no. He's perfectly all right now. I doubt if he really knows how—how near it was. He seemed quite happy when I left him, but I did have to promise to go back and play a game before bedtime."

"Then I won't keep you. But finish your sherry first, won't you?"

I obeyed him, then set the glass down and said carefully, "Monsieur de Valmy, before I go, I have a confession to make."

An eyebrow lifted. I was right. It was amusement.

I said, "No, I'm serious. I—I've been deceiving you and Madame de Valmy, and I can't do it any longer. I've got to tell you."

The glint was still there. He said gravely, "I'm listening. How have you deceived us?"

I said, in French, "This is how I've deceived you, monsieur —ever since I came into the house, and I think it's high time I came clean."

There was a short silence.

"I see," he said. "Not just good French, either; the French of France, Miss Martin. Well, let's have it. Come clean."

The murder was out. It was over. My useless deception was confessed, and nothing had happened except that Léon de Valmy had laughed rather a lot—not only at the shifts I had been put to, but at the idea that my job should be contingent on an ignorance of French. Shamefacedly, I laughed with him, only too ready, in my relief, to admit my own folly. But . . .

Somewhere, deep inside me, something was protesting faintly. But . . .

But now the Demon King laughed good-temperedly, and, thankfully, I laughed with him.

It was into this scene of hilarity that Raoul de Valmy came a few moments later. I didn't hear him come in until he said from the door, "I'm sorry. I didn't know you were engaged."

"It's all right," said his father. "Come in."

With a click, the lights sprang to life. Raoul came around the bookcase into the bay where we sat. "I've just got in—" he began, then saw me sitting, sherry glass in hand, and paused.

"Good evening, mademoiselle." He glanced from me to his father. "I believe you wanted to see me, sir?"

I put down my glass and got quickly to my feet.

"I was just going," I said. I spoke in French, and I saw Raoul's brows lift, but he made no comment. Then I paused, glancing back diffidently at my employer. "Perhaps Monsieur Raoul has found something about the shooting? Has he been out to look for this man?"

"No," said Monsieur de Valmy. He nodded a pleasant dismissal. "Well, Miss Martin, thank you for coming. Good night."

"Shooting?" said Raoul sharply.

He was speaking to me. I hesitated and looked uncertainly at Monsieur de Valmy. Raoul said again, "What's this about shooting? Who should I have been looking for?"

"Oh," I said awkwardly—I had, after all, been already dismissed from the library—"I thought perhaps . . . then you don't know what happened this afternoon?"

Raoul had moved between his father's chair and the fireplace and was reaching for the sherry decanter.

"No. What did happen?"

Léon said coldly, "Some fool out with a rifle in the woods has narrowly missed killing your cousin."

Raoul's head jerked up at that. Some sherry splashed. "What? Philippe? Someone shot at Philippe?"

"That's what I said."

"Was he hurt?"

"He wasn't touched."

Raoul straightened, glass in hand, his shoulders back against the mantel. He looked from one to the other of us. "What did the chap think he was doing?"

"That," said his father, "is what we would like to know." He tilted his head back to look at his son. "You've been out, you say. Did you see anyone?"

"No."

"Which way did you go?"

"East. I told you I was going up through the new plantations. I went up from the kitchen gardens. I never saw a soul. Where did it happen?"

"On the track through the beechwood, half a mile north of the bridge."

"I know the place." He looked at me. "This is . . . shocking. He really wasn't hurt at all?"

"Not at all," I said. "He fell down, and the bullet missed him."

"And you? I take it you were there?"

"I was with him. It didn't go near me."

He stood looking down at the empty glass between his fingers, then set it carefully on the mantelpiece beside him. "Don't go yet, please. Sit down again. D'you mind telling me just what happened?"

Once more I told the story. He listened without moving, and his father leaned back in his chair, one hand playing with the stem of his empty glass, watching us both. When I had finished Raoul said, without turning his head, "I assume you have the matter in hand?"

For a moment I thought he was speaking to me, and looked up, surprised, but Léon de Valmy answered, "I have," and proceeded to outline the various instructions he had given by telephone. Raoul listened, his head bent now, staring into the fire, and I sat back in my chair and watched the two of them, wondering afresh at the queer twisted relationship that was theirs. Today all seemed quite normal between them; last night's perverted cut and thrust might never have been. The two voices, so alike; the two faces, so alike and yet so tragically different . . . my eyes lifted to the devil-may-care young face above the mantelpiece, with the pictured smile and the careless hand on the pony's bridle. No, it wasn't Raoul; it could never have been Raoul. There was something in his face, something dark and difficult that could never have belonged to the laughing careless boy in the picture. I had the feeling, watching Raoul as he talked to his father, that the young man of the picture would have been easier to know. . . .

I came back to reality with a jerk. Léon de Valmy was saying, "We seem to treat our employees a little roughly. I

102

would have liked to persuade Miss Martin to take the evening off, but she feels it her duty to entertain Philippe."

"I must," I said. "I promised."

"Then go out afterward. Not—" that flash of charm again "for a walk, as we seem so determined at Valmy to dog you with malice, but why not shake our dangerous dust from your feet, Miss Martin, and go down to Thonon? It's not late. A café, a cinema—"

"By the time she has put Philippe to sleep there'll be no buses to Thonon," said Raoul.

"It doesn't matter," I said quickly, surprised at the desire to escape that had swept over me. An evening outside Valmy— supper in a crowd, lights, voices, music, the common comings-and-goings of café and street—suddenly I longed desperately for these. I had had enough of drama this last two days. I got to my feet, this time decisively.

"It's very kind of you, but I did promise Philippe, and he's been upset. . . . I mustn't disappoint him. I'll rest after dinner."

"Tea alone in your room again and an early bed?" Raoul straightened his shoulders. "Are you sure you won't go?"

"Well I—" I hesitated, laughing. "I can't, can I?"

"There are two cars at Valmy, and the requisite number of people to drive them." He glanced down at Léon. "I think we owe Miss Martin her escape, don't you?"

"Assuredly. But I'm afraid Jeannot has the big car in Geneva on my business, and the shooting brake isn't back yet from the sawmill."

"Well," said Raoul, "there's mine." He looked at me. "Do you drive?"

"No. But look, you mustn't think—I wouldn't dream—"

"You know," said Raoul to the ceiling, "she's pining to go. Aren't you?"

I gave up. "It would be heaven."

"Then take my car." He looked at his father. "You can spare Bernard to drive it?"

"Of course."

"Where is he?"

"Out. I sent him straight away to look for traces of this fool with the gun, but it's dusk now so he should be back. No doubt he'll be in soon to report. . . . That's settled, then. Excellent. It only remains for me to wish you—what, Miss Martin? A pleasant evening, an evening to remember?"

I said, thinking of Philippe's face streaked with mud and tears, "I thought it was to be an evening to forget."

Léon de Valmy laughed.

Raoul crossed the room and opened the door for me.

"At eight, then?"

"Thank you. Yes."

"I'll see he's there. I—er, I gather we now speak French?"

I said, low voiced, "I told him just now."

I didn't add that I was pretty sure my confession had been quite unnecessary. The Demon King had known already.

Punctually at eight the lights of the car raked the darkness beyond the balcony rail. Philippe was already sound asleep, and Berthe sat sewing beside the fire in my sitting room. It was with a light step and a light heart that I ran downstairs toward my unexpected evening of freedom.

The Cadillac was standing there, its engine running. The driver, a tall silhouette against the lights, waited by the off front door. I got in and he slammed it after me, walked around the front of the car, and slid into his seat beside me.

"You?" I said. "That wasn't in the bond, was it?"

The car glided forward, circled, and dived smoothly into the zigzag. Raoul de Valmy laughed.

"Shall we talk French?" he said in that language. "It's the language I always take girls out in. Construe."

"I only meant that I don't see why you should chauffeur me. Couldn't you find Bernard?"

"Yes, but I didn't ask him. Do you mind?"

"Of course not. It's very nice of you."

"To follow my own inclinations? I warn you," he said lightly, "I always do. It's my modus vivendi."

"Why 'warn'? Are they ever dangerous?"

"Sometimes." I expected him to smile on the word, but he didn't. The light mood seemed to have dropped from him, and he drove for a while in an abstracted, almost frowning silence. I sat there rather shyly, my hands in my lap, watching the road twist and swoop up to meet us.

The car dropped down the last arm of the zigzag, turned carefully off the bridge and gathered speed on the valley road.

He spoke at length in a formal, almost cool tone. "I'm sorry you should have had such a bad two days."

"Two days?"

"I was thinking about last night's episode on the bridge back there."

"Oh, that." I gave a little laugh. "D'you know, I'd almost forgotten it."

104

"I'm glad to hear it. But perhaps that's only because what happened this afternoon has overridden it. You seem to have got over your scare now." He threw me a quick glance and said abruptly: "Were you scared?"

"Today? Ye-es. Yes, I was. Not of being shot or anything, because that part was over before I knew anything about it, but somehow—just scared." I twisted my fingers together in my lap, thinking back to that heart-stopping point of time, trying to explain. "I think it was the moment when I heard the shot and there was Philippe flat on the path . . . the moment before I realized he wasn't hurt. It seemed to last forever. Just the silence after the shot, and the world spinning round out of gear with no noise but the tops of the trees sweeping the air the way you hear a car's tires when the engine's off."

We were sailing up the curve toward Belle Surprise. The trees streamed by, a moment drenched in our flowing gold, then livid, fleeing, gone. I said, "Have you ever thought, when something dreadful happens, 'a moment ago things were not like this; let it be *then*, not *now*, anything but *now*'? And you try and try to remake *then*, but you know you can't. So you try to hold the moment quite still and not let it move on and show itself. It was like that."

"I know. But it hadn't happened after all."

"No." I let out a long unsteady breath. "It was still *then*. I—I don't think I'll forget the moment when Philippe moved as long as I live."

Another of those quick glances. "And afterward?"

"Afterwards I was angry. So blazing angry I could have killed someone."

"It takes people that way," he said.

"Because they've been scared? I know. But it wasn't only that. If you'd seen Philippe's face—" I was seeing it myself a little too clearly. I said, as if somehow I had to explain, "He's so quiet, Philippe. It's—it's all wrong that he should be so quiet. Little boys shouldn't be like that. And today was better; he was playing the fool in that silly maddening way children have, shouting rubbish and hopping about, only I was so pleased to see him like that that I didn't mind. And then . . . out of the blue . . . that beastliness. And there was mud on his face and he didn't want to stop to look at the trout and then he—he cried." I stopped then. I bit my lip and looked away from him out of the window.

"Don't talk about it any more if you'd rather not."

"It . . . gets me a bit. But I feel better now I've told someone." I managed a smile. "Let's forget it, shall we?"

"That's what we came out for." He smiled suddenly, and said with an abrupt, almost gay change of tone, "You'll feel quite different when you've had dinner. Have you got your passport?"

"What?"

"Your passport. I suppose you carry it?"

"Yes, it's—here it is. This sounds serious. What is it, a deportation?"

"Something like that." We were approaching the outskirts of Thonon now. Trees lined the road, and among them globed lamps as bland as melons made fantastic patterns of the boughs. "What d'you say," said Raoul, slowing a little and glancing at me, "shall we make a night of it? Go across into Geneva and eat somewhere and then dance or go to a cinema or something like that?"

"Anything," I said, my mood lifting to meet his. "Everything. I leave it to you."

"You mean that?"

"Yes."

"Excellent," said Raoul, and the big car swept out into the light and bustle of Thonon's main square.

I am not going to describe that evening in detail though, as it happens, it was desperately important. It was then, simply, one of those wonderful evenings. . . . We stopped in Thonon beside a stall where jonquils and wallflowers blazed under the gas jets, and he bought me freesias which smelled like the Fortunate Isles and those red anemones that were once called the lilies of the field. Then we drove along in a clear night with stars aswarm and a waxing moon staring pale behind the poplars. By the time we reached Geneva—a city of fabulous glitter and strung lights whose reflections swayed and bobbed in the dark waters of the Lake—my spirits were rocketing sky-high; shock, loneliness, the breath of danger all forgotten.

Why had I thought him difficult to know? We talked as if we had known each other all our lives. He asked me about Paris and I found myself, for the first time, talking easily—as if memory were happiness and not regret—of Maman and Daddy and the Rue du Printemps. Even the years at the orphanage came gaily enough to hand, to be remembered with amusement, more, with affection.

And in his turn Raoul talked of his own Paris—so different from mine; of a London with which it seemed impossible that the Constance Butcher Home for Girls could have any connection; of the hot brilliance of Provence, where Bellevigne stood, a little jewel quietly ruining down among its dusty vines. . . .

Anything but Valmy. I don't think it was mentioned once.

And we did do everything. We had a wonderful dinner somewhere; the place wasn't fashionable, but the food was marvelous and my clothes didn't matter. We didn't dance there, because Raoul said firmly that food was important and one must not distract oneself with gymnastics, but later, somewhere else, we danced, and later still we drove back toward Thonon, roaring along the straight unenclosed road at a speed which made my blood tingle with excitement, yet which felt, in that wonderful car, on that wonderful night, like no speed at all. The frontier checked us momentarily, then the big car tore on, free, up the long hill to Thonon. Along the wide boulevard that rims the slope to the Lake, through the now-empty market place, past the turning that led up to Soubirous. . . .

"Hi," I said, "you've missed the turning."

"I'm following one of my dangerous inclinations."

I looked at him a little warily. "Such as?"

He said, "There's a casino at Évian."

I remembered Mrs. Seddon, and smiled to myself. "What's your lucky number?"

He laughed. "I don't know yet. But I do know that this is the night it's coming up."

So we went to the casino, and he played and I watched him, and then he made me play and I won and then won again and then we cashed our winnings together and went out and drank café-fine and laughed a lot and then, at last, drove home.

It was three in the morning when the great car nosed its way up the zigzag, and—whether from excitement or sleepiness or the fines—I might have been floating up it in a dream. He stopped the car by the side door that opened off the stableyard, and, still dreamily and no doubt incoherently, I thanked him and said good night.

I must have negotiated the dark corridors and stairways to my room still in the same trancelike daze. I have no recollections of doing so, nor of how I got myself to bed.

It wasn't the brandy; the coffee had drowned that effectively enough. It was a much more deadly draught. There was one thing that stood like stone among the music and moonfroth of the evening's gaieties. It was stupid, it was terrifying, it was wonderful, but it had happened.

For better or worse, I was head over ears in love with Raoul de Valmy.

Sixth Coach

Chapter IX

Never seek to tell thy love,
Love that never told can be . . .

WILLIAM BLAKE: *Poem from MSS.*

It was to have been expected. It would be a very odd
Cinderella indeed who could be thrown out of such dreary
seclusion as the orphanage had offered me, into contact with
Raoul de Valmy, without something of the sort happening. A
man whose looks and charm were practically guaranteed to get
him home without his even trying, had exerted himself to
give a very lonely young woman a pleasant evening. An evening to remember.

That it was no more than that I was fully aware. In spite of
a quantity of romantic reading and a great many wistfully
romantic (and very natural) dreams, I had retained a good
deal of my French common sense. That, along with the nastily-
named English quality called phlegm, would have to help me
to control the present silly state of my emotions. I had had my
evening. Tomorrow would be another day.

It was. Soon after breakfast the big Cadillac disappeared
down the zigzag; Raoul, I supposed, gone back to Bellevigne.
I tore my thoughts resolutely away from a Provençal idyll
where he and I drove perpetually through moonlit vineyards
with an occasional glimpse of the Taj Mahal and the Blue
Grotto of Capri thrown in, and concentrated rather fiercely on
Philippe.

Nobody owned to the rifle incident, and there was little
hope of tracing the culprit. But Philippe seemed to have got
over his fright so the matter was allowed to drop. Life fell back
into its accustomed pattern, except for the exciting prospect of
the Easter Ball, which now provided a thrilling undercurrent
to conversation below stairs. This function had for many
years been held at Valmy on Easter Monday. Mrs. Seddon
and Berthe, when they were about the schoolroom domain,
delighted to tell me of previous occasions when the Château

Valmy had been en fête.

"Flowers," said Berthe (who seemed to have taken serenely for granted my sudden acquisition of fluent French) "and lights everywhere. They even used to string lights right down the zigzag to the Valmy bridge. And there's floodlights in the pool, and they turn the big fountain on, and there are little floating lights in the water, like lilies. Of course," pausing in her dusting to look at me a little wistfully, "it isn't as grand as it used to be in the old days. My mother used to tell me about it when the old Comte was alive; they say he was rolling in money, but, of course, it's not the same anywhere now, is it? But mind you, it'll be pretty grand, for all that. There's some as says it's not quite the thing to have a dance this Easter seeing as Monsieur le Comte and Madame la Comtesse were killed last year, but what I says is them that's dead is dead (God rest their souls)—" crossing herself hastily—"and them that's alive might as well get on with the job. Not wanting to sound hardhearted, miss, but you see what I mean?"

"Of course."

"Anyway, Madame says it'll be just a small private party—not but what they call a small private party'd make your eyes stand out on stalks, as the saying is . . . if you'll excuse the expression, miss. But—" here she brightened, and picked up a brass tray which she began to polish with vigor—"we'll have our dance just as usual."

"You have one, too?"

"Oh yes. All the tenants and the château staff. It's the night after the château dance, on the Tuesday, down at Soubirous. Everybody goes."

This, not unnaturally, left me wondering which dance I would be invited to attend, but it was very soon made clear to me by Madame de Valmy that for this occasion at any rate I was above the salt. . . . So I, too, succumbed to the universal feeling of pleased anticipation, a pleasure shot through with the worry of not having a dance frock to wear.

I didn't worry about this for long. I am French enough where my needle is concerned, and I had been—there was nothing else to do with it—saving the greater part of my salary for the last weeks. I didn't doubt that I could achieve something creditably pretty, even though it might not stand comparison with the Balmains and Florimonds with which the ballroom would probably be crowded. It would be pretty enough to sit out in, I told myself firmly, thrusting back a vision of myself en grande tenue, dancing alone with Raoul in a ballroom about the size of Buckingham Palace. But it would not (this with a memory of Jane Eyre's depressing wardrobe and Léon de Valmy's mocking eye) it would not be "suitable." I wasn't down to bombazine yet.

My next halfday off fell some three days after the incident with the rifle, and I went down to Thonon on the afternoon bus, with the object of buying stuff and pattern for a dance frock. I didn't think it would be much use looking for a ready-made in so small a place as Thonon, and Évian or Geneva prices were beyond me. So I hunted happily about for the best material I could afford, and at last was rewarded with a length of some pretty Italian stuff in white, webbed with gossamer silver threads, at what the saleswoman called a bargain price, but to me represented a horrifying proportion of my savings. I fought a swift losing battle with the remnants of my common sense, and firmly planted the money down on the counter with no trace of regret. Then, clutching the parcel to me, I pushed my way out through the shop door into the windy street.

It was almost five o'clock, one of those dark, rain-laden April days with a warm gusty wind blowing. There had been showers earlier, but now a belated gleam from the west glissaded over the wet housetops and etched the budding chestnuts of the square in pale gold against a salty sky. Many of the shop windows were bright already, harshly lighted grocery stores and boucheries mirrored to soft orange and copper in the damp pavements. Over the flower stall where Raoul had bought me the freesias a naked gas jet hissed and flared in the gusty wind, now a snake-long lash of brilliant flame, now a flattened mothswing of cobalt and sulphur-yellow. The tires of passing cars hissed softly on the wet tarmac. Here and there among the bare chestnuts an early street lamp glowed.

I was longing for a cup of tea. But here my sense of economy, subconsciously outraged, no doubt, by the recent purchase, stepped in to argue the few francs' difference between tea and coffee. A salon de thé would be expensive, while coffee or an apéritif were at once far better quality and half the price.

I abandoned the tea and walked across the square toward a restaurant where a glass screen protected the tables from the fitful wind.

As I gained the pavement and paused to choose a table, a diffident voice spoke beside me.

"Miss Martin?"

I turned in some surprise, as the voice was unmistakably English. It was the fair young man of my encounter in Soubirous. He was dressed in a duffel coat supplemented by a shaggy scarf. His thick fair hair flopped in the wind. I had forgotten what an enormous young man he was. The general effect was that of a huge, shy blond bear, of a bigness incredible, as Philippe would have said.

He said, "D'you remember me? We met in Soubirous."

"Of course I remember you, Mr. Blake." I could have added that I was hardly likely to have forgotten him—the one English lamb in my pride of French tigers—but thought it was, perhaps, not tactful. . . . "I hope you haven't had to use any of those bandages and things?"

He grinned. "Not yet. But I expect to daily. Were you—were you thinking of going in here for a drink? I wonder if you would—may I—I mean I'd be awfully glad if—"

I rescued him. "Thank you very much. I'd love to. Shall we sit out here where we can watch what's going on?"

We settled ourselves at a table next to the glass screen, and he ordered coffee in his laborious English-French. His look of triumph when in actual fact coffee did arrive, made me laugh. "You're coming on fast," I said.

"Aren't I? But really, you know, it's hard to go wrong over café."

"Are you managing your shopping all right today?"

"Oh, yes. You can usually find someone who understands English in Thonon. Besides," he said simply, "it's cheaper. I usually shop in the market. I don't need a lot."

"Are you living up at the hut now?"

"For the time being. I sleep at the Coq Hardi in Soubirous a couple of nights in the week, and I have the odd meal there, but I like the hut. I get a lot of work done, and I can come and go and eat and sleep when I like."

I had a momentary and irresistible vision of him curling up in the straw, nuts in the pocket, like a bear, for the winter. This made me think of Philippe. I said, "Does anyone from your side of the valley ever bring a gun over to Valmy?"

"Only if invited. There are shooting parties in the autumn, I believe."

"I didn't mean that. Would the foresters or keepers or anyone ever go stalking foxes or chamois or something with a rifle?"

"Good Lord, no. Why?"

I told him in some detail just what had occurred on Tues-

111

day afternoon with Philippe. He listened with great attention, shocked out of his shyness by the end into expostulation.

"But that's frightful! Poor kid. It must have been a beastly shock—and for you, too. The best you can say of it is that it's bl——er, criminal carelessness! And you say they've found no trace of the chap?"

"No one admits it, even now it's known that nobody was hurt. But that's easy to understand; he'd lose his job just like *that*, and jobs aren't all that easy to come by up here."

"True enough."

"What's more," I said, "when Monsieur de Valmy sent a couple of men down to look at the place where it happened, they found that the bullet had been dug out of the tree."

He whistled. "Thorough, eh?"

"Very. D'you see what it means? Those men were sent down there as soon as Philippe and I got back to the house. It means, first, that the chap with the gun knew what had happened when he loosed it off; and, second, that he didn't run away. He must have sat tight waiting for Philippe and me to go, then skated down to remove the evidence." I looked at him. "The thought of him hiding up there in the wood watching us is rather—nasty, somehow."

"I'll say. What's more, the man's a fool. Accidents do happen, and if he'd done the decent thing and come tearing down to apologize and see you both home the odds are he'd have got off with just a rocket from the boss. He must have lost his head and then not dared own up. As it is, I hope they do get him. What's de Valmy doing about it?"

"Oh, he's still having inquiries made, but I don't think they'll produce anything now. All we've got so far is lashings of alibis, but the only two I'm prepared to believe are Monsieur de Valmy's and the butler's."

William Blake said, "The son was here, wasn't he?"

His tone was no more than idle, but I felt the blood rushing hotly to my cheeks. Furious with myself, I turned away to look out through the glass at the now twilit square. If I was going to blush each time his name was mentioned, I wouldn't last long under the Demon King's sardonic eye. And this sort of nonsense I couldn't expect him to condone. I fixed my gaze on the brilliant yellows and scarlets of the flower stall, and said indifferently, "He was; he went away the morning after it happened. But you surely can't imagine —" In spite of myself my voice heated. "It certainly couldn't have been *him!*"

112

"No? Cast-iron alibi?"

"No. It—it just couldn't!" Logic came rather late in the wake of emotions: "Dash it, he'd have no reason to sneak about digging bullets out of trees!"

"No, of course not."

I said, rather too quickly, "How are the weevil traps?"

That did it. He was the last person to see a reference to his work, however abruptly introduced, as a mere red herring. Soon we were once more happily in full cry. . . . I listened, and asked what I hope were the right questions, and thought about the Valmy dance. Would he be there? Would he? Would he?

I came out of my besotted dreaming to hear William Blake asking me prosaically which bus I intended to take back to Valmy. "Because," he said, "one goes in about twelve minutes, and after that you wait two hours."

"Oh Lord, yes," I said, "I mustn't miss it. Are you getting the same one?"

"No. Mine goes just before yours. I'm sloping off this week end to meet some friends at Annecy." He grinned at me as he beckoned the waiter. "So forget you saw me, will you, please? This is A.W.O.L. but I couldn't resist it. Some pals of mine are up in Annecy for the week and they want me to go climbing with them."

"I won't give you away," I promised.

Here the waiter came up, and Mr. Blake plunged into the dreadful struggle of The Bill. I could see all the stages; understanding the waiter's total, translating it mentally into English money, dividing by ten for the tip, reckoning to the nearest round number for simplicity, slowly and painfully thumbing over the revolting paper money, and finally handing over a sheaf of it with the irresistible feeling that so much money cannot possibly be the fair amount to pay for so little.

At last it was over. He met my eye and laughed, flushing a little. "I'm all right," he said defensively, "until they get to the nineties, and then I'm sunk. I have to make them write it down."

"I think you're wonderful. By the time you've been here another month you'll talk it like a native." I stood up. "Thank you very much for the coffee. Now you'd better not bother about me if you want to dash for that bus."

"You're right. I'm afraid I'll have to run." But he still hesitated. "It was—awfully nice meeting again. . . . Could we —I mean, when do you have your next afternoon off?"

"I don't quite know," I said, not very truthfully. Then I

113

relented. "But I'm often in Thonon on a Friday afternoon and—look, for goodness' sake . . . isn't that your bus? The driver's getting in! Go on, run! Is this yours? And this . . . ? Good-by! Have a good week end!"

Somehow he dragged his paraphernalia up from the floor, lurched, with rope and rucksack perilously swaying, between the crowded tables, thrust his way through the swing door I grabbed and held wide for him, then waved a hand to me and ran. He reached the bus just as the driver's door slammed and the engine coughed noisily to life. Then wedged—it seemed inextricably—on the narrow steps of the bus, he managed to turn and wave again cheerily as the vehicle jerked and roared away.

Feeling breathless myself, I waved back, then turned hurriedly to cross the road to where my own bus waited. But before I could step forward a big car slid to a halt beside me with a soft hush of wet tires. A Cadillac. My heart, absurdly, began to race.

The door was pushed open from inside. His voice said, "Going my way?"

He was alone in the car. I got in beside him without a word, and the car moved off. It swung around the corner of the square where the Soubirous bus still stood beside its lamp, and turned into the tree-lined street that led south.

It was odd that I hadn't really noticed till now what a beautiful evening it was. The street lamps glowed like ripe oranges among the bare boughs. Below in the wet street their globes glimmered down and down, to drown in their own reflections. *He hangs in shades the orange bright, like golden lamps* . . . and on the pavements there were piles of oranges, too, real ones, spilled there in prodigal piles with aubergines and green and scarlet peppers. The open door of a wine shop glittered like Aladdin's cave with bottles from floor to roof, shelf on shelf of ruby and amber and purple, the rich heart of a hundred sun-drenched harvests. From a bright lighted workmen's café nearby came music, the sound of voices loud in argument, and the smell of new bread.

The last lamp drowned its golden moon in the road ahead. The last house vanished and we were running between hedgeless fields. To the right a pale sky still showed clear under the western rim of the rain clouds, and against it the bare trees that staked the road stood out black and sheer. The leaves of an ilex cut the half-light like knives. A willow streamed in the

114

wind like a woman's hair. The road lifted itself ahead, mackerel silver under its bending poplars. The blue hour, the
lovely hour . . .

Then the hills were around us, and it was dark.

Raoul was driving fast and did not speak.

I said at last, a little shyly, "You're back soon. You haven't
been to Bellevigne, then?"

"No. I had business in Paris."

I wondered what kettles of fish he'd (in Mrs. Seddon's
unlikely idiom) been frying. "Did you have a good time?"

He said, "Yes," but in so absent a tone that I hesitated to
speak again. I leaned back in silence and gave myself up to
the pleasure of being driven home.

It was not for some time that I—absorbed in my dreaming—noticed how he was driving. He always traveled fast
and there was a slickness about the way the big car sliced
through the dark and up the twisting valley that demon-
strated how well he knew the road; but there was something
in his way of handling her tonight that was different.

I stole a glance at his silent profile as we whipped around
and over a narrow bridge that warped the road at right angles.
He had done nothing that was actively dangerous; in the
dark we would have had ample warning of an approaching
car, but we were skirting danger so closely that it now occurred to me a little sickeningly to wonder if he were drunk.
But as our headlights brushed a brilliant arc against the wall
of rock, reflected light swirled through the car and in it I
saw his face. He was sober enough; but that something was
the matter was quite evident. He was frowning at the road
ahead, his eyes narrowed on the flying dark. He had forgotten I was there. It seemed quite simply as if something
had put him into a bad temper and he was taking it out
on the car.

"What were you doing down in Thonon?" The question
was no more than a quid pro quo, but he spoke so abruptly
out of the silence that it sounded like an accusation, and I
jumped and answered almost at random.

"What? Oh, it's my afternoon off."

"What do you usually do on your afternoon off?"

"Nothing very much. Shopping . . . a cinema, anything."

"You go out to friends sometimes?"

"No," I said, surprised. "I don't know anyone. I told you
when we . . . I told you on Tuesday."

"Oh. Yes. So you did."

We had run into another shower, and big drops splashed and starred the windshield. The car slewed overfast around a sharp bend in the road, and rubber whined on the wet tarmac. He hadn't once so much as glanced at me. He was probably hardly aware of who it was he had in the car. So much for Cinderella.

I sat quietly beside him and nibbled the bitter crusts of common sense.

We had gone two-thirds of the way to Valmy before he spoke again. The question was sufficiently irrelevant and surprising.

"Who was that chap?"

I was startled and momentarily at a loss. I said stupidly, "What chap?"

"The man you were with in Thonon. You left the café with him."

"Oh, him."

"Who else?" The phrase, brief to the point of curtness, made me glance at him in surprise.

I said shortly, "A friend of mine."

"You told me you didn't know anyone hereabouts."

"Well," I said childishly, "I know him."

This provoked a glance, quick and unsmiling. But he only said, "How is Philippe?"

"All right, thank you."

"And you? No more mishaps?"

"No."

My voice must have sounded subdued and even sulky, but I was having a fight to keep it level and unbetraying. Pride had joined forces with common sense, and the two were flaying me. The phantoms of those idiotic dreams wavered, mockingly, in the dark. . . . I don't know quite what I had expected, but . . . that man, and this: the change was too great; it was unnerving.

I was also making a grim little discovery that frightened me. The dreams might be moonshine, but the fact remained. I was in love with him. It hadn't been the wine and the starlight and all the trappings of romance. It hadn't even been the charm that he'd been so lavish with that night. Now I was undoubtedly sober and it was raining and the charm wasn't turned on . . . and I was still in love with this cold-voiced stranger who was making futile and slightly irritated conversation at me. At least I'd had the sense all along to try and laugh at my own folly, but it was no longer even remotely amusing.

116

I bit my lip hard, swallowed another choking morsel of that bitter bread, and wished he would stop asking questions that needed answering. But he was persisting, still in that abrupt tone that made his queries—harmless enough in themselves—sound like an inquisition.

It seemed he was still curious about William Blake, which, in view of my promise to say nothing, was awkward.

"Who is he? English?"

"Yes."

"He took the Annecy bus, didn't he? A climber?"

"He's climbing from Annecy this week end."

"Staying there?"

"Yes."

"Did you know him in England?"

"No."

"Oh. Then he's been to Valmy?"

"Not that I'm aware of."

"Is he staying hereabouts for long?"

"Look," I said, cornered, "does it matter? What's the inquisition for?"

A pause. He said, sounding both stiff and disconcerted, "I'm sorry. I wasn't aware I was trespassing on your private affairs."

"They're not private. It's just—I—I didn't mean . . . I didn't want to tell you . . ." I floundered hopelessly.

He threw me an odd look. "Didn't want to tell me what?"

"Oh—nothing. Look," I said desperately, "I don't want to talk. D'you mind?"

And now there was no doubt whatever about his mood. I heard him say, "God damn it," very angrily under his breath. He wrenched the Cadillac around at the Valmy bridge and hurled her up the zigzag about twice as fast as he should have done. The car snarled up the ramp like a bad-tempered cat and was hauled around the first bend. "You mistake me." Still that note of barely-controlled exasperation. "I wasn't intending to pry into what doesn't concern me. But—"

"I know. I'm sorry." I must have sounded nearly as edgy as he did, shaken as I was, not only by his anger and my failure to understand it, but by a humiliation that he couldn't guess at. "I expect I'm tired. I trailed about Thonon for a couple of hours looking for some dress material—oh!" My hands flew to my cheeks. "I must have left it—yes, I left it in the café. I put it on the ledge under the table and then William had to run for the bus and—oh dear, how stupid of me! I suppose if I telephone—oh!"

His hand had moved sharply. The horn blared. I said, startled, "What was that?"

"Some creature. A weasel, perhaps."

The trees lurched and peeled off into darkness. The next corner, steeply embanked, swooped at us.

I said, "Do you have to go so fast? It scares me."

The car slowed, steadied, and took the bend with no more than a splutter of gravel.

"Did you tell him about the shooting down in the beechwood?"

"What? Who?"

"This—William."

I drew a sharp little breath. I said clearly, "Yes, I did. He thinks that probably you did it yourself."

The car whispered up the slope and nosed quietly out above the trees. He was driving like a careful insult. He didn't speak. The devil that rode me spurred me to add, out of my abyss of stupid self-torment, "And I didn't know that I was supposed to account to my employer for everything I said and did on my afternoon off!"

That got him, as it was meant to. He said, between his teeth, "I am not your employer."

"No?" I said it very nastily because I was afraid I was going to cry. "Then what's it to do with you what I do or who I see?"

We were on the last slope of the zigzag. The Cadillac jerked to a stop as the brakes were jammed on. Raoul de Valmy swung around on me.

"This," he said, in a breathless, goaded undertone. He pulled me roughly toward him, and his mouth came down on mine.

For a first kiss it was, I suppose, a fairly shattering experience. And certainly not such stuff as dreams are made on. . . . If Cinderella was out, so decidedly was Prince Charming. . . . Roaul de Valmy was simply an experienced man shaken momentarily out of self-control by anger and other emotions that were fairly easily recognizable even to me. I say "even to me" because I discovered dismayingly soon that my own poise was a fairly egg-shell affair. For all my semisophistication I emerged from Raoul's embrace in a thoroughly shaken state which I assured myself was icy rage. And certainly his

118

next move was hardly calculated to appease. Instead of whatever passionate or apologetic words should have followed, he merely let me go, restarted the car, opened the throttle with a roar, and shot her up the slope and onto the gravel sweep without a word. He cut the engine and opened his door as if to come around. I didn't wait. I whipped out of the car, slammed the door behind me and in a silence to match his own I stalked (there is no other word) across the gravel and up the steps.

He caught up with me and opened the big door for me. He said something—I think it was my name—in an undervoice sounding as if it were shaken by a laugh. I didn't look at him. I walked past him as if he didn't exist, straight into a blaze of light, and Léon de Valmy, who was crossing the hall.

He checked his chair in its smooth progress as I came in, and turned his head as if to greet me. Then his eyes flicked from my face to Raoul's and back again, and the Satanic eyebrows lifted, ever so slightly. I turned abruptly and ran upstairs.

If it had needed anything else to shake me out of my daydreams, that glance of Léon de Valmy's would have done it. I leaned back against the door in my darkened bedroom and put the back of my hand to a hot cheek. There was blood bitter-sweet on my tongue from a cut lip. . . . Léon de Valmy would have seen that too. The whip flicked me again. Not only my face, my whole body burned.

I jerked myself away from the door's support, snapped on the light, and began to tug savagely at my gloves. Damn Raoul; how dared he? How dared he? And Léon de Valmy—here the second glove catapulted down beside the first—damn Léon de Valmy, too. Damn all Valmys. I hated the lot of them. I never wanted to see any of them again.

On the thought I stopped, halfway out of my coat.

It was more than possible that I wouldn't have the chance. The Demon King didn't have to be en rapport with me to guess what had happened tonight, and it was quite probable that he would take steps to dismiss me.

It didn't occur to me at once that, if there were any hint of trouble, Raoul would certainly tell his father the truth, that I had been kissed against my will, and that since for the greater part of the year Raoul was not at Valmy to trouble the waters I would probably be kept on.

I only know that as I hung my coat with care in the pretty

paneled wardrobe I felt depressed—more, desolate—at the prospect of never seeing any of the hated Valmys again.

My lip had stopped bleeding. I put on fresh lipstick carefully, and did my hair. Then I walked sedately out and across my sitting room to the schoolroom door.

I opened it and went in. The light was on, but no one was there. The fire had burned low and the room had an oddly forlorn look. One of the French windows was ajar and the undrawn curtains stirred in a little breeze. On the rug lay an open book, its pages faintly vibrant to the same draft.

Puzzled, I glanced at the clock. It was long past time for Philippe's return from the salon. Madame de Valmy would be upstairs, dressing. Well, I reflected, it wasn't my affair. On this night of all nights I wasn't going to see why he was being kept late below stairs. No doubt he would come up when his supper did.

I was stooping for a log to throw on the fire when I heard the sound. It whispered across the quiet room, no more loudly than the tick of the little French clock or the settling of the wood ash in the grate.

A very slight sound, but it lifted the hair on my skin as if that, too, felt the cold breath from the open window. It was no more than a voiced sigh, but, horribly, it sounded like a word . . . "Mademoiselle . . ."

I was across the schoolroom in one leap. I ran out onto the dark balcony and turned to peer along the leads. To right and left the windows were shut and dark. From behind me the lighted schoolroom thrust a bright wedge across the balcony, making my shadow, gigantic and grotesque, leap and posture before me over the narrow leads.

"Philippe?"

The ends of the balcony were in deep darkness, invisible. I plunged out of my patch of light and ran along past the windows. The balcony floor was slippery with rain.

"Philippe? Philippe?"

That terrible little whisper answered me from the darkest corner. I was beside it, kneeling on the damp leads. He was crouched in a tiny huddle up against the balustrade.

Or rather, where the balustrade had been. It was no longer there. In its place was merely the step-ladder which I had taken from the broom closet that very afternoon to wedge across the unsteady coping. Beyond this frail barrier was merely a gap of darkness and a thirty-foot drop to the gravel and that terrible line of iron spikes. . . .

My hands were on him, my voice hoarse and shaking.

"Philippe? What happened? You didn't fall. Oh, God, you didn't fall . . . oh my little Philippe, are you all right?"

Small cold hands came up and clung. "Mademoiselle . . ."

I had him in my arms, my face against his wet cheek. "Are you all right, Philippe? Are you hurt?" I felt his head shake. "Sure? Quite sure?" A nod. I stood up with him in my arms. I am not big myself, but he seemed a featherweight, a bundle of birds' bones. I carried him into the schoolroom, over to the fireplace, and sat down in a wing chair, cuddling him close to me. His arms came up around my neck and clung tightly. I don't know what I was saying to him; I just hugged and crooned rubbish over the round dark head that was buried in my neck.

Presently he relaxed his strangle hold and stopped shivering. But when I tried to stoop for a log to put on the fire he clutched me again.

"It's all right," I said quickly, "I'm only going to build the fire up. We must get you warm, you know."

He suffered me to lean forward, throw some faggots onto the sullen fire, and stir it until some little tongues of flame crept up around the new wood and began to lick brightly at it. Then I sat back in the chair again. It seemed to me that the reassurance of my arms was of more importance at that moment than bed or hot drinks or any of the remedies that would follow shortly. I said gently, "Was it the car, Philippe?"

That little nod again.

"But I warned you the stone was loose. I told you not to go galloping along there, didn't I?"

He said in a voice that sounded thinner and more childish than ever, "I heard the horn. I thought . . . Papa always used to . . . on the drive . . . to tell me he was coming. . . ."

I bit my lip, then winced. Of course, the horn. I remembered that arrogant blare on the zigzag. I had seen nothing on the road. It had merely been part, no doubt, of the flare of temper and excitement that had driven Raoul to kiss me . . . and driven Philippe out into the darkness, running in a stubborn, passionate hope to fling himself against the rotten stone.

I said, as much to myself as him, "I'd no idea the coping was as dangerous. It only seemed to move such a little. I thought it would hold. Thank God I put the ladder across.

121

Why I did . . . oh, thank God I did!" Then a thought struck me. "Philippe, where was Berthe? I thought she was with you."

"Bernard came for her. Something she'd forgotten to do."

"I see." I waited for a moment, holding him. "Look, Philippe, we've got a lovely fire now. What about warming those frozen paws?"

This time he unclasped himself without demur, and slipped down onto the rug beside me, holding out his hands obediently to the now bright blaze of the fire. I ruffled his hair. "This is wet, too. What a beastly night to go running out in! You are a little ass, aren't you?"

He said, his voice still too tight and sharp, "I hit the stone and then it wasn't there. It went over with a bang. I bumped into something. I couldn't see. I fell down. I couldn't see anything."

"It was the ladder you bumped into, Philippe. You couldn't have fallen over, you know. There wasn't really a gap. You couldn't see the ladder, but it's a very solid one. It was really quite safe. Quite safe."

"It was awful. I was frightened."

"I don't blame you," I said. "I'd have been scared stiff. It was awfully sensible of you not to move."

"I didn't dare. I knew you'd come." The plain, pale little face turned to me. "So I waited."

Something twisted inside me. I said lightly, "And I came. What a good thing I came up in your cousin Raoul's car instead of waiting for the bus!" I got up and bent over him, slipping my hands under his arms. "Now, come and get these things off. Up with you." I swung him to his feet. "Goodness, child, you've been lying in a puddle! What about a hot bath and then supper in bed with a fire in your bedroom as a treat?"

"Will you be there?"

"Yes."

"Have your supper in my room?"

"I'll sit on your bed," I promised.

The black eyes glinted up at me. "And play Peggitty?"

"Oho!" I said. "So you're beginning to make capital out of this, are you? What's more, you're getting too dashed good at Peggitty. All right, if you'll promise not to beat me." I swung him around and gave him a little shove toward the door. "Now go and get those things off while I run the bath."

He went off obediently. I rang the bell for Berthe, and

122

then went to turn on the bath. As I watched the steam billowing up to cloud the tiles I reflected a little grimly that now I should have to face Léon de Valmy again tonight.

Above the noise of the taps I heard a knock on the door that led from my sitting room. I called, "Come in." Berthe had been very quick.

I turned then in surprise, as I saw that it wasn't Berthe, but Madame de Valmy. She never came to these rooms at this hour, and as I caught sight of her expression my heart sank. This, then, was it. And I hadn't had time to think out what to say.

I twisted the taps a little to lessen the gush of water, and straightened up to meet whatever was coming.

"Miss Martin, forgive me for interrupting you while you're changing—" Hardly a frightening opening, that; her voice was apologetic, hurrying, almost nervous. "I wondered—did you remember to get me my tablets in Thonon this afternoon?"

I felt myself flushing with relief. "Why, yes, madame. I was going to give them to Berthe to put in your room. I'm sorry, I didn't realize you'd want them straight away."

"I'm out of them, or I wouldn't trouble you."

"I'll get them now," I said. "No, really, it's no trouble, madame. You're not interrupting me; this bath isn't for me. Philippe!"

I bent to test the water, then turned off the taps. "Oh, there you are, Philippe. Hop in, and don't by-pass your ears this time . . . I'll get your tablets straight away, madame. My bag's through in my sitting room."

As I came out of the bathroom and shut the door behind me I was wondering how to tell her about the recent near-tragedy. But as I looked at her all idea of this melted into a different consternation. She looked ill. The expression that I had thought forbidding was revealed now as the pallor, set lips, and strained eyes of someone on the verge of collapse.

I said anxiously, "Are you all right? You don't look well at all. Won't you sit down for a few minutes? Shall I get you some water?"

"No." She had paused by the fireplace, near a high-backed chair. She managed to smile at me; I could see the effort it took. "Don't worry, my dear. I—I didn't sleep well last night, that's all. I don't manage very well nowadays without my medicine."

"I'll get it straight away." Throwing her another doubtful look I ran toward my sitting room, only to remember that the tablets were after all still in the pocket of my coat. I turned swiftly.

"Madame!" The horrified anxiety of the cry was wrenched out of me by what I saw.

She had put a hand on the chair back, and was leaning heavily on it. Her face was turned away from me, as if she were listening to Philippe splashing in the bathroom, but her eyes were shut, and her cheeks were a crumpled gray. No beauty there. She looked old.

At my exclamation she started, and her eyes flew open. She seemed to make an effort, and moved away from the chair.

I ran back to her. "Madame, you are ill. Shall I call some-one? Albertine?"

"No, no. I shall be all right. My tablets?"

"In my coat pocket in the wardrobe. Yes, here they are. . . ."

She almost grabbed the box I held out to her. She managed another smile. "Thank you. I'm sorry if I alarmed you . . . these things pass. Don't look so worried, Miss Martin." In the bathroom Philippe had set up a shrill tuneless whistling that came spasmodically between splashes. Héloïse glanced toward the noise and then turned to go. She said, with an obvious attempt at normality, "Philippe sounds . . . very gay."

"Oh, yes," I said cheerfully, "he's fine."

I opened the door for her, straight onto Berthe who had paused outside, one hand lifted to knock. . . .

"Oh, miss, you startled me! I was just coming." Her eyes went past me and I saw them widen. I said quickly, "Madame isn't too well. Madame de Valmy, let Berthe see you to your room. I only rang for her to light Philippe's bedroom fire, but I'll do that myself. Berthe," I turned to the girl, who was still looking curiously at Héloïse de Valmy's drawn face, "take Madame to her room, ring for Albertine and wait till she comes. Then come back here, please."

"Yes, miss."

As I knelt to light Philippe's bedroom fire my mind was fretting at a new problem—a minor one, which I suppose I had seized on almost as a relief from the other worries that beat dark wings in my brain. What were those tablets that were apparently the breath of life to Madame? Did she take drugs? The ugly thought swirled up through a welter of ignorant conjectures, but I refused to take it up. The things were only sleeping tablets, I was sure; and presumably some people couldn't live without sleeping tablets. But—the flames

124

spread merrily from paper to sticks and took hold with a fine bright crackling—but why did she want the tablets now? She had looked as if she were suffering from some sort of attack, heart or nerves, that needed a restorative or stimulant. The sleeping tablets could hardly be the sort of lifesavers that her anxiety had implied.

I shrugged the thoughts away, leaning forward to place a careful piece of coal on the burning sticks. I was ignorant of such matters, after all. She had certainly seemed ill, and just as certainly old Doctor Fauré must know what he was about. . . .

Another burst of whistling and a messy-sounding splash came from the bathroom, and presently Philippe emerged, his hair in damp spikes, and his usually pale cheeks flushed and scrubbed-looking. He had on his nightshirt, and trailed a dressing gown on the floor behind him.

Something absurd and tender took me by the throat. I looked austerely at him. "Ears?"

He naturally took no notice of this poor-spirited remark, but came over to the hearthrug beside which the fire now burned brightly. He said, with palpable pride, "I escaped death by inches, didn't I?"

"You did indeed."

"Most people would have fallen over, wouldn't they?"

"Decidedly."

"Most people wouldn't have had the presence of mind to stay quite still, would they?"

I sat back on my heels, put an arm around his waist, and hugged him to me, laughing, "You odious child, don't be so conceited! And look, Philippe, we won't tell Berthe when she comes back, please."

"Why?"

"Because your aunt isn't well, and I don't want any alarming rumors getting to her to upset her."

"All right. But you'll—you'll tell my uncle Léon, won't you?"

"Of course. It's a marvel to me that he didn't hear the coping fall himself. He was in the hall when I got in, and that was only a few moments after—ah, Berthe. How is Madame?"

"Better, miss. She's lying down. Albertine's with her and she knows what to do. She says Madame will be well enough to go down to dinner."

"I'm glad to hear it. She . . . she took her tablets, Berthe?"

"Tablets, miss? No, it was her drops. She keeps them in the cabinet by her bed. Albertine gave her them."

"I . . . see. By the way, Berthe, weren't you supposed to be around the schoolroom wing while I was out?"

"Yes, miss, but Bernard came for me." She shot me a sidelong glance. "There was some linen I'd been sewing. Bernard wanted it for the Master, and couldn't find it, though I'd told him where it was."

"I see. Well, that shouldn't have kept you very long."

"No, miss. But it wasn't where I'd put it. Somebody'd moved it. Took me quite a while to find." She was eying me as she answered, obviously wondering why I questioned her so sharply.

I said, "Well, Master Philippe went outside to play on the balcony and got wet, so he's had a bath and is to have supper in bed. Do you mind bringing it in here, Berthe, and mine as well, please?"

"Not a bit, miss. I'm sorry, miss, but you see Bernard was in a hurry and—" She broke off. She was very pink now and looked flustered.

I thought, but in no hurry to let you go, that's obvious. And I don't suppose you insisted. I said aloud, "It's all right, Berthe, it doesn't matter. Master Philippe's not a baby, after all. It was his own fault he got a wetting, and now he gets the reward, and you and I have the extra work. That's life, isn't it?"

I got up, briskly propelling Philippe toward the bed. "Now in you get, brat, and don't stand about any longer in that nightshirt."

I had supper with Philippe as I promised, and played a game with him and read him a story. He was still in good spirits, and I was glad to see that his own part in the accident was assuming more and more heroic proportions in his imagination. At least nightmares didn't lie that way.

But when I got up to go out to the pantry to make his late-night drink he insisted a little breathlessly on coming with me. I thought it better to let him, so he padded along in dressing gown and slippers and was set to watch the milk on the electric ring while I measured the chocolate and glucose into the blue beaker he always used. We bore it back to the bedroom together and I stayed with him while he drank it. And then, when I would have said good night, he clung to me for a moment too long, so that I abandoned my intention of seeing Léon de Valmy that night, and spent the

126

rest of the evening in my own room with the communicating doors open so that the child could see my light.

When finally I was free to sit down beside my own fire I felt so tired that the flesh seemed to drag at my bones. I slumped down in the armchair and shut my eyes. But my mind was a cage gnawed by formless creatures that jostled and fretted, worries—some real, some half recognized, some unidentified and purely instinctive—that wouldn't let me rest. And when, very late, I heard a car coming up the zigzag I jumped to my feet, nerves instantly astretch, and slid quietly through the shadows to the door of Philippe's room.

He was asleep. I went wearily back into my bedroom and began to undress. I was almost ready for bed when someone knocked softly on the door.

I said in some surprise, "Who is it?"

"Berthe, miss."

"Oh, Berthe. Come in."

She was carrying a parcel, across which she looked at me a little oddly. "This is for you, miss. I thought you might be in bed, but I was told to bring it straight up."

"No, I wasn't in bed. Thank you, Berthe. Good night."

"Good night, miss."

She went. I sat down on the bed and opened the parcel in some mystification.

I sat there for some time, looking down at the silver-webbed folds of Italian stuff that glimmered against the coverlet. Then I saw the note.

It read:

"*For the kiss I can't honestly say I'm sorry, but for the rest I do. I was worried about something, but that's no excuse for taking it out on you. Will you count the fetching of your parcel as penance, and forgive me, please?*"

R.

P.S. Darling don't be so Sabine about it. It was only a kiss, after all.

Before I got to sleep that night, I'd have given a lot, drugs or no, for some of Madame de Valmy's tablets.

127

Chapter X

I told my love, I told my love,
I told him all my heart . . .

WILLIAM BLAKE: *Poem from MSS.*

NEXT morning it might all have been illusion. Raoul
left Valmy early, this time for the south and Bellevigne.
I didn't see him go. Whether or not he and Léon had
spoken of last night's incident I never discovered; certainly
nothing was said or even hinted to me. When I braved my
employer in the library to tell him about Philippe's second
escape, he received me pleasantly, to darken as he listened
into a frowning abstraction that could have nothing to do
with my personal affairs.

He was sitting behind the big table in the library. When
I had finished speaking he sat for a minute or two in silence,
the fingers of one hand tapping the papers in front of him,
his eyes hooded and brooding. I had the feeling that he had
forgotten I was there.

When he spoke it was to say, rather oddly, "Again."

I said, surprised, "Monsieur?"

He glanced up quickly under his black brows. I thought
he spoke a little wearily. "This is the second time in a very
few days, Miss Martin, that we have had cause to be in-
debted to you for the same rather terrible reason."

"Oh. I see," I said, and added awkwardly, "it was nothing.
Anyone—"

"Anyone would have done the same?" His smile was a
brief flash that failed to light his eyes. "So you said earlier,
Miss Martin, but I must insist as I did before that we are
lucky to have so . . ." a little pause . . . "so foresighted
a young woman to look after Philippe. When did you put
the ladder there?"

"Only yesterday."

"Really? What made you do it?"

I hesitated, choosing my words. "The other day I went
out myself along the balcony to—to wait for a car coming.
I remembered the coping had felt a bit loose before, and
tried it. It was loose, but I'd have sworn not dangerously.
I intended to mention it to you, but honestly I'd no idea

128

t was as bad. Then the car came, and . . . I forgot about it."

I didn't add that the day had been Tuesday and the car Raoul's. I went on, "Then yesterday, just before I was due to leave for Thonon I went out again, to see if it was going to rain. I remembered then about the coping, but I was in a tearing hurry for the bus, so I thought I'd just shove something across temporarily to make it safe, and see you when I got in. I'd seen a step-ladder in the schoolroom pantry, so I ran and got that. It seemed secure enough. I—I vowed I'd remember to tell you as soon as I got back. I—I'm terribly sorry." I finished lamely.

"You needn't be. You were not to know that the stone was as rotten as that. I did have a report on the stonework of that balcony some time ago, but there was no suggestion that the repair was urgent. There'll be trouble about this, you may be sure. But meanwhile let us just be thankful for whatever inspired you to put the ladder across."

I laughed, still slightly embarrassed. "Perhaps it was Philippe's guardian angel."

He said dryly, "Perhaps. He seems to need one."

I said, "There's a phrase for it, isn't there? 'Accident prone.'"

"It seems appropriate." The smooth voice held a note that, incongruously, sounded like amusement. I looked sharply at him. He met my look. "Well? Well, Miss Martin?"

"Nothing," I said confusedly. "I . . . it's just that . . . you take it so calmly. I'd have expected you to be angry."

"But I am," he said, "very angry." And meeting his eyes squarely for the first time during the interview I realized with a shock that he spoke a little less than the truth. He smiled again, and quite without amusement. "But being a rational man, I keep my anger for those who are to blame. It would ill become me, mademoiselle, to vent it on you. And I cannot spend it in protests, because that is . . . not my way."

He swung the wheel chair around so that he was turned a little away from me, looking out of the window across the rose garden. I waited, watching the drawn, handsome face with its fine eyes and mobile mouth, and wondering why talking with Léon de Valmy always made me feel as if I were acting in a play where all the cues were marked. I knew what was coming next, and it came.

He said, with that wry calmness that was somehow all wrong, "When one is a cripple one learns a certain . . . economy of effort, Miss Martin. What would be the point

129

of raging at you here and now? You're not to blame. How's Philippe?"

The question cut across my thoughts—which were simply that I'd have liked him better indulging in some of that profitless rage—so abruptly that I jumped.

"Philippe? Oh, he's all right, thank you. He was frightened and upset, but I doubt if there'll be any ill effects. I imagine it'll soon be forgotten—though at the moment he's inclined to be rather proud of the adventure."

He was still looking away from me across the garden. "Yes? Ah well, children are unpredictable creatures, aren't they? *Le pauvre petit*, let's hope he's at the end of his 'adventures,' as you call them."

"Don't worry, Monsieur de Valmy. He's having a bad spell, but it'll get over." I added, inconsequentially, "When does Monsieur Hippolyte get home?"

He turned his head quickly. The chair moved at the same moment so suddenly that the arm struck the edge of the desk. His exclamation was lost in my cry.

"You've knocked your hand!"

"It's nothing."

"The knuckle's bleeding. Can I get you—"

"It's nothing, I tell you. What were you saying?"

"I forget. Oh yes, I wondered if you knew just when Philippe's Uncle Hippolyte gets home?"

"I have no idea. Why?"

My eyes had been on his grazed hand. I looked up now to see him watching me, his face as usual calmly shuttered, but with something in that quiet gaze that held me staring without reply.

Then the brilliant eyes dropped. He moved a paper knife an inch or two and repeated casually, "Why do you ask?"

"Just that Philippe keeps asking me, and I wondered if you'd heard from Monsieur Hippolyte."

"Ah. Yes. Well, I don't know exactly, I'm afraid. My brother has always been slightly unpredictable. But he'll be away for another three months at least. I thought Philippe knew that. I believe his scheduled lecture tour finishes just before Easter, but he plans to stay for some time after that to assist the excavations at—as far as I remember—Delphi." He smiled. "My brother is a remarkably poor correspondent. . . . I imagine Philippe knows just about as much as I do." He lifted the paper knife, placed it exactly where it had been before, looked up at me and smiled again, charmingly. "Well, Miss Martin, I won't keep you. I still have

130

to divert some of that anger into its proper channels."

He was reaching for the house telephone as I escaped.

It occurred to me with wry surprise that "escape" was exactly the right word for my relieved exit from the library. The discovery annoyed me considerably. Damn it, the tiger played velvet paws with me, didn't he?

But, unreasonable as it was, I couldn't rid myself of the impression that some of that much-discussed anger had been—whatever he said, whatever the probabilities—directed straight at me.

It was only a fortnight now to the Easter Ball, and I had to work fast. The weather was bad, so walks with Philippe were not obligatory, and though I took him several times to the stables to play on wet afternoons, we had a good deal of spare time indoors when I cut and sewed. Philippe and Berthe, the maid, both appeared fascinated by the idea of making a dance dress, and hung over me, fingering the stuff and exclaiming over every stage in its manufacture. Berthe was of rather more practical help than Philippe, as she gave me the use of her machine, and—since she was of my height and build—let me fit the pattern on her, never tiring of standing swathed in the glinting folds while I pinned and pulled and experimented.

As the days went by the château hummed with activity and pleased expectation. If there was indeed any shortage of money here, it could not have been guessed at. I did gather, from odd snippets of gossip to which I was careful to pay no attention, that much of the cost for the ball must be borne by Monsieur de Valmy himself. Monsieur Hippolyte, it was whispered, didn't care for such things, and whereas in past years Philippe's father had willingly financed the affair and had invariably, with his wife, come from Paris to attend it, now that Monsieur Hippolyte was Philippe's co-trustee he was, I gathered, inclined to sit down rather tightly on the moneybags. Whatever the case, it seemed that Monsier de Valmy was determined to recall at least some of the splendors of "the old Comte's" time. To my unaccustomed eye the preparations seemed lavish in the extreme. Rarely-used bedrooms were opened and aired—for there were to be guests over Easter week end—the great ballroom and the big drawing room were thrown open, chandeliers were washed, luster by luster, mirrors were polished, furniture and rugs spirited from one place to another, all, it seemed, under the eagle eye of Monsieur de

Valmy. His chair was everywhere; if a servant dropped a piece of silver he was cleaning, the Master heard it; if a table was pushed along a parquet floor instead of being lifted, the Master spoke angrily from a corner of the room; he was even to be seen constantly on the upper corridors, swiftly propelling himself in and out of bedrooms and along corridors not commonly used by the family.

And so, bit by bit, corner by corner, the great house was prepared for the event of the year, and excitement seemed to thicken in the air as Easter drew nearer. Then came the final touches; flowers were carried in from the hot houses, camellias and lilies and gorgeous blooms I didn't recognize, with tub after tub of bluebells and narcissuses and tulips looking cool and virginal among the heavy-scented exotics. In one of the galleries there was even a miniature grove of willows over a shallow basin where goldfish glided, with cyclamens clustering like butterflies at the water's edge. Outside, floodlights had been fitted up, and a fountain like a firework shot its sparkling trails thirty feet toward Saturday's big yellow noon. For on Easter Eve the weather cleared, and Easter itself came in bright and beautiful, with a soft wind blowing that set the wild daffodils dancing in the woods, and put the seal on the success of the affair.

The Château Valmy was en fête.

On Sunday night after Philippe had gone to bed I put the finishing touches to my frock. Berthe had stayed to help me, and now paraded it delightedly before me, while I sat on the floor among a scatter of pins and watched her with critical eyes.

"Ye—es," I said. "Turn round again, will you? Thanks. It'll do, I think, Berthe."

Berthe twirled a curtsy in it, gay and graceful. It was amazing how she had shed her prim servant-maid attitude along with her uniform. In the shimmering dress she looked what she was, a pretty country girl, slim and young and—just now—flushed with excitement.

"It's lovely, miss, it's really lovely." She spun around so that the full skirt swirled and sank. She lifted a fold and fingered it almost wistfully. "You'll look beautiful in it."

"I've an awful feeling it'll look pretty home-made alongside the collection downstairs."

"Don't you believe it," said Berthe stoutly. "I've seen most of them; Mariette and me did most of the unpacking. The prettiest frock I think belongs to the Marquise in the

132

yellow guestroom, and she's no oil painting herself by a long chalk."

"Hush, Berthe," I protested, laughing, "you musn't say things like that to me!"

She began to waltz around the room, humming a tune. "Of course Madame's always nice. She looks lovely in grande toilette—like a queen. And that Madame Verlaine gets herself up very smart, doesn't she? Hers is black."

"Is Monsieur Florimond here?"

"Oh, he always comes. He says he wouldn't miss it for worlds. He dresses half the ladies, anyway."

I began to pick up the scattered pins, asking casually: "And Monsieur Raoul? Does he come to this affair as a rule?"

There was a tiny pause. At the edge of my vision I saw Berthe's circling form check and turn. I looked up to catch a sidelong glance before her eyes slid from mine. She plucked at a fold of the skirt. "He hasn't been for years. But they're expecting him—this time."

I said nothing, and picked up my pins.

She came over to where I sat, her voice warming into naturalness again. "Why don't you try it on now, miss? Don't bother with those, I'll pick them up after."

It's done," I said. "There, that's the lot, I think."

"Don't you believe it," she said darkly. "We'll be finding them for weeks. Go on, miss, put it on, do. I want to see you in it, with the silver shoes and all."

I laughed and got up. "All right."

"It's a shame you haven't got a decent mirror. That one in the wardrobe door's no good at all, not for a long frock."

"It's all right. I told Madame I was making a frock and she said I might use the glass in her room. I'll just go along now and give it the final check-up. Tomorrow night I'll have to make do in here."

She followed me into my bedroom, speaking a little shyly. "May I help you to dress tomorrow?"

"Why, Berthe, how nice of you! But you'll have so much to do! And I could manage quite well, really. I'm not used to luxuries, you know."

"I'd like to. I would really."

"Then thank you very much. I'd be awfully glad to have you."

Back in her uniform, she helped me pleasedly with the dress. At last I stood surveying myself in the narrow wardrobe mirror.

"Oh, miss, it's lovely!"

"We put a lot of work into it, Berthe. I'm terribly grateful to you for helping. I couldn't have managed without you."

I turned this way and that, eying the line and fall of the material, and wondering just how amateurish it was going to look against the other gowns downstairs. Then I saw Berthe's eyes in the glass. They were brilliant with uncomplicated excitement and pleasure. Her delight, it was obvious, wasn't fretted by the shades of Balenciaga and Florimond. "Oh, miss, it's lovely! There won't be one prettier! You'll look a picture! Wait, I'll get the shoes!"

She was scurrying toward a cupboard but I stopped her impulsively. "Berthe. . . ."

She turned.

"Berthe, would you like to wear it too, for your own dance on Tuesday? You've probably got another just as pretty, but if you'd like it—"

"Oh, miss!" Her eyes grew enormous and she gripped her hands together. "Me? Oh, but I couldn't. . . . Could I?"

"Why not? You look lovely in it, and it was practically made on you, after all. If you'd really like it, Berthe, I'd be terribly pleased for you to take it. I don't suppose anyone'll recognize it."

"No, they won't," she said ingenuously. "It'll be hired waiters here tomorrow, and Ber—the servants won't be about. If—if you really mean it—" She began to thank me again, but I said quickly,

"Then that's settled. Fine. Now I'd better fly if I'm to get to that looking glass before Madame comes upstairs."

Berthe dived once more for the cupboard.

"Your shoes! Put on your new shoes with it!"

"No, no, don't bother," I said hastily, making for the door, "I must run. Thanks again, Berthe! Good night!"

Madame de Valmy's bedroom adjoined a small sitting room which she used in the mornings. I went through, leaving the connecting door ajar.

Her bedroom was a beautiful room, all soft lights and brocade and elegant Louis Seize, with a positively fabulous glitter of silver and crystal on the toilet table. An enormous Venetian mirror flanked the bathroom door, apparently held to the silk paneling by the efforts of the whole cherub choir.

I stood in front of this. The long window curtains mirrored behind me were of rose-colored brocade. The lighting was lovely. As I moved I saw the gleam of the cobwebbed silver thread shift and glimmer through the white cloud of the skirt the way sunlight flies along blown gossamer.

I remember that the thought that surfaced first in my mind was that now Cinderella had no excuse to stay away from the ball. And—at midnight?

Impatiently I shook my thoughts free, angry that I could still fool around even for a moment with the myth that I knew was nonsense. I'd burned myself badly enough on that star already.

Someone was at the sitting-room door. Berthe must have come along with the silver sandals. I called, "Come in. I'm through here," and made a face at myself in the glass. Here were the glass slippers. Damn it, I didn't stand a chance. . . .

A quick tread across the sitting room. Raoul's voice said, "Héloïse, did you want me?"

Then he saw me. He stopped dead in the doorway.

"Why—hullo," he said. He sounded a little breathless, as though he'd been hurrying.

I opened my mouth to answer him, then swallowed and shut it again. I couldn't have spoken if I'd tried. I must just have gaped at him like a schoolgirl caught out in some escapade. I know I went scarlet.

Then I gathered up my skirts in clumsy hands and moved toward the doorway which he still blocked.

He didn't give way. He merely leaned his shoulders back against the jamb of the door and waited, as if prepared to settle there for the evening.

I took two more hesitating steps toward him, and then stopped.

"Don't run away. Let me look at you."

"I must. I mean, I'd better—"

He said, "Sabine," very softly, and the laugh in the word brought hotter color to my face and my eyes up to his.

I'm not sure what happened next. I think he moved a little and said, "All right. So you really want to run away?" And I think I said, somehow, "No," and then "Raoul," as his shoulders came away from the doorpost in a kind of lunge, and then he was across the room and had me in his arms and was kissing me with a violence that was terrifying and yet, somehow, the summit of all my tenderest dreams.

I pushed away from him at last, both hands against his chest. "But Raoul, why?"

"What d'you mean why?"

135

"Why me? Your father called me 'Jane Eyre,' and he wasn't far wrong. And you—you could have anyone. So . . . why?"

"Do you want to know why?" His hands turned me around to face the mirror again, holding me back against him. I could feel his heart hammering against my shoulder blade. His eyes met mine in the glass. "You don't have to be humble, ma belle. That's why."

An odd sensation took me, part triumphant and part forlorn. I said nothing. The cherubs peered at us blind-eyed. Behind us the rose and gold and crystal of the lovely room glowed like the Bower of Bliss. Raoul was watching my face.

He opened his mouth as if to say something, but before he could speak there came a slight sound from the other room. He turned his head sharply, and for a moment his hands tightened on my shoulders. Then he let me go and turned, saying coolly, "Ah, Héloïse. I was looking for you. I believe you wanted me."

I jumped and spun around. I felt the quick heat wash and ebb in my cheeks, leaving me cold and pale. We had been standing in full view of anyone entering the sitting room. Héloïse de Valmy was there now, just inside the door, with Albertine beside her. She was speaking over her shoulder to someone—presumably one of the guests—behind her in the corridor, beyond my range of vision.

A woman's voice returned a soft reply and I heard skirts rustle away. It was impossible to tell if Madame de Valmy had seen Raoul holding me, but I knew Albertine had. Avoiding her dark malicious eyes I came quickly out of the bedroom with Raoul behind me.

I said, stammering, "Madame . . . I was using your glass to —to try my frock. You said I might. . . ."

It was still impossible to tell whether she had seen. Her light-gray eyes looked me up and down without expression. As usual, they were unsmiling, but I could detect no hint of displeasure in her face.

She said, in her cold composed voice, "Of course. Is that the dress you have made, Miss Martin? It's very pretty. You must be an accomplished needlewoman. Perhaps one day you might do some work for me?"

So she had seen. I felt Raoul, beside me, make a little movement. The burning color washed back into my face. I said quickly, "It would be a pleasure, madame. Good night, madame. Good night, monsieur."

I didn't look at him. I slipped past Héloïse de Valmy into the dimness of the corridor, and ran back to my room.

The next day passed in a whirl. I spent all my time with Philippe, who, alone of all the people in the house, seemed untouched by the general excitement, and was, indeed, indulging in a bout of the sulks at being left out of the Easter revels.

Luckily I didn't have to face Madame de Valmy. Just after lunch Albertine—was there a spark of malice in the smooth voice and face as she said it?—brought me a message which asked if we could please direct our afternoon's walk to the village to make some small purchases, as none of the servants (had she or had she not hesitated on the phrase "other servants"?) could be spared?

I agreed politely, and chided myself, as I took a reluctant, foot-trailing Philippe down to Soubirous, for being oversensitive. Madame de Valmy would surely not put me so brutally in my place a second time, and as for Albertine, a servant's malice couldn't affect me.

But I began to wonder, a few minutes later, if this last was true. As I paused in the sunshine outside Monsieur Garcin's shop to fish in my bag for Albertine's note, the bead curtains over the chemist's doorway rattled aside, and Albertine herself came out. Albertine, who "could not be spared" today; for whom I was playing errand boy. She must have set out for Soubirous almost immediately after briefing me.

I stared at her in amazement. She showed no sign of confusion, but slipped by me with one of her dark sidelong looks and small-lipped Mona Lisa smiles. She went into the *confiserie* just beyond the café.

When I pushed through the swinging beads myself into the spicy dimness of the shop, I was tense and nervous and very ready to discover in Monsieur Garcin's voice and attitude that same sidelong malice that I had now certainly seen in Albertine.

I told myself firmly that this was only fancy. But as I emerged from the pharmacy I came face to face with Madame Rocher, the curé's housekeeper, and this time there was no doubt about the chilliness of the greeting. If the good Madame could have passed by on the other side she would undoubtedly have done so. As it was she simply stared, nodded once, and gave me *bonjour* in a tone nicely calculated (as from virtuous matron to viper-in-the-bosom) to keep me in my place, while at the same time allowing just the faintest loophole for a possibly legitimate future. Philippe she greeted, quite simply, with pity.

And later, when I bought some chocolate in the *confiserie*,

137

I thought Madame Decorzent's fat smile was a little sti[]
today, and her prune-black eyes were curious, almost avid, a[]
she said, glancing from Philippe to me, "And when are yo[]
leaving us, mademoiselle?"

I said coolly, through the sudden hammering of my hear[]
"We don't go to Thonon for a good while yet, madame. Mon[]
sieur Hippolyte doesn't get back for three more months, yo[]
know."

And I almost swept Philippe out through the tinkling cu[]
tain of beads into the hot sunlight. Albertine had done he[]
work all right. The news, with its attendant rumors, was a[]
over Soubirous.

I ran the gauntlet of sundry other stares and whispers befor[]
I reached the bridge and faced—with poor Philippe madden[]
ingly awhine beside me—the long trudge up through th[]
watermeadows.

I hadn't realized before what hard going it must have bee[]
for Cinderella.

After tea I went to look for Mrs. Seddon, to talk to he[]
about whatever rumors were being put about below stairs, onl[]
to be told that the fuss and overwork occasioned by the ba[]
had brought on "one of her attacks," and that she had gone t[]
bed, unfit to speak to anyone. So I stayed with Philippe, m[]
mind hovering miserably between remembered—and surel[]
disastrous?—ecstasy, and my apparently imminent dismissa[]
from Valmy. I am glad to remember that some of my worr[]
was on behalf of Philippe. . . .

By the time Berthe came up that evening to serve Philippe'[]
supper, I was in a fairly lamentable state of nerves, and mor[]
than half inclined to shirk facing my host and hostess down[]
stairs. Then Philippe chose to throw a tantrum, and refuse[]
with tears to go to bed at all unless I would come up later "i[]
the middle of the night" and take him to peep at the dancin[]
from the gallery. I promised, and, satisfied, he disappeare[]
quietly enough with Berthe.

I shut the door on them, and went to run my bath.

Dressing for my first dance . . . and Raoul somewher[]
among the throng of dancers . . . I should have been happy[]
eager, excited. But my fingers shook as I opened a fresh bar o[]
scented soap, and later on when I was sitting in my petticoa[]
brushing my hair, and a knock sounded on the door, I turne[]
to face it as if it were a firing squad.

"I'll go," said Berthe, who had disposed of Philippe and wa[]
helping me. She opened the door a little way, had a shor[]

138

muffled colloquy with whoever was outside, then shut the door and came back into the room holding a box.

I was still sitting at the dressing table, hair brush suspended. Berthe came over to me. She looked a little flushed as she handed me the box, and she avoided my eye.

"This is for you." Her tone—like her whole bearing that evening—was subdued and a little formal.

For a moment I thought of asking her what was being whispered, then I held my tongue. I didn't want to meet him—and Monsieur and Madame—fresh from Albertine's brand of backstairs gossip. The woman's glance had been smirch enough.

Et tu, Berthe, I thought, and took the box from her.

It was light and flat, with a cellophane lid glassing the dark heartshaped leaves and fragile blossoms of white voilets; milk-white blooms, moth-white, delicate in dark-green leaves. There was the faintest veining of cream on throat and wing.

A card was tucked among the leaves. Without opening the lid I could see the single letter in an arrogant black scrawl:—R.

I finished dressing in silence.

Then I pinned the violets on, said quietly, "Thank you, Berthe," and went toward the music and the laughter.

Chapter XI

I am two fools, I know,
For loving, and for saying so.

JOHN DONNE: *The Triple Fool.*

THE ball was well underway, and I was thankful to see that Monsieur and Madame de Valmy had finished receiving. Their place near the banked flowers at the foot of the great staircase was empty. Now the hall was brilliant with a shifting mass of people. I hesitated on the gallery, having no mind to make an entrance alone down that impressive flight of steps; then three young women came chattering past me from some room along the corridor, and I followed as inconspicuously as I could in their wake.

It was easy enough to slip unremarked through the throng and into the ballroom itself, where I found a corner sheltered

139

by a pillar and a bank of azaleas, and settled down quietly to watch the dancers.

I couldn't see Léon de Valmy's chair anywhere, but Héloïse, looking wonderful in a gown the color of sea-lavender, was dancing with an elderly bearded man on whose breast the blue ribbon of an Order showed. I saw Florimond over by one of the windows talking, or rather listening, to a terrifying-looking old woman with a beak of a nose and improbable blue hair. He was leaning forward slightly, that flattering air of his assuring her that she was the most amusing and intelligent woman in the room. For all I knew she may have been. But had she been the dreariest hag on earth I am sure that Florimond would have looked exactly the same.

I turned to look for Raoul. On a swirl of music the dancers near me swung and parted and I saw him. He was dancing with a blonde girl with slanting eyes and a beautiful mouth. She was in black, with a high neck and a straight-cut skirt that spoke of Madame Fath and made her look incredibly slender and fragile. She was dancing very close to him and talking rapidly, with flickering upward glances through her long lashes. I didn't see him speak, but he was smiling. They were a striking couple, and danced so beautifully that more than one glance was thrown in their direction and—I had nothing else to do but see it—more than one significant eyebrow lifted in their wake. It would seem that Mrs. Seddon had been right: where Raoul went, rumor walked. I wondered who the girl was. When—if—he danced with me, what would the eyebrows do then? Who's the new girl? My dear, nobody, obviously. And my dear, the dress. . . . The governess? . . . Oh. . . . Oh, I see. . . .

The music stopped, and people drifted to the sides of the ballroom. I was hidden by the crowd. Nobody had noticed me. I sat still, glad of the sheltering pillar and the massed azaleas. Beside me a trickle of water ran down a little scale, soulless as the music of a spinet. There was a tank of fish here, too, and the water dripped into it from a bank of moss. The azaleas threw patterns on the water, and gold and silver fish moved warily underneath.

The music started again, obliterating talk, laughter, and the tiny tinkle of water. The glittering dresses took the floor. This time he led out an elderly woman with a dreadful gown of royal blue and magnificent diamonds. And then a dark hawk of a woman with a clever hungry face and hands like yellow claws. And then the lovely blonde girl again. And then a well-corseted woman with dyed hair who wore dramatic black with emeralds. And then a white-haired woman with a gentle face. And then the blonde again.

The fish hung suspended in water green as serpentine, fins moving rhythmically. A petal, loosed from a pink azalea, floated down to lie upon the surface. I remembered my promise to Philippe. I got up, shaking out the folds of my skirt. The fish, startled, shuttled about the tank under the hanging moss.

When a voice said: "Mademoiselle," just behind me, I started like a guilty thing upon a fearful summons, and dropped my handbag, missing the tank by millimeters.

The owner of the voice stooped a little ponderously to pick it up for me. I might have known he would come sooner or later to comfort the wallflower.

"Monsieur Florimond!" I said. "You startled me."

"I'm sorry." He handed me the bag with a smile. "But you must not fly away now, mademoiselle. I'm depending on you for an alibi."

"An alibi?"

He made one of his wide gestures. "My dear, I don't dance, and I've talked myself to a standstill. I thought perhaps if I cornered you quickly we could resume our flirtation, which is something I can do at any time without effort."

"And," I said, watching how his hand hovered already over his pocket, "have a quiet smoke at the same time? All right, Monsieur Florimond, I'll be your chimney corner."

"A sympathetic woman," said Florimond, unabashed, taking out his case, "is above rubies."

"Don't you believe it. No woman is above rubies," I said, sitting down again. "No thank you, I don't smoke."

"Above diamonds, pearls, and rubies," said Florimond, lowering himself into the chair beside me with a sigh, and proceeding, as to an elaborate ritual, to light a cigarette. He beamed at me through the resultant cloud of smoke. "That's a very pretty gown, my dear."

I laughed at him. "Shakespeare," I said, "congratulating Minou Drouet on a neat phrase? Thank you, monsieur."

His eyes puckered at the corners. "I meant it. But you're rather hiding your light under a bushel, aren't you? I've been watching for you, but I haven't seen you dancing."

"I don't know anyone."

"Oh, là-là! And didn't Héloïse introduce any young men?"

"I haven't seen her to speak to. I came down late."

"And now she is—ah, yes, there she is, dancing with Mon-

141

sieur de St. Hubert." He scanned the floor. "Then where's Raoul? He knows everybody. Perhaps he—"

"Oh, no, please!" The exclamation burst out quite involuntarily. I met Florimond's eye of mild inquiry and finished lamely: "I—I was just going upstairs. I promised Philippe to go and see him. I—don't bother Monsieur Raoul, please."

"Upstairs? And not to come down again, is that it?" The kind eyes surveyed me. "And is that also why you came down so late and then hid among the flowers?"

"I don't—what d'you mean?"

His gaze fixed itself on the violets. He didn't answer. My hand moved in spite of me to cup the flowers, a curiously defensive gesture and quite futile. I said, "How did you know?" and touched the violets with a finger tip. "These?"

He shook his head. "My dear," he said gently, "haven't you learned yet that every breath the Valmys take is news in the valley?"

I said bitterly, "I'm learning." I looked away from him. A fish was nosing at the azalea petal, butting it gently from underneath. I watched it absorbedly. The dance music seemed to come from a great way off. Here among the flowers was a little walled garden of silence broken only by the liquid arpeggios of the dripping mosses.

At length he spoke. "You're very young."

"Twenty-three." My voice tried hard not to sound defensive.

"Mademoiselle—" he seemed to be choosing his words— "if you ever thought of leaving Valmy, where would you go?"

I stared at him through a moment of whirling silence. Here, too. It was true. It hadn't been imagination to see those dragon's teeth of scandal springing up in Albertine's malicious wake. Madame de Valmy or (something caught at my breathing) Monsieur himself had said something, hinted something about dismissing me. And Florimond the kind had sought me out to talk to me about it. Everybody, it seemed, was making my connection with Raoul their business.

I don't quite know what I was thinking about it myself. I couldn't see beyond the fact that I loved him; that he had kissed me; that he was here tonight. I wanted to see him; dreaded seeing him. About Raoul's feelings and purpose—his "intentions"—I didn't think at all. He was here, and I loved him. That was all.

I pulled myself together to hear Florimond saying, kindly, "Have you friends in France, or are you on your own over here, mademoiselle?"

I said in a tight little voice, "I don't know anyone in rance, no. But I am not on my own, monsieur."

"What do you mean?"

"Monsieur Florimond, you are being very kind, and don't ink I don't appreciate it. But let's be frank, now that e've gone so far. You are concerned about me because I as seen kissing Raoul de Valmy, and I'm to be dismissed. that it?"

"Not quite."

I said, surprised, "Then what?"

He said gently, "Because you are also in love with Raoul e Valmy, child."

I said, rather breathlessly, "So—what?"

"What I said. You are too young. You have nobody here) run to. You are too much alone."

"No. I told you. I'm not alone."

He looked a query.

I said very evenly, "Is it so very impossible that I should be ble to run—as you put it—to Raoul?"

There was a pause. The words seemed to repeat themselves nto the silence. The clasp of my bag was hurting my fingers vhen I gripped it. I looked at him. "Yes, monsieur. We are eing frank, you and I. Is it so very impossible that Raoul hould—care for me?"

"My dear—" said Florimond, and stopped.

"Yes, monsieur?"

He took a deep breath. "You and Raoul . . . ? No, ma- lemoiselle. No and no and no."

I said, after a little pause, "Just how well do you know im, monsieur?"

"Raoul? Well enough. Not intimately, perhaps, but—" he topped again and one large hand tugged at his collar. He lidn't meet my eyes. He said, "Hell!" unexpectedly and ex- losively, and began to grind out his cigarette in the earth f the azalea tub.

I was too angry to let him off. "Then since you don't now him so very well, perhaps you'll explain what you neant."

He looked at me then. "My dear, I can't. I should never ave said it. I've already done the unforgivable. I mustn't go urther."

"Monsieur de Valmy being your host?"

He almost jumped. "You're a little too quick for me, my lear. Yes, that and other reasons."

Our eyes met, in a curious half-ashamed comprehension.

But I was still angry. I said, "Since we're talking in riddle
monsieur, what makes you think that all tigers breed true?"

"Mademoiselle—"

"All right," I said, "we'll leave it. You've warned me
You've eased your conscience and it was very kind of yo
to bother. Shall we just wait and see?"

He breathed a great, gusty sigh. "I was wrong," he sai
"You're not as young as I thought." He was groping fo
another cigarette, grinning amiably at me. "Well, I've sai
my piece—unwarranted cheek, and you've been very nic
about it. And don't forget, when you do do that running
you've got at least one other person in France to run to."

My anger died. "Monsieur Florimond—"

"There," he said, "and now we'll drop the subject. Wh
about that flirtation we were in the middle of? Do you r
member just where we'd got to? Or would you rather hav
a quick game of chess?"

I gave a shaken little laugh. "It would certainly be quic
Compared with me, Philippe's a master. You'd mop me u
in three minutes."

"A pity. There's nothing like chess and tobacco, jud
ciously mixed, for taking the mind off the advice of a do
dering old fool who ought to know better." A large han
patted mine paternally, and was withdrawn. "Forgive m
child. I couldn't help it, could I, if the advice came too late?"

I smiled at him. "Monsieur Florimond, even if this isn
the right moment in our flirtation to say so, you are a da
ing. But yes . . . much too late."

Raoul's voice said, above me, "So here you are! Carl
what the devil d'you mean by hiding her away in this co
ner? Damn it, I've been watching the doors for a couple
hours! I'd no idea she was finding you and the goldfish suc
fascinating company. What was the somber discussion, mo
vieux? What's much too late?"

"You, for one thing," said Florimond, calmly. "Now tal
Miss Martin away and dance with her and try and atone fo
leaving her to the goldfish."

Raoul grinned. "I'll do that. Linda, come here."

I went.

Florimond's eyes followed me, still with that pucker
trouble about them. Then I forgot them as the music took u

His voice said at my ear, "It's been an age. Had you bee
there long?"

"Not really."

144

"Why were you so late?"

"I was scared to come down."

"Scared? My God, why? Oh, of course, Héloïse."

"She saw us; you know that."

"Yes." He laughed. "D'you mind?"

"Of course."

"You'll have to learn not to."

My heart was beating anyhow up in my throat. "What d'you mean?"

But he only laughed again without replying and swept me around with the music in a quick turn. A pillar swirled past, a group of men, a wheel chair. . . .

Léon de Valmy.

He was watching us, of course. A shadow at the center of the kaleidoscope: a spider at the knot of the bright web . . . the stupid fancies rose from nowhere in a stinging cloud. I shook my head a little, angrily, as if that would dispel them. Damn the man, I wasn't afraid of him . . . was I?

As, momentarily, the dance took me around to face him again, I looked straight at him and gave him a brilliant smile.

He was taken aback: there was no doubt about that. I saw the black brows lift sharply, then his mouth twitched and he smiled back.

The other dancers came between us and cut him off from view. I was left with the sharp impression that my employer's smile had been one of quite genuine amusement, but that it was amusement at some joke I couldn't see. It was an impression that was quite particularly unpleasant.

"Raoul," I said suddenly, urgently.

"Yes?"

"Oh . . . nothing."

"Just Raoul?"

"Yes."

He slanted a look down at me and smiled. "Soit," was all he said, but I had the odd feeling that he understood.

When the dance finished we were at the opposite end of the room from Léon de Valmy, and beside one of the long windows. Raoul showed no sign of leaving me. He waited beside me in silence. He seemed to be oblivious of the crowd surrounding us, though the eyebrows were certainly at work. I caught a few curious looks cast at us, but I wasn't worrying about them. I was busy trying to locate Madame de Valmy in the crowd, and to see her without actually catching her eye. But she wasn't there.

The music started again. Raoul turned back to me.

I said feebly, "Now look, you don't really have to bother about me. I'm—"

"Don't be idiotic," said he crisply, taking hold of me.

This lover-like speech naturally reassured me completely. I laughed. I forgot Héloïse de Valmy, the raised eyebrows, even Léon and his amusement. I said meekly, "No, monsieur," and was swept out onto the floor again.

"I've done more than my share tonight, by God," said Raoul with feeling. "I've danced with every dowager in the place. Don't try and thwart me now, my girl. . . . It's just as well I couldn't find you before or I might have neglected my duty."

We were dancing at the edge of the room, near the French windows which stood open to the mild night.

"As," he finished, "I am about to neglect it now. . . ."

And before I knew quite what he was about we were out of the ballroom and on the loggia, slipping as easily and unnoticeably out of the throng as a floating twig slides into a backwater. The music followed us through the long windows; and there was the Easter moon and the ghosts of jonquils dancing in the dark garden. My skirt brushed the narcissuses on the terrace's edge. Raoul's shoulder touched jasmine and loosed a shower of tiny stars. We didn't speak. The spell held. We danced along the moonlit arcade of the loggia, then in through the dark windows of the salon, where firelight warmed the deserted shadows, and the music came muted as if from a great way off.

We were in the shadows. He stopped and his arms tightened around me. "And now . . ." he said.

Later, when I could speak, I said shakily, "I love you. I love you. I love you." And, of course, after that singularly ill-advised remark it was impossible to speak or even breathe for a very long time indeed.

When at length he let me go and spoke, I hardly recognized his voice. But, slurred and unsteady as it was, it still held that little undertone of laughter that was unmistakably his.

"Well, aren't you going to ask it?"

"Ask what?"

"What every woman in the world asks straight away. The vow returned. 'Do you love me?' "

I said, "I'll settle for whatever you want to give."

"I told you before not to be humble, Linda."

"I can't help it. It's the way you make me feel."

He said, "Oh God!" in that queer wrenched voice and pulled me to him again. He didn't kiss me but held me tightly and spoke over my head into the darkness. "Linda . . . Linda, listen."

"I'm listening."

"This love thing. I don't know. This is honest. I don't know."

Something twisted at my heart that might—if it were not absurd—have been pity. "It doesn't matter, Raoul. Don't."

"It does. You have to know. There've been other women—you know that. Quite a few."

"Yes."

"This is different." A silence. The ghost of a laugh. "I'd say that anyway, wouldn't I? But it is. It is." His cheek moved against my hair. "Linda. That's the hell of a name for a Frenchwoman, isn't it? So now you know. I want you. I need you, by God I do. If you call that love—"

"It'll do," I said. "Believe me, it'll do.

Another silence. The fire burned steadily, filling the room with shadows. In one of the logs I could hear the whine and bubble of resin.

He gave a queer little sigh and then loosed me, holding me at arm's length. His voice was his own again, cool, casual, a little hard. "What were you and Carlo talking about?"

The question was so unexpected that I started. "I—why, I hardly remember. Things. And—oh, yes, my frock. Yes, we talked about my frock."

I saw him smile. "Come now, confess. You talked about me."

"How did you know?"

"Second sight."

"Oh, murder," I said. "Don't tell me you've got it as well."

"As well?"

"Your father's a warlock; didn't you know?"

"Oh? Then shall we just say that I've got excellent hearing. Did Carlo warn you that my intentions were sure to be dishonorable?"

"Of course."

"Did he, by God?"

"More or less. It was done by implications and with the nicest possible motives."

"I'm sure of it. What did he say?"

147

I laughed at him and quoted: "'You and Raoul, no an no and no.' And you are not to be angry. I adore Monsieu Florimond and he was only talking to me for my own good."

He was looking down at me soberly. "I'm not likely t be angry. He was too damned near right. I don't mean abou my motives, but that probably you and I—" He stopped "I've told you how I feel. But you; you say you love me."

I said: "Yes and yes and yes."

I saw him smile. "Again thrice? You're very generous."

"I was canceling Carlo out. Besides, we have a poem ir English which says, 'What I tell you three times is true.''

Another pause. Then he said, still holding me, "Then you will take a chance on marrying me?"

I began to tremble. I said huskily: "But your father—"

His hands moved so sharply that they hurt me. "My father? What's it to him?"

"He'll be so angry. Perhaps he'll do something about it— make you leave Bellevigne, or—"

"So what? I'm not tied to him or to Bellevigne." He gave a short, half-angry laugh. "Are you afraid of harming my position? My prospects? By God, that's rich!"

I said falteringly, "But you love Bellevigne, don't you? You told me you did, and Mrs. Seddon said—"

"So she's been talking about me, too, has she?"

"Everybody does," I said simply.

"Then did she tell you I hadn't any future except Belle- vigne, and that only until Philippe gets Valmy?"

"Yes."

"Well, she's right." He added more gently: "Does that three-times-true love allow you to take a chance on a barren future?"

"I said I'd settle for what you had to give, didn't I?"

Another of those little silences. "So you did. Then you'll marry me?"

"Yes."

"In the teeth of the warnings?"

"Yes."

"And without prospects?"

"Yes."

He laughed then, still on that curious note of triumph. "You needn't worry about that," he said cryptically. "Fair means or foul, I'll always have prospects."

"An adventurer, that's what you are," I said.

He was looking down, and the black eyes were veiled again. "Aren't you?"

148

I said slowly, "Yes, I believe I am."

"I know you are," said Raoul. "Diamond cuts diamond, my darling. Kiss me and seal the bargain."

Afterward he let me go. I said uncertainly, "Do we have to—tell them?"

"Of course. Why not? I'd like to shout it from the housetops now, but if you like we'll wait till tomorrow."

"Oh yes, *please*."

I saw his teeth gleam. "Does it need so much hardihood, ma *mie*? Are you afraid of my father?"

"Yes."

He gave me a quick, surprised look. "Are you? You've no need. But I'll tell them myself if you'd rather. You can just keep out of the way until it's done."

I said, "They'll be—so very angry."

"Angry? You undervalue yourself, my dear."

"You don't understand. I'm—I was due to be sacked anyway. That doesn't make it any easier to tell them."

"Due to be *sacked*? What on earth do you mean?"

"What I say. I was rather expecting to be told tomorrow. That's why I didn't want to come down to the dance."

"But—why? What's the crime?"

I looked up at him and gave a little smile. "You."

It took him a moment to assimilate this. "Do you mean because Héloïse saw me kissing you? You were to be sacked for that? Rubbish," he said curtly.

"It's true. At least I think so. You—well, you heard how Madame spoke to me just afterward, and when I went into Soubirous today it was quite obvious that the story had got around." I told him about the reception I had had in the village. "Albertine—the maid—may just have been scandalmongering because she doesn't like me, but I think she probably knows what Madame intends to do."

He lifted a shoulder indifferently. "Well, it doesn't matter, does it? You needn't let it worry you now. In any case I'm sure you're wrong. Héloïse would never want to let you go."

I said rather shyly, "I thought that myself. I did think it . . . odd, because of Philippe."

He said quickly, "Philippe?"

"Yes. I—don't get me wrong; I don't think I did anything very great for Philippe. The shooting business in the wood was nothing. I just didn't lose my head and fuss him too much, but I—well, I did save him the time he nearly fell off the balcony, and your father said—"

Raoul said, "What time? What are you talking about?"

"Didn't you know?" I said, surprised. I told him about the grim little incident that had crowned my shopping trip to Thonon. He listened, his face turned away from me toward the fire. In the flickering light I couldn't read his expression. He reached abstractedly for a cigarette and lit it. Over the flare of the match I could see he was frowning. I finished: "And your father knew that night that you'd kissed me. I'm sure he did. You remember?"

A glint through the frown. "I remember."

"There wasn't any talk then about sending me away. But there is now, really."

He laughed. "Well, my love, we've given them more cause, haven't we? Let that be a comfort to you. It's very probable that everybody in the ballroom knows by this time that you've gone out with me, and is speculating wildly on the whys and wherefores."

I said tartly, "I don't suppose they have any doubt at all about the whys and wherefores. It's all very well you carrying off your love affairs en grand seigneur, Monsieur de Valmy, but I'm only the governess. No, don't laugh at me. I've got to face them tomorrow."

"With me, chérie, remember. And now let's forget tomorrow. This is tonight, and we are betrothed." He took my hands. "If we can't shout it from the housetops at least we can celebrate it to ourselves. Let's go and get some champagne."

"And some food," I said.

"You poor child! Haven't you fed?"

"Not a bite. I sat in my corner while you danced and drank and enjoyed yourself—"

"More fool you," said Raoul unsympathetically. "You had only to show yourself to be trampled to death by partners avid to let you dance and drink and enjoy yourself with them. Come on, then. Food."

The great dining room was brilliant with people and gay with chatter and the popping of corks. Raoul made his way through the crowd with me in his wake. Several people hailed him, and I saw a few curious glances cast at me, but he didn't stop. As we reached the big table all agleam with silver I remembered something and touched his sleeve.

"Raoul, I'd forgotten. I promised to go up and see Philippe halfway through the dance. I must go."

He turned quickly, almost as if I had startled him. "Philippe? What on earth for?"

"I think he felt left out of things. At any rate I did promise to go up at 'dead of night.' I can't disappoint him."

"You . . . do look after him a little beyond the line of duty, don't you?"

"I don't think so. Anyway I think I ought to go straight away, in case he goes to sleep and thinks I've forgotten."

"But I thought you were starving?"

"I am." I looked wistfully at the laden table. There was a silver dish of crab patties just beside me, creaming over pinkly under their crimped fronds of parsley. "But a vow's a vow."

"And you always keep your vows?"

"Always."

"I'll remember that."

I laughed. "They're only valid if you'll let me keep the one I made to Philippe. His came first."

"Then I suppose I must. But I insist on coming too, and I'm not letting you faint with hunger by the wayside." He glanced at his wrist. "It's close on midnight—that's 'dead of night,' isn't it? Why don't we break a few more rules and take some food upstairs? Then Philippe will get his excitement and we our celebration."

"Oh, Raoul, that's a wonderful idea! Let's do that!"

"All right. I'll fix some food and drink. What d'you like?"

I looked again at the table. "Everything," I said simply.

He looked startled. "You must be hungry!"

"I am. Even if I weren't—" I sighed—"I couldn't by-pass that. I never saw anything so wonderful in my life."

He was looking at me with a curious expression. "Do you mean to say you've never been to a dance before?"

"This sort of thing? Never."

"One forgets," he said.

"I try to," I said lightly, "at any rate the dreary past never produced anything remotely like this. May I have one of those meringues?"

"If you must. And I suppose you've never had champagne either? That's a thought. . . . Well, you shall have it to-night. Meringues and champagne, may God forgive me. Well, you go along up to Philippe and I'll follow as soon as I've organized the food. I'll bring a bit of everything."

"That's a vow," I told him, and made my way out through the crowd.

My main fear was of coming across Léon de Valmy. I turned away from the hall and main staircase and ran down a corridor toward the secondary stair that Philippe and I commonly used.

151

But I needn't have worried. I reached the stairs unnoticed and mounted them hurriedly, holding up my filmy skirts. The staircase gave onto the upper corridor almost opposite Madame de Valmy's bedroom door. I was nearly at the top when I half tripped as the catch of my sandal came loose. The sandal came off. I had to stop to pick it up.

As I straightened up, sandal in hand, two women came out of Madame de Valmy's sitting room. My heart seemed to catch in mid-beat, then I saw that neither was Héloïse. They were elderly women who had not been dancing. I recognized one of them as an inveterate eyebrow-raiser—first at the blond, then at me. I wondered how high her over-worked brows would go if she knew I had an assignation with Raoul upstairs, however closely chaperoned by Philippe.

The sandal was my alibi. I waited politely for them to pass me before I proceeded to my own room for the ostensibly-needed repairs. I smiled at them, receiving in return two courteous and beautifully-calculated inclinations as they sailed by me, making for the main staircase.

The corridor emptied itself of the last rustle. With a wary eye on Héloïse's door I picked up my skirts again and turned toward Philippe's room.

Somewhere a clock whirred to strike. Midnight. I smiled. Dead of night exactly. I hoped Philippe was still awake.

The clock was beating twelve as I moved quietly along the corridor. Then a thought touched me out of nowhere and I stopped short, staring down at the sandal in my hand. Midnight. The dropped slipper. The escape from the ball.

I realized that I was frowning. The thing was so absurd as to be obscurely disquieting. Then I laughed and shrugged.

"Bring on your pumpkins," I whispered cheerfully, and laid a hand on Philippe's door.

Chapter XII

These delicates he heap'd with glowing hand
On golden dishes and in baskets bright
Of wreathèd silver: sumptuous they stand
In the retired quiet of the night . . .

KEATS: *Eve of St. Agnes.*

Drink to heavy Ignorance!
Hob-and-nob with brother Death!

TENNYSON: *The Vision of Sin.*

PHILIPPE was awake. When I let myself quietly into his bedroom I found him sitting bolt upright in bed in his dressing gown, with his eyes on the door. The fire, which should have been out hours ago, was burning merrily. The curtains over the long balcony windows were drawn back, so that the moonlight flowed in bright dramatic slant across the head of the bed.

Full in its path sat the little boy, his skin blanched to a waxy pallor by the white light, the black eyes huge and brilliant. He looked very frail.

But he seemed animated enough. He said immediately, "You've been ages."

"You said 'dead of night,' remember. It's just midnight now."

"Midnight? Is it really?" He looked pleased. "I kept the fire on. I knew you'd come."

"Of course I came. How d'you manage to be so wide awake at this hour?" I saw the untouched tumbler of chocolate on the bedside table, and laughed. "Oh, I see. Cunning, aren't you? Didn't you feel sleepy at all?"

"I did a bit," he confessed, "but it kept me awake looking after the fire."

"Is that why you kept it on?"

The big eyes slid sideways from mine and he plucked at the coverlet. "I sort of hoped—I wondered if you'd stay for a bit now you've come."

I sat down on the bed. "Why, Philippe? Is anything the matter?"

153

A vigorous shake of the head was followed by one of those little sidelong looks that contradicted it. I reached out and laid a hand over his. "What is it, brat?"

He said in a sort of furious mutter, "Nightmares."

"Oh dear, I didn't know. How beastly! What sort of nightmares?"

"People coming in," said Philippe, "and touching me."

This, oddly enough, was more shocking than any more usual horror of pursuit and desperately hindered flight could be. I shifted my shoulders a little, as if with cold, and said rather too heartily, "Oh well, it's only dreams, after all. It's not real—unless you mean me. I come in sometimes after you're asleep."

"No," said Philippe rather wanly, "not you. I wouldn't mind you."

"Do you have the same dream often?"

He nodded.

"It doesn't wake you up? If it does, you should call. I'd come."

"I do call, but there's no noise."

I patted the hand. It seemed very small and cold. "That means you're still asleep. It's a horrid feeling, but it *is* only a dream. And it might easily be me, Philippe; I usually do look in last thing at night. You're always sound asleep."

"Am I?"

"Like a top. Snoring."

"I bet I'm not."

"I bet you are. Now listen, I've a treat for you, Monsieur le Comte de Valmy. Since your honor wouldn't deign to come down for supper on the night of the ball, would you like supper to come up to you?"

"Supper? But I've had supper!"

"That was hours ago," I said, "and I haven't had mine. Wouldn't you like to entertain your cousin Raoul and me to a midnight feast?"

"A midnight feast? Oh, Miss Martin." The big eyes sparkled in the moonlight, then looked uncertain. "Did you say my cousin Raoul?"

I nodded. "He said he'd bring the food, and—oh, here he is."

The door had opened quietly and now Raoul came in, delectably laden with bottles, and followed by one of the hired waiters with a tray. Raoul lifted a gold-necked aristocrat of a bottle in mock salute. "Bonsoir, Monsieur le Comte. Put the tray down there, will you? Thanks. Do you suppose you could collect the debris later on? Secretly, of course."

154

Not a muscle of the man's face moved. "Of course, sir."

Something passed from Raoul's hand to his. "Excellent. That's all, then. Thank you."

"Thank you, sir. M'sieur, 'dame." The man sketched a bow, aimed between the bed and me, and went out, shutting the door.

"Then it really is a midnight feast?" said Philippe, eying his cousin a little shyly.

"Undoubtedly." Raoul was dealing competently with the gold-topped bottle. "As clandestine and—ah, that's it! A grand sound, eh, Philippe?—cozy as one could wish it. That's an excellent fire. Are you warm enough, Linda?"

"Yes, thank you."

He was pouring champagne. Philippe, his doubts forgotten, came out of bed with a bounce. "Is that lemonade?"

"The very king of lemonades."

"It's jolly fizzy, isn't it? It went off like a gun."

"Gun or no, I doubt if its your tipple, mon cousin. I brought some real lemonade for you. Here."

"That's more like it," said Philippe, accepting a tall yellow drink that hissed gently. Mademoiselle, wouldn't you like some of mine?"

"It looks wonderful," I said, "but I daren't hurt your cousin's feelings."

Raoul grinned and handed me a glass of champagne. "I doubt if this is your tipple either, my little one, but I refuse to pledge you in anything less."

"Pledge?" said Philippe. "What's that?"

"A promise," I said. "A vow."

"And there's our toast," said Raoul, lifting his glass so that the firelight spun and spangled up through its million bubbles. "Stand up, Philippe; click your glass with mine . . . now Miss Martin's . . . so. Now drink to our vows, and long may we keep them!"

Philippe, puzzled but game, drank some lemonade, then, hesitating, looked from Raoul to me and finally down at the tray which the servant had set on a low table before the fire. "When do we start?"

"This minute," I said firmly, and sat down.

Even without the influence of the king of lemonades it would have been a wonderful feast. My betrothal supper, held between firelight and moonlight in a little boy's bedroom—to me a feast every bit as magical as the banquet Porphyro spread for his Madeleine on that "ages long ago" St. Agnes' Ave. And the food was a lot better. I don't remember that St. Agnes'

155

lovers—perhaps wisely—ate anything at all, but Philippe and I demolished an alarming number of the delicates that Raoul's glowing hand had heaped upon the tray.

He had made a very creditable attempt to bring "everything." I remember thin curls of brown bread with cool, butter-dripping asparagus; scallop-shells filled with some delicious concoction of creamed crab; crisp pastries bulging with mushroom and chicken and lobster; *petits fours* bland with almonds; small glasses misty with frost and full of some creamy stuff tangy with strawberries and wine; peaches furry and glowing in a nest of glossy leaves; grapes frosted with sugar that sparkled in the firelight like a crust of diamonds.

Philippe and I ate and exclaimed, and chatted in conspiratorial whispers, while Raoul lounged beside the fire and smoked and drank champagne and watched us indulgently for all the world as if I and Philippe were of an age, and he a benevolent uncle watching us enjoy ourselves.

"Or an overfed genie," I said accusingly, having told him this, "bringing a feast to Aladdin starving in his garret, or was it cellar?"

"As far as I recollect he was still," said Raoul lazily, "in his mother's washhouse. Romance is running away with you tonight, Miss Martin, is it not?"

"Remind me to resent that another time when I feel more . . . more earthly."

He laughed. "More champagne?"

"No, thank you. That was wonderful. Wonderful champagne, wonderful supper. Philippe, if you get a nightmare after this, let it comfort you to know that you've asked for it!"

"I rather think," said Raoul, "that Monsieur le Comte is all but asleep already."

Philippe, curled up on the rug with his head against my knee, had indeed been rather silent for some time. I bent over him. The long lashes were fanned over the childish cheeks, and he was breathing softly and evenly. I looked up again at Raoul and nodded. He rose, stretched, and pitched his cigarette into the dying fire.

"We'd better put him to bed." He stood for a moment looking down at the child. He looked very tall in the firelight with Philippe curled at his feet. "Does he have nightmares?"

"He says so. People come in in the night and touch him. Rather horrid."

His eyes rested on me for a moment, but I had the odd impression that he didn't see me.

"As you say." He stopped then and picked the child up,

156

holding him easily in his arms. He carried him toward the bed.

The side of the room where we had been sitting was in deep shadow, lit warmly by the now-fading fire. Behind us the white shaft from the moonlit windows had slowly wheeled nearer. The bed lay now full in the sharp diagonal of light.

Raoul carried the sleeping child across the room. He was just about to step into the patch of light—a step as definite as a chessman's from black to white—when a new shadow stabbed across the carpet, cutting the light in two. Someone had come to the window and stopped dead in the path of the moon.

The shadow, jumping across his feet, had startled Raoul. He swung around. Philippe's face, blanched by the moon, lolled against his shoulder. Héloïse de Valmy's voice said, on a sharp note of hysteria: "Raoul! What are you doing here? What's wrong?"

She was backed against the light, so I couldn't see her face, but the hand gripping the curtain was tight as a hawk's claw. The other hand went to her heart in a gesture I had seen before.

He said slowly, his eyes on her, "Nothing. What should be wrong?"

She said hoarsely, "What's the matter with Philippe?"

"My dear Héloïse. Nothing at all. He's asleep."

I thought it better not to wait for discovery. I got to my feet.

The movement of my white dress in the shadows caught her eye and she jerked around. "Oh!" It was a little choked scream.

"Easy," said Raoul. "You'll wake him up."

I came forward into the moonlight. "I'm sorry I startled you, madame."

"You here? What's going on? Is there something wrong?"

Raoul grinned at her. "A carouse, that's all. An illicit night out à trois. Philippe was feeling a bit left out of the festivities, so Miss Martin and I tried to include him in, that's all. He's just gone to sleep. Turn the bed down, Linda, and help me get his dressing gown off."

Héloïse de Valmy gave a rather dazed look about her. "Then I did hear voices. I thought I heard someone talking. I wondered. . . ." Her eye fell on the tray at the fireside, with its bottles and empty glasses and denuded silver dishes. She said blankly, "A carouse? You really did mean a carouse?"

Raoul pulled the bedclothes up under Philippe's chin and

gave them a final pat before he turned around. "Certainly. He may suffer for those lobster patties in the morning, but I expect he'll vote it worth while." He looked across the bed at me. "Let me take you down again now."

His eyes were confident and amused, but I looked nervously at Madame de Valmy. "Were you looking for me?"

"I? No." She still sounded rather at a loss. "I came to see if Philippe was asleep."

"You . . . don't mind our coming up here . . . bringing him some of the supper?"

"Not at all." She wasn't even looking at me. She was watching Raoul.

He said again, rather abruptly, "Let me take you downstairs," and came around the bed toward me.

Downstairs? Léon de Valmy, Monsieur Florimond, the eyebrows? I shook my head. "No, thank you. I—it's late. I'll not go down again. I'll go to bed."

"As you wish." He glanced at Madame, "Héloïse?"

She bent her head and moved toward the door. I opened it and held it for her. As she passed me I said hesitantly, "Good night, madame. And thank you for . . . the dance. It was—I enjoyed it very much."

She paused. In the dim light her face looked pale, the eyes shadowy. She had never looked so remote, so unreachable. "Good night, Miss Martin." There was no inflection whatever in the formal words.

I said quickly, almost imploringly, "Madame . . ."

She turned and went. The rich rustle of her dress was as loud in the silence as running water. She didn't look back.

Raoul was beside me. I touched his sleeve. "It was true after all. You see?"

He was looking away from me, after Héloïse. He didn't answer.

I said urgently, under my breath, "Raoul . . . don't tell them. I can't face it. Not yet. I . . . just can't."

I thought he hesitated. "We'll talk about it tomorrow."

I said quickly, "Let them send me away. I'll go to Paris. I can stay there a little while. Perhaps then we can—"

His hands on my shoulders turned me swiftly toward him, interrupting me. "My dear, if I'm not to tell Héloïse tonight, I'd better leave you now. Don't worry, it'll be all right. I'll say nothing until we've talked it over." He bent and kissed me, a brief, hard kiss. "Good night, m'amie. Sleep well. . . ."

The door shut behind him. I heard him walk quickly down the corridor after Héloïse, as if he were in a hurry.

Chapter XIII

> "Yes," I answered you last night;
> "No," this morning, sir, I say.
> Colours seen by candlelight
> Will not look the same by day.

ELIZABETH BARRETT BROWNING: *The Lady's Yes.*

NEXT morning a note was brought up to the schoolroom at breakfast-time by Bernard, Léon de Valmy's man.

It looked as if it had been written in a tearing hurry, and it read:

> My dear,
>   I can't stay today as I'd hoped. I find I must go back to Paris—a damnable "must." Forgive me, and try not to worry about anything. I'll be back on Thursday morning without fail, and we can get things worked out then.
>   Héloïse said nothing to me, and (as I'd promised you I wouldn't) I didn't talk to her. I don't think you need worry too much about that side of it, m'amie; if they have anything to say they'll undoubtedly say it to me, not you. Till Thursday, then, pretend, if you can—if you dare!—that nothing has happened. I doubt if you'll see much of Héloïse anyway. She overdid things, and I imagine she'll keep to her bed.
>
> > Yours,
> > R.

As a first love letter, there was nothing in it to make my hands as unsteady as they were when I folded it and looked up at the waiting Bernard. He was watching me; the black eyes in that impassively surly face were shrewd and somehow wary. I thought I saw a gleam of speculation there, and reflected wryly that it was very like Raoul to send his messages by the hand of the man who hadn't been out of Léon de Valmy's call for twenty years. I said coolly, "Did Monsieur Raoul give you this himself?"

"Yes, mademoiselle."

"Has he left already?"

"Oh yes, mademoiselle. He drove down to catch the early flight to Paris."

"I see. Thank you. And how is Mrs. Seddon today, Bernard?"

"Better, mademoiselle, but the doctor says she must stay quiet in her bed for a day or two."

"Well, I hope she'll soon be fit again," I said. "Have someone let her know I was asking after her, will you please?"

"Yes, mademoiselle."

"Bernard," said Philippe, putting down his cup, "you have a dance tonight, don't you?"

"Yes, monsieur."

"Down in the village?"

"Yes, monsieur."

"Do you have supper there as well?"

"Yes, monsieur."

"What sort of things do you have for supper?"

The man's dark face remained wooden, his eyes guarded—unfriendly, even. "That I really couldn't say, monsieur."

"All right, Bernard," I said. "Thank you."

As he went I wondered, yet again, what pretty little Berthe could see in him.

It was a very unpleasant and also a very long day.

I felt curiously bereft. Raoul had gone. Florimond left soon after breakfast. Mrs. Seddon did as Bernard had prophesied and kept to her room, and Berthe went about her tasks all day with that withdrawn and rather shamefaced expression which seemed—if it were possible—faintly to image Bernard's sullen mask.

Small wonder, then, that when Philippe and I were out for our afternoon walk, and a jeep roared past us carrying several men and driven by William Blake, I responded to his cheerful wave with such fervor that Philippe looked curiously up at me and remarked, "He is a great friend of yours, that one, *hein?*"

"He's English," I said simply, then smiled at myself. "Do you know what irony is, Philippe? *L'ironie?*"

"No, what?"

I looked at him doubtfully, but I had let myself in for a definition now and plunged a little wildly at it. "*L'ironie* . . . I suppose it's Chance, or Fate (*le destin*), or something, that follows you around and spies on what you do and say, and then uses it against you at the worst possible time. No, that's not a very good way of putting it. Skip it, *mon lapin;* I'm not at my best this afternoon."

"But I am reading about that this morning," said Philippe. "It has a special name. It followed you comme vous dîtes and when you do something silly it—how do you say it?—came against you. It was called Nemesis."

I stopped short and looked at him. I said, "Philippe, my love, I somehow feel it only wanted that . . . And it's practically the Ides of March and there are ravens flying down on our left and I walked the wrong way around Sainte-Marie-des-Points last Thursday afternoon, and—"

"You didn't," said Philippe. "It was raining."

"Was it?"

"You know it was." He chuckled and gave a ghost of a skip. "You do say silly things sometimes, don't you?"

"All too often."

"But I like it. Go on. About the ravens flying upside down. Do they really? Why? Go on, mademoiselle."

"I don't think I can," I said. "Words fail me."

On our way in from the walk we met Monsieur de Valmy.

Instead of coming up the zigzag itself we took the short cut which ran steeply upward, here and there touching the northerly loops of the road. We crossed the gravel sweep at the top. As we went through the stableyard archway, making for the side door, the wheel chair came quietly out of some outbuilding and Léon de Valmy's voice said, in French, "Ah, Philippe. Good afternoon, Miss Martin. Are you just back from your walk?"

The quick color burned my face as I turned to answer. "Good afternoon, monsieur. Yes. We've just been along the valley road, and we came back up the short cut."

He smiled. I could see no trace of disapproval or coolness in his face. Surely if I were privately under sentence of dismissal, he wouldn't act quite so normally—more, go out of his way to greet us in this unruffled friendly fashion? He said, including Philippe in the warmth of his smile, "You've taken to by-passing the woods now, have you?"

"Well, we have rather." I added, "I'm nervous, so we keep near the road."

He laughed. "I don't blame you." He turned to Philippe with a pleasant twinkle. "And how are you this morning, after your excesses of last night?"

"Excesses?" said Philippe nervously.

"I'm told you had a midnight feast last night . . . an

161

'illicit night out à trois' was the phrase, I believe. No nightmares afterward?"

Philippe said, "No, mon oncle." The amused dark gaze turned to me.

I said, almost as nervously as Philippe, "You don't mind? Perhaps it was a little unorthodox, but—"

"My dear Miss Martin, why should I? We leave Philippe very completely to your care and judgment, and so far we've been amply proved right. Please don't imagine that my wife and myself are waiting to criticize every move that's out of pattern. We know very little about the care of children. That's up to you. And a 'special treat' now and again is an essential, I believe? It was kind of you to spare time and thought to the child in the middle of your own pleasure. . . . I hope you enjoyed the dance?"

"Yes, oh yes, I did! I didn't see you last night to thank you for inviting me, but may I thank you now, monsieur? It was wonderful. I enjoyed it very much."

"I'm glad to hear it. I was afraid you might feel rather too much a stranger among us, but I gather that Raoul looked after you."

Nothing but polite inquiry. No glint of amusement. No overtone to the pleasant voice.

"Yes, monsieur, thank you, he did. . . . And how is Madame de Valmy this afternoon? She's not ill, is she?"

"Oh no, only tired. She'll be making an appearance at the dance in the village tonight, so she's resting today."

"Then she won't expect us—Philippe and me—in the salon tonight?"

"No. I think you must miss that." The smile at Philippe was slightly mischievous now. "Unless you'd like to visit me instead?"

Philippe stiffened, but I said, "As you wish, monsieur. In the library?"

He laughed. "No, no. We'll spare Philippe that. Well, don't let me keep you." The wheel chair swiveled away, then slewed back to us. "Oh, by the way . . ."

"Monsieur?"

"Don't let Philippe use the swing in the big coachhouse, Miss Martin. I see that one of the rivets is working loose. Keep off it until it's mended. We mustn't have another accident, must we?"

"No indeed. Thank you, monsieur, we'll keep out of there."

He nodded and swung the chair away again. It moved off

with that disconcertingly smooth speed toward the gate to the kitchen garden. Philippe ran ahead of me toward the side door with the air of one reprieved from a terrible fate.

He wasn't the only one. I was reflecting that once again my imagination had betrayed me. That smile of Monsieur de Valmy's last night . . . Madame's coldness . . . my interpretation of them had been wildly wide of the mark A guilty conscience, and a too-ready ear for gossip had given me a few bad hours. It served me right. There was obviously no idea of dismissing me; if there had been Monsieur de Valmy would never have spoken to me as he had. All was well . . . and even if there were snags in the future, Raoul would be here beside me.

"Mademoiselle," said Philippe, "you look quite different. Qu' est-ce que c'est?"

"I think I've seen a raven," I said, "flying the right way up."

The rest of the day limped through without incident. I put Philippe to bed a little earlier than usual, and later on, as soon as I had taken him his late-night chocolate, I went thankfully to bed myself and slept almost straight away.

I don't remember waking. Straight out of deep sleep, it seemed, I turned my head on the pillow and looked with wide-open eyes toward the door. The room was dark and I could see nothing, but then there came the stealthy click of the door closing, and soft footsteps moved across the carpet toward the bed. I think that for a moment or two I didn't realize I was awake, but lay still listening to the ghostly approach in a sort of bemused half-slumber.

Something touched the bed. I heard breathing. I was awake and this was real. My heart jerked once, in a painful spasm of fear, and I shot up in the bed, saying on a sharply rising note, "Who's that?"

As I grabbed for the bedside switch a voice that was no more than a terrified breath said, "Don't put the light on. Don't!"

My hand fell from the switch. The intruder's terror seemed to quiver in the air between us, and in the face of it I felt myself growing calm. I said quietly, "Who is it?"

The whisper said, "It's Berthe, miss."

"Berthe?"

There was a terrified sound that might have been a sob. "Oh, *hush*, miss, they'll hear!"

I said softly, "What's the matter, Berthe? What's up?" Then a thought touched me icily and I put a hand to the bedclothes.

"Philippe? Is there something the matter with Philippe?"

"No, no, nothing like that! But it's—it's—I thought I ought to come and tell you . . ."

But here the distressful whispering was broken unmistakably by gulping sobs, and Berthe sat down heavily on the end of the bed.

I slipped from under the covers and padded across the room to lock the doors. Then I went back to the bed and switched on the bedside lamp.

Berthe was still crouched on the bottom of my bed, her face in her hands. She was wearing the silver-netted frock, with a coat of some cheap dark material thrown around shoulders which still shook with sobs.

I said gently, "Take your time, Berthe. Shall I make you some coffee?"

She shook her head, and lifted it from her hands. Her face, usually so pretty, was pinched and white. Her cheeks were streaked with tears and her eyes looked dreadful.

I sat down beside her on the bed and put an arm around her. "Don't, my dear. What is it? Can I help? Did something happen at the dance?" I felt the shoulders move. I said on a thought, "Is it Bernard?"

She nodded, still gulping. Then I felt her square her shoulders. I withdrew my arm but stayed beside her. Presently she managed to say, with rather ragged-edged composure, "You'd better get back into bed, miss. You'll get cold like that."

"Very well." I slipped back into bed, pulled the covers around me, and looked at her. "Now tell me. What is it? Can I help?"

She didn't answer for a moment. Nor did she look at me. Her eyes went around the room as if to probe the shadows, and I saw terror flick its whiplash across her face again. She licked her lips.

I waited. She sat for a moment, twisting her hands together. Then she said fairly calmly, but in a low, hurried voice, "It is Bernard . . . in a way. You know I'm—I'm going to marry Bernard? Well, he took me to the dance tonight, and I wore your frock and he said I looked a princess and he started—oh, he was drinking, miss, and he got . . . you know—"

164

"I know."

"He was drunk," said Berthe, "I've never seen him that way before. I knew he'd taken a good bit, of course, he often does, but he never shows it. I—we went outside together." Her eyes were on her fingers, plaited whitely in her lap. Her voice thinned to a thread. "We went to my sister's house. She and her man were at the dance. It—I know it was wrong of me, but—" She stopped.

I said, feeling rather helpless and inadequate, "All right, Berthe. Skip that part. What's frightened you?"

"He was drunk," she said again, in that thin little voice. "I didn't realize at first . . . he seemed all right, until . . . he seemed all right. Then . . . afterward . . . he started talking." She licked her lips again. "He was boasting kind of wildlike about when we were married. I'd be a princess, he said, and we'd have money, a lot of money. I'd—I'd have to marry him soon, now, he said, and we'd buy a farm and be rich, and we'd have . . . oh, he talked so wild and silly that I got frightened and told him not to be a fool and where would the likes of him get money to buy a farm. And he said . . ."

Her voice faltered and stopped.

I said, wondering where all this was leading, "Yes? He said?"

Her hands wrung whitely together in the little glow of the lamp. "He said there'd be plenty of money later on . . . when Philippe—when Philippe—"

"Yes?"

"—was dead," said Berthe on a shivering rush of breath.

My heart had begun to beat in sharp slamming little strokes that I could feel even in my finger tips. Berthe's eyes were on me now, filled with a sort of shrinking dread that was horrible. There was sweat along her upper lip.

I said harshly, "Go on."

"I—I'm only saying what he said. He was drunk . . . half-asleep. He was—"

"Yes. Go on."

"He said Monsieur de Valmy had promised him the money—"

"Yes?"

"—when Philippe died."

"Berthe!"

"Yes, miss," said Berthe simply.

Silence. I could see sweat on her forehead now. My hands were dry and ice cold. I felt the nails scrape on the sheets

165

as I clutched at them. The pulse knocked in my finger tips.

This was nonsense. It was nightmare. It wasn't happening. But something inside me, some part of brain or instinct listened unsurprised. This nightmare was true, I knew it already. On some hidden level I had known it for long enough. I only wondered at my own stupidity that had not recognized it before. I heard myself saying quietly, "You must finish now, Berthe. Philippe . . . so Philippe is going to die later on, is he? How much later on?"

"B—Bernard said soon. He said it would have to be soon because Monsieur Hippolyte cabled early today that he was coming home. They don't know why—he must be ill or something; anyway he's canceling his trip and he'll be here by tomorrow night, so they'll have to do it soon, Bernard says. They've tried already, he says, but—"

I said, "They?"

"The Valmys. Monsieur and Madame and Monsieur—"

"No," I said. "No."

"Yes, miss. Monsieur Raoul," said Berthe.

Of course I said, "I don't believe it."

She watched me dumbly.

"*I don't believe it!*" My voice blazed with the words into fury. But she didn't speak. If she had broken into protestation perhaps I could have gone on fighting, but she said nothing, giving only that devastating shrug of the shoulders with which the French disclaim all knowledge and responsibility.

"Berthe. Are you sure?"

Another lift of the shoulders.

"He said so? Bernard said so?"

"Yes." Then something in my face pricked her to add: "He was drunk. He was talking—"

"I know. Kind of wild. That means nothing. But this can't be true! It can't! I know that! Berthe, do you hear me? It—simply—isn't—true."

She said nothing, but looked away.

I opened my lips, then shut them again, and in my turn was silent.

I don't intend—even if I could—to describe the next few minutes. To feel something inside oneself break and die is not an experience to be relived at whatever merciful distance. After a while I managed, more or less coherently, to think, spurred to it by the savage reminder that Philippe was what mattered. All the rest could be sorted out, pondered,

166

mourned over, later; now the urgent need was to think about Philippe.

I pushed back the bedclothes. Berthe said sharply, "Where are you going?"

I didn't answer. I slipped out of bed and flew to the bathroom door. Through the bathroom . . . across the child's darkened bedroom. . . . Bending over the bed, I heard his breathing, light and even. It was only then, as I straightened up on a shaking wave of relief, that I knew how completely I had accepted Berthe's statement. What was it, after all? A frightened girl's version of the drunken and amorous babbling of a servant? And yet it rang so true and chimed in with so many facts that without even half a hearing it seemed I was ready to jettison the employers who had shown me kindness and the man with whom an hour ago I had been in love.

Stiffly, blindly, like a sleepwalker, I went back to my own room, leaving the connecting doors ajar. I climbed back into bed.

"Is he all right?" Berthe's whisper met me, sharp and thin. I nodded.

"Oh, miss, oh, miss. . . ." She was wringing her hands again. I remember thinking with a queer detached portion of my mind that here was someone wringing her hands. One reads about it and one never sees it, and now here it was. When at length I spoke it was in a dead flat voice I didn't recognize as my own. "We'd better get this clear, I think. I don't say that I accept what Bernard says, but—well, I want to hear it . . . all. He says there's a plot on hand to murder Philippe. If that's so, there's no need to ask why; the gains to Monsieur and Madame and—the gains are obvious."

The words came easily. It was like a play. I was acting in a play. I didn't feel a thing—no anger or fear or unhappiness. I just spoke my lines in that dead and uninflected voice and Berthe listened and stared at me and twisted her hands together.

I said, "You say 'they've tried already.' I suppose you mean the shot in the woods and the balcony rail?"

"Y—yes."

"So." I remembered then the white expectancy on Madame de Valmy's face as Philippe and I came up from the woods that day. And the night of the balcony rail: she hadn't come upstairs that night to get any tablets; she had come because she couldn't stand the suspense any longer. Léon de Valmy, stationed in the hall, must have heard the crash from the

167

forecourt. My mind leaped on from this to recollect those two interviews with my employer in the library. I said harshly, "This could be true. Oh, my dear God, Berthe, it could be true. Well, let's have it. Who fired the shot? Bernard himself?"

"No. That was Monsieur Raoul. Bernard dug the bullet out."

I forgot about its being a play. "I don't believe it!"

"Miss—"

"Did Bernard say so?"

"Yes."

"In so many words?"

"Yes."

"Then he's lying. He probably did the shooting himself and—" But here I saw her face and stopped. After a while I said fairly calmly, "I'm sorry. I did ask you to tell me just what he said, after all. And I—I'm pretty sure that what he said is true in the main. It's just that I can't quite bring myself to—to believe—"

"Yes, miss. I know."

I looked at her. "Oh, Berthe, you make me ashamed. I was so wrapped up in my own feelings that I forgot the way you'd be feeling, too. I'm sorry. We're both in the same boat, aren't we?"

She nodded wordlessly.

Somehow the knowledge steadied me. I said, "Well, look, Berthe. We've got to be tough about this for Philippe's sake, and because there isn't much time. Later on we can work it out and—and decide who's guilty and who isn't. At present I suppose we must assume they're all in it, whether or not we can believe it in our heart of hearts. And I'm pretty sure that Monsieur and Madame are guilty—in fact I know they are. I'm very much to blame for not seeing it before, but who on earth goes about suspecting an impossible outlandish thing like murder? That's something that happens in books, not among people you know. I suppose I ought to have seen it straight away, when Philippe was shot at in the woods. And Raoul . . . Raoul was out there; he admitted it himself, and Bernard was sent straight out, and I suppose he removed the bullet then and went back later with someone else to 'discover' it. Yes, and I was right in thinking that Monsieur de Valmy knew I spoke French; I'd shouted it at—at the murderer in the beechwood, and talked it to Philippe all the way home. Then the affair of the balcony rail, Berthe—I suppose that and

168

he swing in the barn were extras? Off-chances? Booby-traps that might work sooner or later?"

"Yes."

"And then the Cadillac's horn blasting at—perhaps at nothing—brought Philippe out to his death?" I added shakily, "Do I have to believe that, too?"

"I don't know what you're talking about, miss. What horn? Bernard never said anything about any horn."

"Oh? Well, skip it. It's over, thank God, without harm. Now we have to think what to do."

I looked down at my hands while I tried to marshal my thoughts. And the pattern was forming in a way I didn't want to examine too closely. It was all there. I tried to make myself look at it all quite coldly and in order, from the time when Philippe had been sent up to Valmy and so delivered by the unsuspecting Hippolyte straight into the hands of murder. . . .

The first step—and it was taken immediately—had been to get rid of the only person close to Philippe and trusted by Hippolyte—the child's nurse. Someone must replace her, and it was judged better to find a young woman without family or guardian who, in the event of an "accident" to her pupil, wouldn't be able to call upon friends and relatives to exonerate her from possible charges of carelessness (or worse) should there be a mistake and doubts arise. So Madame de Valmy had made inquiries of a friend in London who was known to supply her friends with domestic help from an orphanage. Who better than an orphan, and a foreigner at that—someone who, in the accumulated bewilderments of a new job, a new country, and a foreign language, would hardly be in a position to observe too much or defend herself too readily. . . . There had in sober fact been that slight overemphasis on my English-ness . . . my instinct to hide my Continental origin had, absurd though it had seemed, been right.

So the scapegoat had been found and brought to France. They waited. There was plenty of time. I had been allowed to settle in; my life with Philippe formed its own quiet pattern, an ordinary day-to-day pattern which appeared pleasantly normal except that Monsieur de Valmy couldn't quite keep his bitter tongue off the child who stood between him and so much. So it had gone on. I had stayed there three weeks, settled and happy, though still not quite at ease with my employers. Then the attempt was made and, by the purest chance, it failed. The second was a longer chance, but quite safe for them—the rotten coping had already been reported, so Bernard had made sure of the stone's collapse and then waited for an accident to happen when none of the interested parties was anywhere near. And the second "accident" failed too, because of me. If the first, or even the second, had come off, "accident" would almost certainly have been the verdict ... and no doubt an entirely baffling series of alibis was in any case available. Certainly the one person who couldn't be found guilty was the interested party, Léon de Valmy. It would have been a tragedy, and it would have blown over, whispers and all, and Léon would have had Valmy. It was even possible that there'd have been no whispers at all. . . . Léon was highly thought of, and a first-rate landlord: the country folk would for many years past have regarded him as the seigneur, and they might have been only too pleased when the custody of Valmy passed unequivocally into his hands.

Berthe was still crouching at the foot of my bed, watching me dumbly. I said, "And now, Berthe, what's next?"

"I don't know. I don't know."

"You must. This is what matters. Think. Bernard let so much out; he must have told you that."

"No. I don't think he knew himself. I think it wasn't to be him. That's all." She floundered, gulped, and began to sob again.

Out of nowhere, unbidden, unwanted, a picture flashed onto the dark screen of my mind. Philippe's sleeping head lolling back against Raoul's shoulder, and Héloïse's voice saying hoarsely: "What's the matter with Philippe?" And Raoul giving her that hard quelling look. "Nothing at all. He's asleep."

I said shakily, "And Bernard said nothing to indicate when? Or how?"

"No, honestly he didn't. But it was to be soon because of Monsieur Hippolyte coming back. The cable came early this morning and it really put the Master out, Bernard said."

"And Hippolyte's coming back tomorrow?" I caught my breath. "Today, Berthe. It's today, d'you realize that? Today?"

"Why . . . yes, I reckon it is. It's nearly one o'clock, isn't it? But I don't rightly know when Monsieur Hippolyte'll get here. I think it won't be till night, and then he mayn't get up to Valmy till Thursday."

I said quietly, "Monsieur Raoul has gone to Paris till Thursday, Berthe. If the cable came 'early' this morning he would probably know about it, but he still went to Paris. So he can't be in it, can he? Bernard was wrong."

She said in that dull voice that was stupid with shock and

succeeded in sounding stubborn, "Bernard said he was in it. Bernard said he fired the shot."

It was useless—and cruel—to spend myself in protests. I said, "All right. The point is that if we're to decide how to protect Philippe we must have some idea where the danger's coming from. I mean, nobody's going to listen to us unless we have some sort of a case which, God knows, we haven't got yet. Let's begin with the things we know. You say it's not to be Bernard."

She gulped and nodded. She was steadier now, I saw, and her breathing was less ragged. Her hands had stopped wrenching at each other. She was listening with some sort of attention.

I said, "I think we can count out the idea that there are any more booby-traps waiting about. They've got to make quite certain this time; they can't wait for chance to act for them. And in any case, too many 'accidents' of the same kind might make people begin to think. That was why Monsieur de Valmy warned me about the swing in the barn . . . yes, he did that this afternoon, after he'd heard that Hippolyte was coming back. He was as nice as ninepence, though I'd been quite sure that he and Madame—oh, well, that doesn't matter. Well, Bernard's out, and booby-traps are out. There are limits to what Monsieur de Valmy can do himself, and from the way things have gone up to now I have a feeling he'll keep well out of it, since he's the person who stands most obviously to gain. And Raoul isn't here, so it can't be Raoul." In spite of myself my voice lightened on the words. I said almost joyously, "That leaves Madame, doesn't it?"

"Are you sure?" said Berthe.

"That it's Madame? Of course I'm not. But—"

"That he's gone," said Berthe.

I stared at her. "What do you mean?"

She gave a little boneless shrug. "It's a big place."

Something crept over my skin like a cold draft. "You mean . . . he may still be here somewhere . . . hiding?"

She didn't speak. She nodded. Her eyes, watching me painfully, were once more alive and intelligent.

I said almost angrily, "But he went. People must have seen him go. Bernard said—oh, that's not evidence, is it? But his car's gone. I noticed that when we came through the stableyard this afternoon."

"Yes, he left. I saw him. But he could have come back. There's such things," added Berthe surprisingly, "as alibis."

I said slowly, "Yes, I suppose there are. But that he should

171

be here . . . hiding . . . no, it's too farfetched and absurd."

"Well," said Berthe, "but it's absurd to think Madame would do it, isn't it?"

"Oh God," I said explosively, "it's absurd to think anyone would do it! But I can't believe the thing hinges on Raoul. No—" as she was about to speak—"not only for the reason you think, but because if he is in it, I can't see where I come in at all. *That's* fantastic if you like."

"How d'you mean?"

"If he was involved in this murder thing, why get involved with me? You know he was, of course?"

"Everybody knew."

I said bitterly, "They did, didn't they? Well, why did he? Surely it was a dangerous and unnecessary thing to do?"

"Perhaps," she said disconcertingly, "he just can't help it. You're awfully pretty, aren't you, and Albertine says that when they were in Paris she heard—"

"Ah, yes," I said. "Albertine hears an awful lot, doesn't she? You mean that he automatically turns the power on for every young female he meets? His father's like that, have you noticed? He's got a technique all his own of disarming you with his affliction and then switching on charm like an arc light. Well, it could be, but I don't think so. Raoul's not like his father; he's got no need to waste himself where it doesn't matter. And in this case it might have been actually dangerous to get involved with me if he was . . . Third Murderer."

"If he is in it with them, and he started to—well, to—"

"To make love to me?"

"Yes, miss. If he did that, and, like you said, it wasn't safe, mightn't that be why Monsieur and Madame were so annoyed about it?"

"I thought they were at first, but they weren't. I told you. Monsieur was awfully nice to me this afternoon."

"Oh, but they were, miss. Albertine said you were to be sent away. Everyone knew. They were all talking about it. And why should they bother to send you away, unless Monsieur Raoul was in with them, and it wasn't safe, like you said? Otherwise you'd hardly think they'd trouble their heads about his goings-on, because—oh, I'm sorry, miss, I do beg your pardon, I'm sure."

"It's all right. 'Goings-on' will do. Well, they might be annoyed even so, because Philippe was in their charge and I —no that won't do. If they're all set to murder the child they won't give a damn about the moral code of his governess. But no, Berthe, it won't fit. It doesn't make sense. I still can't throw Monsieur Raoul in, you know. And not just because of the way I feel, either. It went too far, our affair—beyond all the bounds of reason if he was involved in his father's game. He asked me to marry him."

"Yes, I know."

"You know?"

"Yes, miss. Everybody does."

I don't think I spoke for a full five seconds. "Do they? Second sight or just more gossip?"

"I don't know what you mean. Bernard told Albertine and she told the rest of us."

"When was this?"

She looked uncomfortable. "Well, she'd been saying things about you for quite a time. She'd been saying you were, well—"

"Yes?"

"She said you were out to get him, miss, and that Monsieur and Madame were furious and you were going to be sent away. And then yesterday she was saying it had happened, like."

"Yesterday? You mean after the ball?"

"That's right."

"Did she say she knew for certain?"

"I don't know. She was sounding sure enough about it. She said—oh, well, never mind. She's a nasty one sometimes, that one."

"Yes. Let it pass. I've had my fill of Albertine. But let's think," I said a little desperately, "if she and everyone else were talking about our engagement, then, even if they hadn't been actually told, you'd think Monsieur and Madame would know too?"

"That's right, you would."

"But you said they were genuinely furious before that— when it was known that he and I were, well, interested in each other."

"Oh yes. I'm sure of that."

"But I tell you it doesn't make sense. I told you, I saw Monsieur de Valmy yesterday—when presumably he knew as much about it as everyone else—and he was extremely nice to me. And neither of them sent for me to ask me about it or— or anything. I—I can't work it out, Berthe. My head's spinning and it feels as if it's going to burst. If they knew, and didn't mind, then Raoul can't be in it, can he? When I saw him, Monsieur Léon must have already laid his plans because he'd already had Hippolyte's cable. . . ."

173

My voice trailed away into nothing. I swallowed hard. I repeated, unrecognizably: *"He'd already had Hippolyte's cable."*

In the silence that followed she stirred and the bed creaked.

I said slowly, "He and Madame were angry with me before; I know they were. I believe they were planning to send me away. But Hippolyte's cable changed all that. They had to make a plan in a hurry and that plan included me. How does *that* fit?"

"Well—"

"It does, you know. But how? *How?* Are you sure Bernard said nothing?"

"I'm sure," she said desperately. "Don't you fret, miss. I'd go bail you'll be in no danger."

"What makes you think I'm worrying about that?" I said, almost sharply. "But we must get this straight, don't you see? It's the only way we'll be able to do anything to help Philippe. What can they be planning to do that includes me? What the sweet hell can they be planning?"

She said, "Maybe you've nothing to do with it at all. Maybe they just think it'd look funny if something happened to Philippe the day you were sent off, so they've decided they'll have to keep you."

"Yes, but marriage is a bit—"

"Maybe they want to make sure you'll hold your tongue if you suspect anything," said Berthe.

"Oh, dear God," I said wearily, "they surely can't imagine that I'd suspect a child was murdered and do nothing about it?"

"But if you were going to marry him, and everyone knew—"

"What difference would that make? They'd never be idiot enough to think I'd *help* them? No, it's nonsense. They'd never use marriage as a bait to make me hold my tongue. Why, good heavens—"

"I wasn't going to say that." There was some new quality in Berthe's voice that stopped me short. She was still speaking softly, but there was some curious vibrancy in the tones that held me. She said, "Everybody knows you're engaged to Monsieur Raoul. If Philippe died, you'd be Madame la Comtesse de Valmy one day."

"What do you mean?" Then I saw. I finished in a voice that wasn't a voice at all, "You mean that when the cable came and they made their plan, it *did* include me? That they've given me a motive for murder? That they can't risk another 'accident' without a scapegoat ready to hand in case things go

174

wrong and people ask questions? Is that what you mean?"

Berthe said simply, "Why else should he ask you to marry him?"

"Why else indeed?" I said.

I had checked up again on Philippe. He still slept peacefully. The house was quiet. I tiptoed back into my bedroom and reached for my dressing gown.

Berthe said, "Is he all right?"

I was putting the dressing gown on with hands that shook and were clumsy. "Yes. You realize, I suppose, that the likeliest time for anything to happen is tonight, now, and everybody's out at the dance except Mrs. Seddon?"

"Mr. Seddon didn't go. He stayed with her."

"Oh? Well, I'd trust them all right, but she's ill and I doubt if he'd be much use—even if they'd believe us, which isn't likely." I found my slippers and thrust my feet hastily into them. "Will you stay with Philippe and mount guard over him? Lock his door and window now."

"What are you going to do?"

"The only possible thing. What's the time?"

"Going on quarter past one. I—we came away early."

"Did Bernard come up with you?"

"Yes." She didn't look at me. "I persuaded him to bring me up in the brake. It wasn't difficult. He—he's asleep now in my room." She finished in a thin little voice: "It was awful, driving up that zigzag with him so drunk still. . . ."

I was hardly listening. I was reflecting that, apart from the Seddons, we were alone in the house with Léon de Valmy and Bernard. Thank God the latter still had to sleep it off. I said, "Was Madame de Valmy at the dance?"

"Yes, but she'll have left by now. She never stays long."

"I see. Now can I get to the telephone in Seddon's pantry without being heard or seen? Does he lock it?"

"No, miss. But he goes to bed at midnight and he always switches it through to the Master's room then."

Something fluttered deep in my stomach. I ignored it. "Then I'll switch it back again. How d'you do it?"

"There's a red tab on the left. Press it down. But—he might hear it. Miss—what are you going to do?"

"There's only one thing I can do. We must have help. D'you mean that if I use the telephone it'll ting in the Master's room or something? Because if so I can't use it. And I can't go out and leave Philippe. You may have to go for the police yourself if you can—"

175

"The police?"

I was across at the door that gave on the corridor, listening. I turned and looked back at her in surprise.

"Who else? I must tell the police all this. They may not believe me, but at least I can get them up here and if there's a fuss it'll make it impossible for another attempt on Philippe to be made. And tonight or tomorrow Monsieur Hippolyte gets back and he can take care of Philippe when the row's over and I've been sent—home."

"No!" said Berthe so violently that the syllable rang, and she clapped a hand to her mouth.

"What d'you mean?"

"You're not to go to the police! You're not to tell anyone!"

"But my dear girl—"

"I came to tell you because you'd been kind to me, because I liked you and Philippe. You've been so good to me—always so nice, and there was the dress and—and all. I thought you might have got mixed up in it somehow, with Monsieur Raoul and all that. . . . But you mustn't let on I told you! You mustn't!"

The new fear had sharpened her voice, so that I said urgently, "Be quiet, will you! And don't be a fool! How can you expect me to say nothing—"

"You are not to tell them about Bernard! You can go away if you're afraid!"

I must have looked at her blankly. "Go away?"

"If it's true what we said, and you're likely to be blamed for a murder! You can make an excuse in the morning and leave straight away! It's easy! You can say you don't want to marry him after all, and that you know you can't stay as governess after what's happened. It's likely enough. They can't make you stay anyway, and they won't suspect."

"But, Berthe, stop! That's only guesswork! And even if it's true you can't seriously suggest that I should run away and leave Philippe to them?"

"I'll look after him! I'll watch him till Monsieur Hippolyte gets back! It's only one day! You can trust me, you know that. If you upset their plans and they've nobody to blame, maybe they won't do anything!"

"Maybe they will," I rejoined grimly, "and blame you instead, Berthe."

"They wouldn't dare. Bernard wouldn't stand for it."

"You're probably right. But I'm not risking Philippe's life on any 'maybes.' And you don't understand, Berthe. The thing

176

to be stopped isn't my being involved, but Philippe's murder! I know you came to warn me, and I'm grateful, but there's simply no question of my leaving. I'm going to ring the police this very minute."

Her face, paper-white, had flattened, featureless; starched linen with two dark holes torn for eyes. "No! No! No!" Hysteria shook her voice. "Bernard will know I've told you! And Monsieur de Valmy! I daren't! You can't!"

"I must. Can't you see that none of these things matter? Only the child."

"I'll deny it. I'll deny everything. I'll swear he never said a word or that I spoke to you. I'll say it's lies. I will! I will!"

There was a little silence. I came away from the door.

"You'd do—that?"

"Yes. I swear I would."

I said nothing for a bit. After a few seconds her eyes fell away from mine, but there was a look in her face that told me she meant what she said. I fought my anger down, reminding myself that she had lived all her life in Valmy's shadow, and that now there was the best of reasons why Bernard should still be willing—and free—to marry her. Poor Berthe; she had done a good deal: more I could hardly expect. . . .

"Very well," I said, "I'll leave you out of it and I won't mention Bernard. We'll let the past die and just deal with the future. I'll put it to the police as simply my own suspicions. I'll think of something. And then I'll go straight along to Léon de Valmy and tell him that I've spoken to them. That should finish the matter quite as effectively."

She was staring at me as if I were mad. "You'd—dare?"

I had a sudden inner vision of Philippe in Raoul's arms. "Oh yes," I said, "I'd dare."

She was shivering now, and her teeth were clenched as if she was cold. "But you mustn't. He'd guess about Bernard—and me. Someone'd tell him Bernard was drunk tonight. He'd know. You can't do it."

"I must and will. Don't be a fool, Berthe. You know as well as I do that I've got to. . . ."

"No, no, no! We can look after him! With two of us he'll be all right. It's only for one day. We can watch Bernard—"

"And Madame? And Léon de Valmy? And God knows who else?"

She said blindly, hysterically, "You are not to tell! If you don't swear not to go to the police I shall go to Bernard now! He'll be sober enough to stop you!"

177

I took three strides to the bedside and gripped her by the shoulders. "You won't do that, Berthe! You know you won't! You can't!"

Under my hands her shoulders were rigid. Her face, still pinched and white, was near my own. My touch seemed to have shaken the hysteria out of her, for she spoke quietly, and with a conviction that no scream could have carried, "If you tell the police, and they come to see the Master, he'll guess how you found out. And there'll be a fuss, and he'll just deny everything, and laugh at it. They'll say that you—yes! They'll say you tried to marry Monsieur Raoul and were slighted and you're doing it out of spite, and then the police will laugh too and shrug and have a drink with the Master and go away. . . ."

"Very likely. But it'll save Philippe and a bit more slander won't hurt me."

"But what do you suppose will happen to me when it's all over?" asked Berthe. "And Bernard? And my mother and my family? My father and my brothers have worked at Valmy all their lives. They're poor. They've got nothing. Where can they go when they're dismissed? What can we do?" She shook her head. "You must please—please—do as I say. Between us we can keep him safe all right. It's best, miss, honestly it's best."

I let my hands drop from her shoulders.

"Very well. Have it your own way. I'll keep my mouth shut." I looked at her. "But I swear to you that if anything happens to Philippe—or if any attempt is made—I'll smear this story, and the Valmys across every newspaper in France until they—and Bernard—get what they deserve."

"Nothing will happen to Philippe."

"I pray God you're right. Now go, Berthe. Thank you for coming as you did."

She slid off the bed, hesitating. "The frock?"

I said wearily, "Keep it. I'll have no use for it where I'll be going. Good night."

"Miss—"

"Good night, Berthe."

The door clicked shut behind her, and left me alone with the shadows.

Chapter XIV

Fill the cup, Philip,
And let us drink a dram.

Anonymous Early English Lyric.

THERE was only one possible plan that would make certain of Philippe's safety. He had to be removed from Léon de Valmy's reach and hidden till help came.

There wasn't a minute to lose. Léon de Valmy might well assume that one-thirty would be a dead hour in the schoolroom wing. And the servants would be coming back from the dance between three and four. If anything was to be done tonight it would be done soon.

I was back at my bedside, tearing off my dressing gown with those wretchedly shaky hands, while my mind raced on out of control. I couldn't think; I didn't want to think; there were things I didn't want to face. Not yet. But Philippe had to be got away. That was all that mattered. I had decided that I didn't dare use the telephone; it might somehow betray me to Léon de Valmy, and besides, it was possible that Berthe would wait to see if I approached the pantry—and in her present shaken and terrified mood I couldn't answer for her reactions. And there was no help in Valmy. Mrs. Seddon was ill; Seddon himself was elderly, conventional and, I suspected, none too bright. Berthe and I between us might have guarded Philippe if we had only known from what danger, but as it was . . . no, he had to be got away to the nearest certain help, and then, as soon as possible, to the police. I didn't let the promise Berthe had blackmailed from me weigh with me for a second; being a woman, I put common sense in front of an illusory "honor," and I'd have broken a thousand promises without a qualm if by doing so I could save Philippe.

I had flung my dressing gown down and was reaching for my clothes when I heard the sound from the corridor.

Even though I had been listening for it I didn't at first know what it was. It came as the thinnest of humming whispers through the turmoil of my brain. But at some level it must have blared a warning, for my hand flashed to the bedside light and switched it off just as Philippe's door opened, and I knew what the whisper had been. The wheel chair.

179

I stayed where I was, frozen, one hand still on the light switch. I don't think I was even breathing. If there had been the slightest sound from the other room I think I'd have been through there like a bullet from a gun, but the wheel chair never moved, so I stayed still, waiting.

Nothing. No movement. After a while Philippe's door shut once more, very softly. The whisper was in the corridor again.

I don't know what instinct thrust me back into my bed and pulled the clothes up around me, but when my bedroom door opened I was lying quite quietly with my back to it.

He didn't come in. He simply waited there in silence. The seconds stretched out like years. I thought, I wonder what he'd do if I turned over, saw him, and screamed? The employer caught creeping into the governess's bedroom, the lights, the questions, the scurrying feet in the corridor . . . could you laugh that one off, Monsieur de Valmy? Tiny bubbles of hysteria prickled in my throat at the thought of Léon de Valmy pilloried in the role of vile seducer—then I remembered how pitifully he was insured against the risk, and lay still, all my perilous amusement gone. In its stead came a kind of shame and a pity that, rather horribly, did nothing to mitigate my fear. There was something curiously vile about the mixture of emotions. My muscles tensed themselves against it and I started to tremble.

He had gone. The door had closed noiselessly behind him. I heard the whisper of the wheels fade along the corridor, toward his room.

I slipped out of bed and padded across to the door, where I stood listening until, far down the corridor, I thought I heard another door shut softly. Seconds later, I heard the faint whine of the lift. He had been checking up, that was all. But he had also told me all I wanted to know. The story was true. And I had to get Philippe out of it, and fast. Somehow I was calm again. I shut and locked my door, then with steady hands drew the curtains close and turned on the bedside light. I dressed quickly, picked up my coat and strong shoes, and went through the bathroom into Philippe's room.

This was going to be the hardest part of the job. I put the coat and shoes down on the chair where I had sat for last night's midnight feast, then, with a glance at the sleeping child, I crossed to the door and locked it. Deliberately, I refused to hurry. If this was to succeed at all it must be taken calmly.

The room was light enough. The long curtains hung

slightly apart, and between them a shaft of light fell, as it had done last night, to paint a bright line across the carpet. Something struck my foot as I crossed the floor, and rolled a little way, glittering. A frosted grape. Berthe had scamped the cleaning today, it seemed.

I pushed aside the heavy curtain, and latched the window. Behind me Philippe moved and sighed, and I paused and looked over my shoulder toward the bed, with one hand still on the window catch, and the other holding back the curtain.

The shadow falling across me brought me around again like a jerked puppet to face the window. Someone had come along the balcony, and was staring at me through the gap in the curtains. I stood there, held rigid in the noose of light that showed me up so pitilessly. I couldn't move. My hand tightened on the window catch as if an electric current held it there. I looked straight into Héloïse de Valmy's eyes, a foot from my own.

She showed no surprise at my presence, nor even at the fact that I was dressed to go out. She merely put a hand to the window fastening, as if expecting to find it open. She shook it, and then her hands slid over the glass as if trying to push a way in. Then she took hold of the latch once more, rattling it almost impatiently.

I could hardly refuse to let her in. I noticed that there were no pockets to her long ivory-colored robe, and that her hands were empty. Besides, if she was here to harm Philippe she would hardly demand entry from me in this unruffled fashion. Wondering confusedly how I was going to explain the fact that I was up and dressed at one-thirty in the morning, I opened the window. I said, as coolly as I could, "Good evening, madame."

She took no notice, but walked calmly past me into the room. Her robe whispered across the carpet. She stopped near the head of the bed. In the dim room her shadow threw a yet deeper darkness over the sleeping child. She put out a hand slowly, almost tentatively, to touch his face. It was a gentle touch, a meaningless gesture, but I recognized it. This was Philippe's nightmare. This had happened before.

If she had had some weapon, if her approach had been at all stealthy—anything but this apparently calm and routine visit—no doubt I would have moved more quickly. As it was, her hand was still hovering over the boy's face when I flew after her. I reached Philippe just as her fingers touched him. I went around the bed and reached a protective hand to draw

181

the sheet up to the child's face. I faced her across the bed
He didn't move. She drew her hand back, and straightened up
Whatever my feelings toward the Demon King, I was not
afraid of his wife. I said, "What is it, madame? What do you
want?"

She didn't answer. She hadn't even acknowledged my
presence. This was carrying ostracism a bit too far. I began to
say something angry, then stopped, bewildered, to watch her.

She had turned to the little table that stood beside the bed.
Her hands moved now over the clutter of objects on the table
—a lamp, a book, a little clock, the tumbler that had held
Philippe's chocolate, a couple of soldiers, a biscuit. . . . I
thought she was going to switch the light on, and made a half-
movement of protest. But her hands, groping in a curious
blind fashion, passed the lamp, moved softly over the clock
and the tin soldiers, and hovered over the tumbler. She
picked this up.

"I said, "Madame de Valmy—"

She turned at that. She had lifted the tumbler as if to drink
from it, and across the rim her eyes met mine again. With her
back to the moonlight, her face was a pale blur, her eyes dark
and expressionless, but as I looked at her, bewildered and
beginning once more to be frightened, I understood. The
goosepimple cold slid, ghost-handed, over my skin.

The open eyes, no less than the smooth stealthy hands,
were indeed blind. . . . I stared into the woman's expressionless
face for one eerie moment longer, while the child breathed
gently between us, then, very quietly, I moved to one side,
down to the foot of the bed.

She stood still, with the tumbler held to her face, staring at
the place where I had been. . . . *You see, her eyes are open.*
Ay but their sense is shut. . . . I stood and watched her as if
she were a ghost on a moonlit stage. The verses marched on
through my brain as if someone had switched on a tape
recorder and forgotten it. I remember feeling a sort of numb
surprise at their aptness. *Lo you, here she comes! This is*
her very guise, and upon my life, fast asleep. . . .

So Héloïse de Valmy, like Lady Macbeth, had that weighing
on her heart which sent her sleepwalking through the night to
Philippe's room. And would she, like that other murderess,
give away what she had seen and known? I knew nothing
about sleepwalkers except what I remembered of that scene
in *Macbeth*. And Lady Macbeth had talked. Was it possible
that I could get Héloïse de Valmy to do the same? *Observe*
her, stand close.

I was gripping the rail at the foot of Philippe's bed. Without it, I think I would have fallen.

I said hoarsely, "Madame."

She took no notice. She put the tumbler down surely and quietly, and turned to go. The moonlight rippled along the lovely folds of her robe; it caught her face, gleaming back from eyes wide and glossy as a doll's.

I said, "Héloïse de Valmy, answer me. How will you kill Philippe?"

She was on her way to the window. I walked with her. She went smoothly, and at the right moment her hand went up to the curtain. For one fearful moment I thought I had been mistaken and she was awake, but then I saw her fumble the curtains and hesitate as a fold tangled in her robe. The fixed eyes never moved, but she fetched a sigh and faltered. Heaven knows what she has known. The obsessive question burst from me. "Is Raoul helping you to kill Philippe?"

She paused. Her head inclined toward me. I repeated it urgently in her ear, "Is Raoul helping you?"

She turned away. It wouldn't work. She was going, and her secrets with her, still locked in sleep. I reached an unsteady hand and drew the curtain aside for her.

She walked composedly past me and out of sight along the balcony.

But she had told me one thing. I saw it as soon as I turned. God, God forgive us all. I stood over Philippe in the moondappled darkness, with the tumbler in my hand.

I woke him quietly. I used a trick I had read about somewhere in John Buchan—a gentle pressure below the left ear. It seemed to work; he opened his eyes quite naturally and lay for a moment before they focused on me in the moonlight. Then he said, as if we were resuming a conversation, "I had another nightmare."

"I know. That's why I came in."

He lifted his head, and then pushed himself into a sitting position. "What's the time?"

"Half-past one."

"Haven't you been to bed yet? Have you been to the dance in the village? You didn't tell me."

"No, I haven't been out. I got dressed again because—"

"You're not going out now?" The whisper sharpened so abruptly that my finger flew to my lips.

"Quiet, Philippe. No—that is, yes, but I'm not leaving you alone, if that's what you're afraid of. You're coming, too."

"I am?"

I nodded, and sat down on the edge of the bed. The big eyes watched me. He was sitting very still. I couldn't tell what he was thinking. God knows what my voice sounded like. I know my lips were stiff. I said, "Philippe."

"Yes, mademoiselle?"

"Do you . . . feel all right? Not—not sleepy or anything?"

"Not really."

"Quite fit and wide awake?"

"Yes."

I said hoarsely, "Did you drink your chocolate?"

His eyes slid around in that narrow sidelong look toward the tumbler, then back to me. He hesitated. "I poured it away."

"You *what?* Why?"

"Well . . ." he said uncertainly, eying me, then stopped.

"Look, Philippe, I don't mind. I just want to know. Was it nasty or something?"

"Oh no. At least I don't know." Again that look. Then a sudden burst of candor, "They left the bottle last night and I found it and kept it. I didn't tell you."

I said blankly, "Bottle?"

"Yes," said Philippe, "That smashing lemonade. I had that instead. It wasn't fizzy any more but it was fine."

"You . . . never said anything when I went to make your chocolate."

"Well," said Philippe, "I didn't want to hurt your feelings. You always made the chocolate and—what's the matter?"

"Nothing. Nothing. Oh, Philippe."

"What *is* it, Miss Martin?"

"I guess I'm tired," I said. "I had a late night last night and I haven't slept tonight."

"You don't mind?"

"No, I don't mind."

"Why haven't you slept tonight?"

I said, "Now listen, *mon p'tit.* Did you know your Uncle Hippolyte is coming home tomorrow—today?"

I saw the joy blow across his face the way a gleam runs over water and felt, suddenly, a deep and calm thankfulness. There was port in this storm, it seemed.

Philippe was saying in a quick, excited whisper, "When is he coming? Why is he coming back? Who told you? When can we go to see him?"

"That's what I came to wake you for," I said, as if it was the most reasonable thing in the world. "I thought that we might go straight away. The—the sooner the better,"

184

finished lamely, all my half-thought-out excuses dying on my lips under that steady stare.

"Do you mean we are going to the Villa Mireille now? To meet my Uncle Hippolyte?"

"Yes. He won't be there yet, but I thought—"

Philippe said, devastatingly, "Does my Uncle Léon know?"

I swallowed. "Philippe, my dear, I don't expect you to understand all this, but I want you to trust me, and come with me now as quickly and quietly as you can. Your Uncle Léon—"

"You are taking me away from him." It was a statement, not a question. His face was expressionless, but his eyes were intent, and he was breathing a little faster.

"Yes," I said, and nerved myself for the inevitable "Why?" But it didn't come. The child supplied the terrible answer for himself.

He said in that somber, unsurprised little voice, "My Uncle Léon hates me. I know that. He wishes I was dead. Doesn't he?"

I said gently, "Philippe, mon lapin, I'm afraid he might wish you harm. I don't like your Uncle Léon very much either. I think we'll both be better away from here, if you'll only trust me and come with me."

He pushed back the bedclothes without a second's hesitation, and grabbed at the back of his nightshirt, ready to haul it over his head. In the act he stopped. "The time I was shot at in the wood, that was not an accident?"

The question, coming grotesquely out of the folds of the nightshirt, made me gasp. There was no need, it appeared, to pretend, even about this. I said, "No, it wasn't an accident. Here's your vest."

"He tried to kill me?"

"Yes." The word sounded so flat that I added quickly, "Don't be afraid, Philippe."

"I'm not afraid." He was fighting his way into his shirt now. As he emerged from the neck of it I saw that he spoke the truth. He was taut as a wire, and the long-lashed black eyes—Valmy eyes—were beginning to blaze. "I've been afraid for a long time, ever since I came to Valmy, but I didn't know why. I've been unhappy and I've hated my Uncle Léon, but I didn't know why I was afraid all the time. Now I know, and I'm not frightened any more." He sat down at my feet and began to pull his socks on. "We'll go to my Uncle Hippolyte and tell him all this, and then my Uncle Léon will be guillotined."

"Philippe!"

He glanced up at me. "What would you? Murderers go to the guillotine. He's a murderer."

Tigers breed true, I thought wildly, *tigers breed true.* He had even, for a flash, had a look of Léon de Valmy himself. But he was only a child; he couldn't know the implications of what he was saying. I said, "He's not, you know. You're still alive, and going to stay that way. Only we must hurry, and be terribly quiet. Look, your shoes are here. No, don't put them on. Carry them till we get out."

He picked them up and got up, turning toward me, then, with a sudden duck back into childhood, he reached for my hand. "Where are we going?"

"I told you. To your Uncle Hippolyte."

"But we can't go to the Villa Mireille till he's there," he said uncertainly. "That's where they'll look for us straight away in the morning."

"I know." His hand quivered in mine, and I pulled him against my knees and put an arm around him. "But we'll be quite safe. We'll follow our star, Philippe. It'll not let us down. D'you remember Monsieur Blake, the Englishman?"

He nodded.

"Well, he has a cabin up in Dieudonné woods where he spends the night sometimes. I know he's there tonight, because I saw his light shining like a star before I went to bed. We'll go up there straight away, and he'll look after us and take us to your uncle's house tomorrow. It'll be all right, you'll see. I promise you it will."

"All right. Shall I take this scarf?"

"Yes. Was that your warm jersey you put on? Good. We'll lock the balcony window, I think. . . . Okay now? Be terribly quiet."

I paused by the door, my hand on the key, and listened. Philippe drifted to my elbow like a ghost. His eyes looked enormous in a pale face. I could hear nothing. Beyond the door the great house stretched dark and almost untenanted. And Madame de Valmy was certainly asleep, and Bernard was drunk, and the tiger himself—waiting down there for death to be discovered—the tiger himself was crippled. . . .

With a hand that slipped a little on the doorknob I eased the door open, then took Philippe's hand and tiptoed with him out into the dark corridor. Past the clock that had sounded midnight for us, down the stairs where I had lost my slipper, along the dim stretches of corridor walled with blind doors and the side-long painted eyes of portraits . . .

186

he great house slid past us in the darkness as insubstantial
s scenery in a Cocteau fantasy, until our breathless and
hostly flight was blocked by the heavy door that gave onto
he stableyard and freedom.

It was locked. There must be some other way left for the
ervants to come in, but I didn't dare turn aside to explore.
he heavy key turned easily and quietly, but still the door
vouldn't move. My hands slid over the studded wood in the
arkness, searching for a bolt. Beside me I heard Philippe take
little breath and begin to shiver. Standing on tiptoe, groping
bove my head, I found the bolt, and pulled. It moved with
scream like a mandrake torn up in a midnight wood. The
ound seemed to go on and on, winding back along the cor-
idor in a creeping echo. I pulled at the door with shaking
ands, listening all the time for the whine of the wheel chair.
The door wouldn't budge. Still it wouldn't budge. I tried to
eel if it had a spring lock beside the key, but couldn't find
ne. He would be coming any minute now, to find us cornered
n this dark passageway. It didn't need the shrieking bolts to
ell him where we were and what we were doing. I could
lmost hear my panic-stricken thoughts pouring down the
orridor to shout it at him. He would know. Oh yes, he would
now. We were en rapport, the Demon King and I. . . .

"It's all right," whispered Philippe, "I brought my torch."

He stooped down to the other bolt, drew it quietly, and the
loor opened.

We went out into the night air.

Chapter XV

Enter these enchanted woods,
You who dare.

GEORGE MEREDITH: The Woods of Westermain.

HAD no idea how to find William Blake's forest hut, but
rom my window at Valmy I had noticed that the light
eemed to be very near a broad, straight ride that slashed up
hrough the pines from somewhere near the Valmy bridge.
Philippe and I had only to cross the bridge and climb up from
he road, bearing slightly right, and we were bound to strike
he open ride. Once in this we must follow it up toward the
irst ridge, and no doubt sooner or later the light itself would
guide us to the hut.

It sounded easy, but in practice it was a long and exhausting climb. I dared not use Philippe's torch so near the road, no later in the ride, open as this was to every window on Valmy' west front.

In the forest it was very dark. My eyes had by now adjusted themselves, and we were able to pick our way between the trees without actual mishap, but very slowly, and with many stumbles and grazes, as the thick carpet of pine needles was crisscrossed, and in places piled, with dead and spiky branches left when the woods were thinned. Once Philippe tripped and was only saved from falling by my hand, and once I had to bite back a cry of pain as I stumbled against some fallen snag of wood that stabbed at my leg for all the world like a sword. But Philippe made no complaint and, crazy though it may sound, I myself, with every yard of midnight wood put between me and Valmy, felt safer and happier. This wild mountainside, tingling with the smell of the thick pines, was for all its secret and murmurous life no place of fear, that was Valmy with its lights and luxury. I realized that once again the word in my mind was "escape"; it was as if the brilliance and comfort of life at Valmy had been closing in, subtle, stifling, oversophisticated. Now I was free. . . . The darkness took us. The air was cool and the silence was thick with peace.

My guess had been right. After perhaps twenty minutes of our steep, stumbling progress we came at a climbing angle upon the open ride. This was some fifteen yards wide, and ran in a dead-straight slash from top to bottom of the hillside. I supposed it was a fire-break, or a road left open for tractors— whatever its purpose, it would be easier going for Philippe and myself.

It was, we found, very little better underfoot, as here, too, the dead boughs were thickly strewn. But at least we could see to pick our way. Clutching at my hand, and panting, Philippe climbed gamely beside me. We turned once to look at Valmy. On the far side of the valley the château, catching the moon, swam pale above its own woods, its side stabbed with a single light. Léon de Valmy still waited.

With a little shiver I turned my face back toward the sweet-smelling wild mountain of Dieudonné, and we plodded on up the moonlit canyon between the pines.

"All right, Philippe?"

"Yes, mademoiselle."

If any other creature moved in the forest that night, we never saw it. The only eyes that glittered at us were the stars,

d the million drops of stardew that shivered on the fallen
oughs. The breeze was failing, and in its pauses the breaking
f the dead stuff under our feet sounded like thunder. I
und myself, absurdly, with a quick over-the-shoulder glance
Léon de Valmy's remote little light, trying to tread more
ftly, and eying in some dread the gaunt black shadows that
e moon flung streaming behind us down the open ride.

But no new terror waited under the swimming moon, and,
hen we stopped to rest, no sound came to us except the
bored sound of our own breathing, and the age-old singing
f the pines, and the rustle of wind-made showers as the dew
ook down from the boughs.

It was Philippe who saw the hut. I had been straining my
yes upward through the trees on our left for a glimpse of
Villiam's light, and as we neared the summit of the hill,
ad begun to worry to myself in case we had already passed
hidden from us by the thick pines.

Then, as we stopped for one of our now frequent breathers,
hilippe tugged at my hand.

"There," he said breathlessly, and nodded toward a break
the southern wall of trees.

I turned thankfully, only to pause and stare, while a little
hill slid over me.

It was certainly a hut—the hut, as it was placed pretty well
here I had expected to find it. It was small and square,
eautifully made, chalet-fashion, of hewn pine logs, with a
iled veranda around it, a steep-pitched overhanging roof, and
atted wooden shutters. At back and sides the pines crowded
closely up to the eaves that you would have thought a
mp would be burning even by day.

But now the windows showed no light at all. At one there
as a tiny glow, as of firelight, but the welcoming lamp—the
ar—was out. I stood clutching the boy's hand, and staring
those blank windows.

I noticed all at once how black the trees were and how they
rouched and crowded over the hut. I saw how our shadows
treamed back from us grotesque and ink-black down the
pen ride. I moved, and a giant gesture mocked me. The night
as full of whispering.

"He'll be fast asleep," said Philippe cheerfully, and not
hispering at all.

I almost jumped, then looked down at him. I had to control
n impulse to hug him. "Why, of course," I said, not too
teadily. "Of course. I—I was forgetting it'll soon be day-
ght. I hope he doesn't mind being awakened again! Come

along, Monsieur le Comte!"

He set off sturdily, ahead of me this time, for the hut. I followed him thankfully. We were here, safe, at our star. It was Valmy now whose alien glimmer showed a crow's mile away. I spared a last quick glance for that cold point of light. Already it seemed remote, distance drowned. I would never go there again.

I found my eyes were full of tears. Not one, but a swarm of stars swam in the liquid distance. Angrily, I put up a hand to brush the tears away, and looked again.

Not one, but a swarm of stars.

Three lights now glared from the white bulk that was Valmy. And even as I stared, with the quick hot thrill twisting belly-deep inside me, another window sprang to life, and another. My bedroom, my sitting room, the schoolroom . . . and then I saw two tiny lights break from the shadows below and slide away as a car came out of the courtyard. The alarm had been given. Dear God, the alarm had been given. He hadn't waited till morning. He'd checked on us again, and now Valmy was up. I could almost hear the quick footsteps, the whispering, the whine of the wheel chair, the humming telephone wires. The bright windows stared with their five eyes across the valley. Then, even as I wondered through my sick panic why he should have roused the place, the lights went out quickly, one by one, and Valmy sank back into quiet. Only the single point of brilliance still showed, and below, the car's lamps dropped down two quick flickering curves of the zigzag and then vanished as they were switched off.

I'd been wrong. There had been no alarm. He'd found us gone, made sure, and then gone back to wait by his telephone. He had the rest of the night, and his hound was out after us. Bernard, drastically sobered? Raoul?

I turned and ran in under the darkness of the pines, as Philippe's soft rapping sounded on the door of the hut.

Half a minute went by; three-quarters. I stood beside Philippe, trying to still that little twist of terror deep inside me. In a moment now it would be over; the Englishman's feet would tread comfortably toward the door; the hinges would creak open; the firelit warmth would push a wedge into the cool night across the veranda floor.

The forest was still. The air breathed cold at my back. A minute; a minute and a half. No sound. He would be still asleep.

"Shall I knock again?"

"Yes, Philippe. Harder."

My nerves jumped and tingled to the sharp rap of knuckles on wood. The sound went through the stillness like the bang of a drum. It seemed to me that it must startle the whole forest awake.

In the backwash of the silence that followed I heard, away below us on the road, the snarl of a car going fast.

There was no sound from the hut.

"There's no one in." The quiver in the child's voice—he must be very tired after all—made me pull myself together.

"He's sound asleep," I said calmly. "Let's see if we can get in. He won't mind if we wake him."

Philippe lifted the latch and pushed. A little to my surprise the door opened immediately. He took a step forward, hesitating, but I propelled him gently in front of me straight into the room. The sound of that engine reiterated from the valley was making my skin crawl.

"Mr. Blake!" I called softly as I shut the door. "Mr. Blake! Are you there?"

Silence met us, the unmistakably hollow silence of an empty house.

I knew from what William had told me that the hut only had one room, with a penthouse scullery at the back. The door which presumably led to this was shut. The room in which we now stood was the living, eating, and sleeping room of the place.

He could not have been gone long. It didn't need the memory of the lighted window to prove that he had been there and until quite late. The wood stove still glowed faintly, and the smell of food hung in the air. He must have been working up here, made himself a meal, and then decided, late as it was, to go down to the Coq Hardi. The blankets on the bed in the corner were neatly folded in a pile.

It was a bare little room, its walls, floor, and ceiling all of pine, still, in the heat from the stove, smelling faintly of the forest. There were a sturdy, handmade table, a couple of wooden chairs, and a hard-looking bed with a box underneath. A small cupboard hung in one corner, and a shelf over the bed held a few books. On pegs near the stove was a miscellany of things—ropes, a rucksack, an old khaki coat. Some spare tools lay beneath on a pile of clean sacking. In the far corner an upright ladder led to a small square trap door.

"Can't we stay here?" There was the faintest suspicion of a whine in Philippe's voice; he must be very nearly exhausted, and indeed, the thought of going further appalled me. And

191

where could we go? This must be what the mired fox felt like when it found its way to earth with the last calculated ounce of strength. I glanced at the shut door, at the glowing stove, at Philippe.

"Yes, of course." The car would be raking the road to the Villa Mireille. They would never look for us here. I said, "D'you think you could climb that ladder?"

"That? Yes. What's up there? Why do we have to go up there?"

"Well," I said, "there's only one bed down here, and that's Mr. Blake's. He may come back and need it. Besides, we'd be better hidden away up there, don't you think? Can you keep as still as a mouse if anybody comes in?"

He looked up at me, big eyes in a pinched little face. He was biting his lip. He nodded. I think if Léon de Valmy had come in at that moment I could have killed him with my bare hands. As it was I said briskly, "Well, we mustn't leave any sign we've been here, just in case somebody else comes looking for us before Mr. Blake gets home. Are your shoes wet? Ah, yes, they are a bit, aren't they? So are mine. We'll take them off—no, stay on the mat, *petit*—that's fine. Now, you carry them and perch here by the stove while I reconnoiter the loft."

Luckily the trap door was light, and, it seemed, in frequent use. At any rate it opened easily and quietly, and, standing on the ladder with my head and shoulders through the opening, I raked the loft with the beam of Philippe's torch. I had been praying fervently as I climbed that the place would be not too bad. Now I gave a sigh of relief. The loft was almost as clean as the living room, and quite dry. It was used as a store-room, and I could see some boxes and canisters, some more rope, a drum of wire, and—what was more to the purpose—a pile of tarpaulins and sacking on the chimney side of the steep-roofed little chamber.

I went quickly down again and reported this to Philippe. "It's beautifully warm," I said cheerfully, "right over the stove. Can you shove your shoes in your pockets and swarm away up while I collect some blankets? I'll pass them up to you. I can't spare the torch for a moment, so don't explore too far."

As I had hoped, there were extra blankets in the box under the bed. I dragged these out with wary flashes of the torch, and with some little trouble got them one by one up the ladder and into Philippe's waiting grasp. At last I pulled myself up beside him, and sent a final beam raking the little

192

room. . . . Nothing betrayed us; the floor was dry, the bed undisturbed, the door shut but not locked. . . .

We shut the trap door quietly and crawled—only in the center of the loft could one stand—to make our bed. The warmth from the chimney was pleasant, the blankets thick and comforting; the little dark loft with its steep-pitched roof gave us an illusion of safety.

So presently, having shared a stick of chocolate and said our prayers, from both of which exercises we derived immense comfort, we settled down for what remained of the night.

Philippe went to sleep almost immediately, curled in his usual small huddle up against me. I tucked the blankets thankfully around him, and then lay listening to his light breathing, and to the million tiny noises of the large silence that wrapped us in.

The breeze seemed finally to have dropped, for the forest—so close to us lying up under the shingles—was still. Only a faint intermittent murmur, like a long sigh, came from the pines. Inside the cottage came, from time to time, the tiny noises of a building stirring in its sleep; the creak of a settling board, the fall of charred wood in the stove, the tiny scratching of a mouse in the wall. I lay there, trying to empty my mind of worry and speculation about the coming day. It was Wednesday; only the one day to go and then I could deliver my charge, either at the Villa Mireille itself, or, if that proved difficult, by any telephone. The thing was easy. Easy.

And if, as seemed likely, William Blake called at the mountain hut in the morning, then it became easier still. Once we had him as escort the last shred of danger vanished. All I had to do now was relax and try to sleep. Neither Léon de Valmy nor Bernard would think of looking for us here. I had once spoken of "William" to Raoul (the thought brought me momentarily awake again) and he might connect the name—but of course Raoul wasn't in it. Raoul was in Paris. He had nothing to do with it. We were safe here, quite safe. . . . I could sleep. . . .

The lifting of the door latch sounded, in that sleepy silence, like a pistol shot.

Even as one part of my mind stampeded in panic like the mice now scurrying from the sound, the other rose light and dizzy with relief. It was William Blake, of course. It couldn't be anyone else. I must have slept longer than I'd thought, and now it was early morning, and he had come back.

I lifted my head to listen, but made no other movement. Something else which had nothing whatever to do with my

193

conclusions kept me clamped down like a hare in her form.

I waited. Philippe slept.

Below us the door shut very softly. The newcomer took two or three steps, then stopped. I could hear him breathing hard, as if he'd been hurrying. He stood perfectly still for a long time. I waited for the homely sounds of a log in the stove, the rasp of a match, the opening of the scullery door, but there was nothing except the stillness, and the rapid breathing. And then there was a pause of complete silence, as even the breathing stopped.

I think mine did too. I knew now it wasn't William Blake. I knew why he had paused with held breath, standing with ears at the stretch and probably a torch-beam raking the darkness. He had been listening for sounds of the quarry. It couldn't be true, but it was. The hound was here already.

Then his breath came out again with a gasp, and he moved across the floor.

Now came the quiet chunk of closing shutters, the chink of the lamp globe, the scrape of a match; but the sounds were about as homely as the click of a cocked gun.

I heard the slight clatter of the globe sliding into its socket, then a muttered curse as, I suppose, the wick went out again. Seconds later came the scrape of another match.

It couldn't be morning yet, and it certainly wasn't William Blake. The curse had been in French, and in a voice I thought I recognized. Bernard's. The hunt was up with a vengeance.

The lamp was burning now. I could see, here and there, tiny threads of light between the ceiling boards. He was moving about, with a slow deliberation that was far more terrifying than haste. Only his breathing still hurried, and that, surely, should have been under control by now. . . .

I found that I was shaking, crouched together in my form of blankets. It wasn't the climb up the mountainside that had hurried Bernard's breathing and made his big hands clumsy on the lamp. It was excitement, the tongue-lolling excitement of the hound as it closes in. He knew we were here.

He crossed the floor to the base of the ladder.

But he was only making for the scullery. I heard the door open, then more sounds of that deliberate exploration. A bolt scaped: he was barring the back exit. He was coming back.

My bitten lips tasted salt; my hands were clenched so tightly on a fold of blankets that my nails scored the stuff. I hadn't told Philippe about Bernard, had I? If he should wake, he might not be frightened . . . but let him sleep, dear Lord,

: him sleep. . . . Perhaps Bernard doesn't know about the
't; perhaps he won't notice the ladder . . . if only Philippe
esn't wake up and give us away. . . .

He came out of the scullery and shut the door. This time
didn't pause to look around. He took two unhurried strides
ross to the ladder. I heard the wood creak as he laid hold of

Someone trod rapidly across the veranda outside. I heard
rnard jerk out an oath under his breath. The door opened
ain. A strange voice said, "*Que diable?* Oh, Bernard, it's
u. What the devil are you doing up here?"

The ladder creaked again as Bernard released it. "*Holà,
les.*" He sounded sober enough, but his voice was thick and
t too steady. He seemed disconcerted, almost shaken. "I
ght ask you the same, mightn't I? What brings you up here
this hour?"

The other shut the door and came across the room. "Night
trols, a curse on it. Ever since we had that fire up in Bois-
ussel we've had them. The boss is convinced it's willful
mage and he won't listen to anything else. So I have to
mp up and down between Bois-Roussel and Soubirous the
ole bloody night, and me only a fortnight wed. Dawn's a
sy time to be out in anyway, and when I think where I
ght be—"

Bernard laughed and moved away from the ladder. "Hard
k, friend. I expect you make out, *tout de même.*"

"As to that," said Jules frankly, "I can go to bed the whole
ody day, can't I? Here, let's make this stove up . . . aha,
t's better! Now, tell me what brings you up here at this
ur? It's gone five, surely? If you're wanting the English-
n he's down at the Coq Hardi for the night. What's he
ne?"

Bernard said, so slowly that I could almost hear the calcula-
n clicking behind the words, "No, it's not the Englishman."

"No? What then? Don't tell me you're my fire-raiser,
rnard?" Jules laughed. "Come now, what's up? Come clean
I'll have to take you in for trespass. It's bound to be either
ty or a woman, and I'm damned if I can see why either
uld bring you up here."

"As it happens, it's both," said Bernard. "There's queer
ings at the Chateau Valmy tonight. You've heard of young
ilippe's governess; Martin's her name?"

"The pretty little thing that's been dangling after Mon-
ur Raoul? Who hasn't? What's she done?"

"She's disappeared, that's what she's done and—"

"Well, what if she has? And what the devil would she [be] doing up here anyway? There's an obvious place to look f[or] her, my friend, and that's in Monsieur Raoul's bed, not th[e] Englishman's."

"For God's sake can't you keep your mind out of bed f[or] two minutes?"

"No," said Jules simply.

"Well, try. And let me finish what I was telling you. Her[e.] Have a cigarette."

A match snapped and flared. The sharp smell of th[e] Gauloise came up through the boards to where I lay. I cou[ld] see the two men as plainly as if the ceiling were of glass, the[ir] dark faces lit by the crackling stove, the blue smoke of th[e] cigarettes drifting up through the warm air to hang betwee[n] them. Bernard said, still in that queer note of overmeasure[d] thoughtfulness, "The boy's gone, too."

"The boy?"

"Young Philippe."

A pause, and a long soft whistle. "Great God! Are yo[u] sure?"

"Damn it, of course we're sure! They've both vanishe[d.] Madame went along a bit ago to have a look at the boy—he[']s not strong, you know, and it seems she's been worried abou[t] him. She's not sleeping very well . . . anyway, she went along and he wasn't in his room. She went to rouse the governes[s] and found her gone, too. No word, no note, no nothing. We've searched the château from cellar to roof, the Maste[r] and I. No sign. They've gone."

"But what in the world for? It doesn't make sense. Unles[s] the girl and Monsieur Raoul—"

"You can leave him out of it," said Bernard sourly. "I'v[e] told you she's not snug in *his* bed. For one thing, what woul[d] she want with the boy if that's where she's bound? He'd no[t] be a help, would he?"

"No, indeed," said Jules, much struck. "But—well, th[e] thing's crazy! Where would they go, and why?"

"God knows." Bernard sounded almost indifferent. "An[d] they'll probably turn up very soon anyway. The Master didn['t] seem very worried, though Madame was properly upset. It' made her ill—she has a bad heart, you know—so the Maste[r] told me to get out and scout around the place for them. I've been down to Thonon, but there's no sign. . . . He paused and then I heard him yawn.

Beside me Philippe moved a little and stretched in hi[s] sleep. His shoes must have been lying near him, and throug[h]

196

the blankets his knee touched one of them and pushed it with a small scraping sound over the boards. It was the slightest of noises, but it seemed to fill the pause like thunder.

But Bernard had heard nothing. He was saying, indifferently, "Ten to one it's all nonsense anyway. I probably shouldn't have told you about it, but since you've caught me on your land—" He laughed.

"But why should they be up here?"

"The Master's idea. It seems the girl was seen in Thonon with the Englishman. I tell you, the whole thing's crazy. It stands to reason it's only one of two things; either they're both off together on some silly frolic, or the boy's gone out adventuring on his own and the girl's found him gone and set off to fetch him back."

Jules sounded dubious. "It doesn't seem very likely."

Bernard yawned again. "No, it doesn't, but boys are queer cattle—almost as queer as women, friend Jules. And he and the Martin girl are very thick. The two of them had a midnight feast the other night, so I'm told. They'll not have gone far . . . the boy hasn't got his papers. Depend on it, it'll be some silly lark or other. What else could it be?"

"Well, as long as Monsieur isn't worried," said Jules doubtfully. There was a little silence, through which I heard the hiss of the stove and the shifting of a man's feet. Then Bernard said briskly, "Well, I think I'd better be off. Coming?'

Jules didn't answer directly. He said, in a voice which had a tentative, sidelong sound, "That girl Martin . . . There was talk. A lot of talk."

"Oh?" Bernard didn't sound interested. As if you didn't know, I thought, lying in my form not four feet from his head.

"People were saying," said Jules hesitantly, "that she and Monsieur Raoul were fiancés."

"Oh, that," said Bernard. A pause. "Well, it's true."

"Diable! Is it really? So she got him?"

"If you put it that way."

"Don't you?"

"Well," said Bernard, sounding amused, "I imagine Monsieur Raoul may have had something to say in the matter. You can't tell me that any girl, however pretty, could lead that one up the garden path unless he very much wanted to go."

"There's ways and ways," said Jules sagely. "He knows what he's about, of course, but damn it, there comes a time. . . ."

197

He laughed. "And she's nothing like his usual. That gets us every time, doesn't it? Fools."

"He was never a fool, said Bernard. "And if he wants to marry her—well, that's what he wants."

"You don't persuade me he's really fallen, do you? For the little English girl? Be your age, man. He wants to sleep with her and she won't let him."

"Maybe. But it's quite a step from that to marriage . . . for such as him."

"You're telling me. Well, perhaps the reason's more pressing still. Perhaps she has slept with him and now there's a little something to force his hand. It has been done," said Jules largely. "I should know."

"Oh? Congratulations." Bernard's voice sounded almost absent. "But I doubt if that's it."

That's big of you, I thought, biting my knuckles above him while Jules's words crawled like lice along my skin. The stove top clanked as someone lifted it to drop a cigarette butt on the logs. Bernard said again, "Look, I must go. Are you coming?"

"Bernard . . ." Jules had dropped his voice for all the world as if he knew I was listening. He sounded urgent and slightly ashamed. The effect was so queer, so horrible almost, that my skin prickled again.

"Well?" said Bernard, impatiently.

"The girl—"

"Well?" said Bernard again.

"Are you so sure . . . that she—" Jules paused and I heard him swallow—"that she means well by the boy?"

"What the devil d'you mean?"

"Well . . . I told you there'd been talk. People have been saying that she . . . well, has ambitions."

"Ambitions? Who hasn't? Very likely she has, but why should that make her 'not mean well' by the brat? What d'you—" Bernard's voice trailed off and I heard him draw in his breath. He said on a very odd note, "You can't mean what I think you mean, friend Jules."

Jules sounded defiant. "Why not? Why should her ambitions stop at marrying Monsier Raoul? What does anyone know about her after all? Who is she?"

"An English orphan—I think of good family. That's all I know." A pause. "She's fond of the boy."

Jules said, "The boy will not make her Madame la Comtesse de Valmy."

A longer pause. Bernard's laugh, breaking it, sounded a little strained. "The sooner you get back to that bed of yours

198

the better, mon ami. The night air's giving you fancies. And I must get back. Ten to one the thing's over and they're both safely back in bed. I hope Monsieur gives them hell in the morning for all the trouble they've caused. Come now—"

Jules said stubbornly, "You may laugh. But I tell you that Monsieur Garcin said—"

"That old woman of a chemist? You should have better things to do than listen to village clack."

"All the same—"

Bernard said irritably, "For God's sake, Jules! You can't make every pretty girl a criminal because she makes a play for her betters. Now look, I've got to go. Which way are you bound?"

Jules sounded sulky. "Down toward Soubirous. It's wearing on for morning."

"And your trick's over? Right. I'll go down that way with you. I brought the brake up to the end of the track, so I'll run you down. You go on now while I turn the lamp down and close up."

"Okay." The stove top clanked again as the second cigarette followed the first. I heard Jules tread heavily toward the door. Beside me Philippe stirred again and muttered something in his sleep. The footsteps stopped. Jules said sharply, "What was that?"

"What?"

"I heard something. Through there, perhaps, or—"

Bernard said softly, "Open the door. Quickly." Jules obeyed. The fresh gray-morning smell pierced the blue scent of cigarettes and woodsmoke. "Nothing there." Jules's voice came as if from a distance. I imagined him out on the veranda peering around the wall.

Bernard, just below us still, laughed his short hard laugh. "A mouse, friend Jules. You're seeing a tiger in every tree tonight, aren't you?" He stretched noisily and yawned. "Well I'm for bed as well, though mine'll not be as warm as yours, I'm afraid. What time does the Englishman get up here as a rule?"

"Pretty early—that is, if he's coming up here this morning. I wouldn't know."

"Ah. Well, let's be going. I hope to God the excitement's over down at Valmy. Why the hell the Master should send me up here anyway I can't imagine. Go on, mon ami. I'll turn the lamp down and close up. I'll follow you."

"I'll wait for you."

"Eh? Oh, very well . . . there, that's it. I suppose the

stove's safe? Yes, well . . . I'd have thought that bed of yours would have put a bit of hurry into you, friend Jules." He was going. His voice dwindled toward the door. Beside me Philippe moved his head and his breath touched my cheek softly.

Jules's voice said, with the good temper back in it, "Ah, that bed of mine. Let me tell you, copain . . ."

The door shut quietly, lopping off Jules's embroidery of his favorite motif. I heard his voice faintly, fading off into the dawn-hush that held the forest. I hadn't realized how quiet it was outside. Not a bough moved; not a twig brushed the shingles. Philippe breathed softly beside me. From somewhere a wood pigeon began its hoarse cooing.

Soon the sun would be up. It would be a lovely day. I lay back beside Philippe, shaking as if I had the fever.

The reprieve from terror had been so sudden that it had thrown me out of gear. All through that conversation I had crouched, straining every sense to interpret the two men's intentions, but with my mind spinning in a useless, formless confusion. At one moment it seemed to me that I ought to call out and disclose our presence to Jules, who was not a Valmy employee, and who would at any rate save us from any harm that Bernard might intend. At the next moment I found myself dazedly listening to Jules accusing, Bernard defending me. And what he'd had to say was odd enough: Léon de Valmy was not perturbed; it was known that I was fond of the boy; and Monsieur Raoul "could be left out of it. . . ." Bernard, in fact, had taken some pains to suppress the very gossip that I had imagined he and Albertine had engineered. No wonder I was shaken and confused. Had I been wrong? Could I possibly have been wrong? Surely Léon de Valmy, if he were guilty, must know from my flight with Philippe that I suspected him. If he were guilty, he couldn't be unperturbed; and if he were guilty, why should Bernard defend me to Jules? And Raoul was out of it. Dear Lord, had I been wrong?

But something fretted at me still. The whole conversation had had about it a curious air of inversion, something off-key that had sounded in Bernard's defense of me and in that slow, deliberative tone he had used.

I lay there quietly, savoring our safety and the stillness of Dieudonné, while the pigeon cooed peacefully in the pine-tops outside, and the racing blood in my body slowed down to normal. Philippe stirred again and said, "Mademoiselle?"

and relaxed once more into sleep. I smiled a little, thinking with another quick uprush of relief that, had he spoken so clearly before, Bernard must surely have heard him. After all, he had been standing just below us, while Jules was almost at the door. . . .

On the thought I came upright in the darkness, dry-lipped, my heart going wild again in my breast.

Bernard must surely have heard him. Of course Bernard had heard him.

Bernard had known we were there.

So that was it. No other explanation would fit the facts and explain the curious overtones to the conversation. No wonder it had seemed off-key. No wonder I had been bogged down between friend and enemy.

Bernard had known. And it hadn't suited him to find us while Jules was there. That was why, though he'd been interrupted on his way up to the loft, he hadn't finished the search. That was why he had refused to "hear" what Jules had heard; why he had tried to get Jules to go on ahead while he stayed behind to "close up."

It also explained very effectively his playing down of the effect of our flight at Valmy. Whatever was discovered in the morning, it was obvious that Bernard's presence in the forest would have to be explained. The simplest and safest thing to do was obviously to tell some version of the truth. With me crouched not four feet above his head he'd had to play a very careful game. I was listening, and he didn't want to flush the quarry . . . not before he had a chance to come back alone.

Because of course he would come back. I was out of my blankets almost before the thought touched me, and creeping soundlessly across the floor to the trap door. For all I had heard Jules talking away down the forest path I was taking no risks of a door that closed to leave the enemy inside and waiting. I lay flat beside the trap and slowly, slowly, eased it up till the tiniest crack showed between it and the floor. I peered through as best I could. Some light through the badly-fitting shutters showed an empty room.

I flew back to Philippe's side, but as I put out a hand to shake him awake I checked myself. I knelt beside him, my hands clutched tightly together, and shut my eyes. I could not waken the child on this wave of shaking terror. I must take control again. I must. I gave myself twenty seconds, counting them steadily.

201

He would come back. He would take Jules home in the shooting brake, let himself be seen starting for Valmy, and then he would come back. He would be as quick as he could, because the night was wearing on for morning, and the night and the day were all they had.

I didn't take the thought further; I didn't want it put into words. I left it formless, a beat of fear through my body. How they would get away with it I couldn't—wouldn't—imagine, but in my present state of mind and in that dark hole at the top of the lonely forest anything seemed possible. I knelt there and made myself count steadily on through perhaps the worst twenty seconds of my life, while the terror, pressing closer, blew itself up into fantasy . . . the Demon King watching us from behind that bright window a mile away, hunting us down from his wheel chair by some ghastly kind of radar that tracked us through the forest. . . . I whipped the mad thought aside but the image persisted; Léon de Valmy, like a deformed and giant shadow, reaching out for us wherever we happened to be. Why had I thought I could get the better of him? Nobody ever had, except one.

The silly tears were running down my face. I bent to rouse Philippe.

Seventh Coach

Chapter XVI

Oh Sammy, Sammy, vy worn't there a alleybil

DICKENS: *Pickwick Papers.*

HE came awake instantly. "Mademoiselle? Is it morning?"

"Yes. Get up, chicken. We've got to go."

"All right. Are you crying, mademoiselle?"

"Good heavens, no! What makes you think that?"

"Something fell on me. Wet."

"Dew, mon p'tit. The roof leaks. Now come along."

He jumped up straight away, and in a very short space of time we were down that ladder, and Philippe was lacing his shoes while I made a lightning raid on William Blake's cupboards.

"Biscuits," I said cheerfully, "and butter and—yes, a tin of sardines. And I brought cake and chocolate. Here's riches! Trust a man to look after himself. He's all stocked up like a squirrel."

Philippe smiled. His face looked a little less pinched this morning, though the gray light filtering through the shutters still showed him pale. God knows how it showed me. I felt like a walking ghost.

"Can we make up the stove, mademoiselle?"

"Afraid not. We'd better not wait here for Monsieur Blake. There are too many people about in the wood. We'll go on."

"Where to? Soubirous? Is that where he is?"

"Yes, but we're not going toward Soubirous. I think we'll make straight for Thonon."

"Now?"

"Yes."

"Without breakfast?" His mouth drooped and I'm sure mine did too. There had been a tin of coffee in the cupboard and the stove was hot; I'd have given almost anything to have taken time to make some. Almost anything.

I said, "We'll find a place when the sun's up and have breakfast outside. Here, put these in your pockets." I threw a quick glance around the hut. "All right, let's go. We'll make sure no one's about first, shall we? You take that window . . . carefully now."

We reconnoitered as cautiously as we could from the windows, but anyone could have been hidden in the trees, watching and waiting. If Bernard had taken Jules down to Soubirous he wouldn't be back yet, but even so I found myself scanning the dim ranks of the trees with anxious fear. Nothing stirred there. We would have to chance it.

The moment of leaving the hut was as bad as any we had yet had. My hand on the latch, I looked down at Philippe.

"You remember the open space, the ride, that we came up? It's just through the first belt of trees. We mustn't go across it while we're in sight of Valmy. We must go up this side of it, in the trees, till we've got over the top of the ridge. It's not far. Understand?"

He nodded.

"When I open this door, you are to go out. Don't wait for me. Don't look back. Turn left—that way—uphill, and run as fast as you can. Don't stop for anything or anyone."

"What about you?"

"I'll be running with you. But if—anything—should happen, you are not to wait for me. You are to go on, across the hill, down to the nearest house, and ask them to take you to the police station in Thonon. Tell them who you are and what has happened. Okay?"

His eyes were too big and bright, but he nodded silently. On an impulse, I bent and kissed him.

"Now, little squirrel," I said, as I opened the door, "run!"

Nothing happened, after all. We slipped out of the hut unchallenged, and still unchallenged reached the summit of the ridge. There we paused. We had broken out of our hiding place with more regard for speed than silence, but now we recollected ourselves and moved quietly but still quickly for a hundred yards more of gentle downhill before we halted on the edge of the ride.

Peering through a convenient hazel bush we looked uphill and down. The ride was straight and empty. On the far side the trees promised thick cover.

We ran across. Pigeons came batting out of the pine tops like rockets, but that was all. We scurried deep into the young forest of larch and spruce, still so thickly set that we had to brush a way between the boughs with hands constantly up to protect our eyes.

204

The wood held the wet chill of early morning, and the boughs dripped moisture. We were soon soaked. But we held on doggedly on a long northward slant that I hoped would eventually bring us to a track or country road heading toward Thonon.

It was Philippe who found the cave. I was ahead of him, forging a way through the thick branches and holding them back for his passage, when I pushed through a wet wall of spruce, to find myself on the edge of an outcrop of rock. It was a miniature cliff that stuck out of the half-grown trees like the prow of a ship. The forest parted like a river and flowed down to either side, leaving the little crag with its mossy green apron open to the sky. I could hear the drip of a spring.

I said, "Watch your step, Philippe. There's a drop here. Make your way down the side. That way."

He slithered obediently down. I followed him.

"Miss Martin, there's a cave!"

I said thankfully, "And a spring. I think we might have a drink and a rest, don't you?"

Philippe said wistfully, "And breakfast?"

"Good heavens. Yes, of course." I had forgotten all about food in the haste that was driving me away from Bernard, but now I realized how hungry I was. "We'll have it straight away."

It wasn't really a cave, just a dry corner under an overhang, but it provided some shelter from the gray forest chill, and—more—gave us an illusion of safety. We ate without speaking, Philippe seemingly intent on his food, I with my ears straining for sounds that were not of the forest. But I heard nothing. The screech of a jay, the spattering of waterdrops off the trees, the clap of a pigeon's wing and the trickle of the spring beside us . . . these made up the silence that held us in its safety.

And presently the sun came up and took the tops of the springtime larches like fire.

It may sound a silly thing to say, but I almost enjoyed that morning. The spell of the sun was potent. It poured down, hot and bright, while in front of it the wet grayness steamed off the woods in veils of mist, leaving the spruces gleaming darkly brilliant and lighting the tiny larch flowers to a red flush along the boughs. The smell was intoxicating. We didn't hurry; we were both tired, and, since we had followed no paths, it would only be the purest chance that would put

205

Bernard onto our trail. And on this lovely morning it was impossible to imagine that such an evil chance existed. The nightmare was as good as over. We were free, we were on our way to Thonon, and Monsieur Hippolyte arrived tonight. . . . And meantime the sun and the woods between them lent to our desperate adventure, not the glamour of romance, but the everyday charm of a picnic.

We held hands and walked sedately. In the older belts of the forest the going was easy. Here the trees were big and widely spaced, and between them shafts of brilliant sunlight slanted down onto drifts of last-year's cones and vivid pools of moss. Ever and again the wood echoed to the clap and flurry of wings as the ringdoves rocketed off their roosting places up into the high blue.

Presently ahead of us we saw brighter sunlight at the edge of the mature forest. This ended sharply, like a cliff, for its whole steep length washed by a river of very young firs—babies, in all the beauty of rosy stems and a green as soft as wood sorrel. They split the older forest with a belt of open sunshine seventy yards wide. Between them the grass was thick and springing emerald already through the yellow of winter. On their baby stems the buds showed fat and pink.

We halted again at the edge of the tall trees before braving the open space. The young green flowed down the mountain-side between its dark borders, plunging into the shadow that still lay blue at the bottom of Dieudonné valley. Looking that way I could see the flat fields where cattle grazed; the line of willows that marked a stream; a scatter of houses; a farm where someone—tiny in the distance—stood among swarming white dots that must be hens.

No one was on the hillside. The inevitable wood pigeon played high above the treetops, riding the blue space like surf in ecstatic curved swoops and swallow dives, wings raked back and breast rounded to the thrust of the air.

Nothing else moved. We plunged—Philippe was chest-high—across the river of lovely young trees. The grass-green tufts brushed hands and knees softly, like feathers; they smelled of warm resin. Halfway across Philippe stopped short and cried, "Look!" and there was a fox slipping like a leaf-brown shadow into the far woods. He paused as he reached them and looked back, one paw up and ears mildly inquiring. The sun was red on his fur. Along his back the fine hairs shone like gold. Then he slid quietly out of sight and the forest was ours again.

All morning the enchantment held, our luck spinning out fine and strong, like the filigree plot of a fairy tale. Almost, at times, we forgot the dark and urgent reason for our journey. Almost.

Some time before noon we came, after a slowish journey of frequent stops, and one or two forced diversions, on the road had hoped to find. This was a narrow road between steep banks, that wound stonily the way we wanted to go, high above the valley which carried the main traffic route to the south. Our last stage had taken us through a rough tract of thorns and dead bracken, so it was with some thankfulness that we clambered through the wire fence and negotiated the dead brambles that masked the ditch.

Our luck made us a little careless. As I landed on the gravel surface of the road, and turned to reach a hand to Philippe, the clang of metal and the swish of a car's tires close behind me brought me around like a bayed deer.

A battered Renault coasted around the bend in a quiet whiffle of dust that sounded a good deal more expensive than it looked. She slithered—with a few bangs and rattles that belied that expensively silent engine—to a stop beside us. The driver, a stout gray-stubbled character in filthy blue denims, regarded us benevolently and without the least curiosity from under the brim of a horrible hat.

He was a man of few words. He jerked a thumb toward the north. I said, "S'il vous plaît, monsieur." He jerked the thumb south. I said, "Merci, monsieur," and Philippe and I clambered into the back seat to join the other passengers already there. These were a collie dog, a pig in what looked like a green string bag, and a rather nasty collection of white hens in a slatted box. A large sack of potatoes rode de luxe beside the farmer in the front seat. As I began, through the embraces of the collie, to say rather awkwardly, "This is very kind of you, monsieur," the Renault lurched forward and took a sharp bend at a fairly high speed and still without benefit of engine, but now with such a succession of clanks and groans and other body noises that conversation—I realized thankfully —was an impossibility.

He took us nearly two miles, then stopped to put us down where a farm track joined the road.

To my thanks he returned a nod, jerked his thumb in explanation down toward the farm, and the Renault after it. The track down which he vanished was a dirt road of about one in four. We watched, fascinated, until the Renault skated to a precarious standstill some two inches from the wall of a Dutch barn, and then turned to go on our way, much heartened by an encounter with someone who quite obviously had never heard of the errant Comte de Valmy, and who was apparently content to take life very much as it came. He might also, I thought cheerfully, be deaf and dumb. Our luck seemed to be running strongly enough even for that.

Our road ran fairly openly now along the hillside, so we kept to its easier walking. The lift had done something to cheer Philippe's flagging spirits; he walked gamely and without complaint, but I could see that he was tiring, and we still had some way to go . . . and I had no idea what we might yet have to face.

He set off now cheerfully enough, chatting away about the collie and the pig. I listened absently, my eyes on the dusty length of road curling ahead of us, and my ears intent on sounds coming from behind. Here the road wound between high banks topped with whins. I found myself watching them for cover as we passed.

Half a mile; three-quarters; Philippe got a stone in his shoe and we stopped to take it out. We went on more slowly after that. A mile; a mile and a quarter; he wasn't talking now, and had begun to drag a bit; I thought apprehensively of blisters, and slackened the pace still further.

I was just going to suggest leaving the road to find a place for lunch when I heard another car. An engine, this time coming from the north. She was climbing fast, but for all that, making very little more noise than the old Renault coasting. A big car: a powerful car . . . I don't pretend I recognized the silken snarl of that engine, but I knew who it was. The sound raked up my backbone like a cruel little claw.

I breathed, "Here's a car. Hide, Philippe!"

I had told him what to do. He swarmed up the bank as quick and neat as a shrew mouse, with me after him. At the top of the bank was a thicket of whins, dense walls of green three or four feet high with little gaps and clearings of sunlit grass where one could lie invisibly. We flung ourselves down in one of these small citadels as the Cadillac took a bend three hundred yards away. The road leveled and ran straight below us. He went by with a spatter of dust and the hush of a gust of wind. The top was down and I saw his face. The little claw closed on the base of my spine.

There was no sound in the golden noon except the ripple of a skylark's song. Philippe whispered beside me, "That was my cousin Raoul, mademoiselle."

"Yes."

"I thought he was in Paris?"

"So did I."

"Is he—couldn't we have—wouldn't he have helped us?"

"I don't know, Philippe."

He said, on a note of childish wonder, "But . . . he was so nice at the midnight feast."

A pause.

"Wasn't he, mademoiselle?"

"I—yes. Yes, Philippe, he was."

Another pause. Then, still on that terrible little note of wonder, "My cousin Raoul? My cousin Raoul, too? Don't you trust him, mademoiselle?"

"Yes," I said, and then, desperately, "No."

"But why—"

"Don't Philippe, please. I can't—" I looked away from him and said tightly, "Don't you see, we can't take risks of any kind. However sure we are we've got to be—we've got to be sure." I finished a bit raggedly. "Don't you see?"

If he saw anything odd in this remarkably silly speech he didn't show it. With a shy but a curiously unchildlike gesture he put out a hand and touched mine. "Mademoiselle—"

"I'm not crying, Philippe. Not really. Don't worry. It's only that I'm tired and I didn't get much sleep last night and it's long past time for food." Somehow I smiled at him and dabbed at my face while he watched me with troubled eyes. "Sorry, mon p'tit. You're standing this trek of ours like a Trojan and I'm behaving like a fool of a woman. I'm all right now."

"We'll have lunch," said Philippe, taking a firm hold of the situation.

"Okay, Napoleon," I said, putting away my handkerchief, "but we'd better stay where we are for a little while longer, just to make sure."

"That he's really gone?"

"Yes," I said, "that he's really gone."

Philippe relaxed obediently into the shelter of the whins, and lay chin on hand, watching the road below him through a gap in the thick green. I turned on my back so that the sun was on my face, and closed my eyes. Even then I didn't want to face it. I wanted to go on, blind, cowardly, instinct-driven . . . but as I lay there listening for the engine of his car the thing that I had been trying to keep back, dammed out of mind, broke over me. And before I had thought further than simply his name I knew how very far I was—still was—

from jettisoning him along with the others. Instinct might make me shrink from Léon de Valmy, and keep me a chilly mile away from Héloïse, but—it seemed—whatever evidence, "proof" I was offered, I still sprang without thought straight to his defense.

Because you want it that way. Haven't you been enough of a fool, Cinderella? I stirred on the warm grass with sharp discomfort, but still somewhere inside me hammered the insistent advocate for the defense. . . .

Everything that had happened since Raoul had entered the affair, everything he had said and done, could bear an innocent interpretation as well as a guilty one . . . or so I told myself, groping wearily, confusedly, back through the fogs of memory. A word here, a look there—never did frailer witnesses plead more desperately. He had not known of the attempts to get a non-French-speaking governess; he hadn't been worried, only amused, at the thought that I might have eavesdropped on his father's conversation; he had seemed as shocked as I was over the shooting in the wood; his sharp questions about William Blake, and that curiously touchy temper he had shown, might have been due to jealousy or some other preoccupation, and not to the realization that the "friendless" orphan was in touch with a tough-looking Englishman in the neighborhood; and that blast of the horn that brought Philippe out onto the balcony—that might have been fortuitous. Bernard hadn't spoken of it. As for Bernard's flat statement to Berthe that it had been Raoul who had shot at Philippe in the wood, I didn't regard that as evidence at all. Even in his drunken mood, and however sure he had made himself of Berthe, Bernard might well hesitate to admit that kind of guilt to her. Then at the dance . . .

But here the pleading memories whirled up into a ragged and flying confusion, a blizzard so blinding that, like Alice among the cards, I came to myself trying to beat them off. And I was asked to believe that these, too, were dead and painted like a pack of cards? Something to put away now in a drawer, and take out again, years hence, dusty, to thumb over in a dreary game of solitaire? Yes, there it was. For Philippe's sake I had to assume Raoul's guilt. I couldn't afford to do anything else. The child had only one life to lose, and I couldn't stake it. Raoul was guilty till he could be proved innocent. In that, if in no other part of my crazy fear-driven plans, I had been right. He was here but we couldn't run to him.

Close to my ear Philippe whispered, "Mademoiselle."

I opened my eyes. His face was close to mine. It was scared. He breathed, "There's someone on the hilltop behind. He's just come through the wood. I think it's Bernard. D'you suppose he's in it too?"

I nodded and put a swift finger to my lips, then lifted my head cautiously and peered through the screening whins toward the hill behind us. At first I saw nothing but the trees and the tangling banks of scrub, but presently I picked him out. It was Bernard. He was above us, about two hundred yards away, standing beside a big spruce. There was no need to tell Philippe to keep close; we both lay as still as rabbits in our thickets of green. Bernard was standing motionless, scanning the slope below him. The moments dragged. He was looking our way. His gaze seemed to catch on us, to linger, to pass on, to return . . .

He was coming quickly down the hill in our direction.

I suppose a rabbit stays still while death stalks it just because it is hoping against hope that this is not death. We stayed still.

He had covered half the distance, not hurrying, when I heard the Cadillac coming back.

My hand pressed hard over Philippe's on the short turf. I turned my head and craned to stare up the road. My muscles tensed themselves as if they would carry me without my willing it straight down into his path.

I don't know to this day whether I really would have run to him then or not, but before I could move I heard the brakes go on. The tires bit at the soft gravel of the road and the car pulled up short some fifty yards away from us. I could see him through my screen of whins. He was looking uphill toward Bernard. The horn blared twice. Bernard had stopped. I saw Raoul lift his hand. Bernard changed course and walked quickly down the hill toward the car. He jumped the ditch and hurried up to the door. Raoul said something to him, and I saw Bernard shake his head, then turn with a wide gesture that included all the hill from where we lay back to Dieudonné. Then Raoul gave a sideways jerk of the head and Bernard went around the hood and got in beside him.

The Cadillac went slowly by below us. Raoul was lighting a cigarette and his head was bent. Bernard was talking earnestly to him.

I turned to meet Philippe's eyes.

After a while I got up slowly and reached a hand down to him.

"Come along," I said, "let's get back from the road and

211

find somewhere to have lunch."

After we had eaten we took to the woods again without seeing another soul, and some time in the middle of the afternoon our path led us out of a wild tangle of hornbeam and honeysuckle onto a little green plateau; and there, not so very far to the north of us we saw at last, through the tops of the still-bare trees, the blue levels of Lac Léman.

Chapter XVII

Upon thy side, against myself I'll fight,
And prove thee virtuous. . . .

SHAKESPEARE: Sonnet 88.

"THIS," I said, "is where we stop for a while."

Philippe was surverying the little dell. It was sheltered and sun-drenched, a green shelf in the middle of the wood. Behind us the trees and bushes of the wild forest crowded up the hill, dark holly and the bone-pale boughs of ash gleaming sharp through a mist of birch as purple as bloom on a grape. Below the open shelf the tangle of boughs fell steeply toward Thonon. Those bright roofs and colored walls were, I judged, little more than a mile away. I saw the gleam of a spire, and the smooth sweep of some open square with brilliant flowerbeds and a white coping above the lake. Even in the town there were trees; willows in precise Chinese shapes, cypresses spearing up Italian-fashion against the blue water, and here and there against some painted wall a burst of pale blossom like a cloud.

At my feet a small stream ran, and a little way off, under the flank of a fallen birch, there were primroses.

Philippe slipped a hand into mine. "I know this place."

"Do you? How?"

"I've been here for a picnic. There were foxgloves and we had *pâtisseries belges*."

"Do you remember the way down into Thonon? Where does it land us?"

He pointed to the left. "The path goes down there, like steps. There's a fence at the bottom and a sort of lane. It takes you to a road and you come out by a garage and a shop where they keep a ginger cat with no tail."

"Is it a main street?"

212

He wrinkled his forehead at me. "We—ell . . ."

"Is it full of shops and people and traffic?"

"Oh, no. It has trees and high walls. People live there."

A residential area. So much the better. I said, "Could you find your way from there to the Villa Mireille?"

"Of course. There's a path between two garden walls that takes you to the road above the lake and then you go down and down and down till you get to the bottom road where the gate is. We always went by the funicular."

"I'm afraid we can't. Well, that's wonderful, Philippe. We're practically there! And with you as guide—" I smiled at him—"we can't go far wrong, can we? Later we'll see how much I can remember of what you told me about the Villa Mireille, but just for the moment I think we'll stop and rest."

"Here?"

"Right here."

He sat thankfully down on the fallen birch. "My legs are aching."

"I'm not surprised."

"Are yours?"

"Well, no. But I did miss my sleep last night and if I don't rest this minute I shall go to sleep on my feet."

"Like a horse," said Philippe, and giggled, albeit a little thinly.

I flicked his cheek. "Exactly like a horse. Now, you get tea ready while I make the bed."

"English tea?"

"Of course."

The grass was quite dry, and the sun stood hot overhead in the calm air. I knelt down beside the birch log and carefully removed two dead boughs, a thistle, and some sharp stones from our "bed," then spread out my coat. Philippe, solemn-eyed, was dividing the last of William's biscuits into equal parts. He handed me mine, together with half a stick of chocolate. We ate slowly and in silence.

Presently I said, "Philippe."

"Yes, mademoiselle?"

"We'll be down in Thonon pretty soon now. We really ought to go straight to the police."

The big eyes stared. He said nothing.

I said, "I don't know where the nearest British Consul is, or we'd go to him. I don't suppose there's one in Évian, and we can't get to Geneva because you've no passport. So it should be the police."

Still he said nothing. I waited. I think he knew as well as I did that the first thing the police would do would be to face us both with Léon de Valmy. After a while he asked, "What time will my Uncle Hippolyte get home?"

"I've no idea. He may be here already, but I think we may have to wait till late . . . after dark."

A pause. "Where is this Monsieur Blake?"

"I don't know. He may be out somewhere in Dieudonné, or he may have gone back up to the hut. But we—we couldn't very well wait for him there." He gave me a quick look and I added hastily, "We might telephone the Coq Hardi from Thonon. They might be able to give him a message. Yes, that's a good idea. We can try that."

Still he said nothing. I looked at him a little desperately. "You want to go and look for your uncle first? Is that it?"

A nod.

"Philippe, you'd be quite safe if we went to the police, you know. We—we should do that. They'd be frightfully nice to you, and they'd look after you till your Uncle Hippolyte came—better than I can. We really should."

"No. Please. Please, Miss Martin."

I knew I ought to insist. It wasn't only the eloquence of Philippe's silences, and the clutch of the small cold hand that decided me. Nor was it only that I was afraid of facing Léon de Valmy . . . though, with the anger spilled out of me and dissolved in weariness, my very bones turned coward at the thought of confronting him in the presence of the police.

There was another reason. I admitted it out of a cold gray self-contempt. I might have braved Léon de Valmy and the police, but I didn't want to face Raoul. I was a fool; moreover, if I allowed any more risk to the child I was a criminal fool . . . but I would not go to the police while there was any chance that Raoul might be involved. I wasn't ready, yet, to test the theories of that advocate for the defense who pleaded still so desperately through today's tears. I couldn't bring the police in . . . not yet. If they had to be told, I didn't even want to be there. I was going to wait for Monsieur Hippolyte and, like a craven, hand the whole thing to him. Let the *deux ex machina* fly in out of the clouds and do the dirty work. I was only a woman, and a coward, and not ready, even, to face my own thoughts.

I gave a little sigh. "All right. We'll go to the Villa Mireille first. In any case they've already searched it."

"How d'you know?"

"Eh? Oh, well, I imagine they have, don't you? But your

214

uncle won't be there yet, petit, of that I'm sure. We'll stay here a little while and rest. I don't feel fit for very much more just yet. Here, you may as well finish the last of the chocolate."

"Thank you." He gave me a watery smile. "I'm sleepy."

"Well, curl up there and sleep. I'm going to."

"I'm thirsty, too."

"I imagine the stream's all right. It comes straight down the hillside. Let's risk it anyway."

We drank, and then lay down in the sun, curled close together on my coat, and soon we slept.

I needn't have been afraid that any restless ecstasy of the mind would keep me awake. Sleep fell from nowhere like a black cloud and blotted me out. I never stirred or blinked until the sun had his chin on the hilltop beyond Dieudonné valley, and the shadows of the naked trees stretched long-fingered across the glade to touch us with the first tiny chill of evening.

Philippe was awake already, sitting with knees drawn up and chin on them, gazing a little somberly at the distant housetops, purpling in the fading light. The lake was pale now as an opal, swimming under the faint beginnings of mist. In the distance on the further shore we could see, touched in with rose and apricot, the snows of Switzerland.

Brightness falls from the air. . . . I gave a little shiver, then got to my feet and pulled the silent Philippe to his. "Now," I said briskly, "you show me that path of yours, *petit*, and we'll be on our way."

His memory proved accurate enough. The path was there, and the narrow country road, and the corner with the garage and the shop, past which we hurried in case anyone should recognize him from his previous visits. He never spoke, and his hand in mine had become perceptibly more of a drag. I watched him worriedly. His frail energy was running out visibly now, sand from the brittle glass. I thought of the long wait that probably still lay ahead of us, and bit my lip in a prolonged pain of indecision.

The dusk had fairly dropped now over the town. We walked along a high-walled street where the pavements were bordered with lopped willows. The lamps had come on, and festoons of gleaming telegraph wires pinned back the blue dusk. Few people were about. A truck started up from the garage and drove off with a clatter, its yellow lights like lion's eyes in the half-light. A big car purred by on its own hasty business. Two workmen on bicycles pedaled purposefully

215

home. From a side street came the raucous voice of a radio and the smell of frying.

Philippe stopped. His face, lifted to mine, looked small and pale. He said, "That's the way, mademoiselle."

I looked to my right where a vennel led off the street between two high ivy-covered walls. It was narrow and unlighted, vanishing into shadow within twenty yards. A loose spray of ivy tapped the wall; its leaves were sharp and black and clicked like metal.

From the opposite side of the road came a burst of laughter, and a woman's voice called something shrill and good-natured. The café door clashed, and with the gush of light came once again the heavenly hot smell of food.

The child's hand clutched mine. He said nothing.

Well, what was luck for if it was never to be tempted?

I turned my back on the black little alley. Two minutes later we were sitting at a red-topped table near the stove while a long thin man with a soiled apron and a face like a sad heron waited to be told what we would have to eat.

To this day I vividly remember the smell and taste of everything we had. Soup first, the first delicious hot mouthful for almost twenty-four hours. . . . It was *crême d'asperge*, and it came smoking-hot in brown earthenware bowls with handles like gnomes' ears, and asparagus tips bobbed and steamed on the creamy surface. With the soup came butter with the dew on it, and crusty rolls so new that where they lay on the plastic tabletop there was a tiny dull patch of steam.

Philippe revived to that soup as a fern revives to water. When his omelette arrived, a fluffy roll, crisped at the edges, from which mushrooms burst and spilled in their own rich gravy, he tackled it with an almost normal small boy's appetite. My own brand of weariness demanded something more solid and I had a steak. It came in a lordly dish with the butter still sizzling on its surface and the juices oozing pinky-brown through the mushrooms and tomatoes and tiny kidneys and the small mountain of crisply-fried onions . . . if *filet mignon* can be translated as *darling steak* this was the very sweetheart of its kind. By the time that adorable steak and I had become one flesh I could have taken on the whole Valmy clan single-handed. I complimented the waiter when he came to clear, and his lugubrious face lightened a little.

"And what to follow, mademoiselle? Cheese? A little fruit?"

I glanced at Philippe, who shook his head sleepily. I laughed, "My little brother's nearly asleep. No, no cheese for me, thank you, Monsieur. A café filtre, if you please, and a café au lait. I fingered the purse in my pocket. "And a Bénédictine, please."

"Un filtre, un café au lait, une Bénédictine."

He swept the last crumb from the table, gave the shiny red top a final polish with his cloth, and turned away. I said, "Could monsieur perhaps get me some jetons?"

"Assuredly." He took the money I held out and in a short time the cups were on the table and I had a little pile of jetons in front of me.

Philippe roused himself to blink at them. "What are those?"

I gaped at him. Then it came to me that Monsieur le Comte de Valmy had, of course, never had to use a public telephone. I explained softly that one had to buy these little metal plaques to put in the slot of the telephone.

"I should like to do it," said Monsieur le Comte decidedly, showing a spark of animation.

"So you shall, mon gars, but not tonight. Better leave it to me." And I rose.

"Where are you going?" He didn't move, but his voice clutched at me.

"Only to the corner behind the bar. See? There's the telephone. I'll be back before my coffee's filtered. You stay here and drink your own—and Philippe, don't look quite so interested in those men over there. Pretend you've been in this sort of place dozens of times, will you?"

"They're not taking any notice."

Nor were they—yet. The only other occupants of the little café besides ourselves were a gang of burly workmen absorbed in some card game, and a slim youth with hair cut en brosse whispering sweet somethings in to the ear of a pretty little gipsy in a tight black sweater and skirt. Nobody after the first casual glance had paid the slightest attention to us. The stout patronne who sat over some parrot-colored knitting behind the bar merely smiled at me and nodded as I picked my way between the tables toward her and asked if I might telephone. Nobody here, at any rate, was on the lookout for a young woman with brown hair and gray eyes, on the run with the kidnaped Comte de Valmy.

It wasn't only luck that protected us, I thought, as I fumbled with the half-forgotten intricacies of the telephone; it was common sense to suppose that the chances of our being seen and recognized now, here, were very small. One had read dozens of "pursuit" books, from the classic Thirty-nine Steps

217

onward, and in all of them the chief and terrible miracle had been the unceasing and intelligent vigilance of every member of the population. In sober fact, nobody was much interested. . . .

Here one of the card players raised his eyes from the game to look at me; then he nudged his neighbor and said something. The latter looked up too, and his stare raked me. My heart, in spite of the soothing logic of my thoughts, gave a painful jerk, as with an effort I forced my gaze to slide indifferently past them. I turned a shoulder and leaned against the wall, waiting, bored, for my connection. From the corner of an eye I saw the second man say something and grin. I realized with a rush of amused relief that any pursuit that those two might offer would have other and quite natural motives that had nothing whatever to do with the errant Comte de Valmy.

"*Ici le Coq Hardi*," quacked a voice in my ear.

I jerked my attention back to it, and my imagination back to the teeming little inn at Soubirous.

"I want to speak to Monsieur Blake, please."

"Who?"

"Monsieur Blake. The Englishman from Dieudonné." I was speaking softly, and mercifully the raido was loud enough to prevent my being overheard. "I understand he stays with you. Is he there now?"

There was some altercation, aside, that I couldn't make out. Then it stopped abruptly, as if cut off by a hand over the mouthpiece. To my fury I found that my own hand was damp on the receiver.

Then the voice said into my ear, "No, he's not here. Who's that wanting him?"

"Is he likely to be tonight?"

"Perhaps." Was I being jumpy, or was it suspicion that put the edge on that unfriendly voice? "He didn't say. If you ring back in half an hour. . . . Who is that speaking, please?"

I said, "Thanks very much. I'll do that. I'm sorry to have—"

The voice said, harsh and sharp, "Where are you speaking from?"

Suspicion. It bit like an adder. And the Coq Hardi was on Valmy land and presumably the news would reach the château just as quickly as wires could carry it. If I could put them off—let them think I was safe for another half-hour . . .

I said pleasantly, with no perceptible hesitation, "From Évian. The Cent Fleurs. Don't trouble Monsieur Blake. I'll ring him up later on. Thank you so much."

And right in the teeth of another question I rang off.

I stood for a moment looking unseeingly at the telephone, biting my lip. Needless to say I had no intention of waiting to ring up again, but putting off pursuit I had also put off William Blake. If he got my message at all, and if he was aware of the story that must by now be rife in Soubirous, he might realize I needed help and set straight off for Évian and the huge crowded floor of the Cent Fleurs, which certainly wouldn't remember if a young woman accompanied by a small boy had used the telephone at some time during the evening.

Somehow I was very sure of William Blake's desire—and solid capacity—to help. Now I had had to cut myself off from that, and only now did I realize how much I had depended on the comfort of his company when the inevitable showdown came. I was well aware that even the interview with Hippolyte wouldn't be altogether plain sailing. Never before had I felt so miserably in need of a friend—someone who, even if they could do nothing, would simply be there. I gave myself a mental shake. I mustn't start this. Just because, for a few short hours, I had laid flesh and spirit in other hands, I didn't have to feel so forsaken now. I'd hoed my own row for long enough—well, it seemed I must go on doing just that. What one has never really had, one never misses. Or so they say.

I went back to my table, unwrapped three lumps of sugar, and drank my coffee black and far too sweet. The Bénédictine I drank with appreciation but, I'm afraid, a lack of respect. It was the effect, and not the drink I craved. I took it much too quickly, with half a wary eye on the card players in the other corner.

Then, just as they were nicely involved in a new round of betting, I quietly paid the waiter, nodded a good night to Madame and went—unfollowed except by Philippe—out of the café.

Chapter XVIII

If thou wilt leave me, do not leave me last,
When other petty griefs have done their spite,
But in the onset come. . . .

SHAKESPEARE: *Sonnet 90.*

THE Villa Mireille stood right on the shore of Lac Léman.
It was one of a row of large wealthy houses—châteaux, almost—which bordered the lakeside, being served to land-
ward by a narrow pretty road some two hundred feet below
the town's main boulevards. Most of the houses stood in
large gardens plentifully treed and guarded from the road
by high walls and heavy gates.

It was dark when we reached the Villa Mireille. The gate
was shut and as our steps paused outside there was the rattle of a heavy chain within, and a dog set up a deep barking.

"That's Beppo," whispered Philippe.

"Does he know you?"

"No—I don't know. I'm frightened of him."

Here the door of the concierge's lodge opened, and the
light from it rushed up the trees that made a crowded darkness beyond the gate. A woman's voice called something,
shrilly. The barking subsided into a whining growl. The
door shut and the trees retreated into murky shadow.

I said, "Is there another way in?"

"You can get in from the lake-shore. The garden runs
right down, and there's a boathouse. But I don't know the
way down along the lake."

"We'll find it."

"Are we going further?" His voice was alarmed and
querulous; tears of pure fatigue were not far away.

"Only to find a way down to the lake. We can't go in
past Beppo and Madame—what did you say her name
was?"

"Vuathoux."

"Well, unless you'd like to go straight to her—"

"No."

I said, "You'd be safe, Philippe."

"She would telephone my Uncle Léon, wouldn't she?"

"Almost certainly."

"And my cousin Raoul would come?"

220

"It's possible."

He looked at me. "I would rather wait for my Uncle Hippolyte. You said we could."

"All right. We'll wait."

"Would you rather wait for my Uncle Hippolyte?"

"Yes."

"Then," said Philippe, swallowing, "perhaps we will find the way quickly?"

We did—three houses along from the Villa Mireille. A small wicket, swinging loose, gave onto a dim shrubbery, and as we slipped cautiously inside we could see the dim bulk of a house looming unlighted among its misty trees. No dog barked. We crept unchallenged down a long winding path, along beside a high paling bordering an open stretch of grass, and eventually once again between big trees toward the murmur of the lake.

Neither moon nor stars showed tonight.

Over the water mist lay patchily, here thick and pale against the dark distances, here no more than a haze veiling the lake's surface as breath mists a dark glass, here as faint as the sheen that follows a finger stroking dark velvet. Long transparent drifts of vapor wreathed up from the water and reached slow fingers across the narrow shore toward the trees. The water lapped hollowly on the shingle beside us as we crunched our way back toward the villa's garden. The night was not cold, but the water breathed a chill into the air, and the slowly-curling veils of mist brushed us with a damp that made me shiver.

"That's the boathouse," whispered Philippe. "I know where the key's kept. Are we going to go in?"

The boathouse was a small square two-storied building set, of course, over the water, at the head of an artificial bay made by two curving stone jetties. The shore was very narrow here, and from the yard-wide strip of shingle rose the steep bank crowded with trees that edged the grounds of the Villa Mireille. The rear wall of the boathouse was almost built up against this bank, and the beeches hung their branches right over the roof. Mist and darkness blurred the details, but the general effect of desertion, looming trees, and lapping water was not just exactly what the moment demanded for Philippe and me.

I said briskly, "I want to go up through the garden and take a look at the house. For all we know he's already here. Would you like to stay in the boathouse? You could lock yourself in, and we'd have a secret signal—"

221

"No," said Philippe again.

"All right. You can scout up the garden with me. Very carefully, mind."

"Madame Vuathoux is deaf," said Philippe.

"Maybe. But Beppo isn't. Come on, *petit.*"

The bank was steep and slippery with clay and wet leaves that lay in drifts between the roots of the beeches. Above it was the rough grass of a small parkland studded with more of the great trees. We crept softly from one huge trunk to the next; the spring grass was soft and damp underfoot, and there was, incongruously, the smell of violets. Elms now, and horse chestnuts. I could feel the rough bark of the one, and the sticky buds of the other licked at my hand. The hanging fronds of willow brushed us wetly, clung, hindered us. We pushed through into a grove of willows as thick as a tent, and paused. We were almost at the house now. The willows curtained the edges of a formal lawn; the terrace of the house lay beyond this, thirty yards away. Near us was the metallic gleam of a small pool and I could see something that looked like a statue leaning over it.

I took Philippe's hand and we crept softly up behind the plinth of the statue, where the willows hung like an arras down to the water's surface. I pulled the trailing stems aside and scanned the façade of the house. None of the windows showed light, but there appeared to be a lamp over the front door, illuminating the drive. The door itself was out of our range of vision, but the glow of the lamp showed part of a circular gravel sweep, and banks of rhododendrons. Up here the mist was still only a blurring of the air, a thickening of the lamplight that lay like hoar-frost on the wet leaves.

I said softly, "The windows on the terrace. What room's that?"

"The salon. It's never used. My uncle Hippolyte has his study upstairs. The end window. There's no light in it."

I looked up at it. "Then I'm afraid he's not home yet."

"Are we going in?"

I thought for a moment. "Where's the back door?"

"Round the other side, near the lodge."

"And near Beppo? Then that's out. And I doubt if there are any windows open. And there's that light over the front door. . . . No, Philippe, I think we'll wait. What do you think?"

"Yes. I—there's a car!"

His hand gripped mine almost painfully. The road was not more than twenty yards away on our right. A car was coming along it, slowing down rapidly through its gears. Brakes squealed. A door slammed. Footsteps. A bell changed. Seconds later through the clamor of the dog we heard the chink of iron and the squeak of a hinge, as Madame Vuathoux hastened to open the gates.

Philippe's grip tightened. *"My uncle Hippolyte!"*

A man's voice said something indistinguishable beyond the banked shrubs.

"No," I said on a caught breath. "Raoul."

The cold hand jerked in mine. I heard the concierge say, in the loud toneless voice of the very deaf, "No, monsieur. Nothing, monsieur. And has there been no trace found?"

He said curtly, "None. Are you sure they couldn't have got in here? This is where they'll make for, that's certain. Is the back door locked?"

"No, monsieur, but I can see it from my window. Nobody has been there. Or to the front. Of that I am sure."

"The windows?"

"Locked, monsieur."

"No telephone call? Nothing?"

"Nothing, monsieur."

There was a pause. In it I could hear my own heart hammering.

"All the same," he said, "I'll have a look around. Leave the gates open, please. I'm expecting Bernard here any minute."

Another heart-hammering pause. Then the car started up and the lights turned in slowly off the road, slithering metallically across the sharp leaves of the rhododendrons. He parked it in front of the door, and got out. I heard him run up the steps, and the the door shut behind him. The dog still whimpered and growled a little. Back at the lodge, the concierge called something to it, and after a few moments it fell silent.

I felt the cold hand twitch in mine. I looked down. The child's face was a blur with great dark pools for eyes. I whispered, "Keep close behind the statue. He may put some lights on."

I had hardly spoken before the salon windows blazed to brilliant oblongs, and the light leaped out across the terrace to touch the lawn. We were still in shadow. We waited, tense behind the statue. It was the figure of a boy, naked, leaning over to look at himself in the pool; a poised, exquisite Narcissus, self-absorbed, self-complete. . . .

Room after room leaped into light, was quenched. We followed his progress through the house; light and then black darkness. The windows on the terrace facing us remained lit. Finally they were the only ones. He came to one of the long windows, opened it, and stepped out onto the terrace. His shadow leaped across the lawn to the edge of the water. He stood there for a minute or two, still, staring at the night. I put a gentle hand on Philippe's head, pushing it down so that no faint probe of light would touch his face. We were crouching now. My cheek was against the stone of the plinth. It was cold and smooth and smelt of lichen. I didn't dare lift my head to look at Raoul. I watched the tip of his shadow.

Suddenly it was gone. In the same moment I heard another car come fast along the road. Lights swept in at the gate. The salon windows went black, blank. I lifted my head and waited, straining my ears.

Steps on the gravel. Raoul's voice, still on the terrace, saying, "Bernard?"

"Monsieur?" The newcomer came quickly around the corner of the house. I heard Raoul descending the terrace steps. He said in that quick hard voice he had used to Madame Vuathoux, "Any sign?"

"None, monsieur, but—"

I heard Raoul curse under his breath. "Did you go back to the hut?"

"Yes. They weren't there. But they'd been, I swear they—"

"Of course they had. The Englishman was up there last night till midnight. I know that. They'd go to find him. Have you found out where he is?"

"He's not back yet. He went out with a party up to the plantation beyond Bois-Roussel early this morning and they're not back yet. But, monsieur, I was trying to tell you. I rang up just now, and they told me she'd telephoned him at the Coq Hardi. She—"

"She telephoned him?" The words flashed. "When?"

"Thirty to forty minutes ago."

"Sacré dieu." I heard his breath go out. "Where was she speaking from? Did the fools think to ask?"

"Yes, indeed, m'sieur. They had heard the scandal from Jules, you understand, and—"

"Where was she speaking from?"

"The Cent Fleurs, in Évian. They said—"

"Half an hour ago?"

"Or three-quarters. No more."

"Then the Englishman can't have heard anything. He must be still away with the party. She's not with him yet."

He turned away abruptly and Bernard with him. Their voices faded but I heard him say roughly, "Get over to Évian immediately with that car. I'm going myself. We have to find them, and quickly. Do you hear me? Find them."

Bernard said something that sounded surly and defensive, and I heard Raoul curse him again. Then the voices faded around the corner of the house. Seconds later the Cadillac's engine started, and her lights swept their circle out of the driveway. The dog was barking once more. Madame Vuathoux must have come out of her cottage at the sound of the second car, for I heard Bernard speak to her, and she answered him in that high, overpitched voice, "He said he'd be here at twelve. Twelve at the latest."

Then Bernard, too, was gone. I lifted my head from the cold plinth and slid an arm around Philippe. I waited for a moment.

Philippe said, with excitement coloring the thin whisper, "He's coming at twelve. Did you hear?"

"Yes. I don't suppose it's far off nine now. Only three more hours to wait, mon gars. And they've gone chasing off to Évian."

"He came down the terrace steps. He must have left a window open. Shall we go in?"

I hesitated, then said dully, "No. Only three more hours. Let's play it quite safe and go back and lock ourselves in the boathouse."

The boathouse looked, if possible, rather more dismal than before. Philippe vanished around the back of it and after a minute reappeared with a key which he displayed with a rather wan air of triumph.

"Good for you," I said. "Lead the way, mon lapin."

He went cautiously up the steep outside stair to the loft over the boats. The treads were slippery with moss and none too safe. He bent over the door, and I heard the key grate around in the lock. The door yawned, creaking a little, on a black interior from which came the chill breath of dust and desertion.

"Refuge," I said, with a spurious cheerfulness that probably didn't deceive Philippe at all, and switched on the torch with caution.

The loft, thank heaven, was dry. But that was its only

225

attraction. It was a cheerless little black box of a place, a dusty junk hole crowded with the abandoned playthings of forgotten summers. I found later that one of the concrete piers of the harbor had a flat platform in its shelter which in happier days made a small private lido. Here in the loft had been carelessly thrust some of the trappings that in July's sunshine were so amusingly gay; striped canvas chairs, a huge folded umbrella of scarlet and dusty orange, various grubby objects which looked as if, well beaten and then inflated, they might be air cushions, a comical duck, a sausage-like horse with indigo spots. . . . Seen by flashlight in the chilly April dark, with a vigil ahead of us and fear at our elbow, they looked indescribably dreary and grotesque.

There was a small square window low down in the shore-ward wall. I propped a canvas chair across it to conceal the flashlight from a possible prowler, then turned to lock the door.

Philippe said dolefully behind me, "What are we going to do till twelve o'clock?"

"Failing Peggitty and chess," I said cheerfully, "sleep. I really don't see why you shouldn't. You must be worn out, and there's nothing now to worry you and keep you awake."

"No," he said a little doubtfully, then his voice lightened. "I shall sleep in the boat."

"Little cabbage, the boat isn't there. Besides, how wet. Now up here," I said falsely, gesturing with the light toward the dreary pile, "it's much nicer. Perhaps we can find—"

"Here it is." And Philippe had darted past me and was pulling out from under three croquet mallets a half-deflated beach-ball and a broken oar, a flat yellowish affair that looked like a cyclist's mackintosh.

"What in the wide world—" I said.

"The boat."

"Oh. Oh, I see. Is it a rubber dinghy? I've never seen one."

He nodded and spread his unappetizing treasure out on the unoccupied half of the floor. "You blow it up. Here's the tube. You blow into that and the sides come up and it's a boat. I want to sleep in it."

I was too thankful that he had found something to occupy him to object to this harmless whim.

"Why not?" I said. "It's a good solid damp-proof ground sheet anyway. And after all, who minds a little dust?"

"It's not a ground sheet. It's a *boat*." He was already

226

ootling purposefully behind some dirty canvas in a corner.

"Ça se voit," I said untruthfully, eying it.

"You blow it up," explained Philippe patiently, emerging with an unwonted spot of color in his face, from between an oil drum and the unspeakable spotted horse.

"Darling, if you think either of us has got enough blow left in them——"

"With *this*." He was struggling with some heavy-seeming object. I took it from him.

"What is it?"

"A pump. It's easy. I'll *show* you." He was already down on the floor beside the dismal yellow mass, fitting the nozzle of the pump to the mouth of the tube. I hadn't the heart to dissuade him. Besides . . . I had been uneasily aware for some minutes now of the bitter little draft that crept under the door and meandered along the boards, cutting at my ankles. Philippe was busy with the footpump, which seemed remarkably easy to work. If the blessed boat really would inflate . . .

It would. Presently Philippe lifted a face flushed with pride and effort and liberally festooned with cobwebs from a businesslike rubber dinghy whose fat sausage-like sides would certainly stem any wandering drafts. I praised him lavishly, managed to parry offers to blow up the horse, the duck, and the beachball as well ("just to *show* you") and finally got us both disposed in our draft-proof but decidedly cramped bed, curled up for warmth together in our coats and preparing to sit out the last three hours or so of our ordeal.

The ghastly minutes crawled by. The night was still, held in its pall of mist. I could hear the occasional soft drip of moisture from the boughs that hung over us, and once some stray current of air must have stirred the trees, for the budded twigs pawed at the roof. Below in the boathouse the hollow slap and suck of water told of darkness and emptiness and a world of nothing. . . . Compared with this burial in the outer dark last night's lodging had had a snug homely quality that I found myself remembering—Bernard or no Bernard—with longing.

And it was cold. Philippe seemed warm enough, curled in a ball with his back tucked into the curve of my body and my arms over him; at any rate, he slept almost straight away. But as the minutes halted by I could feel the deadly insidious cold creeping through me, bone by bone. It struck first at my exposed back, then, slowly, slithered through my whole

227

body, as if the blood were literally running cold through the veins and arteries that held me in a chilled and stiffening network. Cramped as I was, I dared not move for fear of waking the child. He had had, I judged, just about as much as he could take. Let him sleep out the chilly minutes before the final rescue.

So I lay and watched the darkness beyond my canvas barrier for a glimpse of light from the villa, and tried not to think, not to think about anything at all.

It was the beachball that put an end to the beastly vigil. Disturbed from its winter's rest and moved, I suppose, by some erratic draft, it finally left its place on a pile of boxes and rolled, squashily elliptical in its half-deflated state, off its perch and down onto the floor. It fell on me out of nowhere with a silent, soggy bounce, and jerked me with a yelp out of my stiff, half-dozing vigil. I sat up furiously. Philippe's voice said, sounding scared, "What was that?"

I reached clumsily for the flashlight. "The beachball, confound it, I'm sorry, Philippe. Don't be frightened. Let's have a look at the time. . . . Quarter to twelve." I looked at him. "Are you cold?"

He nodded.

I said, "Let's get out of here, shall we? There's no light up at the villa yet, so I vote we try that terrace window. Only a few minutes more now. . . ."

The mist was thicker now. Our little light beam beat white against it. It lay heavy as a cloudbank among the trees, but over the lawn near the house it showed only a pale haze that thinned and shifted in the moving light.

The lamp still glowed over the front door. Its circle of light seemed to have shrunk as the trees crowded and loomed closer in the mist. No other light showed.

We slipped quietly across the lawn and up the terrace steps. The long window stood ajar, and we went in.

The salon was a big room, and in the light of a cautious torch it looked even bigger. The little glow caught the ghostly shapes of shrouded furniture, the gleam of a mirror, the sudden glitter of the chandelier that moved with a spectral tinkle in the draft from the window. The meager light seemed only to thicken the shadows and make the room retreat further into dusk. It smelled of disuse, melancholy, dry as dust.

We hesitated just inside the window.

I whispered, "We'll go to your Uncle Hippolyte's room. That'll have been prepared, surely? There'll be a fire or a stove. And is there a telephone in it?"

He nodded and led the way quickly across the salon. If he was scared he didn't show it. He moved almost numbly, as if in a bad dream. He pushed open a massive door that gave onto the hall and slipped through it without a look to right or left into the shadowed corners. I followed.

The hall was a high dim square where I could just make out a graceful branching staircase. Tiles echoed our quick footsteps hollowly. No other sound. We fled upstairs. Philippe turned left along a wide gallery and finally stopped before a door.

"It's Uncle Hippolyte's study," he whispered, and put a hand to the knob.

The room, sure enough, was warm. Like pins to a magnet we flew across the carpet to the big stove and hugged it as closely as we could with our chilled bodies. I said, sending the flashlight raking around the room, "Where does that door lead?"

"There's another salon. Bigger. It's never used now."

I went across and pushed the door open. The flashlight once more probed its way over the ghosts of furniture. Like the room downstairs, this was still shrouded in its winter covers. It smelled musty, and the silk-paneled walls, as I put up a gentle finger, felt dusty and brittle, like a dead moth's wing. From the empty darkness above came the now familiar phantom tinkling of a chandelier.

I crossed the carpet softly and paused by a shrouded shape that seemed to be a sofa. I lifted the dust cover and felt underneath it . . . damask cushions fraying a little, silk that caught on the skin and set the teeth on edge. "Philippe," I called softly.

He appeared beside me like a smaller, frailer ghost. He was shivering a little. I said very matter-of-factly: "I don't suppose it'll be needed, but every fighter has to have a possible line of retreat worked out. If for any reason we still want to hide, I'd say this is as good a place as any. Under the dust cover. It makes a tent, see? And you'd be pretty snug underneath and quite invisible."

He saw. He nodded without speaking. I cast him a look as I covered the sofa again and followed him back into the study. I pulled the salon door almost, but not quite, shut behind me.

I glanced at my wrist. Five minutes to twelve. The window

looked out over the drive. No sign of a car. I turned to Hippolyte's desk and picked up the telephone.

Chapter XIX

So, uncle, there you are.

SHAKESPEARE: *Hamlet.*

A MAN'S voice said, "Coq Hardi."

At least it was not the same unpleasant and suspicious voice, but there was no harm in trying to disarm it further. It was five minutes to twelve, but just in case. . . .

I said quickly, eagerly, "Guillaume? Is that you, *chéri?* It's Clothilde."

He said blankly, "Clothilde?"

"Yes, yes. From Annecy. You haven't forgotten? You told me to——"

The voice was amused. "Mademoiselle, a moment. Who is it you want?"

"I—isn't that Guillaume? Oh mon dieu, how silly of me!" I gave a nervous giggle. "I am sorry, monsieur. Perhaps—if he isn't in bed?—if you will fetch him. . . ."

He was patience itself. "But of course. With the greatest of pleasure. But Guillaume who, Mademoiselle Clothilde? Guillaume Rouvier?"

"No, no. I told you. Monsieur Blake, the Englishman. Is he there? He did tell me——"

"Yes, he's here. Content yourself, Mademoiselle Clothilde. He's not gone to bed. I'll fetch him." I heard him laugh as he moved away from the telephone. No doubt William's stock would soar at the Coq Hardi. . . .

Philippe had moved up close to me. In the faint glow that the front door light cast up through the uncurtained window his face looked small and pale, the eyes enormous. I winked and made a face at him and he smiled.

William said in my ear, sounding bewildered and suspicious, "Blake here. Who is that, please?"

"I'm sorry if I've embarrassed you," I said, "but I had to get you somehow, and that seemed the best way. Linda Martin."

"Oh, it's you. The barman said it was a *petite amie.* I

230

couldn't think—what's been going on? Where are you? Are you all right? And the boy—"

"For heaven's sake! Can anyone hear you, William?"

"What? Oh yes, I suppose they can. But I don't think they know English."

"Never mind, don't risk it. I daren't call you for long because it mayn't be safe, but I . . . I need help, and I thought—"

He said quietly, "Of course. I heard the local version of what's happened, and I've been hop—expecting you'd get in touch with me. I—I've been terribly worried—I mean, you being on your own, and all that. What is it? What can I do?"

I said gratefully, "Oh, William . . . Listen, I can't explain now, it would take too long. Don't worry any more; we're safe, both of us, and I think the whole thing will be over in a few minutes, but . . . I'd be awfully grateful if you'd come along. There's no danger now, but there'll be . . . scenes, and I don't somehow feel like facing them alone. I know it's a lot to ask of someone you hardly know, and it's a shocking time of night, but I wondered—"

"Tell me where you are," said William simply, "and I'll come. I've got the jeep. Is it the Cent Fleurs?"

"No, no. So they told you I'd rung up before?"

"Yes. I've just got back from Evian."

"Oh, William, no!"

"Well," he said reasonably, "I thought you were there. I didn't know anything about this business till we got in tonight, you know. I was up at the hut till late last night, working, but I was due today to go with a couple of men over to the south plantations and we had to make an early start, so I slept at the pub. We were out all day and got back lateish, and then I was told you'd rung up from the Cent Fleurs, and of course I heard all the stories that were going around. I rang up the Cent Fleurs and they didn't remember you, so I skated down to Evian in the jeep—"

"Did you see Raoul de Valmy there?"

"Don't know him from Adam," said William simply. "Is he looking for you, too?"

"Yes."

"Oh. I thought you might have—I mean, someone said—" he stopped, floundering a little.

I said, "Whichever of the stories you heard, it isn't true. We're on our own."

231

"Oh. Ah. Yes. Well," said William cheerfully, "tell me where you are now and I'll be straight over."

"We're in Thonon, at the Villa Mireille. That's Hippolyte de Valmy's place; he's the brother—"

"I know. Have you seen him?"

"He's not back yet. Expected any minute. We're waiting for him. I—I'll explain when I see you why we didn't go straight to the police. Just for the time being, will you not say anything? Just—come?"

"Sure. I'm halfway there already. Repeat the name of the place, please."

"The Villa Mireille. Anyone'll tell you. It's on the lakeside. Take the lower road. M-I-R-E-I-L-L-E. Got it?"

"Yes, thank you . . . sherry."

"What? Oh, I see. Is the barman listening?"

"Yes."

"Then you'll have to say good-by nicely, I'm afraid."

"I don't know how."

"Say 'à bientôt, cherie.' "

"Ah biang toe sherry," said William grimly, and then laughed. "I'm glad you're in such good spirits, anyway," he added.

"Yes," I said drearily. "See you soon. And thank you, William. Thank you a lot. It's nice not to be . . . quite on one's own."

"Think nothing of it," said William, and rang off.

The handset was hardly back in its cradle when the car came down the road. We stood together, just back from the dark window, and watched the lights. It slowed and changed gear for the gate. Its lights swung around in the mist and slid across the study ceiling.

Philippe's hand slid into mine, and gripped. My own was shaking.

He said inadequately, "Here he is."

"Yes. Oh, Philippe."

He said wonderingly, "You have been afraid too, all the time?"

"Yes. Terribly."

"I didn't know."

"I'm glad of that."

The car had stopped. Lights were cut, then the engine. Feet crunched on the gravel and the car door slammed. Steps, quick and assured, mounted to the front door. We heard the rattle of the handle. Then the sounds weren't out-

232

side the house any longer, but inside; the slight sound of the big door opening, a step on the tiled floor. . . .

He had come. It was over.

I said shakily, "*Dieu soit béni,*" and made for the door.

I hadn't even considered what I was going to say to Hippolyte. It was possible that in some fashion he had already been greeted with the news. It was also possible that he had never even heard of me. I didn't care. He was here. I could hand over.

I flew along the carpeted gallery and down the lovely curve of the stairs.

The hall lights were not on. The front door was ajar, and the lamp that hung outside it over the steps cast a long panel of gold across the tiles. Outside I saw the car gleaming in the mist. The newcomer stood just inside the door, one hand raised as if in the act of switching on the lights. He was silhouetted against the lamplit haze beyond, a tall, powerfully-built man, standing stock-still, as a man does when he is listening.

On the thick carpet my feet made little more noise than a ghost's. I reached the center stair and hesitated, one hand on the balustrade. I started slowly down the last flight toward him.

Then he saw me, and raised his head.

"So you are here," he said.

That was all, but it stopped me as if he had shot me. I stood clutching the banister till I thought the wood would crack. For one crazy moment I wanted to turn and run, but I couldn't move.

I said, in an unrecognizable voice that broke on the word, "Raoul?"

"*Lui-même.*" There was a click as the lights came on—a great chandelier that poured and flashed light from a thousand glittering crystals. They struck at my eyes and I flinched and put up a hand, then dropped it and looked at him across the empty hall. I had forgotten all about Philippe, about Hippolyte, about William Blake even now tearing down from Soubirous; I could see nothing but the man who stood there with his hand on the light switch, looking up at me. There was nothing except the thing that lay between us.

He dropped his hand, and shut the door behind him. He was quite white, and his eyes were hard as stones. There were lines in his face I hadn't seen before. He looked very like Léon de Valmy.

He said, "He's here? Philippe?" His voice was very even and quiet, but I thought I could hear the blaze of anger licking through it that he didn't trouble to suppress.

The question was answered by Philippe himself. He had followed me as far as the gallery, and there had stopped, prompted by a better instinct than my own. At his cousin's question he must have moved, for the stir in the shadows above him made Raoul lift his head sharply. I followed his look just in time to see Philippe, a small silent wraith, melt back into the darkness of the gallery.

Then Raoul moved, and fast. He took the hall in four strides and was coming upstairs two at a time. His leap out of immobility had been so sudden that I reacted without reason, a blind thing in a panic. I don't remember moving, but as I let go the banister I fled—was swept—up the stairway in front of him, only to check desperately on the landing and whirl to face him.

I shrieked, "Run, Philippe!" and put up frantic, futile hands to break the tempest.

They never touched him. He stopped dead. His arms dropped to his sides. I moved back till I came up against the curve of the banister rail and leaned there. I don't think I could have stood unsupported. He wasn't looking after Phillipe. He was looking at me. I turned my head away.

Behind me, along the gallery, I heard the study door shut, very softly.

Raoul heard it too. He lifted his head. Then he looked back at me.

"I see," he said.

So did I. I had seen even while shock reacting on weariness had driven me stupidly and headlong from him up the stairs. And now I saw the look that came down over his face, bleak bitter pride shutting down over anger, and I knew that I had turned my world back to cinders, sunk my lovely ship with my own stupid, wicked hands. I couldn't speak, but I began to cry—not desperately or tragically, but silently and without hope, the tears spilling anyhow down my cheeks, and my face ugly with crying.

He didn't move. He said, very evenly, "When I reached the Château Valmy this morning and my father told me that you had gone, he seemed to think you would have come to me for help. I told him no, you thought I was in Paris till Thursday, but I'd left my apartment there on Tuesday evening, and you couldn't know where I was. It was only later that I found you hadn't tried to get in touch with me there at all."

His voice was quite expressionless. "There was only one reason I could think of why you hadn't telephoned me. When I .. put this to my father he denied that any harm had come to you. I didn't believe him."

He paused. I couldn't look at him. I put up a hand to wipe away the tears that streaked my face. But they kept falling.

"I told him then I intended to make you my wife, and that if anything happened to you, or to the boy and through him to you, I would kill him—my father—with my own hands."

I looked at him then. "Raoul . . ." But my voice died away. I couldn't speak.

He said slowly, answering my look, "Yes. I believe I did mean it," and added one word, one knell of a word, "then."

We had neither of us heard the other car. When the hall door swung open to admit two people—a man and a woman—we both jumped and turned. The woman was Héloïse de Valmy; the man was a stranger to me, but even if I had not expected him I would have known that this was Hippolyte. In him, too, the Valmy likeness was strong; he was a younger, gentler edition of Léon de Valmy—Lucifer before the fall. He looked kind, and his voice as he addressed some remark to Héloïse sounded pleasant. But for all the gentleness and the marks of anxiety and fatigue, I thought I could see in him the same hard force as in the other men —cooler, perhaps, and slower, but in the circumstances none the worse for that. My deus ex machina would be capable enough, thank God.

Neither he nor Madame de Valmy had seen us above them on the landing, because at that moment Madame Vuathoux, who must this time have seen the lights of the car, came bustling into the hall from the back regions, vociferous with welcome.

"Monsieur—but you are welcome! I was so afraid that, with this mist—oh!" She stopped and her hands went up as if in horror. "Tiens, madame—she is ill? What is the matter? Of course, of course! What horror! Has there still been no word?"

I hadn't noticed till she mentioned it, but Héloïse de Valmy was indeed clinging to Hippolyte's arm as if she needed its support. In the merciless light from the chandelier her face looked ghastly, gray and haggard like the face of an old woman. The concierge surged forward with cries of commiseration.

235

The little boy—nothing was heard yet, no? And of course Madame was distracted. *La pauvre* . . . Madame must come upstairs . . . there was a stove lit . . . a drink . . . some bouillon, perhaps?

Hippolyte de Valmy interrupted her. "Monsieur Raoul is here?"

"Not yet, monsieur. He came this evening, and then left for Évian. He said he would be back at midnight to see you. It is after—"

"His car's outside."

Raoul moved at that, almost idly. He said, "Good evening, mon oncle."

Madame Vuathoux gaped up at him, at last stricken dumb. Hippolyte turned, eyebrows raised. Héloïse said, "Raoul!" just as I had done, and with no less horror in her voice. New lines etched themselves in her face and she swayed on her feet, so that Hippolyte tightened his grip on her arm. Then she saw me shrinking behind Raoul against the banister and she cried my name, almost on a shriek, "Miss Martin!"

Madame Vuathoux found her voice again at that. She echoed the cry. "*La voilà!*" There she is! In this very house! Monsieur Raoul—"

Hippolyte said curtly, "That will do. Leave us, please."

There was silence until the door had shut behind her. Then he turned again to look up at us. He surveyed me without expression, then he gave a formal little nod and looked at Raoul. "You found them?"

"Yes, I found them."

"Philippe?"

"He's here."

Héloïse said hoarsely, "Safe?"

Raoul's voice was very dry. "Yes, Héloïse. Safe. He was with Miss Martin."

Her eyes fell before his and she gave a little moaning sigh. Hippolyte said, "I think we had better talk this thing out quietly. Come up to the study. Héloïse, can you manage the stairs, my dear?"

No one looked at me, or spoke. I was a shade, a ghost, a dead leaf dropped by the storm into some corner. My story was over. Nothing would happen to me now. I would not even be called upon to explain to Hippolyte. I was safe, and I wished I was dead.

Héloïse and Hippolyte were coming slowly up the stairs. Raoul turned past me as if I didn't exist and began to mount the flight to the gallery. I went after him quietly. I had stopped crying, but my face still stung with tears, and I felt tired, so tired. I found I was pulling myself up by the banisters as if I were an old woman.

Raoul had opened the study door and switched on the light. He was waiting. I didn't look at him. I passed him with my head bent, and went straight across the study to the door that gave onto the salon.

I pushed it open.

I said wearily, "Philippe? It's all right, Philippe, you can come out." I hesitated, conscious that Raoul, too, had crossed the room and was standing just behind me. Then I said, "You're quite safe now. Your Uncle Hippolyte's here."

For some reason—no reason at all—the others had followed us into the salon, ignoring the comfort of the study stove.

Hippolyte had taken the cover from the sofa, and now sat there, with Philippe in the crook of his arm. On the other side of the empty grate Héloïse sat huddled in a small chair of golden brocade. Someone had twitched the dust sheet off that and it lay in a bundle at her feet.

With its light on, the salon seemed more ghostly than ever. The light of the big chandelier dripped icily from its hundred glittering prisms. It fell coldly on the white shrouds that covered the furniture, and struck back from the pale marble of the fireplace where Raoul stood, one elbow on the mantelpiece, as I had seen him stand in the library at Valmy.

I sat as far away from them as possible. At the end of the long room was a piano, a concert-sized grand encased in green baize; to this I retreated in silence, and sat down on the long piano bench with my back to the instrument. My hands clutched at the edge of the bench. I felt numb and unutterably weary. There was talking to be done—well, let them do it, the Valmys, and get it over and let me go. It was no longer anything to do with me. I raised my head and looked at them down the length of that beautiful dead room. They might have been a million miles away.

Hippolyte had been talking to Philippe in an undertone, but now he looked up at Raoul and said in his quiet voice, "As you may have guessed, Héloïse drove into Geneva to meet my plane. She has told me a rather . . . odd story."

Raoul was selecting a cigarette. He said without raising his eyes, "You'd better tell me what it was. I've heard several versions of this odd story lately, and I confess I'm confused. I'd like to know which one Héloïse is trying to sell now."

She made a little sound, and Hippolyte's lips tightened. "My dear Raoul—"

"Look," said Raoul, "this thing has gone a long way beyond politeness or the conventions of—filial duty. We'll get on a lot better if we simply tell the truth." His eyes rested indifferently on Héloïse. "You know, you may as well cut your losses, Héloïse. You must know my father was pretty frank with me this morning. I suppose he may intend to deny it all now, but I confess I can't see where that'll get him—or you. I don't know what he sent you down to Geneva to say, but the thing's over, Héloïse. You can abandon your—attitudes. There are no witnesses here that matter, and you'll certainly need my Uncle Hippolyte to help you if the hell of a scandal is to be avoided. Why not give it up and come clean?"

She made no reply, but sat there in a boneless huddle, not looking at him.

He watched her for a moment without expression. Then his shoulders lifted a fraction and he turned back to Hippolyte. "Well," he said, "since it appears that Héloïse isn't playing, you'd better let me start."

Hippolyte's face, as he glanced from one to the other looked suddenly very tired. "Very well," he said. "Go ahead. You rang me up in Athens in the small hours of Tuesday morning to ask me to come home as you were anxious about Philippe. You spoke of accidents, and insisted that Philippe might be in some danger. You also said something not very clear about Philippe's governess. Héloïse, too, spoke of her tonight—also not very clearly. I take it that this is the young woman in question, and that there have been recent and alarming developments which Héloïse has been attempting to explain to me. I must confess to some confusion. I am also tired. I hope you will be very brief and very lucid."

Raoul said, "You can forget Philippe's governess." (That was me—"Philippe's governess." He hadn't even glanced at me. He was a million miles away.) He went on, "She never was in it, except incidentally. The story begins and ends with my father. That was why I said this thing had gone beyond convention. Because your starting point, mon oncle, is this: Your brother—my father—with the help or at any rate the connivance of his wife—has been trying for some time past to murder Philippe."

I heard Héloïse give a faint sound like a moan, and I saw the child turn his head to look at her from the shelter of Hippolyte's arm. I said in a hard little voice I didn't recognize

238

s my own, "Philippe is only nine years old. Also he has ust been through a considerable ordeal and is very tired and robably hungry. I suggest that you allow me to take him ownstairs to some reliable person in the kitchen."

They all jumped as if one of the shrouded chairs had poken. Then Hippolyte said, "Certainly he should go down-tairs. But I should like you to remain here, if you will. ting the bell, please, Raoul."

Raoul glanced at me, a look I couldn't read, and obeyed.

We waited in silence, and presently the door opened. It vasn't Madame Vuathoux who stood there, but an elderly manservant with a pleasant face.

"Gaston," said Hippolyte, "will you please take Master 'hilippe downstairs and see he gets something to eat? Have Madame Vuathoux or Jeanne get a room ready for him . . . he little dressing room off my own, I think. Philippe, go vith Gaston now. He'll look after you."

Philippe had jumped up. He was smiling. The gray-haired ervant returned the smile. "Come along," he said, and put ut a hand. Philippe ran to him without a backward look. The door shut behind them.

Hippolyte turned back to Raoul. I could see, I'm not sure ow, the rigid control he was exerting over face and hands. Iis voice was not quite steady, but it was as pleasant and entle as ever. He said, "Well, Raoul, you'd better go on with our story. And I advise you to be sure of your facts. 'ou . . . he's my brother, remember."

"And my father," said Raoul harshly. He knocked the ash ff his cigarette into the empty fireplace with an abrupt novement. "As for my facts, I haven't a great many, but you an have them. I only really came into the story myself"— ere his eyes lifted and met mine; they were like slate—"this norning."

He paused for a moment. Then he began to talk.

He said, "I don't have to tell you the background to the tory; that my father, if Philippe had never been born, would ave succeeded to Valmy, where he has lived all his life and vhich he loved with what (particularly since his accident) is n obsessive love. When his elder brother didn't marry he ssumed that Valmy would be some day his, and he never esitated to divert the income from his own estate, Belle-igne, into Valmy. I have run Bellevigne for him since I was ineteen, and I know just how steadily, during those early ears, the place was milked of everything that might have nade it prosperous. My father and I have fought over it time

and again . . . after all, it is my heritage as well, and I wasn
as sure as he that Étienne wouldn't get himself a son on
day."

Hippolyte said, "I know. Léon would never listen."

"Well," said Raoul. "Étienne did marry, and got Philippe
I don't intend to distress you with my father's reactions t
that fact; mercifully he had the sense to keep them fro
Étienne . . . possibly so that Étienne would let him go o
living at Valmy. But the immediate result was that Bell
vigne's income was put back where it belonged, and I ha
the job to build up what had been steadily ruined for years.
Something like a smile touched the hard mouth. "I may sa
I enjoyed the fight. . . . But last year, Étienne was killed.

He looked down at Hippolyte. "And immediately Valm
started to take the money out of Bellevigne again."

The older man made a little movement. "As soon as that?

Raoul smiled again. It wasn't a nice smile. "I'm glad you'r
so quick in the uptake. Yes. He must have decided then an
there that something had to be done about Philippe. Ther
were six years before the child inherited. The chance woul
come."

Hippolyte said, hard and sharp, "Be sure of your facts.

"I am. It'll save time and heart-searching if you know her
and now that my father has admitted his intention of mu
dering Philippe."

A pause. Hippolyte said, "Very well. I'll accept that. T
whom did he admit this?"

Raoul's mouth twisted. "To me. Content yourself, mo
oncle, it's still only a family affair."

"I—see." Hippolyte stirred in his chair. "And so I went o
to Greece and handed Philippe over."

"Yes. Somewhat naturally I hadn't tumbled to the signi
icance of what had happened over Bellevigne. One doesn't,
said Raoul evenly, "readily assume one's father's is a mu
derer. I was merely puzzled and furious—so furious at bein
thrown back to the foot of the cliff I'd been climbing that
didn't stop to think out the whys and the wherefores. I ju
spent all my energy on one blazing row after another. Whe
I went up to Valmy at the beginning of April I thought I'
find out how Philippe was getting on there. I don't preten
for a moment that I thought there was anything wrong;
told you, one doesn't think in that sort of way of one's ow
family and the people one knows. But . . . anyway, I wer
up to Valmy to 'sound' things, as it were. And things seeme

240

all right. I'd heard Philippe had a new governess, and I wondered . . ." Here his glance crossed mine momentarily and he paused. He added, "Valmy was never a house for children, but this time it seemed all right. Then, next day, there was an accident that might have been fatal."

He went on, in that cold even voice, to tell Hippolyte about the shooting in the woods, while Hippolyte exclaimed, and Héloïse stirred in her chair and watched the floor. She made no sound, but I saw that the fragile gold silk of the chair arm had ripped under her nails. Raoul was watching her now. There was no expression whatever on his face.

"Even then," he said, "I didn't suspect what was really going on. Why should I? I blamed myself bitterly for that later, but I tell you, one doesn't think that way." He dropped his cigarette stub onto the hearth, and turned away to crush it out with his heel. He said a little wearily, as if to himself, "Perhaps I did suspect; I don't know. I think I may have fought against suspecting." He looked at his uncle. "Can you understand that?"

"Yes," said Hippolyte heavily. "Yes."

"I thought you would," said Raoul. "A damnable exercise isn't it?" He was already lighting another cigarette.

Hippolyte said, "But you suspected enough to make you go back pretty soon? And again at Easter?"

Raoul's attention was riveted on lighting the cigarette. "It wasn't altogether suspicion that drove me back. Nor did I see anything to rouse me into active worry until the Easter Ball—the night I rang you up. But that night two things happened. Miss Martin told me that there'd been another accident—a coping of the west balcony was suddenly dangerously loose overnight, and only the fact that she noticed it and shoved something across the broken bit saved Philippe from a particularly nasty end on some spiked railings underneath."

This had the effect of making Hippolyte turn and look at me. The expression in his face made me wonder, for the first time, what Héloïse had been telling him about me on the way from Geneva. From the look on his face it had been nothing to my credit. As Raoul went on to speak of the midnight feast with Philippe I saw the expression deepen —as if Hippolyte were being given a very different picture of me from the one he had got from Héloïse. "And there was something so odd about Héloïse that night," said Raoul. "She seemed frightened, if that were possible, and then there was Miss Martin's talk of nightmares. . . . But it was really

241

the second accident that shook me. I went straight to the telephone in the small hours, and eventually got hold of you. It seemed the best thing to do, for us to tackle him together and find out what was going on and force him to . . . see reason. I thought you might also hand the child over to my care if you had to leave again. I've no authority at all where Philippe's concerned, and for obvious reasons I preferred not to enlist official help at that point. Hence the SOS to you." He gave his uncle that fleeting, joyless smile. "In any case, as far as the police were concerned, my father still held the winning card, which was that nothing had happened. He had, and has, committed no provable crime. But I thought that if you cabled you were coming home it would put paid to whatever he might be planning. If even then," he finished very wearily, "he really was planning anything."

There was another of those silences. Hippolyte looked across at Héloïse. Raoul went on, "It seems odd, now, that I should ever have been so slow to believe him capable of murder. I should have known . . . but there it is. I tell you it's not the sort of thing one readily accepts. It certainly wasn't the sort of thing I felt I could tax him with . . . and I doubt if that would have done much good anyway. If the interview I had with him this morning is anything to go by—" He broke off, and then gave a little shrug. "Well, I had sent for you. I'd done what I could to silence my own uneasiness, and I knew Miss Martin was dependable. I told myself I was being a fool. I didn't want to leave Valmy next morning, but I got an early call from Paris, and had to go. It was to do with some money I'd been trying to raise on Bellevigne, and the chap I wanted was passing through Paris that afternoon. I had to catch him. So I went. I'd intended to stay in Paris till Wednesday afternoon, then to come over here and meet you when you got in from Athens, and go up to Valmy with you on Thursday. But once I got away from Valmy I found I was worrying more and more; it was as if, once I got out of his range, I could see him more clearly. Anyway, I think I saw for the first time that this impossible thing might be true, and there might really be danger—immediate danger. I did ring up Valmy in the afternoon and got my—got him. I made some excuse—I forget now what it was—and asked a few questions. He told me about your cable, and I'll swear he even sounded pleased at the prospect of seeing you. Everything seemed to be normal, and when I rang off I was convinced yet again that the whole thing was bag of moonshine." He drew on his cigarette and the smoke came out like a sigh. "But . . . well, by the evening I couldn't stand it any longer. I rang up the airport and was lucky. There was a seat on a night flight. I'd left my car at Geneva, and I drove straight up to Valmy. I got there early this morning, to find that Miss Martin and Philippe had disappeared."

He flicked ash from his cigarette. "Just as a matter of interest, Héloïse, how did you account for that to my uncle when you met his plane?"

Still she didn't speak. She had turned away her head so that her cheek was pressed against the wing of the chair. She looked as if she were hardly listening. Her face was gray and dead. Only her fingers moved, shredding, shredding the gold silk under them.

Hippolyte began, looking so uncomfortable that I had a rough idea what the story had involved: "It wasn't very coherent. I did gather—"

I said, "It doesn't matter. I'll tell you what did happen. I found out on Tuesday night what Monsieur de Valmy was planning. Bernard got drunk at the dance and told Berthe, one of the maids. She told me. I had to get Philippe away. I—I didn't know where to go. We hid, and then came here to wait for you. That's all."

I could feel Raoul's eyes on me. Between us stretched the empty ghost-filled spaces of that alien room. I said no more. If I never told him the rest, I couldn't do it here.

Hippolyte turned back to Raoul. "Go on. You got back and found them gone. I assume that at this point you did tackle Léon?"

"I did." Something new had come into the even voice, something that made me stir on my bench and look away. I didn't want to watch his face, though heaven knew, there was nothing there to read. He said, "There were various—theories as to why the two had run away, but to me it only meant one thing; that Miss Martin had had some proof that Philippe was in danger, and had removed him from harm's way. I blamed myself bitterly for not having let my own suspicions take root. So I attacked my father."

"Yes?"

Raoul said, "It wasn't a pleasant interview. I'll cut it very short. He started by denying everything, and—you know him —he denied it so well that he made me look a fool. But the fact remained that Lin—Miss Martin had bolted. I kept at him and eventually he changed his ground. He suggested

243

then that as far as Philippe's fate was concerned Miss Marti
mightn't be entirely disinterested." He flicked ash off hi
cigarette, not looking at me.

Hippolyte said, "What do you mean?"

Raoul didn't answer. I said briefly, "Monsieur de Valmy
had reason to believe I was in love with Monsieur Raoul."

I saw Hippolyte raise his brows. In his own way he was a
quick as Léon. He said, "So you might have had an interes
in disposing of Philippe? A very longsighted young lady. And
what was your reaction to this—suggestion, Raoul."

"It was so absurd that I wasn't even angry. I laughed.
then told him that he had got the facts right only so far. The
interest was on both sides and it was serious—in other word:
that I intended to make Miss Martin my wife, and if any
harm came to her or to Philippe he'd have me to answer to
as well as the police."

Hippolyte flashed a look from Raoul to me, and back
again, then his eyes dropped to his hands. There was a long
pause. Something in the way the interview was going must
have prompted him to ignore the information in Raoul's last
speech, for all he said was, "And then?"

Raoul said, in a very hard, dry voice, "I'll cut this short.
It's pretty unspeakable. He changed his ground again, and
suggested cutting me in. Yes. Quite. He pointed out the
advantages that I and my wife would get from Philippe's
death. He didn't seem to understand that I might be able to
resist them. And he was convinced I would be able to
persuade her too, as my wife, to acquiesce in his plans.
Between us we could pacify you when you arrived, see you
back to Greece, and then take our time over Philippe. We
could cook up some story of Linda's having run away to me
—everyone was saying that anyway—and get through the
bigger scandal by making it a purely sex affair. He then suggested that I find Linda and allow people to believe she had
run off to meet me."

"Yes?"

It was, perhaps, the most horrible thing about the interview that neither Léon's son nor his brother showed surprise.
Distress, yes; horror, perhaps; but not surprise. Not even at a
wickedness that couldn't conceive of disinterested good.

Raoul said, "I didn't say much. I—couldn't, or I'd have
laid hands on him. I merely said that neither of us would
ever connive at harming Philippe, and we had better stop
talking nonsense and find the pair of them, or there might
be a scandal he'd find it hard to get out of. I thought that

Linda might have tried to get in touch with me in Paris, and rang up there and then in front of him, but there hadn't been a call. I left a message with the concierge in case Linda rang up later, but I'd been so sure she'd ring me up that I thought my father had lied about their escape from Valmy, and that something had happened to them, so—oh well, never mind that now. I knew I was wrong almost straight away, because Bernard—you know his man?—came in. Apparently he'd been out looking for them. He got a bit of a surprise to see me, and I lost no time in making it very plain that it was in his best interest to find Linda and Philippe quickly. I thought they might have gone for help to the Englishman who works over on Dieudonné—I'd discovered that Linda knew him, and was glad she had at least one friend in the district. I rang up the Coq Hardi at Soubirous, where he sleeps sometimes, but he'd already gone out, and he wasn't expected back till dinnertime. I told Bernard to go up to the hut where the Englishman keeps his things, but he said he'd been already and they weren't there. He told me where else he'd been. I sent him out again with instructions to report to me, and some sort of plan of search, the best I could devise with the little I knew . . . well, none of this matters now. He knew very well he'd better play in with me, and play safe. When he'd gone I told my father again, quite plainly, that if any harm came to those two even if it looked like the most obvious accident in the world, I would kill him. Then I went out with the car." His voice was suddenly flat and very tired. "That's all."

I sat still, looking down at my feet. That was all. Only another fifteen hours or so spent combing the valleys, ringing up Paris, making carefully casual inquiries (I found later) of the Consulate, the hospitals, the police. . . .

One or two things became plain: first, that Léon de Valmy had had no idea that the convenient rumor of my engagement was, in fact, true; second, that Raoul knew nothing of the final hurried poison plot, and was unaware that Léon de Valmy had ever had any positive intention of harming me; Bernard, coming in on the interview, must have realized immediately that his master's guns were spiked; somehow, Léon de Valmy had tipped him the wink that the hunt must be called off, and from then on the man had, perforce, cooperated with Raoul in his search. Whether or not I had been right about our danger last night in the woods, we had been safe since early this morning . . . since Raoul had come home. Because of Raoul, the dogs had been called off. We had been quite safe all day, because of Raoul. I sat very still, watching my feet.

The silence was drawing out. I heard the lusters quiver like the music of a ghostly spinet. I looked down the length of the lovely dead room toward the group by the fireplace.

Both men were watching the woman in the chair.

She was sitting very still, but her stillness wasn't even a travesty of the poise I knew. The delicate flower had wilted to pulp. She lay back in her chair as if she had no bones, and her hands were motionless at last on the shredded silk of the chair arms. Her pale eyes were fully open now; they moved from Raoul's face to Hippolyte's painfully. There was no need for her to speak. It was all written in her face, even, I thought, a dreadful kind of relief that now it had all been said.

The door opened and Philippe came in. He was carrying a steaming cup of bouillon very carefully between his hands. He brought it to me and held it out. "This is for you. You had an ordeal too."

I said, "Oh, Philippe . . ." and then my voice broke shamefully. But he didn't appear to notice this. He was looking at Héloïse, silent and slack in her chair. He said doubtfully, "Aunt Héloïse, would you like some too?"

That did it. She began to cry, on a thin dry note that was quite horrible to listen to.

I leaned forward, kissed Philippe's cheek, and said quickly, "Thank you, p'tit, but Aunt Héloïse isn't well. Better just run along. Good night now. Sleep well."

He gave one wondering look, and went obediently.

Héloïse didn't put her hands to her face. She lay back in her chair and sobbed tearlessly on that dreadful, jerky note. Hippolyte de Valmy, now as gray-faced as she, watched her helplessly, touching a handkerchief to his lips with an unsteady hand. Then, after a few moments' hesitation, he moved to a chair beside her, took one of her unresisting hands and began, rather feebly, to pat it. He was murmuring something through her sobs, but the uncertain comfort had no effect.

Raoul stood apart from the two of them, silent, and with the shutters still down over his face. He didn't look at me.

I believe I opened my lips to say something to him, but at that moment Héloïse began at last to speak. Her voice was terrible, thin and shaken and breathless.

She said, "It's true, yes, it's true what he says, Hippolyte.

246

He made Léon tell him . . . there was a scene . . . dreadful things . . . he had no right. . . ." She turned suddenly toward him and her free hand closed over his, clutching at him. "But I'm glad you know, Hippolyte. You'll get us out of it, won't you? You'll see there's nothing said? You won't take it further? It's not a police matter! You heard what Raoul told you—it's only in the family! That's it, it's only in the family! Bernard won't dare speak, and Raoul can't say anything; how can he? Léon's his father, isn't he? Surely that means something?" She shook his arm, leaning nearer, her voice hurrying and breathless: "You can't let it all come out, you know that! You can't do that to Léon, you and Raoul! There's no harm done . . . the boy's safe and the girl's all right. Don't look like that, Raoul. You know you can put it right between you if you want to! The Martin girl's in love with you; she'll keep her mouth shut, and—"

"Héloïse, please!" This, sharply, from Hippolyte. He had freed himself and moved slightly away from her. He was looking at her almost as if he'd never seen her before. "You say it's all true? You did know of it? You?"

She had sunk back in her chair. She swallowed another of those sharp convulsive sobs and moved her head to and fro against the chair-back. "Yes, yes, yes. Everything he told you. I'll admit everything, if only you'll help." Something in his tone and look must have got through to her here, for her voice changed. "I—I'm not wicked, Hippolyte, you know that. I didn't want to hurt Philippe, but . . . well, it was for Léon's sake. I did it for Léon." She met his stony look and added sharply, "You know as well as I do that Valmy should be his. Surely he has the best right to it? It's his home. You know that. Why, you've said so yourself! And he's not like other men. You know that, too; you should realize he's not like other people. He should have had Valmy. He should! He'd had enough to bear without being turned out of his home!"

Her brother-in-law moved uncomfortably. "I cannot see that Léon would be grateful for this special pleading, Héloïse. And at the moment it's beside the point. What we're discussing is a good deal more serious. Attempted murder. Of a child."

"Yes, yes, I know. It was wrong. It was wrong. I admit that. But it didn't happen, did it? There's no harm done, Raoul said that himself! That doesn't have to be taken any futher! Oh, you'll have to talk to Léon about it, I can see that, but you'll see he stays on at Valmy, won't you? There's no reason why he shouldn't! People are talking, but it'll soon be forgotten if you stand by us and don't bring things into the open. And I know you won't! You know how Léon feels! You'll see he keeps Valmy, won't you? He should have talked to you before—I wanted him to, instead of trying to arrange things this way. I was sure you'd see his point of view, and you do, don't you? I'm sure there's some way things can be fixed! You can come to some arrangement, can't you? Can't you?"

He started to say something, then bit it back, saying instead, calmly enough, "It's no use discussing it any more here. This is getting us nowhere. Héloïse—"

"Only promise me you won't take it to the police!"

"I can't promise anything. All I can say is that we'll try and compromise between what's right and what's best."

She seemed not to be listening. Something had broken in her, and now she couldn't stop. She was out of control; her hands and lips were shaking. The pleading voice poured on, admitting with every desperate syllable what must never— even in her mind—have been in words before.

"It'll kill him to go to Bellevigne! And all our money's in Valmy! We looked after Valmy, you can't say that we didn't! Every penny went into the estate! You can't say he was a bad trustee!"

"No," said Hippolyte.

She didn't even notice the irony. The dreadful single-mindedness she showed was ample explanation of how Léon had persuaded her to help him against what better instincts she must have possessed. She wept on, "It was for Léon's sake! Why shouldn't he get something—just this thing—out of life? Valmy was his! You know it was! Étienne had no right to do this to him, no right at all! That child should never have been born!"

Raoul said suddenly, as if the words were shaken out of him, "God pity you, Héloïse, you've begun to think like him."

This stopped her. She turned her head quickly toward him. I couldn't see her eyes, but her hands clenched themselves on the arms of the chair. Her voice went low and breathless, "You," she said, "you. You always hated him, didn't you?"

He didn't answer. He had taken out another cigarette and was making rather a business of lighting it.

"He's your father," she said. "Doesn't that make any difference? Can you stand by and see him ruined? Doesn't it

248

mean anything to you that he's your father?"

Raoul didn't speak. For all the expression on his face he mightn't even have been listening. But I saw his brows twitch together as the match burned him.

Suddenly her hands hammered the chair arms. She shouted at him, "Damn you, are you condemning your own father?" Even the vestiges of common self-control had gone; her voice rose to the edge of hysteria. You to stand there and call him a murderer! You who have everything, everything, and he a cripple with nothing to call his own but that ruined relic of a place in the south! You condemn him, you talk fine and large of right and wrong and murder and police, and who's to say what you'd have done if you'd been in his place? How do you know what you'd have been if you'd smashed your car up one fine day on the zigzag and cracked your spine and two lives along with it? Yes, two! Would she have looked at you then? Ah yes, it only takes one look from you now, doesn't it, but would she? Would she have stayed with you and loved you the way I've loved him all these years and done for you what I've done for him—and glad to, mind that, glad to? Oh, no, not you!" She stopped and drew a long shivering breath. "Oh, God, he's a better man with half a body than you'll ever be, Raoul de Valmy! You don't know . . . oh dear God, how can you know . . .?"

Then she put her hands to her face and began to weep.

Quite suddenly, the scene was unbearable. And I didn't belong in this anywhere any more. I stood up abruptly.

It was at this moment that the door went back with a slam against the silk-paneled wall, and William Blake came in with a rush like an angry bear.

Eighth Coach

Chapter XX

Death has done all death can.

BROWNING: After.

"WHO the devil are you?" said Raoul.

Since he said it in French, William Blake took not the slightest notice. He stopped just inside the door, breathing hard. He looked, as ever, enormous; very English, with the untidy blonde hair, and very safe. He looked down the room at me, ignoring everyone else.

"Linda? What's going on here? Are you all right?"

I said, between a laugh and a sob, "Oh, William!" and ran to him down the length of the room, bouillon and all.

He didn't exactly fold me in his arms, but he did catch me, and, with some presence of mind, hold me away from him, so that the bouillon didn't spill all over his ancient jacket, but only on the priceless Savonnerie carpet.

"Here, steady on," he said. "Are you sure you're all right?"

"Yes, quite all right."

Hippolyte had turned and risen in surprise at the interruption, but Héloïse was past caring for the presence of a stranger. She was weeping freely now, the sobs tearing at the atmosphere of the beautiful overcivilized room. Hippolyte paused, looking helplessly from the newcomer back to her. Raoul said, without moving, "It's the Englishman. I told you about him."

I saw William wince from the sound of sobbing, but he stood his ground, his jaw jutting dangerously. "Did they hurt you?"

"No, oh no. It's not them, William, it's all finished, honestly."

"Anything I can do?"

"Not a thing, except . . . take me out of here."

Behind me I heard Hippolyte say with a kind of controlled desperation, "Héloïse, please. My dear, you must try and pull yourself together. This is doing no good, no good at all. You'll make yourself ill. Héloïse!"

William said, "Okay. We'll get you out of this. And fast." He put an arm around my shoulders, and turned me toward the door. "Let's go."

I saw Hippolyte take a half step toward us. "Miss Martin—"

But here Héloïse sobbed something incoherently and caught at his sleeve, a desperate little gesture that broke something inside me.

I said, "I can't stand this, William. Wait."

I thrust the half-empty pot of bouillon into his hands, and went back to Madame de Valmy. Hippolyte stood aside and I went down on my knees in front of the little gold chair. I was kneeling at Raoul's feet. I didn't look up at him, and he never moved. Her hands were still over her face. The sobs were less violent now. I took her wrists gently and pulled them down and held her hands.

I said, "Madame, don't. Don't cry any more. We can talk this thing over quietly when you're feeling better. It won't do any good to make yourself ill." Then to Hippolyte, "Can't you see she's beside herself? There's no point in letting this go on. She doesn't know what she's saying. She must be got to bed. . . . Madame, there'll be some way to arrange everything, you'll see. Don't cry any more. Please."

The sobbing caught in her throat. She looked at me with those pale, drowned eyes. The beauty had all gone. The delicately rouged cheeks sagged slack and gray, and her mouth was loose and blurred with crying. I said, "There've been enough tears over this, madame. Don't distress yourself any more. Nothing's going to happen to you. It's all over now. Here, take my handkerchief. . . . Why, you're cold! I don't know why you're sitting here when there's a stove in the study; and you haven't been well lately, have you? Shall we go in there, and perhaps we can get Gaston to bring some coffee? Can you get up? Let me help you. . . ."

She got to her feet slowly, stiffly, and I led her across to the study door. She came obediently, as if she were sleepwalking. The others followed. Nobody spoke. She was weeping still, but quietly, into my handkerchief. I put her into a chair near the stove, and knelt again beside her on the rug.

I don't know quite what else I said to her, but the sobbing stopped, and presently she lay back in the chair quietly, and looked at me. She looked exhausted, dazed almost. She said abruptly, in a flat, sleepwalker's tone, "I liked you, Miss Martin. I liked you from the first."

I said soothingly, "I know you did. It's all right. Don't worry now. We'll get you home, and—"

"You wouldn't really have been blamed for the accidents, you know. We didn't mean to blame you. We never meant at the beginning to make you responsible."

"No."

"Léon liked you too. He said you were gallant. That was the word. He said, 'She's a gallant little devil and it'd be a pity if we had to bring her down.' "

Raoul said very quietly, from behind me, "And just what did he mean by that?"

Madame de Valmy took no notice. She seemed oblivious of anyone but herself and me. She held my hands and looked at me with those pale dazed eyes, and talked in that tired monotone that she didn't seem to be able to stop. "He said that just a day or so ago. Of course, after the second accident on the balcony we were going to have to dismiss you, you know. He said you were too wide-awake and now you'd begin to suspect us if anything else happened. We were pleased when you gave us the excuse to send you away. You thought I was angry, didn't you?"

"Yes, madame."

"Then we got the cable. We had to do something in a hurry. There were the rumors in the village about you and Raoul, and about your being dismissed, but Léon said it might come in useful later anyway, if the village had been linking your names."

Behind me I heard Raoul take in his breath as if to speak. I said quickly, to divert her, "Yes, madame, I know. Albertine started to talk, didn't she? Well, don't think about that now."

"She never knew what we were trying to do," said Madame de Valmy. "But she didn't like you. She never liked you. It was she who told me about the muddle you'd made with the prescriptions that time. She only told me to show you up. She thought I'd think you careless and silly. It was only spite. But that's what made us think of the poison, you see. That was the only reason we thought of using those pills. We weren't trying to fix it on you, Miss Martin. It was to have looked like an accident. It was in the glucose, you understand. The poison was in the glucose that you used every night to make his chocolate with."

"Madame—"

"Luckily there wasn't much left in the tin, so we soaked the blue color off the tablets and powdered them up and made a

252

strong mixture. Too strong perhaps. It may have been bitter.
He didn't take it, did he?"

"No. But that wasn't why." I turned desperately to Hippolyte, who was standing silently over by the desk. "May I ring and ask for some coffee, Monsieur de Valmy? I really think—"

"We hadn't time to think of anything better," said Héloïse. "It was to look like an accident. If he had taken it and died they might not have thought of murder. Those antihistamine pills are blue. The doctor might have thought he'd taken them as sweets. Children do. We meant to empty out the rest of the glucose and leave one or two pills by his bed. There were some in a jar on your mantelpiece, where he might have found them and eaten them. You mightn't have been blamed. They would have thought you'd forgotten to give them to Mrs. Seddon. Léon said you might not be blamed even then."

Behind me Raoul said, "Just what are you talking about, Héloïse?"

She looked up at him with that dead, sleepwalker's look. She seemed to have forgotten her outburst. She answered him mechanically, "The poison. It wasn't a very good plan, but we had to be sure and it was all we could think of that might look like an accident. But he didn't take it. It's all right. She said so. I was just explaining to her that we didn't mean her any harm. I like her. I always did."

I said quickly, "Madame, you're upset. You don't know what you're saying. Now we're going to have some coffee, and we'll see you home."

Across me Raoul said, "And if Miss Martin *had* been blamed? If murder *had* been suspected? You had made it common knowledge, hadn't you, that she and I—that there might be an interested reason to get rid of Philippe?"

She said nothing. She stared up at him.

"Was that what my father meant when he said that the gossip 'might have been useful later'?"

I heard Hippolyte begin to say something, but Raoul cut across it. "On Tuesday night, Héloïse . . . who was it found Philippe had gone?"

"Léon did. He stayed awake. We were going to empty out the rest of the glucose and—"

"So you said. He found Philippe gone. And then?"

"He thought he must have felt ill and gone for Miss Martin. But there was no light there. She'd gone too."

"And when he couldn't find them, what then?"

253

"He sent Bernard out to look for them."

Raoul said, "With what instructions?"

She said nothing. Under the hammering of his questions she seemed to have come partly to life again. Her eyes were conscious now, blinking nervously up at him.

"With what instructions, Héloïse?"

Still she didn't answer. She didn't need to. Her features seemed to flatten out and melt like candle grease. Hippolyte said, harshly, "That's enough, Raoul."

"Yes," said Raoul. "I think it is."

He walked out of the room and shut the door behind him. For a moment nobody moved. Then Héloïse came to her feet, thrusting me aside so that I fell over on the rug.

She stood there with her hands slack at her sides. She said, almost conversationally, "Léon. He's gone to kill Léon." Then she crumpled beside me on the rug in a dead faint.

I left her there. I remember leaping to my feet, to stand like a fool on the rug beside her, gaping at the shut door. I remember Hippolyte starting forward and shouting, "Raoul! Come back, you fool!" He was answered by the slam of the front door. He turned with a sound like a groan and jumped for the telephone. I remember that, as he touched it, it began to ring.

Before it had threshed once I was out on the gallery and racing for the head of the stairs. There were steps behind me and William's hand caught at my arm. "Linda, Linda. Where are you going? Keep out of this. You can't do a thing."

Outside, an engine roared to violent life. A door slammed. The Cadillac gained the road, paused, whined up through her gears, and snarled away into the silence.

I shook off William's hand and fled down the curving stairs. Across the hall, and struggling with the heavy door . . . William reached over my shoulder and yanked it open. The lamp over the door showed the dark circular drive walled in with misty trees . . . a big black car . . . a battered jeep . . . the scored grooves in the gravel where the Cadillac's tires had torn their circle. The smell of her exhaust hung in the air.

I ran out.

William caught at my arm. "For God's sake, Linda—"

"We've got to stop him! We've got to stop him!"

"But—"

"Didn't you understand? He's gone to kill Léon. He said he would, and they'll have to kill him for it. Don't you understand?"

254

He still held me. "But what can you do? You've been mixed up in enough of their dirty game as it is. Let me take you away. There's nothing you can do. You said yourself it was finished. What's it to you if they murder each other?"

"Oh, dear God, what's it to me? William—" I was clinging to him now—"William, you have to help. I—I can't drive a car. Please, William, please, *please*—"

The night, the misty trees, the solitary lamp in its yellow nimbus, were all part of the roaring horror that enveloped me, that was only my own blood pounding in my ears. . . .

He said quietly, "Very well, let's go," and his hand closed over mine for a moment. As the world steadied around me I saw that he was opening the door of the jeep.

I said shakily, "No. The other." I ran to the big Daimler and pulled the door open. It was the Valmy car. Héloïse must have had it down to the airport to meet Hippolyte.

William followed me. His voice was doubtful. "Ought we to?"

"It's faster. The key's in. Oh, William, hurry!"

"Okay."

And then we were away. Our wheels whined around in the same circle, skidding on the gravel. Our lights raked the trees, the lodge, the willows fronded with weeping mist. . . . We took the gate cautiously, gained the road, and swung right.

Along the narrow, fog-dimmed road with its soaring dark trees; a sharp turn left, a steep little climb between echoing walls; right again, then a series of dizzy, whipping turns through the steep streets that climbed up to the town. Now we had reached the upper level, and were clear of the mist. We swept along a wide curved boulevard where lamps flickered by among the pollard willows. . . . A sharp swing right, and we scudded across the empty market place where cobbles gleamed damply and a few flattened cabbage leaves lay in a gutter like a drift of giant leaves. William had got the feel of the car now. We swirled righthanded into a badly-lighted avenue and gathered speed. The lopped chestnuts flicked past us one by one, faster, faster, faster. . . .

We were out of the little town. Our headlights leaped out ahead of us, and the engine's note rose powerfully, and held steady.

Ahead of us the road forked. A signboard flashed up in the white light and tore toward us.

We took the left for Valmy.

William was, I thought, as good a driver as Raoul, but

Raoul had not only a start, but a faster car which was, moreover, the one he was accustomed to drive. But after a while I began to hope that even these advantages might not help him too much, for very soon after leaving Thonon we met the mist again. Not the tree-haunting gray mist that had risen from the lake to moat the Villa Mireille, but little clouds and clots of white brume, breathed up from the river to lie in all the hollows of a road that was never far from the water. Each time the car's nose dipped a dazzling cumulus of white struck back the light at us, swept over us, blinded, engulfed us, then even as the engine slowed and hesitated we roared up out of cloud again into the calm black air. At first the experience was unnerving; the moment of blindness was like a great white hand thrust against your face, so that you flinched backward against the upholstery, and were conscious of your eyes' catlike dilation. But with each succeeding dive into the cloud the car's hesitation became less apparent and after a while I realized that William was losing very little speed. He seemed to know unerringly just how the road lifted and curved, where the mist would lie for fifty yards and where for five, and he sliced through the fog patches with the confidence of the man who—literally—knows his road blindfold. He must have driven up and down it scores of times in the course of his job; it was even probable that he knew it better than Raoul, who for some time had lived most of his year between Bellevigne and Paris. We might catch him yet . . .

So at any rate I told myself, huddled down in the seat beside William and staring with eyes that winced through the marching clouds of mist to catch a glimpse of a vanishing taillight around some curve ahead.

William said, "What was all that about, Linda?"

"What d'you mean? Oh—I keep forgetting you don't speak French." I gave a shaky little laugh. "I'm sorry, William. I—I'm not thinking very clearly tonight. I haven't even said thank you for coming. I've just rushed you into my affairs and used you like this. I—I'm terribly grateful. I really am."

"Think nothing of it. But you'd better put me in the picture, hadn't you?"

So I told him the story from the beginning—not very clearly, I'm afraid, and with halts and pauses due to weariness and the fear that clawed at me, while the car roared on up that wicked valley road and the night went by us smoothly as a dream. The dark road fell away, steamed, poured away

256

behind us; the thin gray trees reeled past us into nothingness; the mist clouds marched, fled, broke and streamed away from us in mackerel flakes like rack in the wind.

The red tail-light struck at my eyes like a dagger.

I said hoarsely, "There. William. Look, there."

He didn't answer, but I knew he'd seen it. Then it vanished and a moment later the blinding white swamped us again. Out into a patch of clear darkness, and then another cloud was on us, but this time thin, so that our yellow-dimmed lights made rainbows in it that wisped away along our wings, and we were through.

The car gathered speed up a steady straight rise. And the fleeing red light was there, not three hundred yards ahead.

He didn't seem to be traveling so very fast. We were gaining, gaining rapidly. Two hundred yards, a hundred and fifty . . . the gap dwindled. We were coming up fast. Too fast.

"It's only a truck," said William, and lifted his foot.

We ran up close behind it and asked to be let by.

It was one of those appalling monsters so common in France, far too high and wide for any road, and far too fast for their size. And it became obvious very soon that this one had no intention of allowing us the road. Ignoring the flickering of our lights it roared along, rocking a little on the bends, but never yielding an inch of the crown of the road.

I don't know how long we were behind it. It seemed a year. I sat with my nails driving holes into the palms of my hands, and my teeth savaging my lip while I stared with hatred at the dirty blackboard of the truck held in our lights. It was carrying gravel, which dripped through the cracks onto the road. Someone had chalked a face like a gremlin on the left-hand panel. To this day I can see the license plate with the chip off the corner and read the number. 920-DE75. . . . I stared at it without consciously seeing it at all, and thought of the Cadillac roaring on ahead, of Raoul and Léon and the terrible little scene that, unbelievably, was so soon to be acted out in the Valmy library.

I said again, "William. . . ."

"If the Caddy passed him," said William calmly, "we can. Hold on."

There wasn't even a trace of impatience in his voice. He drew out to the left, flickered his lights again, and waited. The truck lumbered on. We were on an upgrade now, and the truck was slowing. It held the road, and once again we drew patiently in behind it.

So we went in procession up the hill. A sob rose and burst in my throat and I put the back of my hand hard against my teeth in an effort for self-control.

The truck slowed, slowed again, and checked as it was rammed into bottom gear. We crawled toward the head of the rise.

The trees that crowned the hilltop swelled into light that soared toward us. Lights were coming up the other side of the hill, and coming fast. Their gray aurora spread, splayed brighter, lifted into gold. The truck topped the crest of the road, black against the approaching glare, and swung sharply over to its right to make way for the oncoming car.

Our own lights flashed once, and dimmed. Something hit me in the small of the back as the Daimler shot forward like a torpedo into the gap.

Lights met lights with a clash that could be felt. Then we whipped to the right almost under the truck's front bumper. I heard the yell of a horn and something that might have been a shout, but we were through with a little to spare and dropping downhill with the rush of a lift.

"Oh, you honey," said William affectionately to the car, and then sent me a grin. I had bitten the back of my hand but his breathing wasn't even ruffled. "It's nice," he said mildly, "to have the horses. . . ."

The road lifted once more, to shake itself clear of mist. William's foot went down and those horses took hold. My eyes strained through the darkness ahead for that telltale light among the trees.

But no light showed till we rounded the curve where the road begins the long drop to the Valmy bridge, and saw the lurch and sway of lights that cut their way up the zigzag nearly half a mile ahead.

I must have made some small sound, for William gave me a glance and said, "Don't fret, my dear. They'll talk it over, surely?" But he didn't sound convinced, and neither was I. We'd both seen Raoul's face. And the way those distant headlights now slashed their way up the zigzag was some indication that the mood still held.

I saw them vanish at the top under the château's bright windows. William accelerated, and we shot down the last hill, met a wall of mist hood-high, slowed, sang down to second for the turn onto the bridge—and then stopped short, with brakes squealing.

I said breathlessly, "What is it?"

258

"Can two cars pass on that road?"

"The zigzag? No. But—"

He nodded toward it. I followed his gaze and said, "Oh, dear Lord," on a dreary little sob. A car had nosed its way down off the driveway and was taking the first hairpin with some caution. It got around, and came on its decorous way down. . . .

"Where are you going?" asked William sharply.

I was fumbling with the door. "There's a path straight up from the bridge through the wood . . . steps . . . I think I could—"

He reached across and his hand closed over mine. "Don't be silly. You'd break your heart and I'd still be there before you. Sit still."

"But William—"

"My dear girl, I know. But there's nothing else to do." His voice was calm. "Look, he's nearly down. Sit still."

I was shaking uncontrollably. "Of course. It—it doesn't matter to you, does it?"

His eyes were grave and gentle. "And it does to you? It really does?"

I said nothing. The descending car swung around the last bend, and her lights sank toward the bridge. There was mist lying as it had lain that night.

William said gently, "I'm sorry, Linda."

The car was crossing the bridge, nosing through the mist. It paused, and moved out into the road with a lamentable crash of gears. William's hand shifted and the Daimler leaped for the gap and went over the bridge with the mist flying out from the headlamps like spray in the teeth of a destroyer.

For a fleeting second before the cliff cut it off from view I lifted my eyes and saw the Château Valmy, brightly lighted against the night sky. That was what William meant; I knew it. The castle in the air, the Cinderella dream—nonsense for a night. *Banquets abroad by torchlight, music, sports, nine coaches waiting!*

Not for you, Linda my girl. You get yourself back to North London.

The Daimler lurched up and around the final curve, and skidded wildly as her wheels met the gravel of the drive. She came to a rocking halt just behind the parked Cadillac.

There was another car in the drive and a van of sorts, but I hardly noticed them. I had my door open before our wheels had shrieked to a stop, and was out and stumbling up the steps to the great door.

Seddon was in the hall. He started forward when he saw me and I heard him say, "Oh, Miss Martin—" but I fled past him as if he didn't exist, and down the long corridor that led to the library.

The door was slightly ajar and a light showed. As I reached it my panic courage spilled out of me like wine from a smashed glass and I stopped dead with my hands actually on the panels ready to push.

Inside the room there was no sound.

I pushed the door open softly, took three steps into the room, and stopped short. There were several men in the room, but I only saw two of them.

Raoul de Valmy was standing with his back to the door, staring down at his father.

For once Léon de Valmy was not in his wheel chair. He had fallen forward and out of it onto the floor. His body lay clumsily, pulled a little crooked by whatever harness he wore under his clothes. His head was turned to one side, his cheek against the carpet. His face was smooth, wiped clean of every line and shadow; beauty and evil had emptied themselves from it together. Now there was nothing there at all.

From where I was you could hardly see the blackened hole in the temple.

I would have fallen where I stood but that William's arms came around me from behind and swept me up and out of the silent room.

Ninth Coach

Chapter XXI

Look you, the stars shine still.

JOHN WEBSTER: *The Duchess of Malfi.*

. . . Warmth, and the sound of liquid, and the smell of azaleas . . . And someone was patting my hand. But there was no music, and the voice that said my name was not Florimond's. Nor was Raoul there waiting to sweep me out onto the terrace and under the moon. . . .

William said, "Here, Linda, drink this."

The liquid burned sourly on my tongue and made me gasp. I opened my eyes.

I was in the small salon, lying on the sofa before the fire. Someone had made this up recently. Tongues of pale flame licked around the new logs. I stared at them dazedly. I had never fainted before, and the memory of the roaring dizziness frightened me and I put an unsteady hand up to my eyes. The salon still swam around me, too bright and out of focus.

"Finish it," urged William.

I obeyed him meekly. It was detestable stuff, whatever it was, but it ran into my body warm and potent, so that in a few moments more my eyes and fingers and even my brain were mine again. And my memory.

"How d'you feel now?" asked William.

I said drearily, "Oh, fine. Just fine. I'm sorry, William. That wasn't a very useful thing to do."

He took the glass from my hand and put it on the mantelpiece. Then he sat down on the sofa beside me. "Nothing we've done tonight has been so terribly useful, has it?"

I found myself staring at him in a kind of daze. Of course. It was nothing to him. I said, dragging the words up from the depths, "Have they . . . taken him away yet?"

"Not yet."

"William. I've got to . . . see him. Just for a moment. I've got to."

I heard stupefaction in his voice. "But, my dear Linda—"

"When will he go?"

"I've no idea, the police are still busy. The ambulance is waiting."

I gave a little gasp and turned my head sharply. "Ambulance? Is he hurt? What's happened?" I sat up and gripped his arm. The bright roaring mist was there again. Dimly through it I saw William's eyes, puzzled and a little shocked. Dimly I heard him say, "But Linda. Didn't you realize? I thought you knew. He's dead."

My grip must have been savaging his sleeve. His hand came up to cover mine, quietly. "He shot himself," said William, "some time before Raoul and you and I got here."

"Oh," I said, in a silly high voice, "Léon. Léon shot himself. The ambulance is for Léon."

"Why—who else?"

I heard myself give a cracked breathless little laugh. "Who indeed?" I said, and burst into tears.

It was hard luck on William. And for a shy British amateur, he was certainly doing very well. He produced some more of that filthy drink, and patted my hand some more too, and put a large comforting arm around me.

"I thought you'd grasped the situation," he was saying. "I thought it was just the shock of seeing, er, Monsieur Léon that made you faint. . . . The butler chap was telling me all about it just now when he brought the drink for you. I thought you heard. I'd no idea you were right out."

"I—I wasn't really. I heard you talking. But I didn't take it in. It was like voices in a dream . . . coming and going."

The arm tightened momentarily. "You poor kid. Better now?"

I nodded. "Go on, tell me. What did Seddon say?"

"Is that his name? Thank God he's English! Well, he told me he'd gone in to look at the library fire soon after eleven, and found him dead on the floor, the way you saw him. Nobody heard the shot. He called the police and the doctor first, and then the Villa Mireille, but got no answer there."

"That would be before Philippe and I got into the house."

"Oh? They tried again later, twice. I suppose the first time was while you were telephoning me, and then they finally got Monsieur Hippolyte. That would be the call that came through as we left the house. Hippolyte's on his way up. He'll be here before long."

"If he knows how to drive the jeep."

"Oh, murder," said William. "I never thought of that."

I said, "Are they sure it was suicide?"

"Oh, quite. The gun was in his hand, and there's a letter."

"A letter. Léon de Valmy left a letter?"

"Yes. The police have it. Seddon didn't read it, but from what the police asked him he pretty well gathered what it said. It admitted the first two attempts to murder Philippe, involving Bernard, but nobody else. He states categorically that neither Raoul nor Madame de Valmy knew anything about them. He never mentions this last affair of the poison— I suppose that would almost certainly involve his wife. He simply says that Bernard must have let something out to you about the two early attempts, and you got in a panic and bolted with Philippe. I think that's about the lot. You've certainly nothing to worry about."

"No." I was silent for a moment. "Well, I shan't volunteer anything else unless they ask me. I don't somehow want to pile anything more onto Madame de Valmy, whatever she did. *He's* dead, you see. She's got that to go on living with. Funny, one somehow imagines her snuffing quietly out now, the way the moon would if the sun vanished. Somehow it's like Léon to let her out, and me, and yet to turn the wretched Bernard in . . . though I suppose it was impossible to hide his part in it. And Bernard failed, after all. "

"That's not why," said William. "When Bernard found you both gone and Raoul on the trail he must have realized that Léon de Valmy's bolt was shot and that there'd never be a future and a fortune for him the way he'd been promised. He moved onto the winning side, probably with an eye to the future, and played in with Raoul all day, looking for you and Philippe. Then last night—three or four hours ago—he came and tried to retrieve the lost fortune by putting the black on Monsieur Léon."

"Blackmail?"

"Yes. It's in the letter. He threatened to turn informer. If you ask me, that's what tipped Léon de Valmy's scales toward suicide in the end. I mean, there's no end to blackmail, is there?"

I said slowly, "You're probably right. I was wondering what had made him kill himself instead of waiting to see what Raoul and Hippolyte would do. After all, it was still all in the family. But when one thinks about it . . . Even if Raoul and Hippolyte and I had agreed to hush the whole thing up for Philippe's sake and the sake of the family—what was there left for Léon de Valmy? Hippolyte would be able to put any sort of pressure on that he liked, and he might have insisted on Léon's leaving Valmy. Even if Leon was allowed to stay, Hippolyte would start sitting down tight on the moneybags, and presumably Raoul would be in a position to stop Léon milking Bellevigne any more. . . . And in any case Léon would have had to get out in six years' time. And we all—even Philippe—knew what he'd done and what he was. . . . And then, finally, the wretched tool Bernard started to blackmail him. Yes, one can see a desperate moment for Léon, and no future. Certainly he wasn't the kind of man to submit to blackmail; he'd literally die sooner, I'm sure of it. It only surprises me that he didn't kill Bernard first, but I suppose Bernard would be on guard against that, and he did have certain physical advantages. What did happen to Bernard anyway? Did Léon kill him?"

"No, he's disappeared. There'll be a hue and cry, but I suppose it's to be hoped that he gets away, and the rest of the story with him."

I said, "Yes. Poor little Berthe."

"Who's that?"

"Oh, nobody. Just one of the nobodies who get hurt the

263

most when wicked men start to carve life up to suit themselves. You know, William, I doubt if I was altogether right about why Léon de Valmy killed himself. . . . I imagine all those things would be there, part of it, in his mind, but it would be something else that tipped him over. I think I knew him rather well. He'd been beaten. He'd been shown up. And I don't think he could have taken that, whatever happened later. He was—I think the word's a megalomaniac. He had to see himself as larger than life . . . everything that happened was seen only in relation to him. . . . He sort of focused your attention on himself all the time, and he could do it, William. I believed he liked to think he could play with people just as he wanted to. He *couldn't* ever have taken second place to anyone. To shoot himself, making that magnanimous gesture with the letter . . . yes, that was Léon de Valmy all right." I leaned back wearily. "Well, whatever his reasons, it made the best end, didn't it? Oh, William, I'm so tired."

He said anxiously, "Are you all right? What about some more brandy?"

"No, thanks. It's all right. Just the anticlimax hitting me."

"D'you want to go now? Perhaps we could—"

"Go. Where to?"

He pushed his fingers through his hair. "I—yes, I hadn't thought of that. They didn't exactly get the red carpets out at the Villa Mireille, did they? Though if you ask me they owe you a ruddy great vote of thanks, and I'll tell them so myself if nobody else does!"

"They know, for what it's worth," I said.

"But you don't want to stay here, do you?"

"What else can I do? When Monsieur Hippolyte gets around to it, he'll see that I get my passage paid home."

"You'll go home?"

"Yes." I looked at him and gave a smile of a sort. "You see, when you're in my position you can't afford to make the grand gesture, William. I can't just sweep out. I'm afraid I must wait here till the police have asked all their questions. I think I'll go along and see Berthe now, and then come back here and wait for them."

"Hang on, here's someone coming," said William. "Yes, here they are."

I must still have been in a semidazed condition, because, although I remember quite well exactly what the police inspector looked like, I can't recall our interview with any accuracy. I did gather that after Léon de Valmy's death the frightened servants had poured out the story of Philippe's and my disappearance and all the accompanying rumors, but that the suicide's letter, together with what Hippolyte de Valmy had said over the telephone and—finally—an interview with Raoul, had strangled stillborn any doubts about myself. This much I understood soon enough: the inspector's manner with me was gentle and even respectful, and I found myself answering his questions readily and without any anxiety other than the dreadful obsessional one—the fox under my cloak that kept my eyes on the open door all through the half-hour or so of question and answer, and made my heart jump and jerk every time anyone passed along the corridor.

The inspector left us eventually when Hippolyte arrived. I saw them pass the door together on the way to the library. Hippolyte was still pale and tired looking, but very composed. It was easy to suppose that, once the shock was over, the news would prove a relief.

I wondered fleetingly about Héloïse, and then again, sharply, about Berthe. But as I got to my feet to go in search of her Seddon came in with coffee, and in response to my inquiries told me that the police had dealt with her very kindly, and had (when the interview was over) sent her in one of their cars down to her mother's house in the village. I supposed this was the car that had held us up at the zigzag. There was nothing more to be done for Berthe except to hope that Bernard could be forgotten, so I sat wearily down again while Seddon poured me some coffee. He lingered for a while, asking me about Philippe, to vanish at length in the direction of the hall when Hippolyte came into the room.

William got to his feet a little awkwardly. I put my coffee cup down on the floor and made to follow suit, but Hippolyte said quickly, "No, please," and then, in English, to William, "Don't go."

I began to say, "Monsieur de Valmy, I—we're awfully sorry—"

But he stopped me with a gesture, and coming over to the sofa he bent over me and took both my hands in his. Then, before I knew what he was about, he kissed them.

"That is for Philippe," he said. "We owe you a very great deal, it seems, Miss Martin, and I have come belatedly to thank you and to ask you to forgive me for my rather cavalier treatment of you at the Villa Mireille."

I said rather feebly, "You had other things on your mind, monsieur." I wanted to tell him not to bother about me but to go back to his own worries and his own personal tragedy, but I couldn't so I sat and let him thank me again with his

265

grave courteous charm, and tried not to watch the door while he talked, or to think how like Raoul's his voice was.

I realized suddenly that he had left the past and was talking about the future.

". . . He will stay with me at the Villa Mireille for the time being. Miss Martin—dare I hope that after your very terrible experience you will stay with him?"

I stared at him for some time, stupidly, before I realized what he was asking me. He must, in his own tragic preoccupation, have forgotten Raoul's confession concerning me. I said, "I—I don't know. Just at the moment—"

"I quite see. I had no right to put it to you now. You look exhausted, child, and no wonder. Later, perhaps, you can think it over."

There was a queer sound from the corridor, a kind of slow, heavy shuffling. Then I knew what it was, Léon, leaving the Château Valmy. I looked down at my hands.

Hippolyte was saying steadily, "If under the circumstances you prefer not to spend the night here, there's a place for you as long as you choose to stay at the Villa Mireille."

"Why, thank you. Yes, I—I would like that."

"Then if we can find someone to take you down—"

He had glanced at William, who said immediately, "Of course." Then he stammered and added awkwardly, "I say, sir, I'm terribly sorry about taking the car. We thought—that is, we were in a hurry. I really am awfully sorry."

"It's nothing." Hippolyte dismissed the theft with a gesture. "I believe you thought you might prevent a tragedy— a worse one than what actually happened." His eyes moved somberly to the door. "I'm sure you will understand me when I say that . . . this . . . was not altogether a tragedy." Another glance at William, this time with the faintest glimmer of a smile underlying the somber look. "You'll find your own— extraordinary vehicle—outside. And now good night."

He went. I picked up my coffee cup absently, but the stuff was cold and skinning over. I set it down again. A log fell in with a soft crash of sparks. No movement now outside in the corridor. I looked at the clock. It had stopped. *The world-without-end hour. . . . Nor dare I chide the world-without-end hour, whilst I (my sovereign) watch the clock for you. . . .*

"Linda," said William. He came and sat beside me on the sofa. He reached out and took both my cold hands in his. Safe, gentle hands; steady, sensible hands. "Linda," he said again, and cleared his throat.

I woke to the present as to a cold touch on the shoulder. I

266

sat up straighter. I said, "William, I want to thank you most awfully for what you've done. I don't know what I'd have done without you tonight, honestly I don't. I'd no business to call you in the way I did, but I was so terribly on my own, and you were my only friend."

"It's a friend's privilege to be used," said William. He loosed my hands. There was a pause. He said, "If you are going to stay with Philippe, I might see you now and again, mightn't I?"

"I don't suppose I'll be staying."

"No?"

"No."

"I see." He got to his feet and smiled down at me. "Shall I run you down to the Villa Mireille now in the jeep?"

"No, thanks, William. I—think I'll wait."

"Okay. I'll say good night, then. You'll look me up before you leave, won't you?"

"Of course. Good night. And . . . thanks a lot, William. Thank you for everything."

I forgot him almost as soon as the front door shut behind him. Someone had come out of the library. I could hear Hippolyte's voice, and Raoul's, talking quietly. They were coming along the corridor together.

My heart was hurting me. I got up quickly and moved toward the door. Hippolyte was talking, saying something about Héloïse. I shrank against the wall to the side of the door so that they wouldn't see me as they passed.

". . . A nursing home," said Hippolyte. "I left her with Doctor Fauré. He'll look after her." There was something more—something about a small allowance, a pension, and "somewhere away from Valmy, Paris or Cannes," and finally the words, dimly heard as they moved away along the corridor, "her heart," and "not very long, perhaps. . . ."

They had reached the hall. Hippolyte was saying good night. I went softly out into the corridor and hesitated there, waiting for Hippolyte to leave him. I was shaking with panic. Léon and Héloïse might have faded already into the past, poor ghosts with no more power to terrify, but I had a ghost of my own to lay.

Raoul's voice, now, asking a question. Seddon's answer, almost indistinguishable. It sounded like "Gone." A sharp query from Raoul, and, clearly, from Seddon, "Yes, sir. A few minutes ago."

I heard Raoul say, grimly, "I see. Thank you. Good night, Seddon."

Then I realized what he had been asking. I forgot Hippolyte's presence, and Seddon's. I began to run down the corridor. I called, "Raoul!"

My voice was drowned in the slam of the front door.

I had reached the hall when I heard the engine start. Seddon's voice said, surprised, "Why, Miss Martin, I thought you'd gone with Mr. Blake!" I didn't answer. I flew across the hall, tore open the door, and ran into the darkness.

The Cadillac was already moving. As I reached the bottom of the steps she was wheeling away from the house. I called again, but he didn't hear—or at least the car still moved, gathering speed. Futilely, I began to run.

I was still twenty yards behind it when it slid gently into the first curve of the zigzag, and out of sight.

If I had stopped to think I should never have done what I did. But I was past thinking. I only knew that I had something to say that must be said if I was ever to sleep again. And I wasn't the only one that had to be healed. I turned without hesitation and plunged into the path that shortcircuited the zigzag.

This was a footway, no more, that dived steeply down the hillside toward the Valmy bridge. I had taken it with Philippe many a time. It was well kept, and the steps, where they occurred, were wide and safe, but it could be slippery, and in the dark it could probably be suicide.

I didn't care. Some kind freak of chance had made me keep Philippe's torch in my pocket, and now by its halfhearted light I went down that dizzy little track as if all my ghosts hunted me at heel.

Off to the left the Cadillac's lights still bore away from me on the first long arm of the zigzag. The engine made very little sound. I hurtled, careless of sprains and bruises, down through the wood.

It couldn't be done, of course. He was still below me when he took the first bend and the headlights bore back to the north, making the shadows of the trees where I ran reel and flicker so that they seemed to catch at my feet like a net.

The path twisted down like a snake. The whole wood marched and shifted in his lights like trees in a nightmare. Just before he wheeled away again I saw the next segment of my path doubling back ten feet below me. I didn't wait to negotiate the corner with its steps and its handrail. I slithered over, half on my back, to the lower level, and gained seven precious seconds before the dark pounced again in the wake of the retreating car.

268

The third arm of the zigzag was the longest. It took him away smoothly to the left without much of a drop. I flung myself down a steep smooth drop, caught at a handrail to steady myself, and then went three at a time down a straight flight of steps. The rail had driven a splinter into my hand, but I hardly felt it. A twig whipped my face, half blinding me, but I just blinked and ran on. Down the steps, around, along over a little gorge bridged with a flagstone . . . and the great headlights had swung north and the shadows were once more madly wheeling around me. They blurred and wavered, caught at me like the ropes of a great web. My breath was sobbing; my heartbeats hammered above the sound of the oncoming car, and there was a silly little prayer on my lips. "Please, please, please," it was, and it spun in my brain like a prayer wheel to the exclusion of any kind of sense or thought.

I didn't stop. Two more sweeps of the zigzag and the Valmy bridge and—he was away. I left the path and simply went down the shortest way between the trees, a steep slope ending in a rocky drop below which was the bridge itself. I fetched up hard against the trunk of a beech at the very edge of the drop. The mist lying over the river swirled up into silver as the Cadillac wheeled and then dived smoothly for the last bend.

I went over the drop. The stone was glowing queerly in the light that came off the mist. I suppose I got scratches and knocks, I don't know. I do know that I slipped once and gripped at a holly bush to save myself and even as I bit the cry off I heard the shriek of the Cadillac's brakes.

I found out later that something had run across the road. I like to think it was the same anonymous little creature that had been there the first time Raoul kissed me. At any rate it stopped the car for those few precious seconds.

I dropped into the road just as his lights swept around the last curve.

I ran onto the bridge. The mist swirled up waist-high. It was gray, it was white, it was blinding gold as the glare took it.

I shut my eyes and put both hands out and stayed exactly where I was.

Brakes and tires shrieked to a stop. I opened my eyes. The mist was curling and frothing from the car's hood not three yards from me. Then the headlights went out and the grateful dark swept down. In the small glow of the car's sidelights the mist tossed like smoke. I took three faltering, trembling steps forward and put a hand on her wing. I leaned against it, fighting for breath. The little prayer wheel still spun, and the prayer sounded the same: "*Please, please, please. . . .*" But it was different.

He got out of the car and walked forward. He was on the other side of the hood. In the uncertain, fog-distorted light he looked taller than ever.

I managed to say, "I was . . . waiting. I've got to . . . see you."

He said, "They told me you'd gone." He added unemotionally, "You little fool, I might have killed you."

My breathing was coming under control, but my legs still felt as if they weren't my own. I leaned heavily on the wing of the car. I said, "I had to tell you I was sorry, Raoul. It's not exactly—adequate—to tell a man you're sorry you suspected him of murder . . . but I am. I'm sorry I even let it cross my mind. And that was all it did. I swear it."

He had his driving gloves in his hand and he was jerking them through and through his fingers. He didn't speak.

I went on miserably, "I'm not trying to excuse myself. I know you'll not forgive me. It would have been bad enough without what—was between us, but as it is . . . Raoul, I just want you to understand a little. Only I don't somehow know how to start explaining."

"You don't have to. I understand."

"I don't think you do. I was *told*, you see, told flatly that you were in it, along with your—with the others. Bernard had said so to Berthe. He told her that you had done the shooting in the wood. I imagine he realized, even when he'd gone so far, that he'd better not own to *that*. And he may have thought you *would* condone the murder once you saw the advantages of it. I didn't believe it, even when she told me flatly. I couldn't. But the rest was so obvious, once I knew, about . . . them, I mean, and there was nothing to prove you weren't in it with them. Nothing except the—the way I felt about you."

I paused, straining my eyes to see his expression. He seemed a very long way away.

I said, "I don't expect you to believe it, Raoul, but I was fighting on your side. All the time. I've been through a very private special little hell since Tuesday night. You called it a 'damnable exercise,' remember? Everything conspired to accuse you, and I was half silly with unhappiness and . . . yes, and doubt, till I couldn't even trust my own senses any more. . . . Oh, I won't drag you through it all now; you've had enough, and you want to be done with this and with

270

me, but I—I had to tell you before you go. It was simply that I couldn't take the chance, Raoul! You do see that, don't you? Say you see that!"

He jerked the gloves in his fingers. His voice was quite flat, dull, almost. "You were prepared to take chances—once."

"Myself, yes. But this was Philippe. I had no right to take a chance on Philippe. I didn't dare. He was my charge—my duty." The miserable words sounded priggish and unutterably absurd. "I—was all he had. Beside *that*, it couldn't be allowed to matter."

"What couldn't?"

"That you were all I had," I said.

Another silence. He was standing very still now. Was it a trick of the mist or was he really a very long way away from me, a lonely figure in the queerly-lighted darkness? It came to me suddenly that this was how I would always remember him, someone standing alone, apart from the others even of his own family. And, I think for the first time, I began to see him as he really was—not any more as a projection of my young romantic longings, not any more as Prince Charming, the handsome sophisticate, the tiger I thought I preferred. . . . This was Raoul, who had been a quiet lonely little boy in a house that was "not a house for children," an unhappy adolescent brought up in the shadow of a megalomaniac father, a young man fighting bitterly to save his small inheritance from ruin . . . wild, perhaps, hard, perhaps, plunging off the beaten track more than once . . . but always alone. Wrapped up in my loneliness and danger I hadn't even seen that his need was the same as my own.

I said gently, "Raoul, I'm sorry. I shouldn't have bothered you with this just now. I think you've had about all you can take. What can I say to you about your father, except that I'm sorry?"

He said, "Do you really think I would have shot him?"

"No, Raoul."

A pause. He said in a very queer voice, "I believe you do understand."

"I believe I do." I swallowed. "Even the last twenty-four hours—with the world gone mad and values shot to smithereens—I must have known, Raoul, I want you to know, that you were you, and that was enough. Raoul, I want you to know it, then I'll go. I loved you all the time, without stopping, and I love you now."

Still he hadn't moved. I turned back toward the château. I said, "I'll leave you now. Good night."

"Where are you going?"

"Someone'll take me to the Villa Mireille. Your Uncle Hippolyte asked me to go there. I—I don't want to stay at Valmy."

"Get into the car. I'll take you down." Then, as I hesitated, "Go on, get in. Where did you think I was going?"

"I didn't think. Away."

"I was going down to the Villa Mireille to look for you."

I didn't speak; didn't move. My heart began to slam again in slow painful strokes.

"Linda." Under the quiet voice was a note I knew.

"Yes?"

"Get in."

I got in. The mist swirled and broke as the door slammed. Swirled again as he got in and slid into the seat beside me. It was dark in the car. He seemed enormous, and very near.

I was trembling. He didn't move to touch me. I cleared my throat and said the first thing that came into my head. "Where did you get this car? Roulette?"

"Écarté. Linda, do you intend to stay at Villa Mireille for a while with Philippe?"

"I don't know. I haven't thought things out yet. I'm awfully fond of him, but—"

Raoul said, "He'll be lonely, even with Hippolyte. Shall we have him with us at Bellevigne?"

I said breathlessly, "Raoul. Raoul. I didn't think—" I stopped. I put shaking hands up to my face.

"What is it, sweetheart?"

I said, very humbly, into my hands, "You mean you'll still . . . have me?"

I heard him take a quick breath. He didn't answer. He turned suddenly toward me and pulled me to him, not gently. What we said then is only for ourselves to remember. We talked for a long time.

Later, when we could admit between us the commonplace of laughter, he said, with the smile back in his voice, "And you've still not made me own it, my lovely. Don't you think it's time I did?"

"What are you talking about? Own what?"

"That I love you, I love you, I love you."

"Oh, that."

"Yes, damn it, that."

"I'll take a chance on it," I said. And those were the last words I spoke for a very long time.

And presently the car edged forward through the mist and turned north off the Valmy bridge.